The Sound at the Edge

ANGELA DAY

ISBN-13: **978-0-9885995-4-3**

DEDICATION

To my Gaidin, as always, for always. Ani l'dodi

And

To my Grandpa, Parley Newman, for being unbreakable in hope, courage, and faith, and for being my pal my whole life.

To my dad, for being a secret superhero and teaching me it's okay to be passionate about something.

And my mom, my aunts, and all Foutz women, who taught me that intelligent, strong women are also kind.

ACKNOWLEDGMENTS

This book and my life in general would not have been possible without the help of brilliant, kind people. Special thanks to everyone at Bricken & Associates for putting up with me for hours at a time, especially Dr. Glenn Bricken for his line editing assistance and boundless enthusiasm for my work. Dr. Bricken, Thane would've liked you. Thanks to all my readers who've sent me emails and tweets asking when this book is coming out and I promise the next one won't take so long. Thanks also to my family for their endless support, especially my Grandma Foutz for reading my book over and over and telling everyone else about it and my brother who told me my first book was so good that he forgot I wrote it, and thanks first, best, and most of all to my husband who is always my most valiant supporter and champion.

And thanks to the SMG. This is, after all, our story.

PROLOGUE

The memory of fleas still made his scalp itch, and Broussard scratched his head without thinking. Of course the fleas were gone; the prissy prudes of Sanctum were strict about hygiene, and he pondered his fate while staring at his close-cropped nails. He'd never bathed so much in his life. Not that he'd enjoyed being filthy, but as he hadn't much choice in the matter he'd gotten used to it. He leaned back against the solid stone wall of his cell. It was cold, but not unpleasant. Broussard ran his calloused fingers absently along the soft felt of the blanket he sat on. It was comfortable, serviceable, but not plush.

The bunk that folded down was bolted to the wall with thick chains and large screws that had been specially made by Sanctum to deflect the Song. Broussard thought those represented all of Sanctum pretty aptly. Functional, strong, and songless.

He stretched and stood to pace the length of his cell. Broussard walked three times a day, twenty laps each time. Keeping limber was important, because you never knew what might happen. Best to be ready.

In the cell across, the gorgeous leggy redhead looked up from the book she was reading and frowned. "Do you have to do that?"

Broussard was years younger than her, but flirted anyway. Where was the harm? "I don't have much else to do. Unless you'd like to suggest a change of activity, Cressida?"

Her eyes narrowed as she glowered at him. Broussard had heard the guards say her name, Cressida Ras-something, and had only paid attention to it because she'd refused to tell him. She'd refused to talk to him at all for the first week. That'd hurt his feelings, because Broussard was a social young man who craved interaction with others. And when those others were as beautiful as this redhead, well, you knew there was some dragon involved. He liked that sense of danger. But what he admitted to himself was he only liked the danger because he knew she was harmless. This was a facility for those with heavily diluted blood and only slight access to their songs so even if she was a dragon, she was too weak to be a threat.

Cressida had gone back to reading, not deigning to respond to his attempt at banter. Broussard resumed his walking, pacing out his eight by eight cell with three walls of stone and one wall of bars. No windows. They were a safety hazard, and Broussard's earth sense told him they were at least thirty feet underground anyway. He might have enjoyed looking at a window full of dirt, but his Shae heritage leaned him in that direction and even though Sanctum made sure each cell was appropriately comfortable, they weren't personalized.

A muffled and distant boom interrupted his pacing. He halted mid-step, reaching out with his mind to the ground beyond the stone. It was difficult and he couldn't get a solid sense of it until the boom repeated. Blasting. Like miners sometimes used to open up a tunnel. The soil vibrated with the feel of marching feet, and Broussard was suddenly very glad that he was both limber and short.

A final explosion shot stone and rubble into the hallway between cells, and guards shouting and gunfire echoed through cell block Two One November. Broussard dove under his bunk while the groans of the injured and dying filled his ears.

"Dear Cressa, we have found you," a smooth male voice spoke through the setting dust. Broussard peeked out from under his low-slung bunk and saw an inconceivably handsome man with olive skin and an expensive white suit step out of the chaos, his arms spread wide. The earth under the well-dressed man's feet thrummed with the power of his song. Broussard pulled back under the bunk and rolled in on himself. Whatever that guy was, he was pure Shae. And

Broussard had too strong a sense of self-preservation to want anything to do with whatever was going on out there.

He would have pulled his ears inside his head if he could have, but instead he heard every word. Cressida's smooth, dark voice was warm like velvet. "I like a man who knows how to make an entrance. I assumed you'd come for me."

The man clucked his tongue. "Of course I would come. I sent you out, after all. And I hear you've had quite the adventure. But there's one thing I haven't been able to learn for certain," there was a long pause in which Broussard counted his rapid heart beats, feeling uncommonly fond of them. "Did you find him?"

"I did."

"Get her out of there," the man ordered, and Broussard heard the high buzzing whine of metal being cut. This lasted long enough for the little man to breathe deeply ten times, and then there was a loud clang as something large and metallic- presumably her cell bars- hit the stone floor. There were footsteps, then the sound of a passionate kiss, wet and smacking. The little man wiggled uncomfortably under the bunk. "Dearest Cressa, what a treasure you are," the man said. "Now tell me my son's name."

Cressa sounded breathless as she said, "Thane Whitaker."

"Thane..." the man caressed the name with his voice, then repeated it quietly. "Thane. A good name, if somewhat common. And Sanctum apprehended you before you could contact me? Those arrogant fools. What charge did they invent?"

"Apparently attempting to contact you was enough of a crime," Cressida said.

"Surprising, considering our channels are secure. I was told Sanctum apprehended you while you were attempting to make a tear in the weave." There was silence as those words hung in the air. Broussard wished he could chew through the stone like a full Shae Gnorf.

"And if I was, what concern of yours is that?" Cressida said. She sounded unconcerned, but from his vantage point on the floor, Broussard could see her trembling below the knees.

"It is my concern because there were children with you. Two children. One of them was damaged, and one of them was partially transformed." There was another pause, which Cressida did not choose to fill. "Were you perhaps attempting to flee with my son into the Shaerealm?"

"Why would I want to take him to Shae?" Cressa was startled enough that her legs stopped trembling.

"For ransom. For leverage. For power. If you had only come to me immediately you would have been rewarded with power. And I would have my son. Instead," the man's voice grew harder than the stone, "I must dig a hole to find you to learn the name of my son, who is currently being indoctrinated by the very imbeciles he was going to help me destroy. Their time is past. And so, my sweet girl, is yours."

Broussard squeezed his eyes shut as someone snapped their fingers. The sharp crack and rattle of semi-automatic gunfire burst for half a heartbeat, and a muffled thud sounded. "Pity," the man said, and his footsteps and the footsteps of several others faded into the distance as the sound of Sanctum guards shouting grew louder. Broussard swore he was never coming out from under his bunk again.

CHAPTER 1

The sun was only beginning to rise when Thane snuck out of his dorm building with his backpack. Twitch's modified and startlingly violent alarm clock hadn't even fired yet. It was unusually quiet on Sanctum's still dark campus and Thane hoped the combination of the early hour and it being a weekend would finally grant him some privacy.

He moved along the side of building four, crouching low and trying to make as little noise as possible. The student dorms weren't far away and all he had to do was get in, take a shower, and get back without running into anyone. It wasn't that his building didn't have a locker room- it did, and a much nicer one than the student dorms- but it was impossible to wrap his mind around the idea of being that close to so many of the mercenaries from the differing SMG teams. Taking a shower next to someone who could kill you with their mind if they didn't like the way you hung your towel was terrifying.

Staying in the team dorms was hard for more than just that. Because he was more than half Shae- blue dragon, specifically, with an affinity for electricity- the Sanctum regulations prohibited him from staying in the student dorms. But it also let every Shaeling student know that he could access more Song than they could. Naturally only those who had a problem with that ever brought it up, and he didn't have as much chance to bond with the rest of the students because he wasn't around them outside of class.

Then there were his hands. Or what used to be his hands. The thick black rubber gloves he wore were unwieldy and made him clumsy, but what was underneath was even more difficult to maneuver. Thick fingers covered in bright scales ended in curved and wickedly sharp talons that were so dark blue Thane had assumed they were black. His hands had transformed when he'd allowed the song to engulf him to save Remi's life. He could not make them change back. Thane hadn't even been able to hear the Song since that night, and so he was isolated from the other students for being too much Shae and isolated from his Shae heritage by not having his Song. Knowing where he'd come from, who his father was, and what it meant for him had only made Thane feel more alone than ever.

The locker room in the student dorms was empty. Thane found a locker on the bottom row that was smaller than the others and stuffed his backpack in it. Then he grabbed a towel and turned on the hot water.

He stood under the stream, allowing the heat to relax his tense muscles. It was the end of his second week at Sanctum, and thus far the only bright point was Remi. She was thriving here, and making friends with everyone. The fallout from lying that General Gage had been so afraid of had never happened, because Remi was so thrilled to finally be in a school permanently. They couldn't move her now that she was in on the secret. Twitch had even arranged it so Thane and Remi had most of their classes together, and they ate lunch together in the student cafeteria every day with an ever-changing group of Remi's new friends.

The locker room door opened with a loud bang, and male voices burst into the quiet of the morning. Loud laughter and insults echoed as more boys joined the cacophony. Thane shut off his water and listened, but apparently they hadn't heard him over their own noise. Maybe he could sneak out without drawing too much notice. He pulled his towel behind his curtain and wrapped it around his waist. Thane thought that Sanctum would be so much better than Payson High. It wasn't. If anything, it was worse.

"Hey! Who put their songless trash in my locker?" Thane heard the angry question through the curtain. The acoustics of the voice were strange in the tiled room, but Thane didn't have time to think about it. He stepped out into the back of a gathering half circle of boys.

6

In the center was Thane's open locker, and standing in front of it was a... boy? The deepness of his voice, his well-defined muscles, and the red stubble on his chin that ran from ear to ear said he had to be at least 18. But he was less than four feet tall. Not squat or horned or an unusual color, he looked like he would be a linebacker on a senior football team except for being only as high as Thane's bottom rib. Thane would've laughed, or come forward and admitted his mistake immediately, but his subconscious was screaming at him.

Thane's instinct saw what his conscious mind was too busy to note. All the other boys in the room, eight of them, weren't laughing. They weren't joking or ignoring the angry short linebacker. Every single one of them stared at their feet, shuffling or looking nervous and not making eye contact with little red beard. Even the two teens who were both taller and thicker than Thane, one of them with grey skin that Thane thought he recognized, were looking down and away.

Linebacker red beard jerked out Thane's backpack and shook it. "So no one claims it? Some farting flogger snuck in here and stuffed their oversized smelly crap into my locker and left it?" As he got angrier, his vowels stretched longer and flatter and the hard rolling 'r' sound became more pronounced. "Well then, I suppose no one would object to it being incinerated?"

Thane's head snapped up and he watched the short muscular arms hold up his backpack and carry it over to a metal door in the wall he hadn't seen anyone use. With one hand the little man slid the door open and a wave of heat and the acrid smell of burning garbage rolled into the room. "One," red beard began. Thane swallowed. Most of the clothing that he owned was in that bag. "Two," the little linebacker swept the room with his eyes, and no one dared look back. That backpack was one of the few possessions he had, and if he didn't speak up he'd only have a towel to wear back to his dorm. If he spoke up now, every eye in the room would be on him. At least Jaeger wasn't here. "Thr-"

"It's mine," Thane whispered to his feet.

The grey-skinned boy heard him. "It's his, Kearney," he said, jerking a thumb at Thane. All eyes in the room turned to Thane, standing between the end of the lockers and the tile wall.

Kearney glowered at Thane. "This trash is yours?"

"Yes," Thane said, loudly enough to be heard while keeping his gaze down and away. He watched with his peripheral vision as the little man sauntered over, swinging the backpack roughly by a strap. Kearney came forward until Thane, still looking down, was staring straight into his green eyes.

"You want it back?" Kearney asked. The room was too still as everyone seemed to hold their breath, waiting to see how exactly this bomb would explode.

Thane sighed. He knew there was no answer he could give that would get his backpack back in one piece. No answer but one.

He held the thick rubber glove on his right hand by pinching it between his arm and body and pulled slowly, revealing the dragon claws underneath. "Do you want to make me try and take it?"

"Shredding--" Kearney swore and stepped back. Thane stood there with one hand exposed and the other still in its glove, holding his towel in place. "You're that Song-broken dragon freak."

The insult felt harsher coming from the clearly Shae-blooded Kearney. "Yeah," Thane said. "That's me." He held out his clawed hand toward the short man, his cobalt blue claws glistening and still wet.

Kearney blinked, then laughed. "Songless trash," he mocked, and threw the backpack over the row of lockers towards the door. "Get it yourself."

Thane turned away from the sounds of their laughter. For a brief moment his eyes met those of the boy who'd spoken up. His grey face was carefully expressionless. He gave Thane a brief nod, whether of respect or commiseration Thane couldn't tell and didn't really care about at the moment. He was just grateful to escape.

Thane retrieved his backpack from the floor and dressed in the bathroom, away from the showers. Putting his glove back on was tricky, and he hissed as one of his talons left a dark red line across his left arm. He used the faded towel to clean the blood after drying off his hair, then stuffed everything back into his backpack and put his shoes back on. He stared at the damp and blood streaked towel. Leaving it in the bathroom made him feel guilty, but he didn't want to walk back through the locker room to drop it in the laundry bins.

"I'll take it," a voice said behind him, and a door closed. Thane glanced back and saw the boy with grey skin, dressed now with damp hair that was only slightly darker than his skin. The two boys stood and stared at each other in silence, until Thane tossed the towel over. The other boy caught it in the air. If he saw the blood, he didn't comment.

"Thanks," Thane said.

"Have you ever had a small dog?" the boy asked. Thane shook his head. "My sister had one. Never shut up. Always tried to sound dangerous, and attacked anything that moved. I hated that dog." Thane blinked, and waited. "Kearney's like that. Feels small, inside. Barks a lot. Makes me want to punt him sometimes. Not all Chauns are like that."

"That's a Chaun?" Thane asked. The boy nodded.

"They're all short, mostly red or blonde hair. You really want to make him mad, mention gold or rainbows. Drives him crazy. Best line I've ever heard on him was Twitch. Asked Kearney why he wasn't in a tree somewhere making cookies." The corner of the grey mouth lifted a little, and Thane gave a small smile back.

Hearing about Twitch and the Chaun reminded Thane of something Twitch had said. "Why are Chauns angry at amusement parks?"

The grey skinned boy laughed. "They're too short to ride the rides."

Thane laughed despite himself.

The other boy lifted the dirty towel in a small salute, and went back into the locker room. The small act of kindness made Thane feel better, and he went back to his dorm room to drop off his backpack before going to breakfast. Twitch was already gone. As Thane was leaving the room the cell phone in his pocket buzzed, a location based alert that Thane had not set on it.

It was a message from Twitch. "Don't touch the project on my bed. General Gage wants to see you after breakfast in the overseer's office. I'll be back tonight. Don't touch my stuff."

Thane glanced at the jumble of gears, wires, twisted metal, old cell phones, and other things he couldn't begin to identify that covered Twitch's cot. A soldering iron sat on the end table, still plugged in and smoking. Thane looked at the message again, then sighed and unplugged it. Twitch might get mad, but Thane's stuff was in here.

Thane left the building again and exited into bright morning sunlight. Even this early on a Sunday morning in November, the air was humid and warm and he was glad he'd left his hoodie behind. Thane walked toward building five, the cafeteria, and circled to the back. The entrance to the student cafeteria stood open and Thane could hear the wall of sound from all the students inside having breakfast. He paused before the door and took one deep breath. In and out slowly, through his nose. Thane walked in.

The noise of hundreds of voices all talking at once enveloped him. The student cafeteria wasn't quite the cacophony of noise, color, and surrealism that the team mess hall provided, but it was easily twice as intense as the Payson High lunchroom. The bright fluorescent lights bore down leaving no shadows to hide in. The enhanced or varied abilities of the students made everyone stand out, with flashes of color or patterns to draw the eye. Thane stayed next to the wall and made his way to the end of the line.

"Thane!" Remi's voice carried over the general tumult, and Thane glanced around until he saw her waving at him from a table. Her bright smile warmed him, and he held up his hand in acknowledgement. Satisfied, she sat back down and resumed talking.

Thane filled his tray with scrambled eggs, pancakes, biscuits, and a banana so Remi wouldn't tease him about never eating fruit. He passed between the lunch monitors-- a pair of bored looking Felidae with wrinkled noses-- who scanned the implant in his forearm and waved him onward.

"Scoot over, Naessa," Remi instructed, and she and her blue-haired roommate inched over to make room for Thane. The boy that had been sitting on Remi's other side gave him a dirty look. Thane ignored it. He saw Remi look at his tray and deliberately picked up the banana and peeled it before taking a large bite.

His best friend grinned at him before resuming her conversation. "No, Axial History is a million times more interesting than American Civ., I promise. You're not missing anything," she said to Naessa, who looked relieved.

"But what about dances?" another girl asked. She was new to the table, and Thane didn't know her name. There was something about her that unsettled him, but he couldn't decide exactly what.

"What do you mean?" Remi asked. She loved this topic of conversation, Thane knew. Remi had attended three different high schools and so everyone considered her the authority on what normal human high school was like, even though she was still a sophomore.

"Dances, like the prom. Don't you miss that?" the girl pressed.

"You don't have dances here?" Remi looked shocked. Thane was immeasurably relieved.

"They say it isn't safe for us because we haven't mastered all our affinities yet," the girl whined. The others around the table nodded, their feelings of annoyance or dismay expressed by furrowed eyebrows and downturned lips.

Remi patted the girl's hand consolingly. "I'm sure we can do something about that. I'll talk to my--"

"I have to go to the overseer's office after breakfast," Thane cut in, preventing Remi from referring to her father, General Gage. She was supposed to keep their relationship a secret, so she had registered here as Remi Quinn. She had initially resisted the use of her mother's maiden name, but acquiesced when Thane pointed out this wasn't really a lie, and when General Gage had said it was a choice between using Quinn or not attending Sanctum.

The new girl glanced at him, her eyes narrow, and Thane realized her pupils were slitted vertically like Jaeger the imp. Remi was surprised by his outburst too, but she smiled at him while the widening of her eyes told Thane she realized her almost verbal slip. "What does the overseer want? Maybe you could ask her about the dances," Remi suggested. The rest of his peers at the table added their support to this idea, and the girl with the cat eyes smiled at him. He felt like a mouse.

"I don't know what she wants. I just had a message that she wanted to see me." Remi's friends were looking at him expectantly, so he added, "I'll ask about dances if I can." That pleased them, and they returned to their conversations. He had taken several bites when he heard his name. Thane looked up and saw Naessa watching him, clearly waiting for something. "What?" he asked.

"I asked how Twitch was," the tall blue-haired girl repeated. Thane suddenly remembered where he had seen her the first time. When Twitch had given him a tour of Sanctum, Naessa had been in a group of students that walked by. Thane remembered she'd been the one that had smiled at the tech genius. He was suddenly sure that this girl being Remi's roommate wasn't random, and wondered what else Twitch had arranged when he'd been in the student system setting Remi and Thane's classes.

"He's fine. Gone today, but he'll be back tonight," Thane responded. The answer seemed to satisfy her, and she turned to the girl on her other side. Briefly Thane and Remi were the only two not engaged in talking, and Remi dropped her napkin with the pretense of leaning closer to Thane.

"I always forget that stupid rule. I hate not being able to talk about my dad," she whispered towards the ground next to him.

"Your welcome," he replied. "I'm meeting your dad in the overseer's office. Twitch left me the message." She frowned at him as she straightened.

"Well, I'm done," she announced. "Thane, I'll walk with you to the office. Give you moral support before you go and face the thunder queen." The others around the table snickered. The thunder queen was the student body's nickname for the overseer, who was a cross between principal and military leader for the Shaelings. Although not draconic herself, any student who'd ever been to her office would swear that she could send a group of dragons to detention and make sure they went. She was infamous for strict adherence to rules and when the matter concerned the students under her care, her word was law. Even the Guardian Council members would tread cautiously with her.

Thane rose, stuffing the last few bites of pancake into his mouth before lifting his tray. He followed Remi to the door and dumped the trash and handed in the plates and silverware, getting a nod from the Felidae standing watch at the exit. The best friends emerged into the sunlight outside. The humidity left a sheen of water on their cheeks, and the sound from the cafeteria faded behind them as they walked towards the administration building, which was the western wing of Building 1. The significance of having the principal's office as part of the infirmary was not lost on Thane. You step out of line, we send you down the hall. Or we have someone carry you there.

Remi glanced around before speaking in a low whisper. "You really have no idea why my dad wants to see you?" Thane shook his head and Remi pursed her lips, brow furrowing. "I don't like this. I thought we were both supposed to cut off contact with him once we started school here. Him wanting to talk to you can't be anything good."

"Maybe he wants to talk about you," Thane suggested. "The two of you can't be seen together here, and calling you to the office might be too dangerous. Most people remember me from the week I spent here before," he flinched at the memory of Corellian and his friends calling him tadpole every time they saw him, "so him talking to me isn't that strange."

Remi shrugged. "Maybe. But it doesn't seem like him. If he was worried about me, he'd talk to me, not you." She nodded with a firm jerk of her chin. "I'm waiting for you outside."

"But you'll miss class--"

"And they'll report me," she cut him off, "and I'll get written up, and I'm new so maybe I got lost and they'll talk to me then it'll be over." She squared her shoulders and walked a little faster. "I'm waiting."

Thane didn't argue further. He knew it was pointless, and a small part of him was worried enough to be glad she would be there when he got out. They arrived at the doors to the administration wing of the infirmary and Thane paused. "Wait out here?" he asked.

"Outside? Bit it's so hot..." Remi began, then looked at him more closely. "Why?"

Thane tried to explain. "If it's something really bad, or if they're going to kick me out because I don't have my song anymore, I don't think you... I don't want..." he struggled to articulate his concern. "You shouldn't be seen with me in case I'm in trouble," he finished lamely.

She raised one eyebrow at him and narrowed one eye. "It isn't your job to protect me," she said, and breezed past him into the building. Thane sighed, and followed. He was never going to learn how to get her to do things for her own good.

Outside the overseer's office the secretary was rapidly filing away documents and working on the computer. Thane tried not to stare as unsuccessfully as last time. Besides the woman's striking dark features and cocoa colored skin, her eight arms that moved independently around the room made her stand out as something more than human. She glared at them around her computer monitor. "Yes?" she said, the chill in her voice strong enough to make Thane shiver.

"He's supposed to see the overseer, Ms. Tagore," Remi said when Thane didn't respond.

"And you?" Ms. Tagore's dark eyes raked up and down Remi.

"I'm waiting for him," Remi said. Before the secretary could object or bathe her in more disdain, Remi spun on her heel and sat on one of the chairs in the hallway.

All eight hands still engaged in other tasks, Ms. Tagore turned the full force of her gaze on Thane. He waited, looking down. After a moment, he heard her snap, "Name?"

"Thane Whitaker."

"Oh," the tone of her voice changed drastically, the cold brusqueness gone. Even her hands on the keyboard paused, the absence of clicking keys jarring. He glanced up at her sideways and saw her studying him. Ms. Tagore's frown was gone. "She's waiting for you. Through there."

Thane had one awkward moment when he wasn't sure which hand she was using to direct him, but one paused in filing papers and pointed to a door until he began to walk towards it. Then the hand resumed working, and Thane opened the door and went through, shutting it behind him.

He was in a narrow antechamber, the waiting area beyond the guard secretary. The room had no windows and was small enough that Thane could walk the entire length and width in four, maybe five steps. The lights here were dim and the only thing in the room were two chairs, one pressed against either wall. The thunder queen's office was just past the second doorway, which stood ajar. Light and sound spilled out from that small gap, and Thane paused to listen.

"I don't like this," the overseer's clipped tones were audible. "First you bring that criminal in to my office, and now you want to bring one of my students in here with him?"

"These are unusual circumstances, Ms. Yemaja," General Gage sounded confident and calm, and Thane was relieved the general was already there.

"Fine," she said, although she sounded anything but fine, "on one condition. Mr. Whitaker has to choose to stay. I won't force him."

"Agreed," General Gage said. What was going on? Thane knocked on the door and waited.

"Come in," Ms. Yemaja ordered. Thane entered the room and closed the door behind him. His eyes swept the room, searching for General Gage's solid, comforting presence.

He hadn't been in the overseer's office before, but it was immediately apparent that her reputation was not unfounded. Thane stood at the bottom of the room near the door. Three feet in front of him was a platform at about the height of his waist, upon which sat a row of five chairs. Beyond that was another raised platform on which sat an enormous dark wooden desk. Ms. Yemaja sat behind it, staring down at him, her large white eyes starkly contrasted by her smooth, dark skin.

"Thane Whitaker," when she spoke the words echoed through the room. Thane glanced up at the ceiling and noticed the unmistakable ridges of a room designed for acoustics. It was an impressive bit of theatrics. "You have been summoned because General Gage wishes to speak with you. Will you hear him?"

Where was the general? "Yes," he answered, speaking quietly into the corner nearest him. His glance around the room and up to the ceiling told him where the sound would carry best, and he knew his whisper would sound as loud as to her as a normal voice. Thane hated yelling.

He had the satisfaction of seeing her jump. "Well," she said, and then glared at him. Making her jump may not have been a good idea. "Fine. Take a seat," and she indicated the row of chairs below her. Thane climbed up onto the raised platform and sat down.

General Gage's voice came from somewhere behind him. "It's good to see you, son," he said. Thane craned his neck around and saw Remi's father coming down a short set of stairs on the far left of the room. He must have been standing behind Ms. Yemaja.

"You too, sir," Thane said, rising to his feet and taking the general's outstretched hand.

"Sit boy, sit," Gage waved him back to his chair. "We have to talk about something that happened yesterday evening. I've brought someone for you to listen to, and you can ask him questions, if you like. But first I want you to hear everything he has to say."

"General Gage, I must object," Ms. Yemaja cut in. "This young man is underage to be in our program as is, and I don't believe exposing him to further trauma is a good way to serve his interests--"

"The truth is in everyone's best interests, Ms. Yemaja," Gage interrupted, his face not changing expression. "This young man, more than almost any other, is someone who deserves the truth." She didn't respond, and Gage pressed his earpiece. "Bring him in."

A side door opened and Brennan Taylor entered, escorting a man with dirty brown hair who couldn't be more than twenty. Brennan was holding the younger and much shorter man by the shoulder. Thane noticed that the other man was in handcuffs, and Brennan gave the prisoner a baleful glare before turning to Thane and winking.

"Thane, this is Broussard," General Gage began. "He has been a guest of ours in a holding facility for a little more than twelve weeks now. Last night he witnessed something that I feel would be of interest to you. Broussard, tell us what you saw."

"Didn't see anything," Broussard responded, his brows drawn down and mumbling his words.

"Fair enough," General Gage conceded. "Tell us what you heard."

"I'd rather not," Broussard said.

"You have served approximately half your sentence, is that correct?" Gage asked. The short man nodded. "Then what happens to you?"

"I go to a rehabilitation facility to learn to use my affinity without exploitation or exposure," Broussard mumbled. He kept his shoulders hunched and down, never looking up at anyone directly.

"What if we were to arrange for your transfer to that facility tomorrow?" General Gage asked. "After all, no crime that you were convicted for was violent or dangerous."

"If I tell you about last night, I can get out of holding tomorrow?" Broussard asked. He looked at Gage sideways without raising his head. He seemed to stand balled up on himself, as if expecting to be beaten at any moment.

"That's right. Tomorrow. And you wouldn't go back to holding tonight, you could stay under supervision here," General Gage added.

"Can I get your word on that?" Broussard's voice was timid and shook slightly.

"You have my word," Gage confirmed.

"Lovely," Broussard said, standing straight and stretching. He locked eyes with General Gage. "On to business. Last night I was taking my usual walk around my cell, stretching my legs, and then I felt the earth shake. Someone had set off an explosion, and a big one." He rolled his shoulders and glanced at Brennan. "Get me a chair, would ya? It's hard to stand up like this while relating such a traumatic event."

Brennan rolled his eyes and shook his head. "Go on," Gage prompted.

"It's hard to remember all the details, being so tired," Broussard looked back at Brennan again. "A chair sure would help."

Brennan cuffed him on the back of the head. "I'll be the one supervising you tonight. This could be a very unpleasant twenty-four hours if I'm grumpy."

"Point taken." The man ran his fingers through his hair, the handcuffs dragging his other hand along with the motion. "There was a boom. Then another one, and someone blew a hole in the wall. While the dust was flying around I got under my bunk. Not many would fit under a space like that, so they likely wouldn't look for anyone there. I heard footsteps coming closer, and then a man's voice. He was dressed in a really nice suit, I mean, tailored and worth at least a couple grand."

"I thought you didn't see anything," Brennan cut in.

"I peeked, okay?" Broussard grinned. "I was curious. It's my curse. Anyway, so this guy and his guards come through the hole and they start talking to the redhead across the aisle from me."

Thane blinked. Redhead? Did he mean...

"He called her 'Dearest Cressa,' or some sap like that, and made a big deal out of her finding somebody. She said she had, and they cut out the bars to get her out. The guy in the suit asked her what his name was, and she said 'Thane Whitaker.'" Broussard blinked and looked at Thane. "Is that you? He called you Thane," the short man jerked his head at General Gage.

"Go on," Gage ordered.

"Fine, need to know, whatever. So anyway, she said 'Thane Whitaker' like she was saying 'The Holy Grail' or 'Endless Bacon,' then they get all kissy-face." Broussard puckered his lips, and Thane felt sick inside. This couldn't be real; it couldn't be what he thought. "Then the suit guy started asking her how she got caught and about trying to escape with his son to the Shaerealm and demanding ransom. She tried to deny it, but he wasn't listening. Then his guys shot her and they left before the guards came." Broussard yawned and looked back at Thane and General Gage. "You may want to get that kid a bucket."

Thane could feel the sweat on his face and the knot in his belly, "You okay, kid?" Brennan asked.

"Who... who was the man? In the suit?" Thane asked. It was hard for him to get the words out. Why didn't anything ever get to be easy for him?

"Get that criminal out of my office," Ms. Yemaja hissed.

"Take him away, Mr. Taylor," General Gage ordered. Brennan gave Thane one more concerned look as he grabbed Broussard's shoulder and steered the short man back out the side door, and closed it behind him.

"Who?" Thane asked again.

"I must protest this again, General Gage," Ms. Yemaja said.

"Thane, the man who broke into the holding facility and extracted information from Cressida Rasmussen was looking for you. It was Ruan de Argos." Thane's stomach flexed and the air whooshed out of his lungs as if Remi's father had punched him in the gut. "Your father knows where and who you are."

He knows who I am, Thane thought. *I wish I did.*

20

CHAPTER 2

"I'm glad she's dead," Remi growled. She absently rubbed the scar on her leg just above her knee. "She deserved it. That psychopath tried to kill me and used you."

Thane didn't answer her. Instead he rewound the video feed again, and watched from the high vantage point as Broussard paced his cell and Ms. Rasmussen read a book. There was no sound, so the explosion manifested with the camera shaking and dirt and stone flying through the air. The hole in the wall appeared through the dust on the very edge of the picture. Men with large guns came through and immediately one aimed and fired at the camera just as the man in the suit entered the frame. Then the screen went dark.

Twitch's hand appeared as he leaned over Thane's shoulder, pressing a few keys in quick succession. The film went back frame by black frame until the last visible image reappeared. Twitch paused the video feed.

"That's him," he said, stepping back.

Thane leaned forward. The man's face was small and in the background of the shot. He squinted, trying to get a better look and tapped the screen twice on the man's face so the image would zoom in on that spot. The resolution was poor and the screen pixelated, but Thane could see the strong jawline and dark hair of the man who was his father. The man who sent Ms. Rasmussen to look for him, then killed her. The man who's spoken name brought legions of minions to attack. The man who was really a dragon.

Ruan de Argos.

This blurry image was as close to his biological father as Thane had ever been. It was a lot to process. He touched the image again, and it zoomed in closer so that Ruan's head filled the screen. At that resolution, it was hard to tell what the shape even was. Thane felt like that, like his whole world had gotten so blown out that it was hard to tell what anything was anymore.

"What are you going to do?" Remi asked him.

Thane shrugged. "Nothing."

"Nothing? How can you do nothing?"

Thane double tapped the screen to make the picture return to normal size. "What can I do?" He pushed back from the computer terminal and swiveled his chair to face her, looking up into her eyes. "He knows I'm in Sanctum but not what I look like. He can't get in here to get me and no one is going to let me out to find him, even if I wanted to."

"You don't want to meet him?" Remi asked, one eyebrow raised.

"I don't know," Thane admitted. "I was relieved when Bert wasn't my father. I don't have to be like him. But..." he trailed off and looked back over his shoulder at the screen and the image of the man in the suit. "He's no hero either. If I don't ever meet him, maybe I won't find out he's evil. Chaotic I can deal with. Charlie's chaotic," he heard Remi snort and turned back to her. "Charlie's not so bad. He's--"

"Creepy," Remi interjected.

"You haven't seen him since the cave," Twitch said. "Where we saved your life."

"Yeah, but he kept calling me 'love' and hovering and he's like a million years old. I don't like the way he looks at me. I mean, he's your great grandpa." Remi scrunched up her nose. "You saved my life the most, Thane, and it didn't make you all weird and possessive."

Thane shifted in his seat. He wanted to defend Charlie, say that he really was a great person, but the conversation rubbed him the wrong way. Not because of Charlie, but because of Remi. When Remi had been lying on the ground and bleeding out, Thane, Charlie, and Twitch had seen her soul. Physically she was human, but her soul was a phoenix. She had lived for hundreds of years, being reincarnated every lifetime. The phoenix-souled couldn't remember their past lives, and so Remi didn't remember that she was Charlie's truest love, the woman he searched for and was not complete without.

Thane knew the whole story, because Charlie had told him all about the phoenix. Neither of them knew then that it was Remi. After the fight with Ms. Rasmussen at the cave, Charlie had pulled Thane aside and made him swear not to tell Remi about their history or her past lives. Thane had argued, but Charlie said it would hurt Remi to know. It would put too much pressure on her, trying to remember. Or she wouldn't believe him, and would be angry. She never needed to know, because frankly to her it didn't matter. It wouldn't change who she was, it could only hurt her.

In the end, Thane had agreed. But he didn't like it. Especially knowing how important the truth was to Remi, and how she usually didn't forgive those who lied to her. Thane assumed Twitch was under a similar oath not to say anything because the tech savvy teenager was tapping his leg with two fingers and counting under his breath. Twitch was the twitchiest when he felt uncomfortable.

Thane tapped the mouse and the image on the screen vanished. "Creepy's still better than evil," he finally said and pushed away from the terminal. He rose to his feet and addressed Twitch. "You aren't going to be in trouble for showing me that?"

Twitch snorted. "Who would know?" He took the seat Thane had vacated and scooted forward. "You guys should get going. I have work to do."

"Okay," Thane said and he and Remi turned to leave.

"Bye Twitch!" Remi called. "Oh, and Naessa asked about you."

"Hang on, there's a message coming through- she did?" Twitch spun to face them. "Asked what about me?"

"What message?" asked Thane.

"She asked Thane how you were doing. It was this morning at breakfast," Remi answered.

"What did she say?" Twitch asked, and added to his left, "No, I don't care, but if people are talking about me I should know."

"Who are you talking to?" Remi asked.

Twitch's eyes widened and his whole body froze except for his left eyelid, which began spasming. "What? No one. You. There's a priority message that just came through and it involves you two." He turned back around and clicked the mouse a few times.

A message window popped up on the large overhead left monitor of the three-screen array. The subject line said, "MANDATORY HAND-TO-HAND COMBAT CLASS" in all capitals, and it was sent to a long list of email addresses. Twitch opened the message for Thane and Remi to read.

"Attention teachers, councilors, advisors, and Shaeling representatives: there has been a mandatory hand-to-hand combat class added to the curriculum for students who have either been at the primary Sanctum training facility for less than six months, are level two or lower, or have a phasic ability of 10% or less. This class will be taught three times per week beginning tonight at 19:00. The following students are required to attend."

Remi's name was at the top of the list, and Thane's was about a third of the way down. "Have they done this before?" Thane asked.

Twitch shrugged. "Everyone is required to take combat training from the second year on. They're starting you guys earlier, that's all."

"Wonder why," Thane said, looking at the list again.

Remi jabbed her finger towards her name. "That's why. I'm why." She shook her head. "You men. You're all still trying to protect me."

"We protect each other," Thane amended. "I need this more than you do."

She grinned and made a playful jab at him. Her fist found his shoulder easily. "Yeah, that's true. Let's go; we'll just have time to grab some food before this new class. You want to come?" Remi added that last to Twitch.

He shook his head. "I was serious about having work to do. I'm behind since I've been gone all day."

"I'll tell Naessa hi for you," Remi said. Twitch flinched and blushed.

"Whatever," he said, and added, "you shouldn't think this is so funny," towards his left knee.

After dinner Remi and Thane made their way across the compound with several other students from the cafeteria who'd been notified of their mandatory enrollment in the combat class by a general announcement. Naessa wasn't there since she was level three and had been at Sanctum for over a year now, but several of Remi's other friends came and Thane was caught up in the chatter of a much larger group of peers than he'd ever been in before. For the first time in his life he found himself wishing he had something to say to them. He couldn't think of anything. So he walked silently among them in the middle, because every time he tried to trail behind Remi would alter her pace to match his and the group would follow her lead.

Building eleven loomed large ahead of them and Thane tried to muster some enthusiasm. Thane flexed his talons inside the black rubber. He needed to learn to defend himself and the class promised to be interesting, but his thoughts kept turning back to that pixilated image of the dragon who was his biological father. Now that Ruan de Argos knew where Thane was, would Ruan attack Sanctum? Both General Gage and Twitch thought that was unlikely. Ruan was too smart to try something that risky and with so little chance of success. No, General Gage had assured Thane that so long as he stayed within the protective dome of Sanctum, he would be safe.

No matter how large the cage, Thane was still trapped. He glared resentfully at the distant shimmer of the shield high overhead, only visible because the fading rays of the setting sun refracted against it instead of shining though as usual. Not for the first time Thane wondered just where in the world Sanctum was, that the air inside the dome was balmy and warm even in late November.

The students filed inside building eleven and walked along the hallway and up the stairs, the enclosed concrete walls bouncing and echoing their voices back. The hand-to-hand combat class was going to take place in the third floor gym. Thane tried once last time to drop back so he could enter near the tail end of the group as Remi and the rest of her friends entered.

Remi hissed. "No way," she said.

Thane's head jerked up and he ran into the room. She'd sounded so angry he thought she was in trouble, and he stopped next to her with his hands in a defensive position. He checked to see where the danger was coming from. Remi stood with her hands on her hips and her eyes narrowed, staring at the middle of the huge room and the instructor who waited there.

Thane glanced at the man and back at Remi, and then looked again without quite understanding. The man was lean and muscular and all the female students in the room, except notably Remi, immediately started whispering to each other and gazing at him. He was talking to someone else with his back to Thane, but the shaved clean head looked familiar. It wasn't until he turned around that everything clicked.

"Charlie," Thane said, feeling his lips stretch into a smile and walked forward. His sometime mentor and grandfather grinned at him and clapped him across the shoulders, pulling him in for a brief rough embrace.

"Tadpole. Missed me?" Charlie grinned at him.

Thane grinned back and shrugged. "No. Didn't even recognize you at first." Saying it out loud, Thane realized why. Charlie was a centuries old dragon who, like all dragons, could transform himself to look human. Every other time Thane had seen him Charlie had looked in his late thirties to early forties. Right now he looked barely twenty. Glancing back to where Remi stood glaring at them both he understood why. "Laying it on a little thick, don't you think?"

"I dinnae ken what you're on about," Charlie said. The ancient blue dragon clapped his hands together twice. "Oi! Let's get fair tae walkin'. Get yer bahookies lined up in six rows of five each, littles in the front."

The students milled around, and it took several minutes before they'd managed to comply with his instructions. Thane found himself near the back of his line with one boy and two girls in front of him. Remi was in the line next to him, second from the front. Even from behind Thane could see how tense she was, her hands clenching and unclenching in fists. He didn't understand what about Charlie discomfited her so much since she didn't know about her lifetimes of history with the dragon, but he wished he could help her somehow.

"All right, then, eyes tae the front!" Charlie said, his command echoing off the far walls. "I'm sure yer all guddle when it comes tae protecting yerselves from the baddies, which is why yer in here. I'm cried Charlie, and I'm here at the special request of yer own headmistress and make no mistake-- if yer failing in my class it'll be her yer answering tae. I've not the time tae coddle ye along. Ye ken?"

There was a general mumble in response. Thane was positive that most the students had no idea what his grandfather had just said. He sighed inwardly and hoped that Charlie wouldn't--

"Tadpole! Bring yerself tae the front."

Groaning inwardly, Thane trudged to the front of the room without looking up. "Ye'll all be with a partner, and this laddie here is mine. Get yer feet set," Charlie added in a more normal voice, and helped Thane set his feet in a boxing stance, with his right foot in front. "The first step in fighting is lowering yer center. Ye'll be harder tae knock down if yer already lower tae the ground, so." The dragon man placed his feet in the same boxing stance and bent his knees, placing one hand over his stomach to indicate where his center was.

"There's only three good rules to fighting, and it'll be yer job tae memorize 'em. Lower yer center. Keep up yer guard. And dinnae get killed."

A few snickers and eye rolls followed his statement, and Charlie straightened and turned to face them. "Think it's funny, eh? Well sure, it sounds so simple. Would anyone like tae volunteer tae try?" He was smiling, but the look in his eyes was cold and although he didn't move, the front row of students shied away. "I'll tell ye survive. But ye'll get others who'll say different, leaders who'll say dinnae lose sight of the mission and encourage ye tae sacrifice. I'm telling ye now, yer mission," and he put a disdainful emphasis on the word, "is tae get away."

"Wimp," Remi said. It was under her breath, but it wasn't exactly quiet. The few noises the class had been making stopped as if someone had turned the sound off. All eyes snapped to their combat instructor to see how he would react.

There was a slight tightening of the skin around his eyes, but he continued speaking as if he hadn't heard. "If ye want tae keep hammering away at the grand evil yer sent tae fight, stay living. There's no shame in running off, so long as yer full well able tae come back fit like." Charlie's gaze swept over them all. "Now that's clear, we'll start at the beginning again. Lower yer center."

"Chicken," Remi's voice was slightly louder. Charlie's jaw went rigid, but he ignored her again. Thane's heart was hammering in his chest. What was she doing? Did she want to make him mad? He looked over at her, standing in the second row and glaring at the dragon man with her fists clenched at her sides. Thane recognized the expression on her face with her eyes narrow and the way she held her shoulders hunched and forward. Remi was furious.

Charlie continued with his lesson. "Lowering yer center makes ye more balanced and harder tae knock down. If ye--"

"You really think we should just run away?" Remi wasn't trying to whisper anymore. "Just because we're too terrified to stand and take it?"

Thane's grandfather's hands were shaking and his voice was tight. "Ye must bend yer knees while keeping yer feet ahead--"

"There's no shame in abandoning the people depending on you?" Remi was speaking loudly enough that each word echoed once off the far wall. The students had given up all pretense of following Charlie's instructions, and instead were riveted on the rising confrontation with those closest to Charlie and those closest to Remi edging away. "You're a coward, worse than a deserter, because when things get hard you leave!"

"Yer the one who always dies!" The echoes of Charlie's bellow bounced around the room and the cowering students.

"She didn't die!" Thane looked at Remi's face as she shrieked back, the defiance in her voice undercut to anyone who could see the tears in her eyes.

Charlie could, and his angry posture evaporated. "Love, what are ye--"

Before he could finish Remi spun on her heel and fled the room. Thane followed, catching the door as it bounced and closing it, catching one last glimpse of the stunned class. He chased Remi down the hall and out of the building until they burst through the doors and into the cooling night beyond.

Remi didn't look at him. She also didn't slow down, but Thane didn't have any problems keeping up. He ran alongside her shoulder and waited. They continued to run, Remi breathing heavier than the running would need and Thane staying quiet beside her.

"I'm going to get him fired," she announced. "He has no business being here." The only response he could think of, that Charlie couldn't actually be fired since he didn't work for Sanctum, seemed unwise. Thane didn't say anything.

She slowed to a walk and Thane did too, watching her as she looked around. He wanted to ask if she was all right, what was wrong, or how he could help, but he was fairly certain that any of those questions would get him punched. So he asked the only other thing he really wanted to know. "Where are we going?"

She picked a direction and started jogging, heading roughly in the direction of building nineteen and the far edge of Sanctum. "I'm going to see my father."

"What?" Thane stumbled, then corrected and caught up. "You're not supposed to do that," he began, and then paused. "How are you going to find him? Where are we going?"

"Building twenty," Remi answered. "That's Sanctum's main headquarters. The war room is there, and all the general's offices. The Guardian Council chambers are there too."

"How do you know that?"

"He told me." Remi looked at Thane sideways, an almost smile shadowing her lips. "He felt so guilty about lying to me that when I found out about all this he gave me ten minutes to ask any questions I could think of." She gave a tiny laugh. "He had no idea how much I already knew from you and Twitch, so he was really surprised by what I wanted to know. Including where his office was and how to find it. And how to get in."

She stopped at the hill between building nineteen and the rest of Sanctum, the grass covered hill where Thane had learned to scream with Paka and Jaeger and had a picnic with Charlie after destroying building fifteen. "What are you doing?" Thane asked as Remi studied the side of the hill nearest the barrier dome.

"Knocking," she said, and placed her hand in a small indent in the grass. "*Enim bonum omnium.*" As she spoke, the indent around her hand began to glow with a blue light. There was a click, and a grinding sound like metal against dirt, and a piece of the hillside the size of a large door slid away. Behind it was a short staircase that broadened into a set of wooden double doors engraved with a huge seal.

"Their building is underneath my hill?" Thane asked in disbelief.

Remi looked at him. "Your hill?"

Thane shrugged, embarrassed, and started down the stairs. Remi went with him, and as they neared the seal the large wooden doors slid apart silently. Beyond them was a startlingly normal hallway. Carpeted flooring and bare walls were lit by florescent lights, with doorways at regular intervals. Remi strode ahead of him, her short black hair bouncing around her ears as she walked past the first section of doorways and into a larger lobby area beyond.

"My mom didn't abandon us," Remi suddenly said. "She wasn't like that. Isn't like that. No matter what that creep says."

"Right," Thane agreed, because he didn't know what else to say. Remi had told him that her mother had been military too, like her dad, but she had left on a classified mission when Remi was six. She hadn't ever come back. Thane wanted to ask Remi what the other choice was, if her mother hadn't abandoned her mission but still hadn't come back but wasn't dead. He also wanted to keep his friendship with Remi, so he changed the subject.

"Elevators?" Thane asked. Remi pushed the call button and the light above the far left door lit up with a ding. They stepped inside, and she looked at the bay of buttons, considering.

"They go to twelve," Thane said. "There are twelve floors? This goes under ground for twelve floors?"

"Apparently," Remi said as she pushed the button with a "9" on it. "I don't know. He only told me he was in section nine." The elevator door shut with a small whoosh of compressed air, and then began to descend.

"Section?"

"Yeah, that's what--" The floor underneath them shuddered and jolted to a stop before suddenly throwing itself forward. Thane was thrown off balance and grabbed onto a bar, and Remi's shoulder hit into his sternum with a hard thud.

"Are we going sideways?" Thane asked, rubbing his chest.

Remi stood up. "It feels like it." She placed her hand against a wall and Thane did the same, feeling the vibrations of the metal underneath his hand. "It feels like..."

"We're moving really fast," Thane finished. Almost in response, the elevator slowed again and halted. Everything was silent and still.

"Why aren't the doors--" Remi began, but before she could finish the floor shot upwards with such force they were both thrown to the ground. It went faster, nearly shivering under the stress of speed and Thane could feel each tremor with his face. His nose was pressed flat against the floor and it scraped against the carpet as he tried to turn his head to see Remi.

She was sprawled on the floor also, but her head was turned towards him. She reached out towards him and he tried to grab her hand, but his thick rubber gloves had gotten skewed so he couldn't hold onto her.

"I'm going to try--" suddenly his stomach heaved and crawled into his throat as the elevator slowed so quickly that he and Remi rose into the air for several feet before slamming back down. The hand that had been reaching for Remi ended up underneath him, and he got the wind knocked out of him with his own fist. The elevator slowed gently to a stop, and then opened with a cheerful sounding ding.

"Can I help you?" a sweet female voice asked. Thane twisted his head around from where he lay gasping for air and saw an attractive blonde woman seated behind a desk. Her fingers hovered over her keyboard and she had one eyebrow raised behind thin wire glasses. Thane struggled to rise, pushing himself up on one knee.

Remi had no such difficulties. "We're here to see General Gage. Is he in his office?" she demanded. The woman blinked, but otherwise her expression didn't change.

"General Gage is in a meeting right now. You can wait, or I can take a message," she offered, her voice pleasantly helpful.

Thane cringed. He knew Remi was feeling neither pleasant nor willing to be helped. "I don't care," Remi said through clenched teeth. "I am going to see *my father*, and unless you'd like to find out what defenestration means, I recommend you get him or get out of my way."

"Remi," Thane wheezed, pushing himself to his feet. "You're not supposed to tell people--"

"The act of throwing something or someone out a window, usually motivated by politics," the woman said. Thane blinked at her. "It may also refer to the condition of being thrown out a window," she continued, and then turned back to her computer. "You've both placed me in and freed me from a difficult situation, Ms. Gage. I am General Gage's aide-de-camp, meaning that it is my directive to carry out all his wishes. I have strict orders to not give anyone access to General Gage or his office until otherwise specified. However, I also have equally concrete and standing orders to assist you and allow you access to your father whenever and wherever you demand it of me."

The tightness in Thane's chest lessened enough that his lungs began to work again. He took a deep, shuddering breath and both Remi and the General Gage's aide looked at him, Remi with concern and a flicker of annoyance, and the woman as if she was only just acknowledging his existence. "So what are you going to do?" Remi asked, her hands in fists and tossing her hair back.

"I am not going to give you access to General Gage or his office. However, should you decide you want to take it, I will allow you to do so. His office is the third door on the wall behind me. You'll need a keycard," without taking her eyes from her computer screen she pointed to a small white rectangle on her desk, "which I will also not give you nor prevent you from taking. Have a lovely evening, Ms. Gage." The woman continued typing as though there was no one else in the room with her.

Remi only hesitated for a moment before grabbing the keycard and walking past the aide. Thane followed gingerly behind her, but stopped next to the woman. "How could you stop someone who wanted to see General Gage?" he asked, curious.

The clicking of the keys stopped as she paused with her head cocked to one side, then turned it on that angle to face him. She raised one eyebrow again. "Your burnout persists, Mr. Whitaker," she stated. "Had you currently the capabilities listed in your file, you would not ask so impertinent a question."

He opened his mouth, then closed it again as she turned away and resumed typing. He almost wanted to poke her with his finger just to see if she was real, but something about the way she held herself in her chair suddenly made him think of Raven, the deadly Sang Evarish bartender at The Leaf and Dagger.

"Are you coming?" Remi asked, holding open the door to her father's office.

"Yeah," Thane said with one more look at the aide. Then he followed Remi into General Gage's office and was smacked in the face by the smell.

"Perfekt head," said a weak, familiar voice from a pile in the corner. "Do hyu haf something to drink?"

CHAPTER 3

"Jaeger?" Thane said, gagging on the smell of iodine and blood and viscera, along with a sweet, sticky scent he couldn't place. The red imp unwound himself from where he huddled on a small pile of cloth in the corner, clutching a small stuffed toy dog in one hand. It was brown and black and missing an eye, with a drying streak of purplish blood diagonally across its back. Jaeger pulled it close and sighed, shuddering. "What are you doing here?"

The last time Thane had seen the devilish imp he had been climbing into a tear in the Weave, quite literally wiggling through a hole in the universe. General Gage had torn that hole. Jaeger had gone on a secret mission into the Shaerealm, the universe that had gotten tangled with our own, and had somehow found a way back.

With a stuffed dog. Jaeger sighed again, licking a wound on his arm with a long forked tongue while he cuddled the toy and held his wings slightly open, protectively. "Aye cannot say." He swallowed. "No one was to know Aye was here. Aye may only speak to the general--"

"That's mine," Remi spoke, seeming to come out of the shock she'd been in ever since Jaeger had first spoken. Thane forgot she hadn't met Jaeger yet. The imp was quite a surprise the first time, as most of the Shae were only part Shae-blooded, and most were more than half human. Full blooded Shae were rare and most of those that crossed over were still humanoid in size and form. Jaeger was about the size of a monkey, the kind that would sit on your shoulder, but a dark scarlet red color with a face like a wrinkled old man and disproportionally large leathery wings. Those wings immediately closed around his body and the little dog.

"Is not. It's mine. Aye founds it, Aye gets to keep it," his voice sounded strange coming from the inside of his wings, like someone talking through a cardboard tube. "Dids hyu bleed to bring it back? No. It is mine. Ask perfekt head. Those are the rules."

Remi glanced at Thane. He hadn't told her about Jaeger's strange mission and Gage's directive for secrecy. It had seemed so important that even though Gage didn't know Thane was there, Thane protected the knowledge. Not that it'd been difficult; Thane had been busy moving to Sanctum and starting school, and no one had asked him anything about it anyway.

"Where did you get it?" Thane asked the imp.

"It is secret. Aye can only talk to General Gage. That is also a rule." The cocoon of imp trembled. "Aye don't care if Aye stole it, Aye don't care that hyu got back first. Aye haf rescued Caspian and he is mine."

"Caspian?" Remi took a step towards the whimpering imp. "He's mine! From when I was little, I lost him!"

"What do you mean, you got back first?" Thane asked.

"And rescued him from what? Give him back, you're getting your icky demon blood all over my dog," Remi demanded.

"He isn't a daemon, he's an imp," Thane corrected, thinking of Rip, the man who truly was possessed by a daemon. "Jaeger, why are you bleeding?"

The little imp wailed and his wings drooped, revealing his tear-stained face. "Aye am bleeding because Aye fought to save Caspian my puppy from the Sang, and now General Gage will be mad because she escaped and made it back first and Aye wasn't supposed to let her see me," he sniffed, pointing at Remi. "Now Andrus will be angry and he won't let me keep Caspian because she has crossed time and space before Aye could report and please perfekt head Aye am so thirsty."

"What are you talking about?" Thane and Remi asked together.

"Are you hurt anywhere else?" Thane added.

36

Remi grimaced. She stepped forward and Jaeger hissed, pulling the little dog further away. "Stop it," Remi said, but gently, as she reached out. "Give me your arm, the one that's hurt."

Tentatively Jaeger held out his cut arm, still trying to lick it. "Don't do that," Remi instructed. "Thane, find some water."

"Um," Thane said, looking around the room. He stuck his head out into the lobby area, opening the door just barely enough for his head to fit through. "Do you have any water?"

The woman at the computer continued to type with one hand while reaching into a desk drawer with another. She pulled out a bottled water and tossed it to Thane without looking. He held out a hand to catch it, and fumbled it in his glove before trapping it between his body and arm. "Thanks."

He shut the door again and turned back. "I have--" he stopped. Remi was sitting cross-legged on the floor with Jaeger on her lap like a child, cuddling the well worn and battle scarred Caspian. She was wrapping his arm with some of the cloth from the pile he'd been laying on.

"--the water," Thane finished lamely, and handed it over. Jaeger grabbed it with his other hand and rather than trying to open it, just bit the entire top off and guzzled the contents.

"Ah. Better. Not good yet, but better. Hyu are nice here," Jaeger said, flicking his tongue to lick Remi on the cheek. "And prettier. And younger!"

"Who do you think I am?" Remi asked.

"Aye cannot tell hyu who hyu are. Aye can only tell General Gage," Jaeger insisted. "He sent me to find hyu and Aye found hyu and took my puppy as proof."

"I'm not whoever you're thinking I am," Remi insisted. "I haven't crossed anything. I've been here."

"But hyu are just like hyu. Hyu could not be anyone else," Jaeger insisted.

"I--," Remi paused, unsure how to argue against that logic.

Thane decided to try something else. "Jaeger, I know about your mission, the one that Gage sent you on," he began. The imp stared at him from Remi's lap, his yellow eyes wide and black vertical slits tightening. "I know about the tear, Jaeger, I know he sent you into the Shaerealm."

Both Jaeger and Remi gasped.

"How did hyu know--"

"How could you not tell me--" they both began, but Thane held up a hand for silence.

"I also know he sent you to find someone but not make contact with her. You were to not be seen, and were to come back and report as soon as you found her." Thane held Jaeger's gaze, and Jaeger blinked first. The imp nodded acknowledgement. Remi just stared at Thane, her eyes wide and a strange sick expression beginning on her face. "This is not her. This is my friend Remi."

"I'm General Gage's daughter," Remi whispered. Thane hadn't been going to reveal that piece of information, but there it was. She tore her eyes from Thane and focused on Caspian, loose strings and worn fur visible under Jaeger's grip.

Jaeger chuckled, then giggled, then threw his head back and laughed. "Andrus Gage has a child?" he wheezed through his mirth. "The iron general is a papa? No, hyu are trying to make me a fool. Aye don't know how hyu know about my mission, but here she is and better proof than puppy," and he cuddled the toy under Remi's hungry gaze.

"Think," Thane encouraged. "Which is really more likely? That you found her and she crossed time and space and came back prettier and younger and got here first? Or that Gage has a daughter?"

"The first," Jaeger giggled. "By all the fates, the first."

"Who were you looking for?" Remi asked. Her voice was strange, and strained, and Thane looked at her face. It was pale, so pale he almost thought he could see through it. She locked eyes with Thane. "Make him tell us who he was looking for."

"Are you okay?" he asked.

"Make him tell us," she said, and Thane saw tears in her eyes. He felt his chest tighten and his lungs constrict.

"Aye will not tell," Jaeger asserted. "Aye must only speak with Andrus."

Thane looked around the room for something, anything that might help. Two walls of the office were made of clear glass, and Thane realized they weren't underground anymore. They were high up, and the visible sky was full of stars but no moon. The stars reminded Thane of the last time he'd been at the hill before tonight.

"Jaeger," he began, and something in his tone made the imp sit straighter and look at him as though he might bite. "Am I a present?"

The little imp's face fell, and he gathered in his tail and brought his wings closer. "No, hyu are a human boy and a Shaeling, Aye know this is a truth fact."

"I am. And you owe me," Thane bent down until his face was level with the imp's wrinkled old man face. "You owe me a debt that you promised to repay."

"Ye-es," Jaeger added a syllable, squirming now and not meeting Thane's eyes.

"Who were you looking for?"

"Aye don't see why it matters," Jaeger dodged, extricating himself from Remi's lap and scampering back to the cloth pile. "Just ask her. She is herself."

"I'm Remi Quinn Gage," Remi said.

Jaeger growled and shook his head. "No, no, her real name. The other one. Aye am very tired," and he laid down, tucking Caspian under one arm and wrapping himself in his wings. "Aye must sleep now."

"Jaeger," Thane said, and the imp opened one eye and squinted at him. "You made me run across Sanctum in a towel. Then you rode me like a pony and forced me to watch my friends die. You left scars across my back." Jaeger twitched and flinched with each accusation.

"Aye said Aye was sorry," he mumbled.

"Prove it," Thane said. Jaeger shuddered, then sighed.

"Fine," he snapped. "But hyu do not tell General Andrus Gage that Aye spoke this. Hyu do not tell him that we spoke at all."

"Deal," Remi agreed before Thane could respond. Jaeger glanced and him, and he nodded.

"Aye was sent to find someone who was lost in the Shaerealm nearly a decade ago. Aye was sent to find hyu, even if hyu don't remember here who hyu are," he flicked his tail at Remi.

"The name, Jaeger," Thane pressed.

The imp squirmed more furiously, as though the words burned inside. "General Andrus Gage sent me to find his wife," he finally breathed out through four rows of clenched and bared teeth. "Aye was supposed to go to the Shaerealm and find Major Meagan Quinn Gage. And now Aye am asleep and hyu were never here." Jaeger pulled his wing over his eyes and began to snore loudly.

"We have to get out of here," Remi said.

"What?" that hadn't been the reaction Thane was expecting.

"Now. Before he gets back." Remi snatched the keycard from where it lay on the floor and jumped to her feet. "Now. Come on."

"But what about--" Thane made a vague gesture towards Jaeger.

"Leave me alone, Aye am sleeping," Jaeger snapped, and then resumed snoring.

Remi didn't answer either of them. She rushed to the door and yanked it open, then grabbed Thane's upper arm. "Come on," she urged, and dragged him out of the room.

"General Gage's meeting should adjourn in a few minutes," the blonde woman at the desk said. Remi tossed the keycard back near where it had been before. She ignored her father's aide as though the woman had been a chair, and instead hurried to press the elevator button.

"Thanks anyway," Thane said, but the woman barely spared him a glance before returning to whatever she'd been typing. The elevator bay dinged and a door slid open. Remi went inside and jabbed a button without waiting, and Thane ran across the lobby and jumped in as the door closed.

Her fist filled his vision as he threw himself backwards against the elevator door to avoid her swing. "How could you not have told me about that?"

"About what?" he tried to dodge again, but the elevator dropped out from under his feet and suddenly they were both falling, with the floor moving away faster than gravity could pull them down to it.

"About my father sending a flying monkey into another universe," she tried to punch him again, but the speed of their descent pressed them against the ceiling instead.

This was going to hurt. Thane frantically searched the walls for something to hold on to, knowing that once the elevator slowed he and Remi would hit the floor like bugs on a windshield. The walls were smooth and completely useless. He ground his teeth.

"We need a rope or something," he tried to push himself off the ceiling to reach the bar. He could hear Remi moving around and spared a thought to hope she wasn't going to punch him again, but the hand he used to push against the ceiling touched something that moved sideways.

He grabbed it and yanked. With a click, a harness came loose from the panel in the elevator ceiling. "Here," Thane shouted, shoving his arm behind Remi's back and jerking out a second harness. He thrust it at her and she took it, then he wrapped the straps around himself and buckled furiously, tying the ends together in knots if the buckle didn't fit.

Remi didn't finish in time. When the elevator slowed her harness was only half together, and Thane's arm shot out to grab her before she fell. The elevator came to a gentle stop at the bottom of its descent, and then there was a grinding of gears before it began sliding sideways again. Thane's arm and legs dangled, while he held tightly across Remi's shoulders with the other arm. Straps crisscrossed his chest from his collarbone to his belt. She was only held twice around the waist, her eyes wide and staring down.

"We've been a little busy," he said.

She looked up at him. "We need to talk to Jaeger."

Thane blinked. "We just were."

Remi pushed his arm away and started to undo the buckles at her waist. "Somewhere my dad isn't going to show up at any moment." She loosened one and the second snapped open.

Remi grabbed Thane's arm and used it to get her feet underneath her and dropped lightly to the ground. "Why?" he asked, staring down at her.

Her assisted descent had loosened his glove, and it dropped to the ground before he could grab it. Remi picked it up and twisted it in her hands for a moment before answering. "My mom," she said, "We have to rescue her."

"How?" he asked, putting his talons next to his waist and trying to hide them with the straps.

She looked up at him and held the glove out. "We have to find a way into the Shaerealm."

He took it wordlessly and stared down at her.

Remi gazed back, her eyebrows drawn together and her mouth set in a hard line.   Without changing expression, tears filled her eyes and overflowed, running down her cheeks and dripping onto the floor. Thane noticed her hands were shaking. Her jaw flexed, and she spoke through her teeth. "My mom is alive," she said. Saying the words out loud seemed to unlock something inside her and she started crying in earnest, gasping for breath between shuddering sobs. She collapsed on the floor, and Thane fumbled with the straps that held him suspended.

He'd forgotten to put his glove back on. The moment he tugged with his claws the straps tore and he fell forward, sliding out of the harness and landing hard in front of Remi with an impressively loud thud. The stinging in his elbows and knees was worth it; she gave a slight gasping giggle and then a slow deep breath. On talons and knees he looked into her wet face.

"I don't care how you feel about your dad, Thane," she said, hiccupping and wiping her eyes with her sleeve, "but we are going to go get my mom."

Thane nodded. "Tell me what you need me to do."

"Get Jaeger. We'll start there," she said, and then dove forward and threw her arms around him and buried her face in his shoulder.

He carefully wrapped his arms around her, balling his uncovered hand into a fist so the dark blue claws dug into his palm instead of risking them touching her. Then he held her like he would Lanie if she'd had a bad dream.

They stayed like that until the elevator slowed to a halt, the doors opening with a ding and the colder air of the underground lobby whooshed in around them. "Oi, what's this?" Thane's head shot up and he saw Charlie, standing in front of the open elevator and glaring down at them. The dragon man's wide eyes narrowed. "What are ye two about in there?"

Thane dropped his arms. "That's none of your business," Remi snapped and pushed herself to standing. She swept past Thane's grandfather and out the huge doors that slid open before her without deigning to look at Charlie again.

Charlie sighed, and held out a hand to Thane. "I cannae do good for her," he said as he pulled Thane up. Thane stood and put his glove back on. "Will ye tell me what she's on about, tadpole?"

Thane paused, considering what he could say that would be the truth. "She misses her mom."

"That's true enough, but it isnae all." Charlie looked at him, his bald head tilted to one side and with an eyebrow raised. "I'll leave ye younglings tae yer secrets, but remember; if she has need, ye bring it tae me. Ye ken?" Thane shrugged and started past him, trying to follow Remi out the door. Charlie stepped in front of him again to bar the way.

"Thane." The dragon man stood between Thane and the only visible way out, waiting. Thane raised his chin to look his grandfather in the eye. "I've waited half a century tae find her, and now that I have, she'll have naught tae do with me. I cannae make her love me, but I'll be stripped of my Song before I'll stand aside and let her be hurting. Now, in th' names of all the moons, ye will tell me what's going on."

"No, I won't," Thane answered, suddenly sick of the man's posturing. Charlie stiffened, an angry blue light flashed in his eyes and his hands tightened in sudden fists. Thane was unimpressed. "I'm already keeping your secrets which by rights she should know, and that's hard enough. I'm not going to tell you hers." He held up one hand placatingly. "I'll let you know you if you can help. Until then, back off."

The dragon man shrugged, then sighed. "This gets harder every time. Have any sense of yer Song coming back, lad?" he asked, gesturing towards Thane's gloved hand.

Thane quickly shoved the telltale black rubber glove behind his back and looked down. "Not yet."

"Aw, yer not the first dragon with burnout. Give it time-- the wound'll heal," Charlie said, resting his hand on Thane's shoulder. Thane snorted.

"Really? That's your advice, that time heals all wounds?" he asked, unsure how to respond to the comforting gesture from someone he didn't want to admit that he looked up to.

"Not all," Charlie answered, a brief grimace crossing his face. His grandfather stepped aside and used the hand on his shoulder to propel Thane towards the door. "Get on. If I know that lass at all, she'll be waiting outside and wondering what's dragging yer feet."

Thane went through the double doors and up the staircase back into the cool night air, his eyes adjusting to the darkness around him. Remi wasn't there. He blinked, surprised, and started back towards his own dorm, the silence of the night unnatural beneath the protective dome.

"What did you say to him?" Remi asked, stepping out of the shadows next to the charred and roped off remains of building fifteen.

"Nothing," Thane answered. "Why are you hiding?"

"I didn't want him to see me if he came back out that way," she said. "What did he want?"

"He said he wanted to help you, if he could." She snorted and made a dismissive wave of her hand.

"Forget him. We need to find out everything Jaeger knows. Can you get him to talk to us?"

"Where?" Thane asked. "There's surveillance everywhere."

Remi looked around at the debris of the fallen building behind her. The seven stories of building fifteen had collapsed after Thane had blown a giant hole in one of the walls. The destruction of the building might not have been as complete if Gideon, the gold dragon of Alpha Team, and Charlie in his blue dragon form hadn't torn up and carried away the floor of the top level to save General Gage. And if Thane hadn't made the hole using an impressively large electrical charge which, in addition to making the hole, had blown up or burst every transformer in the building. As a result the seven stories of training building fifteen had been reduced to half of the first floor and a pile of cement, twisted metal, and wood shrapnel. In the darkness of the night it really did look like the corpse of some enormous monster.

"Here," she faced the building. "Nothing electrical would've survived. If we go in no one can see or hear us unless they're in the room with us. Tell Jaeger to meet us here tomorrow."

"Tomorrow? When? What if the rest of the building falls?" Thane asked, eyeing the remaining structure skeptically.

"It'll be fine. Nathiel told me that people sneak in there all the time to make out without the teachers knowing," Remi said, still studying the building.

Thane did not like that piece of information. "Who's Nathiel?"

"He's a friend," Remi placed her hands on her hips and turned to look at Thane. "We have to do this."

"I know," Thane said.

CHAPTER 4

"Shredding holes, you can't be serious," Twitch had said when Thane had come back to their dorm that night. Remi hadn't made him promise not to tell, and Thane needed help contacting Jaeger so Thane had filled in his bunkmate on where Remi had gone after leaving class and how they'd gotten into General Gage's office. "I haven't even been there."

"Jaeger has," Thane continued, "he was in there."

Twitch nodded. "I thought he'd have to get back soon. Gage hates it when Jaeger goes off on his own, and we'd usually have a tracker on him before now. I bet Gage is going to be furious--"

"Jaeger was in the Shaerealm," Thane interrupted. Twitch's mouth snapped shut as his eyes widened. "And Gage sent him there."

Twitch didn't so much sit down as he was lucky his cot was behind him when his knees gave out. He stared at Thane. "That can't-- it isn't-- how would-- yes, I know I'm stuttering," he snapped at Thane's right shoulder. His eyes met Thane's again. "That isn't possible. Gage doesn't have the authority to open a hole, and even if he did, a mission like that would require weeks of training and paperwork and you wouldn't know about it." Twitch's eyes narrowed as he watched Thane. "Did Jaeger tell you all this? He is shade--"

"I saw it," Thane said. Twitch stopped talking and waited. Thane held his gaze and continued. "At the cave, after they took Ms. Rasmussen away, I was looking for Gage and Kari said he was inside. I went in but he didn't see me because he was giving Jaeger orders. Orders to go through the hole."

"But there wasn't a hole, we stopped the tear event..." Twitch began, but then paused and seemed to be thinking. "Yes, but it was unstable and the proximity of the guardian bone tore a small hole anyway." He blinked several times, looking at Thane's face. "It, it wasn't proximity?"

"It was Gage." Thane almost rubbed his face with his rubber gloves but thought better of it. "Gage ordered Jaeger into the Shaerealm to locate a target. It was supposed to be a secret. Jaeger had to find his own way back and then report directly to Gage and to no one else. But Remi and I found him first." Thane sighed and sat on his own cot, facing Twitch. "I wish we hadn't."

"Why?" Twitch was getting twitchier. He pinched the edge of his nose several times and ran his hand through his dark brown hair. "Was he all right? Did he find his target? Who was he looking for?"

"Remi's mom," Thane said. Twitch froze like a rodent caught in a flashlight beam. "Jaeger found General Gage's wife, Major Meagan Quinn Gage."

Twitch exploded into activity. He jumped up and grabbed Thane by the shoulder, dragging him out of the room and babbling to himself. "This isn't possible. This isn't happening. Get the video feeds and get rid of them!" he shouted, pulling Thane along until they were standing outside in the darkest part of night. "Replace them with something boring from last week."

"Who are you talking to?" Thane asked as Twitch shoved him roughly ahead until they were several yards away from any of the standing buildings.

"Do you have any idea what kind of trouble we're in?" Twitch asked, ignoring Thane's question completely. "General Gage committed a huge breach of protocol. No one, not even members of the council send people into the Shaerealm without permission and vetting and a huge need. Every time," and Twitch grabbed Thane's collar with both fists and put his face close to Thane's, "every time someone passes through the Weave from our world to theirs the Weave separating the two worlds weakens a little more. A little more of our reality seeps into theirs and theirs into ours."

"So what?" asked Thane, knocking Twitch's hands loose and stepping away. "What does it matter? There's magic leaking through all the time. I thought that was how the Shae here used their Songs anyway, because of the leaks."

"You're an idiot." Twitch started pacing. "Do you think it's that simple? Their reality is different than ours. The frequency of their Song is different. And as long as the two worlds stay touching but not too closely, they both exist. They create harmony that every living thing can be a part of. But the more the worlds intertwine, the more they leak into each other, the greater the amplitude of the other world affects us."

"You mean it gets louder?" Thane asked.

"Yes, moron, it gets louder," Twitch's pacing increased, as did his agitated hand motions so that it almost looked like he was conducting an invisible orchestra. "We are a part of the sound of the Song of our world, so it doesn't affect us. We're inside the wave. But if another wave comes along and gets too close, the volume of that other Song that we aren't a part of will get too loud. And if it gets too loud, if their world bleeds too much into ours--"

"The amplitude will blow out our brains," Thane finished the thought.

"Not just ours, but every living thing in both our worlds. That's why the balance is so important to maintain! We're different, but close, and the frequencies would end up canceling each other out if we let them overlap too much. And that, of course, would be after we all bleed our brains out through our ears." Twitch rubbed his face with both hands and then threw them apart. "This is why they've vetoed every rescue mission before, because there was no proof to justify the risk!"

"They tried to do rescue missions before?" Thane asked, watching Twitch pace.

"Of course! Major Gage and her team were lost on a priority one mission almost a decade ago, and the then Colonel Gage immediately applied for a rescue mission and was denied. He proposed six more that year and seven the year after that and was severely reprimanded. After that, he stopped going through official channels and became Sanctum's go-to commander. What was he thinking?" Twitch's arms flailed.

"How do you know all that?"

"I read his file, we read everybody's file, you knew that," Twitch shot back. "But this, if this is true, this is huge. They'd have to mount a rescue now with proof that the team is alive and especially if Jaeger has any evidence that they completed their mission the Guardian Council would have to send a team after them but that would take weeks to arrange and no I don't think that's why he requested Omega Team, why would you bring that up?" Twitch paused in his pacing, his head tilted to one side.

Thane ignored the change in topic. "Why would they approve a mission at all if sending people through would destroy both worlds?"

"What?" Twitch's eyes refocused on Thane. "No, one mission or even one hundred wouldn't do that. But over time it would happen. Not allowing any crossovers is a precaution, because they can't control what the Shae outside of Sanctum do but they discourage it to prevent the worlds from collapsing because people want to open trade with the other side." He paused, cocking his head again. "Weapons, probably. I don't know, I've never been there."

"So if we go to rescue Major Gage it isn't going to destroy the world?" Thane asked.

"What?" Twitch seemed truly shocked. "They're not going to send you. There's no way they'd let you leave Sanctum, not now that they know Ruan is looking for you. They wouldn't send you anyway, you're not on a team. You haven't even graduated."

"Twitch," Thane said, but the other boy kept pacing. "Twitch!" Thane grabbed him by both shoulders, the dragon talons pressing uncomfortably against the thick black rubber of his gloves.

Twitch stopped squirming and looked at him. "What?"

"Remi knows about this," Thane said. Twitch groaned. "Remi knows about her mom being in the Shaerealm. Jaeger said she was in trouble, that he'd rescued some stuffed animal from the Sang and that's where Remi's mom was. She's not going to let this go, not until she gets answers. She wants to talk to Jaeger."

"She can't," Twitch protested, "she shouldn't even know who he is, and team members aren't supposed to interact with students unless we're helping with a class or training. There's no way she'll get a meet with Jaeger. Gage won't allow it."

"If she doesn't meet with Jaeger, she'll hunt him down. Then General Gage will find out that she knows, and everyone will find out that General Gage sent Jaeger into the Shaerealm. What fallout will that get?" Thane let go of Twitch with a small shove.

"The worst kind," Twitch smacked his forehead and let his headrest in his palm for a moment. "How do we stop her?"

"We let her talk to Jaeger. You said now that he has proof they'll have to send a rescue. You get Jaeger to a place where she can talk to him and tell her. That should be enough to get her to calm down," Thane said it because he wanted it to be true, but he didn't really believe it.

"No shredding way. I'm not getting involved," Twitch protested, waving his hands back and forth.

"You're already involved," Thane said. He held up his fingers and counted them off. "You know that Remi is General Gage's daughter. You know about Major Gage. You know that Jaeger's been gone, and now you know where. And," Thane held up a final finger and pointed it at his roommate, "if you don't help, I'm going to mess with every piece of equipment you leave in the room, starting with the alarm clock. Every night."

Twitch stared at Thane with his mouth hanging open. "You wouldn't--"

"I would." Thane stared at the computer genius.

"Shredding holes burn you songless," Twitch swore at him.

Thane held up his gloves. "Already did."

Twitch grimaced. "Fine. I'll see what I can do."

Thane nodded. "Can we go to bed now?"

Twitch paused, listening for something that Thane couldn't begin to hear. "Yeah, it's all right. The surveillance cameras in the halls are down for the next eighty-six seconds."

"How do you do that?" Thane asked.

Twitch started running. "Did you not hear me? Seventy-eight seconds. Move it or explain this all to General Gage tomorrow."

Thane ran.

According to Twitch, Jaeger was detained with the medics in building one for two days as part of a quarantine protocol before resuming to active duty. Every day Remi asked Thane when Jaeger was coming. And Thane asked Twitch every night if the meeting with the imp was set up yet. Five days after finding Jaeger in General Gage's office, Twitch finally slipped Thane an infopad during a break between his classes. There was an archaic screen saver playing on it, the kind where straight sticks of different colors slid across or spun around and rebounded off the edges. Thanes reached down to touch the screen and activate the pad, but Twitch knocked his hand away.

"Don't touch it, just look," he hissed under his breath.

Thane glanced at Twitch with one eyebrow raised and then stared at the pad, waiting. The little lines dancing across the screen seemed random until suddenly they all moved inward, and words snapped into view. "Tomorrow two hours before dawn. Follow the signs." The message was only clear for half a heartbeat before the lines separated to continue bouncing and spinning across the pad.

Thane handed it back. "What about security?"

Twitch twitched. "I don't know what you're talking about," he said, but he rolled his eyes and looked offended. Thane assumed that meant Twitch had it under control, and went to find Remi.

She was having lunch in the cafeteria, surrounded by friends and admirers. Naessa sat next to her, chatting, and the boy who kept glaring at him, the boy who Thane assumed was Nathiel, sat on her other side. He scribbled the message onto a napkin from the stack he took and grabbed a soda, striding quickly between the two humans scanning food in the student lunchroom.

"Hi," he said, standing behind her and popping the can open. He took a drink and bumped his elbow into the head of the boy next to Remi.

The boy reacted immediately. "Hey!" he swung his arm back, knocking the soda can out of Thane's hand and onto Remi's lap, spraying both Remi and Naessa with brown sticky liquid.

"Weaver's pits, Korey," Naessa snapped, jumping to her feet. Remi rose too. "Look what you did."

"It wasn't my fault--" Korey protested, clenching his teeth and narrowing his eyes at Thane.

"Here," Thane cut in, offering Naessa and Remi each some of the napkins he was holding. The one with the note was the second down in the handful he gave Remi, and he watched her closely as she started to clean the root beer off her pants. The liquid soaked up through and Thane saw her eyes widen slightly as the message became visible as the paper it was written on grew translucent with saturation. Remi blinked, then scrubbed her pants with enough force to shred the napkins.

"Give it up, Korey," Naessa and the boy continued arguing. "It doesn't matter."

Korey was grinding his teeth as he rose to his feet. Thane hadn't noticed just how tall the other boy was, just that he was skinny. "He ran into me first!" Korey insisted, his chin level with Thane's forehead which meant that even tilting his head back, Thane was looking straight into the boy's mouth. The most prominent feature of Korey's mouth were his four canine teeth, longer and sharper than any human's teeth should be. Thane stiffened. Whatever Shaeblood Korey had, it was some kind of predator.

"And here I thought pulling student lunch duty would be dull. You still having trouble with root beer cans, kid?" a familiar voice spoke behind Thane. Korey immediately backed down as Thane turned and saw Brennan Tayler, still missing fingers on his right hand and his red hair visible under his flat cap. As a full member of the Shaerealm Mercenary Guard, even the most aggressive student in Sanctum would back away from a direct confrontation with this man. As a member of the Omega Team, most other mercenaries would think twice, too.

Brennan smiled at them all, displaying his perfectly human teeth. "How's lunch?" he asked amicably.

Naessa answered. "Sticky, Mr. Tayler," she said as she indicated the wet spots on her pants and on Remi's.

Brennan flinched sympathetically, but Thane noticed how the skin tightened around the man's eyes and his smile seemed forced. "Just Brennan. Why don't you girls go get cleaned up and I'll take this one with me," he put his left hand on Thane's shoulder and shook the right hand at him, the absence of a pointer finger making the gesture comical and threatening at the same time. "You should know better. Come on, kid," and Brennan steered Thane towards the doors while Korey mumbled something sullen behind them.

"So you have been paying attention," Brennan observed once they were outside. He let his hand drop off Thane's shoulder and stretched in the bright sunlight. "That was a pretty slick piece of work, passing Remi a message in the middle of a crowded room. One she could destroy while people watched. What did it say?"

Thane froze for an instant and then tried to play it cool, walking away. "You're crazy. That kid just made me spill my drink, that's all."

"Yeah, and Paka's just a housecat," Brennan retorted, referring to Usiku Paka, the jungle panther that could talk and think as well as any human and who walked primarily on her hind legs. She was also a vicious fighter. When people spoke about "cat-like reflexes," Paka was the gold standard. "Was it a love note? You making a play for Gage's daughter? Not smart, kid." Brennan grinned.

"What? No! You shouldn't talk about that," Thane hissed, trying to look everywhere to make sure no one was close enough to overhear. "What do you know about it, anyway?"

"I know plenty, kid. Omega Team rescued you both, remember?"

"Charlie and Twitch showed up at the last minute and got all the credit. You weren't even there," Thane responded.

"Maybe, but I read the report. And I listened to my instincts; know what they're telling me?" Brennan looked at Thane, who shrugged. "They're telling me this girl is trouble and you're up to something big enough that you're scared."

"I'm not scared."

"Aw kid, the only person you're good at lying to is yourself." Brennan's slightly mocking tone changed, and his forehead wrinkled as he continued to watch Thane. "Look, kid, remember when I told you not to jump to conclusions because you might know the what but not the why?" Brennan waited for Thane's nod. "Well I've got another piece of brilliant advice for you. Don't do something stupid just because she's pretty. Or a damsel in distress. The consequences last longer than the relationship, and they're usually bigger than you expect." Brennan's right hand curled and relaxed once, the fingers making an approximation of a fist.

Not for the first time, Thane wondered how the one hundred percent human Brennan Tayler had gotten mixed up in Sanctum and the Shae. "Brennan--"

And not for the first time, Brennan wouldn't talk about it. "Later, kid. You've got class and some big secret, and I've got yet another training mission with my finally complete again team." The man made a gesture of farewell with his left hand and walked off, adjusting his hat.

Thane shook his head and started off in the direction of his next class. Brennan was right. Thane was scared and what they were planning was possibly very stupid. But he wasn't doing it because Remi was pretty and Thane was sure she would throw a punch at Brennan for suggesting even the possibility of her being a damsel in distress, Omega Team membership notwithstanding. He was doing it because she was his best friend, and because he was mad at Charlie and Brennan and General Gage for all their dumb secrets that he kept getting tangled in.

For a moment he missed his mattress on the floor of the unfinished basement. It hadn't been fun, but it had been simple. Get seen, get hurt. Don't be seen, don't be hurt. He flexed his claws inside their black rubber, staring down at his hands. Oh well. He hadn't run screaming from Remi when Mr. Hoffman introduced them, so it was already too late.

Brennan was right. The consequences lasted a lot longer.

Thane went to class and planned on getting to bed early. Tomorrow was going to be a very long day.

And start very early, apparently. He felt like he'd barely been asleep when someone grabbed his shoulder and shook it once, hard. Thane shot forward, reflexively covering his face with his arms and his elbows.

"Get up, it's time," Twitch's voice spoke from the darkness.

Thane opened bleary eyes and lowered his arms. Twitch stood in the middle of the room, fully dressed and waiting. "We have one hour and forty-eight minutes from right now to get back here like nothing happened," Twitch spoke without looking at Thane; instead the tech genius was focused on setting the watch on his wrist. "The video feed will loop for that long, but then everything resets the moment the sun breaks the horizon."

"Why?" Thane asked, throwing back the covers and swinging his feet onto the ground.

"Moronic questions later, silence and speed now," Twitch said, and then added under his breath, "it isn't about being polite, it's about getting results. Yes I am bad with people."

Thane was getting used to Twitch's conversations with his left shoulder, and didn't comment. Instead he pulled on a T-shirt and his old ratty sneakers. "Let's go."

Twitch led Thane out of the team's dorm building and into the chill and dark before dawn. There was no moon tonight and so the stars gleamed brighter in contrast, and for the first time since coming to Sanctum Thane wished he'd brought a jacket or something. They moved at an erratic pace, stopping or starting or running with no pattern Thane could see.

"Where are the signs?" Thane whispered. Twitch glanced back at him. "You said there'd be signs. Where are they?"

The other boy snorted softly. "Those were for Remi. You don't need them because you have me, and I can't believe I'm doing this." He turned back and suddenly sprinted across an open area of grass, Thane following as best he could.

They came to the edge of the wreckage of building fifteen, the perimeter outlined by ropes wrapped around poles. Twitch pointed and Thane nodded, following. The two crept around the side of the building until they came to a still intact doorway on the side furthest from the dorms. The ropes here were slack, and Twitch easily lifted one and slid underneath it, holding it up so Thane could do the same.

The door didn't even squeak as Twitch pushed it open, and as Thane stepped inside he saw Twitch duck behind the door and come up with a small can. "It's considered polite," the tech genius said as he sprayed down the hinges of the door with oil. "Anyone who comes in or out greases the door."

Thane suddenly thought of what Remi had said about Nathiel saying this was a make-out spot for students and felt his teeth clench. Before he could comment, though, Twitch was walking into the darkness of the hall. He hurried to catch up and the faint light of the stars fell behind and a thin strip of dim green-grey light outlined a doorway ahead on the right. Twitch paused in front of the door and Thane strained his ears, listening. There was someone inside.

Twitch eased the door open and Remi spun around, her eyes wide as she jumped to her feet. "Oh!" she squeaked, covering her mouth with both hands. The wheeled chair she'd been sitting on slid away from her and Twitch jumped to catch it before it ran into the wall of monitors to the side. "It's just you," she said, lowering her hands and peering at them both in the gloom. "Where are we?"

"This was one of the command observation rooms for the training areas in this building," Twitch explained, pulling the chair back to the middle and sitting on it. "The tech consoles in this room are all blown, thanks so much," he directed that at Thane, who shrugged and held out his hands in a helpless gesture before shutting the door, "but there are no windows and all the cables in the walls can act as a heat shield against any thermal scanners. The walls are also thicker to make room for the wiring."

"If there's no power, what's that?" Thane asked, pointing to what looked like a small statute of peace lily flowers made of metal. At the cusp of each flower was a sphere about the size of a baseball, and each spheres was glowing.

"These are Jaeger's idea," Twitch said, pushing against the floor with one foot and making the chair roll across the floor until it stopped next to the lamp.

He gently picked one up and held it out. "They're bioluminescent, create almost no heat signature, and require no power. They're brilliant."

"They are also not for hyu to touch," Jaeger's voice came from above them, and all three jerked in surprise and looked up. The red imp crawled out of the shadows in the corner of the ceiling furthest from the shining spheres, his claws piercing the sheet rock and his wings tucked close while his red scales of his hanging tail reflected the light on dizzying patterns. The greenish light reflected in his yellow eyes and off his many rows of pointed teeth as he smiled threateningly down on them.

Remi and Thane sat perfectly still, like sparrows facing a snake. Twitch was not as affected. "Knock it off, Jaeger. They're not going to let you get out of this just because you think you're scary. You couldn't intimidate Thane's little sister."

Thane's mind was suddenly filled with the image of Lanie, his six-year-old sister, meeting Jaeger. He burst out laughing and everyone looked at him. "Sorry," he said, still chuckling. "She'd have you in a pink dress and being polite at tea with Twitch Monkey in five minutes."

"Twitch Monkey?" Remi asked.

"Don't ask," Twitch cut in, his cheeks flushing.

Jaeger let go of the ceiling and twisted around to land on his feet on the floor. He curled his tail so it wrapped around him and hunched his shoulders forward. Thane tried not to laugh at the imp again, even though Jaeger had a full pout lip and furrowed brow. "Aye used to terrify entire villages in the old country," he muttered, yellow eyes watery.

"I'm sure you were terrifying," Remi said placatingly, crouching down near him. "I bet you gave all the children nightmares."

"Really?" he brightened, and lunged at her. Remi squeaked and flinched away, but Jaeger's arms pulled around her neck tightly. Thane had already taken a step towards them to stop the imp when he realized it wasn't an attack, it was a hug. The little red head was buried in her shoulder.

"Hyu are nice," the words were muffled. "They are not." Jaeger pulled his head up and stuck his tongue out at the two boys.

Twitch glanced at his watch. "We're running low on time, here. Sixty-five minutes more."

"Jaeger, what happened in the Shaerealm?" Thane asked.

"Not telling," Jaeger put his face against Remi's shoulder again. "Can't make me."

"You owe me," Thane began, but Jaeger interrupted.

"Yes, yes, Aye abused hyu because Aye thought hyu were not sentient. Aye remember. But Aye owe hyu action, Aye owe hyu reparations, Aye do not owe hyu my rank and loyalty." Jaeger looked at Thane, the vertical black slits in his eyes widening and narrowing with the imp's agitation. "Aye haf made a promise to the General, and Aye do not break promises."

Thane growled in frustration, especially since if he had been in Jaeger's position he would've felt the same way. He tried desperately to think of an argument that might work but came up blank.

Remi raised her arms and placed them slowly around the imp that hung from her neck. She tightened them until she was hugging Jaeger tightly. "Jaeger," she began, and then swallowed. "I'm glad you're so loyal to my dad. He's a good person." She gulped again, and Thane was startled to see the green-grey light of the orbs reflecting off the tears on her face. Jaeger saw them too; he hesitantly raised one claw and traced a tear down her cheek, and then stuffed his finger in his mouth.

"Hyu have a face leak," he said, sounding curious.

Remi sniffed. "My dad sent you to find my mom, Jaeger. That means a lot to me. What exactly did you promise my dad?"

Sucking on his finger, the imp considered. "Aye was ordered to find the target in the Shaerealm, not to make contact, and to only report to General Gage about what Aye found." His tail twitched a little, and he brushed her face with the tips of several claws. He held them close to his eyes. "Hyu are still leaking. Are hyu sad?"

"Yes," Remi answered with a slight shrug of her shoulders. "I miss my mom. She used to hold me like this when I was scared. I don't want you to break a promise to my dad, Jaeger," she said, looking the imp straight in his alien face. "I don't need you to report to me. I just want you to tell me about my mother. Like a friend would."

"Hyu are sad for mama, who would hold hyu when hyu was scared." Jaeger seemed to be considering. He pushed himself out of her embrace and sprang into the air, gliding to the wall and digging his claws in and twisting his neck so his head turned to face her. "I do not report to hyu, Gage girl. Hyu do not haf a rank. Aye will not tell hyu about what Aye found."

The imp let go of the wall and flapped his wings until he was near the ceiling, and then tucked his wings in close and shot downward directly at Thane. Thane jumped out of the way and Jaeger landed neatly on the desk behind them and faced them. "Aye will tell hyu who. Major Meagan Gage, hyu's mama. She is captive of Sang Evarish Terracatan with several hundred other humans and those with songless blood. Several members of her original team are with her."

Remi grabbed Thane's arm and dug her fingernails in. He winced and glanced at her, but his irritation changed to concern when he saw that her face was so pale the only color it had was the dim green light shining on it. Was she going to faint?

"Will they, will Sanctum..." she began, but Twitch cut her off.

"How many members of the team?" he leaned forward.

"That is part of the reporting, and Aye will not tell hyu," the imp responded, flexing and relaxing his claws, which left little gouges in the wood desk underneath him.

"Jaeger," Twitch leaned down close and lowered his voice, "did they find it?"

The imp's tail lashed and his eyes narrowed. "Yes."

The thing about the exchange that terrified Thane the most was Twitch. The moment Jaeger had answered, the tech genius went as still as though he'd been flash frozen.

"Will Sanctum send a team to rescue my mother?" Remi finally asked, breaking whatever moment Twitch and Jaeger were having. The imp blinked and sat back, and Twitch immediately began muttering and tapping his fingers together while pacing and ignoring everyone else.

Jaeger shrugged, and the very human gesture looked awkward against a backdrop of red wings. "They will haf to. The General Andrus will haf to take my report to the Council, and there are strict rules about keeping Sanctum personnel captive. It is not allowed."

"Why wouldn't they allow the report?" Twitch said out loud to the wall. The others all looked at him. "What do you mean, contraindicative? I know Jaeger isn't making it up!" he growled, then looked at Jaeger, "Andrus didn't ask you to make this up, right?"

"No," Jaeger's wings flapped once in emphasis. "Why would he?"

"Because he wants to rescue his wife. Because he wants to believe she's out there. Because of what they were looking for." Twitch ticked the reasons off on his fingers while he paced, then stopped and stared at Jaeger. "There's no record of you being in the Shaerealm."

"But I saw him go," Thane argued. "I saw General Gage order him in and make the hole."

"Which makes Gage a criminal," Twitch answered, "and at best they would strip him of his rank and force him to retire."

"Then why would he do it?" Thane asked. "If he knew he couldn't tell anyone about it, why send Jaeger?"

"For my mom," Remi said. "To see if she was still alive. And she is. So what will he do now? What can he do?"

"He can say new information has been brought to light concerning their mission," announced a familiar if muffled voice. The door to the hallway opened and Brennan stood there, leaning against the wall with his arms folded across his chest. Jaeger hissed and Twitch looked startled.

"How--" he asked, but Brennan didn't let him finish.

"I saw the kid here passing secret notes and it felt like something I should look into," he said, jerking a thumb towards Thane.

"But there was no surveillance, I checked every type of signature," Twitch's fingers were a blur and the tick in his left eyelid started.

"I did it old school," Brennan explained, "I watched him with my eyeballs."

Jaeger giggled. "Eyeballs," he sniggered.

CHAPTER 5

"The issue here is the voices in Twitch's head are right," Brennan said, coming into the room and shutting the door behind him.

"Hey!" Twitch protested.

"There are peoples in his head?" Jaeger asked.

"General Gage can't go to the Guardian Council with Jaeger's report, because there were no official channels and therefore no way to verify the story. Plus there's the matter of breaking those rules would earn our dear general a court martial instead of a commendation. No, Gage is too smart for that." Brennan pulled the empty chair over and sat down in it. "All he can do is report a rumor, or even a lead, and use the evidence Jaeger has given him to make it plausible. Then after a lengthy deliberation, the Council will decide to send someone in for reconnaissance in conjunction with another mission so holes in the Weave will be kept to a minimum."

"How long before they decide to send someone?" Remi asked.

"How often are there missions into the Shaerealm?" Thane added.

Brennan glanced at Jaeger. The imp launched himself into the air and flapped, spinning small figure eights close enough to the ceiling that his wings brushed against it and spoke as if reciting from a lesson. "On average the Guardian Council of Sanctum requires ninety-four and one half days to reach a consensus of non-critical issues. Clearance for opening or widening holes in the Weave is approximately fifteen and three quarter days, and sanctioned missions into the alternate song universe of the Shae depart with no less than seven hundred eighty-four and five eighths days between them."

"Um," Thane said.

"What?" Remi finished.

"About two years and four months at maximum before they send a recon team," Twitch translated.

"What about at minimum?" Remi asked.

"About six months less than that."

"But you said she was captured, a prisoner," Remi pled with Jaeger. "Can't they do it faster? Can't my dad bribe someone or call in favors or something?"

"Not for this," Brennan said, his voice barely carrying. "I'm sorry, Miss Gage."

"What are you going to do about what you've heard, Mr. Tayler?" she asked, the chill in her voice reminding Thane of Ms. Rasmussen. That was just creepy.

"This is clearly information above my clearance level, so I must not know it." He grinned, but underneath the pleasant expression his jaw was tight. "And more trouble than the knowing is worth, from the sound of it. The question is, what are you going to do about it?"

Remi squared her shoulders and the look on her face gave Thane a brief flash of deja vu. "I'm going to rescue my mom. With or without Sanctum."

"It will have to be without Sanctum," a voice came from underneath the desk, in the deep shadows where the light could not penetrate. It spat a growling word. The accent was strange, as though the words fit oddly in the speaker's mouth and the "s" sound hissed harshly. "Without their knowledge or permission. If they knew, they would only stop you."

If a shadow had a shadow, it would look like what was moving underneath the desk. Thane took a step forward. He knew if he tried to place himself between whatever was under there and Remi she would get mad at him, but he hoped that if he was closest he could still do something. He also hoped it wouldn't kill him.

A black head slid from the darkness into the weak light and two green eyes turned upward, and Thane was again impressed by how expressive a feline face could be. Paka was annoyed. She spat out a short word that Thane didn't need to speak Felidae to know was a curse.

"Knotted threads!" Twitch nearly fell over, leaning against a wall for support. "Is the whole shredding team here?"

"I hope Turcato shows up, he owes me ten bucks," Brennan added.

"Aye asked Paka to come with me," Jaeger admitted, settling down on the desk again next to the glowing spheres. The imp looked shyly up towards Remi. "Aye thought she could make a distraction if hyu were too angry with me."

"You brought backup to talk to us?" Thane was surprised and secretly pleased. He liked the idea that he could make Jaeger nervous. Paka growled, dangerous and hungry and wild. Thane stifled a flinch.

"I was not intending to speak," she seemed frustrated with herself, as if uncertain why she was talking now. The panther with fur blacker than shadow or darkness rose up on her hind legs and shook herself from head to tail. Usiku Paka's green eyes and white fangs glowed in the bioluminescence, suddenly reminding Thane of old cartoons when you could still see the character's eyes and mouth in a pitch-black room. She spoke again, addressing Remi and lashing her tail.

"Sanctum is uninterested in your personal feelings. They will stop you from creating a hole and will punish you for trying to save your family." Thane suddenly got the feeling Paka wasn't talking about Remi. He remembered what the panther had told him on the hill about not having a name until she avenged her parents and her people, and realized he'd never asked her anything more about it. The human-feline paused, and looked Remi slowly up and down. "You can not do this. You are untrained, untried, and barely beginning to be aware of the world around you. Go home, kitten. You are not yet even a cub." Her tail punctuated each sentence, and she sneered at Remi with one lip pulled back to expose her pointed teeth.

Remi and Paka were the same height, Thane noticed, and then wondered why he'd noticed. Maybe it was because Remi's dark hair was almost the same color as Paka's fur. Or maybe it was because they were standing the same way, shoulders slightly turned and leaning forward with their feet spread apart and both looking like they'd like to tear each other's throat out.

"Um," Thane began, but Remi ignored him completely.

"Why don't you run home, if you're so afraid of Sanctum," Remi spoke through her teeth without opening them. "I'm not, and I'm going to get my mother with or without them. And if you try to stop me you're going to need a bigger litter box, because you'll regret it, kitty."

Thane flinched. He knew how Paka felt about being called "kitty." Apparently so did Twitch because he started forward from the back of the room with both hands out. "No, Paka, don't-"

The Pantera Felidae lunged forward and swung. Remi blocked the swing with her forearm and jabbed with her other hand at Paka's stomach. Instead of blocking, the panther grabbed Remi's wrist. It was only with that motion Thane realized Paka's paws were velveted; her claws were in.

Remi struggled against Paka's grip for a moment before the panther released her and stepped back. "You are in earnest. I will go with you."

"What?" Remi said, dropping her stance. Paka cocked her head.

"You cannot do this alone, you cannot even get out of this facility without help, and it is not possible to tear the Weave from inside the dome. You have no team, no plan, and no resources. What were you going to do?"

"I... didn't know yet," Remi admitted. "But I would figure something out."

"And she isn't alone," Thane said, stepping forward. "I'm going."

"Thane, dragon-son," Paka turned her gaze to him. "Going how? Do you even know how to get to the Shaerealm?"

"Um," Thane said, then looked at Twitch.

"Yes, of course I know," Twitch said. "You haven't asked me that yet, and I'm not supposed to tell you, anyway. You don't have clearance."

"I think we're past clearance now, Twitch," Brennan said, still leaning back in the chair. "After all, you brought them here to talk to Jaeger. You're in it just as deep as the rest of us."

"I know that," Twitch snapped. "I just hoped that they'd forget about it once they heard how impossible it is."

"Even for you?" Brennan asked.

"Do you have any idea how hard it is?" Twitch's fingers started tapping against his thumb and his eyelid spasmed. "To get to the Shaerealm we'd need either a full mage circle, a guardian bone knife and the blood of both worlds and the guardian scroll, or trade favors with one of the ancient ones and we don't have anything they would want! Plus," Twitch continued, his words picking up speed as he became more agitated, "did you know, didn't you know that we can't even breathe over there? The atmosphere," he elongated the word for emphasis, "is different there."

"There's no oxygen?" Thane asked, interrupting.

"How do the Shae breathe over here, then?" Remi added, indicating Jaeger and Paka with her thumb.

"There's oxygen, and going this way is easier than going back. The air there is heavier and the most humid day in the world here wouldn't come close to their driest! You have to take medication with DNA stabilizers, and be inoculated, and have specific types of oxygen tanks with you or you'll die. He," Twitch said, jabbing a finger towards Thane, "has enough Shaeblood to probably survive, but we," and he made a circle with his finger that encompassed Remi, Brennan, and himself, "would drown on dry land before having enough time to adapt." His indignation deflated, and Twitch leaned against the wall and slid to the floor. "I'm sorry."

Remi, Paka, Jaeger, Brennan, and Thane looked at him in silence for a moment. Thane had no idea what everyone else was thinking, but his own thoughts were subdued and defeated.

"That was actually... very helpful," Remi said, nodding to herself. "I'll admit, it seemed hopeless, but now knowing what we're up against, I think we could do it."

"What?" Thane and Twitch said together.

"Yeah," Remi continued. "Paka says she'll come, and so will Thane and they'll both be fine on the Shae side. So I'm the only one who'll need the medicine, and I'm sure Paka can get those for me. She has the clearance?" she spoke this last as a question, looking towards the panther, who nodded confirmation. "Great. And Jaeger already told us who's holding my mom hostage, so we just have to ask around to find this Terracatan."

"He will kill hyu," Jaeger spoke up. He launched himself off the desk and landed on Remi's shoulder, wrapping his tail around her neck like a large lizard in a zoo Thane had seen once on a field trip. "He will know hyu are coming and kill hyu, and hyu," and he pointed to Thane and Paka in turn, "and then hyu will be reunited with hyu's mother and be a slave for him too." Jaeger's sigh seemed to come from his whole body. "Hyu are going, perfekt head?" Thane nodded. "Then Aye am going too. Aye cannot repay my debt to hyu with words, but hyu will take me somewhere dangerous and horrible like Aye did to hyu, and we will be even."

Somehow that description of the Shaerealm frightened Thane more than any other so far. He still had nightmares about the Omega Team training session that Jaeger had driven him into, about seeing his new friends die horribly and knowing at any moment he could be stabbed, eviscerated, or blown up, and most of his nightmares ended now with Rip opening black eyes and the daemon that possessed him tearing Thane and Iselle to shreds. He hadn't had the nightmare about turning into a monster and destroying everyone since the cave, where he lost his ability to hear the music. The Song of the universe was silent to him now, and sometimes the ache of that loss would wake him up at night.

"I guess I'll go too, then," Brennan's voice snapped Thane out of his revere. "I get the feeling you're going to need my help if any of you are going to make it back."

"Fine," Twitch snapped. "Fine. I'll help. You'll need me to access the files on where the weakest points in the Weave are, and cover your tracks, and who knows what else. Shae magic is wonderful and all," he muttered to himself, "but this world runs on tech. You can't get through without it."

"Well, now you have a team," Paka observed. "And they have some resources. Do you have a plan?"

"First we need to get out of Sanctum, apparently," Remi said. "And they don't let us just leave. Is it hard for you?"

Twitch shook his head. "As full members of the Shaerealm Mercenary Guard, we can request leave whenever we want. It has to be approved, though," he paused, looking around the room, "and I doubt they'd give leave to so many members of the same team at once."

"What about Winter Break?" suggested Brennan. "Most of the students go home to spend time with family. Multiple team members getting leave for the holidays are pretty common. That's in two weeks, should give us some time to prepare."

Remi made a face. "My dad is planning some trip for just the two of us. We're leaving right after the end of class when the break starts. I think we have to leave before that."

Thane nodded. "Yeah, if you're not with him he'll send out a search party like last time. We need an excuse to leave that's going to give us a few days head start, something where they think they know where we are."

Paka stiffened, her tail whipping back and forth. "I have an idea." She looked at Jaeger, then Twitch. "It will need your help."

"What?" Remi asked.

Paka looked at Thane and Remi for a long moment before speaking. "It may be better if you don't know. It will be surprising, and possibly dangerous, and the more honest your reactions the better."

Thane didn't like the sound of that at all, but Remi nodded. "Do you think it will work?" she asked the panther.

The Felidae made a noise somewhere between a growl and a purr. "The trouble might be that it works too well," she answered.

Thane opened his mouth to ask a question, but Remi cut him off before he could speak. "All right, that's taken care of. What about getting into the Shaerealm? Twitch, you said we'd need a circle of mages. How hard would that be to get together?"

"Well," Brennan answered before Twitch could respond, "the issue there would be the mages themselves. Since we're doing this without Sanctum's blessing, we can't use any of the mages registered or associated with Sanctum. And those who aren't are of, shall we say, questionable morality."

"Meaning they'd be more likely to scam us and dismember us for spell components than actually help," Twitch cut in. "We don't have the money or the manpower to ensure their cooperation."

"I'm afraid our techie has the right of it," Brennan agreed. "A mage circle isn't a viable option."

"What about the guardian bone and scroll? Isn't that what Ms. Rasmussen used?" Remi asked. "That can't be as hard if she did it."

"I still don't know how that happened," muttered Twitch. "That shouldn't have been possible. The guardian scroll was a protected secret and it was kept in a secure facility, and the guardian bone should have been magically booby-trapped to kill anyone who came near without the proper Sanctum issued wards." He put his head down in his hands and rested his elbows on his knees. "Everything about that should never have happened."

"But it did," Remi pointed out, "so there must be a way."

"There must have been a way," Twitch corrected. "Since that disaster, the guardian scrolls have all been relocated to different secure locations that have not been registered in the Sanctum computer system and are only known by select members of the Guardian Council. The Bones of the Guardians had their spell work tripled and now Sanctum graduates are assigned guard duty in temporary training teams before taking the entrance exams for the SMG."

"Meaning that the four of us could take a team of them, but I'm not going to injure students," Brennan added.

"Meh," Jaeger shrugged.

"We do not fight cubs," Paka admonished, glowering at him. Jaeger grumbled.

"And I'm not killing anyone to get their blood," Thane said, giving Remi a pointed look.

"So the guardian bone is out," Remi continued. "What was the last one? The ancient ones? Who are they?"

There was a long, silent pause as the members of the Omega Team looked at each other. No one seemed to want to answer the question. Twitch sat sullenly with his head in his hands, Jaeger buried his face in his wings, and neither Paka nor Brennan would meet Thane's eyes.

"Somebody just tell us already," Remi burst out. Everyone else flinched.

Twitch seemed to whisper something, then said, "Shut up," slightly louder. With his face covered, Thane couldn't see Twitch's mouth, but the whisper came again and sounded like someone far away was shouting. "Shut up," hissed Twitch, and cupped a hand over his left ear.

"Are we hearing the voices in Twitch's head?" Remi whispered to Thane. Thane shrugged.

"Twitch, are you... all right?" Thane asked.

Twitch sighed and rolled his eyes with pointed exasperation. "The dragons," he said. "Happy now? The ancient ones are the dragons. They're the only ones with enough Song to open a gateway through the Weave without help. You have to ask one of the seven full-blooded dragons, and you have to have something to bargain with. Even with the golds. It's the way they are. I wish you would just shut up."

"Is that true?" Remi asked Brennan.

"I'd assume he wishes we'd have all shut up an hour ago," Brennan answered. Remi glared at him, and he sighed, sitting forward in his chair and resting his elbows on his knees. "It's true. We'd have to find, and then bargain with, a dragon."

Remi growled under her breath, and Thane was close enough to be shocked at her choice of words. Paka wrinkled her nose at the girl. "Gage-cub, those are words used to taunt an enemy. Why does having an answer anger you?"

"Because I already know two dragons," she spat. "And one of them works for Sanctum."

"And the other?" Paka pressed. Thane cringed and didn't even try to hold it back. He knew who the other dragon was, and he knew how Remi would feel about asking his grandfather for help. About owing Charlie. Moving quiet and slow, he tried to edge out of Remi's punching range.

To his surprise, she smiled. There wasn't any humor or warmth in it, though. "The other would like nothing better than to have me ask him for something." She turned to Thane. "We need to talk to your grandfather."

"I was afraid of that," sighed Thane. "When do you--"

Twitch's watch stared beeping. He jumped and looked at it, then leapt to his feet. "We have to go," his voice sounded strained. "We have five minutes before our security hole closes."

"But we're not--" Remi began.

"Five minutes isn't enough--" Thane spoke at the same time.

Paka hissed at them both. "Humans always want to talk when action is needed." She lunged forward, grabbing Remi and Thane each by a shoulder and shoving them towards the door. "Our locations will draw interest but perhaps not comment. Your being out of bed will draw both punishment and questions, neither of which we can afford unless you would care to abandon all planning now."

Remi took off running down the hall, Jaeger still perched on her with his tail around her neck. "Aye will make sure she is safely returned," he called back, waving and smiling like a demented beauty queen.

Thane and Twitch ran the other direction, only slowing when they arrived at the door and pausing to check outside first. "Clear," Twitch whispered, and as the sun began to break across the horizon the first beams of daylight shone on the closing door to their dorm building.

Twitch's watch started beeping faster as they dove into their cots. "Shoes!" hissed Twitch, and Thane kicked his worn tennis shoes onto the floor and lay down as the watch gave a final three quick beeps, then went silent.

Laying in bed with his eyes mostly closed, Thane rolled on his side to look at Twitch. The seventeen year old was gently snoring. Thane was impressed at how well his roommate faked sleeping; even he almost believed it. He tried to relax and allow his lids to close but he didn't think he'd fall asleep again. The glowing red numbers of the clock on Twitch's nightstand read 7:02 a.m. and Thane wondered if Twitch had disabled the caffeine darts for the day.

Then he remembered it was Saturday. No classes today, except for hand-to-hand combat at noon. They held that class six days a week, with Tuesday being their day off. Ever since their argumentative first class Remi and Charlie had carefully avoided any contact, and Charlie hadn't even called on Thane again, for which Thane was grateful. He didn't want to be the center of attention, not even to help Charlie.

Thane missed the private lessons they used to do. Doing the Taijiquan forms with his dragon grandfather had felt like it was bringing them closer, where everything since then felt like it was pushing them apart. He wondered how Charlie would react to Remi's request; he wondered if Charlie would want to go with them. It would've been best to ask the Scotsman about the Shaerealm while they were doing the kata as it always kept him calm. Opening posture...

Thane fell asleep thinking about his grandfather and the memory of the kata, and the memory blended seamlessly into his dream. Except in his dream instead of the Taijiquan form bringing them closer, Charlie used it to channel his Song into a huge ball of lightning. He threw it at the Weave where it burned a huge hole in reality, fragments of burning threads wafting in the air. Thane frantically tried to pull the threads back together before the two worlds shattered under the sound waves that crashed through and disintegrated everything they touched. He looked back at Charlie to ask for help, but instead of his grandfather there was a man made all of blurry pixels who laughed and laughed while the world fell apart around them.

CHAPTER 6

"Are ye gaun fair doolalley? D'ye think I'm daft-- I'm taken a pure maddy ye'd even consider I'd be so gormless!" Charlie was furious, and the more angry he became the fewer words Thane understood.

Thane and Remi were in Charlie's rooms in Sanctum after their hand-to-hand combat lesson. The class itself had gone fairly well, with Remi trying to participate and not antagonize the blue dragon man to the point where she'd almost smiled at him once.   Almost. And she made a face at Thane afterward. But Charlie had been pleased, and even more so when Thane and Remi asked to speak to him privately after class. Incorrigible and irrepressible, he'd grinned at them and asked, "How privately?"

"Somewhere not everyone in the facility can hear us," Remi had responded. Thane shot his grandfather a serious glare, warning him not to take them lightly. Charlie had taken the hint and invited them back to his guest suite and offered them seats in his front room while he leaned against a wall and watched them.

"Are we safe here?" Thane asked tentatively.

Charlie barked a laugh. "Aye, tadpole, there's naught a camera or bug in here. Twas part of my agreement in coming, and I reinforced it with a little electrical Song once I took up residence. There's nary a tech device in this universe that could survive it. What's on yer mind?" He'd tried to seem casual, but Thane could see the tension in his grandfather's shoulders and the concerned way he looked at Remi whenever she wasn't looking at him.

Thane had wanted to explain, to give reasons and backstory before coming to the point, but Remi had jumped right in. "I know you think you care about me," she began while Thane flinched, "and I understand that dragons are willing to trade favors."

Charlie's eyebrows had nearly crawled up onto his bald scalp with that statement, but he'd waved to her to continue.

"You know I don't like you," she said, and Thane winced again, "but I need something that only you can help with, and I'm going to offer you a chance. A clean slate with me the moment I get back. And I would be in your debt, past forgiven, previous offenses forgotten." Charlie breathed in sharply and leaned away, eyes widening, something about that statement affecting him more strongly than Thane thought it warranted.

"Back from where?" he'd asked.

"From the Shaerealm. I need a way in, and I understand that you can provide one."

That's when the dragon man started swearing. The first thing he'd said sounded like several anatomical and biological slang words strung together, and hearing them while he sat next to Remi made Thane's face flush with heat and embarrassment. He hoped she hadn't caught what his grandfather said. Then he'd alternate the swearing with increasingly obscure Scottish words, and Thane was starting to lose track of what they all might mean.

"Charlie," Thane tried to interrupt.

"Shut yer gob, ye bawheid," Charlie whirled to snarl at him, jabbing a finger downward. "I dinnae ken what ye think ye've got her mixed up in, but I'll nip the de'il afore I'll let ye go traipsin' off tae get her kilt!" The dragon man was panting as if his heart was going to explode and the hand that pointed accusingly at Thane was shaking.

Through all this Remi had sat calmly, not blinking or blushing at even the most colorful and imaginative curses Charlie had effortlessly flung at them. Instead she waited and watched. For the space of two heartbeats it looked like the man began to expand, a faint bluish color rising under his skin, and then he deflated and collapsed onto a seat that looked like some cross between an overstuffed easy chair and a reclined deck chair. He put his elbows on his knees and ran both of his hands over his bald scalp under her scrutiny before looking up at them again.

"But why d'ye want tae go tae that midden?" he asked, resting his chin on two fists. "Ye ken it's like ye'll be deid within minutes of crossing over?"

"We're aware of the differences in atmosphere," Remi kept her voice cool and professional, and it suddenly reminded Thane of Teresa LaPointe, the uptight and distant Sanctum representative who'd first come to get him from his home. And who'd shot him execution style for being part blue dragon. Thane tried and failed to repress a shiver. That was twice in two days Remi had sounded like a woman who'd tried to kill him. He hoped it wouldn't become a habit. "We aren't going just because it sounds like fun."

"Why in the Weaver's needles are ye, then?" Charlie pressed.

Remi took a deep breath, and Thane noticed her hand. It was trembling. He wanted to hold it and his own hand twitched in response, the rubber sliding against the scales underneath. Right. No hand holding without hands. Thane looked back up in time to notice Charlie's eyes flick away from Thane's gloves, an unspoken question for another time.

"We are going to the Shaerealm on a rescue mission." She took another shaking breath and tried to keep the shards of her cool detachment from breaking away.

Charlie stared at her, his breathing becoming more even. "Ah. That's more like. Who're ye looking tae rescue, then?"

"Major Meagan Quinn Gage," Remi answered, and lifted her chin. "My mother."

"Yer..." Charlie was so flabbergasted that his elbows slid off his knees and he fell forward a bit. "Her mum?" The dragon man looked at Thane for confirmation.

Thane nodded. "But how d'ye know she's there? The realm's a big place; ye cannae be guddling about and hope tae find her," Charlie asked.

"We have a guide who knows where she is," Remi said, regaining her composure. Charlie raised his eyebrows.

"Jaeger found her," Thane added. Remi shot him an angry glare but Charlie nodded.

"So that's where the wee beastie has been." Thane was surprised that Charlie knew the imp had been gone, and that must've shown on his face because Charlie added, "I was playing a hand of cards with a few of yer Omega boys. The Persian was belly aching about team practice being thrown as the flying monkey was naught tae be found." The dragon man looked at Thane with a raised eyebrow. "Bit of advice, lad; dinnae play cards with Brennan. The de'il hisself couldnae win."

"Um, okay," Thane said.

"Will you help me?" Remi asked, clasping and unclasping her hands while trying to look like she didn't care.

Charlie took a deep breath and let it out slowly. "Yer mum," he said as he exhaled. "There's naught as means more tae ye than yer family." He rested his head in his hands for a moment before continuing. "I know ye cannae ken how much it fashes me tae deny ye anything." His words were hesitant, but not unsure. "I know ye'll hate me, but I cannae do this. I cannae let ye go and be killed."

"We're not going alone," Thane protested, and Remi elbowed him. "What? He'd have to find out eventually. Brennan, Paka, Twitch, and Jaeger are going with us. We'll be fine. Half of the Omega Team has got to be better than all of any others."

"I dinnae care if ye've got all the mankey SMG going, I'll not be helping ye cross over!" Charlie snapped, his nostrils flaring and eyes narrowing. "I cannae risk it. I cannae allow her tae be in such danger," he gestured at Remi.

"How dare you." Thane stiffened. Charlie couldn't have said anything to make Remi angrier than to imply someone else could "allow" her to do or not do anything. Her jaw clenched and her eyes opened wide, glaring as she rose to her feet. "I don't need you," she put a scornful emphasis on the pronoun, "to protect me. I don't need you at all. Thane said you'd offered to help me if I needed it. Well I need it, but not from you. I wouldn't let you help if your life depended on it, you disgusting, gutless monster."

With that, she stormed out of the room and slammed the door behind her hard enough to make it vibrate on its hinges. Thane stood up too and took a step to follow her, but his grandfather reached out a hand to restrain him.

"Thane, lad," Charlie didn't sound hurt, or angry. If anything he seemed to have found the self-possessed calm Remi had been trying so hard to maintain. The dragon's blue eyes looked up at him, and Thane flinched at the eternity of grief that lay exposed in that gaze. None of it showed in his voice. "She'll not forgive me this. And I cannae say I blame her. Her mither. Crivvens. For anything less I'd move the stars tae make her smile, but I cannae send her there."

"She isn't going to give up," Thane said. Charlie nodded.

"I ken it, lad. Did the imp tell ye where her mum is?"

"Yeah," Thane said. Maybe telling him the rest would change his mind. "Jaeger said Major Gage is being held captive by a Sang Evarish named Terracatan. He was going to show us where--"

Charlie swore. Not in Scottish or English, but with words Thane felt more than understood. The sound of the words thrummed like the lightning Song, filling Thane's mind with images of hunting and killing, of power beyond words and fury beyond sight. Thane felt himself growl in response. He flushed; why had he done that? That was stupid, and the whatever influence Charlie's words had snapped under the pressure of Thane's self-consciousness.

"Sorry, lad," Charlie said, noting Thane's embarrassment. "Dragon-tongue is not for every ear tae hear. But that toerag Terracatan has hold of her mum, and I ken why yer all so keen tae get her back. I'll not help ye," the dragon said, holding up a hand against Thane's suddenly hopeful face, "but I'll do whate'er I can without placing her or yerself in danger. That's a promise."

Thane shook his head. It wasn't going to be good enough, but it was all he was going to get out of his grandfather. He was certain of that. He stood to go, and Charlie rose also and laid a hand on Thane's shoulder.

"How's yer Song, lad?"

Thane shrugged. "Burned out." He moved his gloved hands around slightly. "I'm dealing."

"It'll come back, tadpole, dinnae fash yerself about it. Ye cannae do aught for it now." Charlie squeezed Thane's shoulder sympathetically. "At least I can count on that ba-heid Gideon being even more against this manky plan than I. She'll be safe. There's none in Sanctum that'll help ye cross over, so's ye'll have tae trust me." Charlie ruffled his hair and Thane cringed and pulled back.

"I'll see you in class," he said, and left Charlie's rooms. Once he was out of the building, he pressed a small ear-com stuck to the back of his right earlobe. "Twitch, did you get any of that?"

"Not a word," the tech genius' voice spoke right into his ear. "He wasn't kidding about spell security, I don't think there's anyone who could've overheard that. Well, yes, of course except for you," he added.

"Me? Why me?" asked Thane.

"What? Not you. Why you what?" Twitch was obviously flustered. "Never mind. So what did he say? Is he in?"

"No." Thane's shoulders slumped as he walked away. "He's not going to help."

"What? Did Remi ask him?" Thane flinched at Twitch's surprise.

"Yes. Told him about her mother, too. He still said no."

"Shredding holes." Twitch paused, then added so quietly that Thane had to strain to hear, "But she's his phoenix. I didn't think he'd say no to her about anything."

"Me too." Thane realized he'd stopped walking and saw a few other people glancing at him, where it looked like he was standing and talking to himself. He hunched his shoulders and began moving again. "Apparently keeping her safe is more important than giving her what she wants."

"Huh," Twitch sounded like he didn't quite believe that.

"I'm almost there," Thane said, glancing around. He was outside building fifteen again, in the dark about an hour before curfew.

"Wait, there's a merc on the south side, looks like Rho," Twitch whispered. "Hang on, he's walking, going around a corner... now!"

Thane sprinted down the sidewalk towards the remains of the structure that he'd blown up, sliding into the darkened recess of the doorway. He paused for two breaths. No one else moved; no one had a clean line of sight to where he hid. Thane gripped the door handle and opened it barely enough for his thin frame to squeeze through. On the other side he shut it gently and picked up the oilcan in the corner behind it. He oiled the hinges. As he did so, he wondered again just who Nathiel was.

Down the hall in the room where they'd met before waited Remi, Twitch, and Paka. Remi was fuming, and both Twitch and Paka were watching her while trying to make it look like they weren't watching her. It wasn't working. "Brennan is almost here," Paka said after Thane had entered. He nodded acknowledgement and leaned against a wall to wait.

He didn't have to wait very long, as only minutes after he'd entered Brennan strolled in with Jaeger on his shoulder. "We have to stop meeting like this," he said to the room in general. Remi snorted and rolled her eyes. Brennan looked at her with one raised eyebrow. "One, maybe two more, but we're pushing our luck as it is. Someone reported that the students are using this as a make-out spot," Remi flushed and Thane pretended not to notice, "and the overseer already has plans to raze the place."

"When?" Thane asked.

Twitch's eyes snapped back into focus. "Three days. If she didn't need permission from the Guardian Council it would've been done today. She doesn't like-- what the knotted threads does canoodling mean?" he asked no one in particular.

Paka growled something under her breath. "So we are on a stricter deadline. There is no other place to meet under the dome where they cannot hear us. Plans must be made and acted upon now." She turned her green eyes on Remi. "Is the chaos dragon in?"

"Charlie? He's a coward and a liar," Remi said, folding her arms and hugging herself a little with them.

Paka turned to Thane with a puzzled look. "He won't help," Thane translated.

Jaeger heaved a sigh that was disproportionally large for his body. "Aye am sorry, Remi girl. We tried."

"This isn't over," Remi snapped. "We'll find another way."

"How?" asked Brennan. He wasn't being unkind, and his eyes were mournful as he looked at her. "Charlie was our only hope. There aren't any other full dragons we can ask."

"Gideon--" Remi began, but Brennan cut her off.

"--won't get near this, and if we tell him what we were planning he'll be honor bound to tell General Aileen, who at best will only tell your father instead of the entire council." Jaeger climbed down Brennan's arm and flung himself into the air while Brennan spoke. The imp beat his wings twice and landed on Remi's shoulder, wrapping his wing around her head in a pseudo-Jaeger hug. "I'm sorry, but without one of the ancient ones to open a way, we're stuck."

"But..." Remi's face began to crumple and she hid it in Jaeger's outstretched wing. But not before Thane had seen the tears in her eyes. Remi was crying. Twitch backed away and Paka gave him a disgusted glare before stepping closer and placing a furred paw on Remi's other shoulder.

"You would have gone," Paka said, the thrumming in her voice not quite a growl and not quite a purr. "Your honor is unblemished. Take comfort in that."

"I'm not worried about my honor," Remi's voice sounded strained. She took several deep breaths to calm herself and turned to face them again. "There has to be another way."

"There is." Thane almost looked around to see who had spoken before he realized it'd been him. The others all stared at him, and he cleared his throat. He hated being the center of attention. "There is another way. We could ask, um, ask my father." He had to swallow three times to get that sentence out.

Their reaction was immediate. "What?" Twitch shouted, pinwheeling his arms to keep from falling over backwards. Jaeger launched himself off Remi's shoulder and clung to the ceiling, while Paka hissed and Brennan looked dumbfounded, then thoughtful.

Remi just blinked at him. "Your-- what? You mean it?"

"Well, he is one of the ancient ones," Thane defended, not sure whether he wanted them to talk him out of it or not. His father. Whom he had never met, and who sent psychos to find him and then killed them when they did. Who wanted him and had searched for him for years, if what'd he'd heard was true.

"No," Twitch regained his balance and punched a finger at Thane. "Remember the viper birds? And nearly dying? That was from your father."

"He is pretty unpredictable," said Brennan. "But as far as Sanctum can tell, he's done some good throughout his stay here in this universe. It hasn't all been viper birds and killing."

"Like what?" Thane grasped that statement and held on. His father was a blue, like Charlie. Chaotic, but could honestly care about people. Cressida Rasmussen had tried to kill him, after all, and maybe his father was only trying to protect Thane when he'd had her shot her in the holding cells...

"Later, kid, I promise," Brennan said. "Right now we need to decide whether we're moving forward with this or not and get out of here before someone notices."

Paka moved to the window. "There are people out there now. Students, but they still should not hear what we are doing." She turned back to face them. "We would have to break you two out of Sanctum to find him. Break you out with only a hope of finding and asking, and with almost no hope of being helped. And if we find him, even before we ask about opening a tear, he may kill us all." Her green eyes gleamed in the semi-darkness of the room, studying Thane and Remi. "Is this what you wish for us?"

"Not to die," said Remi. "But it is a chance." She turned to Thane. "Are you sure? What do we have to bargain with?"

He could still see unshed tears swimming in her upturned eyes. Suddenly his conversation with Brennan from days ago flashed into his mind. "Don't do something stupid just because she's pretty. The consequences last longer than the relationship." Thane stood there, looking back at her.

"I'm sure."

She closed her eyes, and one remaining tear pushed its way out and ran down her cheeks. She punched his arm with her eyes closed. "Then you're an idiot. And so am I. Let's do this."

"There is a shipment of refugees arriving tomorrow afternoon," Paka said. She looked at Jaeger and then Twitch, who both nodded. "They have been recently recovered from a human trafficking operation in southern Texas, but were kidnapped and captured in South America. There is always a crowd who gathers to watch the arrival of new Shae and Shaelings. Be in that crowd. Twitch will find you."

"Too late," Brennan spoke up and rose to his feet. "You two come with me," he said sternly, grabbing Thane and Remi each by one shoulder and propelling them out of the room.

"What--" Thane began, but glancing behind him he did not see Twitch, Jaeger, or Paka anywhere. It seemed deserted.

"You'll get the chance to defend yourself later. For right now, I suggest you be quiet," Brennan said in that same I'm-not-angry-but-I'm-disappointed voice. He steered them down the hallway towards the door, which was completely blocked by the immense and terrifying presence of Ms. Tagore.

She wore a dress that wrapped around her neck and covered the front, but left the back and sides open to give room for her arms. The skirt billowed around her legs as she stood in the open doorway. The look on her face was dark and terrifying, like an angry goddess ready to descend and destroy. "What are you doing here, Mr. Tayler?" she asked in a silky sweet voice that defied her expression. Thane felt Brennan's hand tighten on his shoulder.

"Felt like something was amiss, so I thought I'd check it out," Brennan responded, and shook Thane and Remi's shoulders for emphasis. "Found these two in one of the rooms. I caught them before they had time to get very far."

Remi started fussing with her hair to play along with Brennan's ruse, but Thane felt his face flush so hard that his toes were probably red.

Ms. Tagore's narrowed eyes relaxed after seeing Thane's blush. "Well caught, Mr. Tayler," she purred, and Brennan's hand tried to make a fist through Thane's shoulder joint again. "I will take it from here. Disciplining the Shaelings is one of my responsibilities after all."

"You discipline after curfew?" Brennan sounded disapproving and surprised, and the small part of Thane's brain that wasn't terrified was impressed by Brennan's acting skills.

"What?" Ms. Tagore drew back, off guard. "It isn't--"

At that moment, the three sharp tones that announced curfew for the Shae students sounded over the speaker system outside. The multi-armed woman's eyes narrowed again as she looked them. "Fine. First thing in the morning, then. Report to Ms. Yemaja's office."

"I can't, I have a test in Axial History," Remi protested. "They don't let you do make ups."

"Me too," Thane said weakly.

"Don't you talk back to her," Brennan shouted at them, shaking them again by the shoulders.

"Mr. Tayler!" Ms. Tagore's voice was sharp. "I will handle the Shaelings, thank you. Please let them go." The threat implied in her tone was doubled by her four highest arms rising up and taking a battle ready stance.

Brennan let them go. Thane and Remi stood halfway between the two adults, unsure what to do next. "Go to bed," instructed Ms. Tagore, and the other two sets of hands balled up in fists and rested on her hips. "And you had both better be sitting in chairs in front of me tomorrow before dinner. If not, you'd better be dead or in a medical ward." After one last look to make sure they believed she was serious, she stepped aside and they ran out the door past her.

"Brennan is brilliant," hissed Remi to him as they ran.

Thane nodded. "He calls it directed luck. Paka had better get us out of here tomorrow before we have to go see Ms. Tagore."

"She will," Remi said. "And then we'll be on our way."

She stopped running so immediately that Thane flew past her, and had to turn around and come back several feet. "What's wrong?"

"Are you sure?" Remi asked him. She took a step closer to him and looked up into his face. "This is for my mom, and I would do anything to save her. But that doesn't mean you have to do anything to save her too. Are you sure you want to find your father? Is this how you want to meet him?"

"I don't know," Thane said. She was standing so close it made him... not uncomfortable, but distracted. "I don't know if there is a good way for me to meet him. Everything about this is going to be weird." He sighed and looked down and felt her lean forward until her forehead rested against his.

"Thank you," she whispered.

"Thank me after we get back," Thane said. "After we don't die, then you can thank me."

CHAPTER 7

It was mid-December so Thane thought it should've been at least a little cold. But not, apparently, under the dome. The next day dawned bright and sunny and just as warm as all the others had been since Thane came to Sanctum. Twitch's alarm clock went of exactly at seven, waking him up, and the sound of Twitch flying out of bed usually woke up Thane.

"So, um, anything I should be ready for?" Thane asked Twitch on their way to the cafeteria.

Twitch shot him an annoyed look. "I hear you have a history test. Be ready for that."

Thane wasn't. His first classes were a blur, and he couldn't remember what the test was even about by lunchtime. He and Remi sat with their usual group in the cafeteria but Thane didn't even make a pretext of being involved, while Remi seemed to be trying harder than ever to keep up the conversation. She talked so fast that Thane couldn't catch half of it if he'd been trying.

"There's a refugee group coming in after lunch," Naessa commented as she sipped her lemonade. "We should go watch."

"What?" her comment immediately arrested both Thane and Remi's attention enough that everyone else stopped chatting. Remi continued. "What refugee group? How did you hear about it?"

Naessa blinked. "They sent out an email about it to the Shaelings who are graduating this year. They want us all to see the good work Sanctum does hoping that we'll all sign up and become good little soldiers. It's supposed to be really sad," she added, taking another drink, "but they bring in refugees every other week or so and it's getting pretty boring."

"So why do you want to go this time?" Remi asked, too brightly. Thane winced and tried to mentally tell her to back it off a little.

Naessa gave Remi a strange look. "Because this time there are full blooded Shae in the group. They found a whole colony of Felidae somewhere in South America, and these poachers in Texas were going to sell tickets to hunt them on some game preserve. Sanctum found out, they didn't say how, and rescued them right off the ship. They're having all the Felidae who are already in Sanctum greet them and help them adapt. I think they're going to send them back eventually."

"Why would they send them back?" asked Korey, eyes wide.

"Why wouldn't they? It's their home," snapped Naessa.

"But they would be safer here," said the girl with vertical slitted eyes, and the rest of the table erupted in a discussion about whether it would be better for the refugees to be returned to where they came from or have Sanctum relocate them to a safer facility.

Remi took the opportunity to whisper to Thane. "Those must be our refugees. We'd better go with Naessa."

"Shouldn't we go on our own?" Thane asked in an undertone.

"Twitch will find us faster if we're with her," Remi answered quickly, and then turned to face Korey, who'd been trying to pull her back into the conversation. Thane wasn't sure Remi was right, but it didn't end up mattering because the entire group decided to go with them.

Besides Remi, Naessa, Thane, Korey and the girl with the imp eyes, there were two other girls Thane couldn't remember having ever spoken to and one other boy named Carl who was a friend of Korey's, all of them excited at the chance to skip classes and not get in trouble for it. A large crowd had already gathered around the landing area for building three, but Remi and her friends weaved their way through the crowd until they stood near the front.

The wide expanse of space before him reminded Thane of his first day at Sanctum, when Gideon the gold dragon had landed while Thane had been on his way to building five. Even now after seeing Gideon in his dragon form and Charlie as a full blue dragon more than once, Thane's mind shuddered away from the idea that something so huge could also be so intelligent.

Like Ruan de Argos. Thane let the crowd jostle him as he was lost in thoughts about his biological father. The father Thane had known all growing up was Robert Whitaker, Bert to his friends, and as a parent Bert had been every type of abusive. Verbal, physical, and emotional, and Thane had spent nearly his whole life trying to avoid that man's notice.

Until Thane had burned out his memory with a lightning bolt. It had been an accident, but the moment Bert had forgotten Thane it was as though Bert was an entirely new person. This man who didn't know him anymore was kind and soft-spoken. What had Thane done in the past to make Bert hate him so much? And would he alienate his real father the same way?

"Oof," Remi elbowing him in the stomach broke his chain of thought. He looked around and saw Twitch standing behind her, trying to be nonchalant while chatting with Naessa.

"Twitch says we need to move," Remi whispered. She started sliding along the crowd, moving parallel to the edge of the landing area. Almost subconsciously, Naessa and her other friends moved with her so they all ended up standing at the edge of the landing area closest to the dome.

"We're not going to see anything from here," complained the girl with imp eyes.

"Twitch knows what he's doing, Bailey," Naessa replied.

Twitch flinched and looked guilty. Naessa gave him a sideways glance and then pointed towards the other side of building three.

An immense semi was driving across the pavement, pulling past the building and out onto the landing area. It turned in an arc until it slowed to a stop in the center of the landing area, facing away at a diagonal to where Thane and Remi were so they had an excellent view of the large doors. Thane saw Naessa give Bailey a smug look. Bailey ignored it.

A procession of individuals were making their way across the tarmac to where the truck waited. Even from the distance, Thane recognized Paka, the black jungle panther and Haider, the golden lion who was also a medic. He was holding an infopad and looking down at it and then up at the truck. He seemed unhappy.

Trailing after him were three more Felidae that Thane had never seen before and the two he remembered from lunch duty. Those two were spotted leopards that seemed to match and moved in harmony with each other. The line of cat people switched back and forth between walking on their hind legs and walking on all fours. They seemed nervous, Thane thought. Their tails were lashing and several of them kept baring their teeth with all their ears flicking back and forth.

The leopards reached the truck first and pulled down a wide ramp from the back. Haider was still studying his infopad and frowning. Paka, wearing a supple sort of full leather armor, strode up the walkway and gripped the door handles.

"Wait, don't!" growled Haider, but too late. Paka had already swung wide open both doors and bared her teeth at whoever was on the other side.

A strange, echoing growl answered her. It didn't rise and fall with someone's voice, but rather stayed constant in pitch and grew louder. Paka's green eyes widened and she dove off the ramp and tucked and rolled under the truck.

People were milling about, shoving each other to get a better view and asking, "What happened? Do you see anything?" over and over. The humming growl grew louder and the noise from the crowd quieted. Everyone tensed. And suddenly a swarm of insects burst from the back of the semi.

The insects flew higher into the sky and spread out, forming a delicate humming net over the now fleeing onlookers. "You have to move," Twitch shouted at Naessa, grabbing her arm and trying to drag her away.

She grabbed Remi's hand and Remi grabbed Thane, and together they took off running from the long-contained insects. "Go," shouted Twitch again, pushing Naessa ahead of him and dropping back next to Remi and Thane.

"Sorry about this," he whispered, and then seized them each on the forearm.

Two sharp pricks and a burning sensation followed. "Ouch!" shouted Remi, and Thane grunted. Twitch held onto their arms for another few seconds as the burning continued, then he let go.

"Everyone will be fine," he promised, "just go to building one with everyone else!" and then sprinted away after Naessa.

Less than an hour later Thane and Remi were sitting in the waiting room outside the main medic area along with several others who had suffered insect bites. He rubbed absently at the red and swollen puncture Twitch had given him. Everyone who had been bitten was considered contaminated until the medical staff could clear them, although no one had specified to Thane what the contamination was.

Haider came into the waiting room with his infopad. "Thane Whitaker," he called, and Thane rose to follow the lion into the examination room. Thane self-consciously covered his arm when Haider turned to look at him.

"Well, this was a disaster," the lion man growled in his deep and resonant voice. His tail lashed and Thane winced.

"Sorry," Thane mumbled. It was a reflex. He couldn't help it.

"Hmm? Why?" Haider glanced at Thane's face with one arched eyebrow. "You didn't do anything wrong, except that you weren't cleared to be there in the first place. But Shaelings will always show where they're not invited, it is the curse and the privilege of the young. Now, show me where the creature bit you."

Thane's grip tightened on his arm, but the black rubber chafed against the inflamed skin. Haider looked down at the glove and then back at Thane. With a sigh, Thane released his arm and held it up for the lion's inspection. "It's no big deal," he began, feeling uncomfortable allowing the assumption that one of the insects had done it.

"That's for me to decide, son," Haider replied, studying the wound. He gently laid the padded tip of one finger, claw retracted, on the lump. "Is it painful? It's very warm," Haider said, making some notes on the infopad.

"It is?" Thane asked. He couldn't feel it through the thick gloves. Haider nodded and indicated that Thane should feel it for himself. He hesitated.

"Go on," encouraged Haider. "It's just you and me in here."

Thane glanced at him and contemplated. Could he even feel things like heat and cold through the dragon scales that transformed his hands? He was curious, and Haider was busy with the infopad. Maybe if he was very careful, and didn't take long.

Thane gripped the glove between his knees and slid his hand out. It had been weeks since he really looked at it, the blue scales that were light in the center and darkened towards the edges and the wickedly curved talons that seemed pitch black unless you studied them. Only then could you see the cobalt streaks winding through like veins in marble.

He flexed his hand experimentally, and then glanced at Haider. Still typing on the pad. Delicately he extended what would normally be his index finger and angled it so the sharp claw wouldn't touch his skin. He lowered just the tip of his finger onto the flushed and puffy puncture wound.

It was warm. Warmer than the pad of his scales, anyway. But the sensation felt strange; although he could feel the pressure of someone touching his arm and the scales felt cold on his skin, he could barely feel his arm under his finger.

It felt like someone else was touching his arm and like he was touching someone else's arm at the same time. The sensation was disorienting enough that he jerked his finger away and accidentally drew a line of blood across the injury, and he hissed with the pain.

"Hmm?" Haider said, looking up at him. Thane hurried to put his hand back in the glove. "Hang on, there," the lion caught his arm and held it before he could hide away the half transformed limb. Thane was mortified; was Haider going to start lecturing him about safety? Or even worse, try to be supportive and sympathetic?

"No, I'm fine," Thane began before Haider could say anything else and tried to pull his disfigured hand away.

"Hang on there, boy," there was enough growl in his voice and strength in his hand to stop Thane from struggling. Haider watched him a moment to make sure Thane wasn't going to move again, and then pulled a sterile white gauze out of a drawer. "You never put away your claws without cleaning them," Haider instructed, handing Thane the gauze. Thane paused before taking it.

The lion man let go of Thane's arm and flexed his own paw in front of Thane's face, extending and then retracting the claws. "They are a tool like any other. Care for them properly, and they will be ready when you need them." Thane nodded and wiped his blood of the index finger talon, and then gripped the bloody gauze in his other hand.

Haider began to inspect the puncture and the inflamed tissue around it. "It looks like an allergic reaction," he said in a conversational tone, "but the mosquitos we trapped all tested positive for yellow fever. That normally isn't any concern because we can treat it effectively, but this was a particularly virulent strain. We're going to need to quarantine those affected for at least 72 hours to ensure they get the treatment they need. Those who are already showing reactions, like you, will be here in building one."

"What about the others?" Thane asked, thinking of Remi and trying to remember if her arm was swollen too. He wasn't sure.

"The rest will be placed in the medic wings of training buildings seventeen and eighteen. I believe you're familiar with building seventeen's medical wing," Haider accompanied his comment with a raised eyebrow. Thane shrugged and nodded. "Yellow fever usually presents in three to six days, but this strain is strong enough that we're expecting symptoms after the first twenty-four hours. Most cases only cause a mild infection with fever, headache, chills, back pain, loss of appetite, nausea, and vomiting, and they last for about a week. That's what we're hoping this will be like."

"Hoping?" Thane asked. He didn't flinch as Haider prodded the cut with a finger and then swabbed it with something that left a yellow smear and had a sharp, metallic smell. Haider wrapped his arm in gauze before looking up to meet Thane's hazel eyes with his deep golden ones.

"This strain of yellow fever has mutated. Did you know that there are places in our world where the Weave is not just thin, but unstable?" Thane blinked, surprised, and shook his head. If he had known that, he didn't remember. "These places sometimes form rifts or holes, and people on one side can get pulled to the other. Sanctum has been trying to stabilize the Weave for three centuries, now, and they've made some progress, but these events still happen. That's why there can suddenly be an entire village of Felidae deep in South America that haven't been discovered before. And some of them were already sick when they arrived." Haider sighed, deep and resonant.

"Was that why you didn't want the truck opened?" Thane asked.

"Yes. I noticed on the pad that they hadn't been through decontamination yet. I have no idea how that happened. Everything is electronic here- it's nearly impossible to mix up paperwork. But because this strain of yellow fever from the mosquitos has been mixed with a virus type from Shae, we have to give everyone a broad set of Shae specific inoculations. And we don't have enough."

He rubbed his eyes and pinched the bridge of his noise with his paw. "We almost never use it, because Sanctum rarely sends teams into Shae. So priority cases get it first, and priority cases are those already showing symptoms." Haider lowered his paw and looked at Thane again. "Like you."

"Oh," said Thane. He couldn't think of anything else to say, and absently reached out to rub his arm again.

"I wouldn't," Haider interrupted and Thane froze, realizing he hadn't put his glove back on. "Yours aren't retractable. I don't know how dragons manage." Haider smiled, and Thane almost managed to smile back.

"And orderly will be here in a moment to assign you a bed," the lion man said, holding out Thane's rubber glove and helping him put it back on. "Then after you're settled, a medic team will come through to give you each your shots."

"How many?" Thane wasn't sure he wanted to know.

"Five," Haider said.

Thane opened his mouth right then to say that he was fine, thank you, and that it had been Twitch who gave him the wound, not a mosquito, and he would be happy to go back to his dorm now. But two things stopped him; one, what Remi would say, and two, he wasn't sure that Twitch hadn't actually infected him with the mutant yellow fever. He had no idea what the tech genius had injected into his arm, and he wasn't positive that Twitch was totally sane.

"Ms. Tagore," Thane said instead. Haider raised an eyebrow. "She's expecting me this afternoon."

"I'll tell her you're under medical care and in quarantine. She can't be upset with you for that," Haider reassured him.

"For Remi, too?"

"Remi?" Haider asked, looking down at his notes. "Remi Quinn? Yes, she'll need to be quarantined too. I'll make sure Ms. Tagore knows."

"Thanks," Thane said.

Haider nodded in response. The orderly knocked. "One moment," called Haider, and then leaned closer to Thane. "Your claws are very impressive," said the lion in a low voice. "Retractable or not, you should be proud of them."

Thank blinked, but before he could respond Haider was opening the door to allow the orderly in. "I'll be in tonight to check on you," said Haider as a dismissal, and Thane followed the orderly down the hall and into the medic ward.

He was given a white bed with clean white sheets and surrounded by curtains that could be dragged along tracks in the ceiling to separate each patient with the illusion of privacy. Thane sat on the edge of the bed eyeing the flimsy hospital gown they had given him to change into. He decided he wasn't going to put it on unless Haider told him he had to.

The door at the end of the hallway opened and Thane turned, hoping for Remi.

An orderly came in first, followed by a tall boy with grey skin. Thane recognized him immediately. The boy from the locker room, the one who'd taken his towel and called the Chaun Kearney a little yapping dog. The grey boy saw Thane staring at him and nodded before the orderly sat him down on a bed two away and across the aisle from Thane.

The orderly spoke to the other boy too quietly for Thane to hear, and then handed over an identical hospital gown and left the room. The other boy waited until the door was closed and then picked up the gown.

"Yeah, that's not going to happen," he said, and tossed it away on another bed. Thane decided they could be friends. "I remember you," the boy said to Thane.

"Yeah," Thane acknowledged. "How's Kearney?"

"Still angry," the boy shrugged. "You got bit too?"

"Something like that," Thane shrugged off the question. "They said worst cases get put in here."

"This room's just for students," the boy corrected. "SMG members get the larger room down the hall."

Thane wondered how the other boy knew that, but before he could say anything else the door banged open and Remi rushed in. "Are you okay?" she asked Thane before the harried looking orderly could show her to her bed. "They said we have yellow fever. What was--" she cut off when she saw the grey boy. "Nathiel? You're here too?"

That was Nathiel? The companionable feeling Thane had for the other boy vanished, replaced with a sullen kind of resentment. This was the guy that told Remi about building fifteen being the make-out spot for students. Had he been inviting her to go?

"--standing in the back of the crowd, but those suckers were fast," Nathiel was saying to her. The orderly was trying to shoo Remi down to the other end of the room, but she wasn't paying attention to her.

"You can chat with your friends later," the orderly was getting irate. "Right now I need you to get to your bed."

"Of course, I'm sorry," Remi said, smiling at the orderly apologetically. "I'm just a little scared with everything that's happening." Her lower lip trembled a little.

Thane was impressed. "Oh, sweetie, it's all right," the orderly gushed, completely taken in by Remi's sweet vulnerability. "You'll be fine. We'll take great care of you, let's get you settled." They walked down the aisle between the beds and the orderly set Remi up on the far end of the room. Then she walked back to the middle and glared at both Thane and Nathiel before drawing a white curtain sharply across the width of the room so they couldn't see Remi anymore. The orderly turned to face them again.

"This room is monitored at all times," she said, the sweetness she'd used for Remi gone from her voice. "This is the boys side. That is the girls side. Don't cross the center line," and she glowered at them again before leaving.

"Whatever," Remi said, pulling the curtain back and coming to sit on a bed halfway between Thane and Nathiel. "And I'm not wearing that hospital robe thing. So, we're sick, huh?"

The three of them made small talk while the orderly came in and out of the room, bringing more students and shooting the boys dirty looks. There ended up being four girls and three boys in their room, leaving five of the beds empty. No one wanted to wear the hospital gowns. Instead they all sat on beds, holding quiet conversations and trying to hide their fear, which only made it more obvious. At least Thane thought so. None of these others were nearly as practiced at hiding their emotions as he was, and he scowled at them all mentally.

"Please return to your assigned beds," announced Haider as he came into the room, followed by six or seven masked orderlies. The students slowly shuffled around until they were each sitting on one bed, the girls on one end of the room and the boys on the other. Haider looked around the room with a raised eyebrow and a knowing half-smile. "So, no one wanted to put on the hospital gowns? Pity. It would have been easier for us to give you your shots. Ah well. Medics?" Haider made a small circling motion with one finger, and the team of people behind him began to spread out in twos throughout the room.

Thane had been wrong. There were eight of them, and they circled the room in pairs pushing small carts and stopping at a bedside, then closing the curtains around it. A few moments later he could hear hisses and grunts and short gasps of pain from behind the thin hanging cloth. Before Thane could wince or panic, there were two of the masked and robed figures before him, yanking the curtains around the tracks and shutting the rest of the world away.

He shrank back a little onto his bed, and the taller of the two medics looked at him. The skin around his eyes wrinkled as if he was smiling, but Thane couldn't see his mouth. The eyes looked familiar, though...

"Hey kid," Brennan Tayler said. "How're you holding up?"

"We're not supposed to talk to them," the other man said, and it took Thane a few moments to place the voice and the Middle Eastern accent.

"Lighten up, Turcato," Brennan rolled his eyes. "We know this kid."

"You know him," Turcato corrected. "I've met him twice and didn't really like him either time."

"You're just grumpy because we pulled medic support," Brennan said, grabbing one of Thane's arms and holding it up, inspecting the still swollen lump.

"Just because Paka screwed up doesn't mean Omega Team should've had to jump the line and be med support again," Turcato continued to complain. "We shouldn't have had med duty for another three weeks. I have other things to do."

Omega Team was giving the shots? Thane considered that, and then realized something. If the whole team was here, Rip was here. The man possessed by a daemon, although no one had explained to him how that was possible. Thane couldn't decide whether to glance around to figure out which one of these masked men was Rip, or if he'd rather not know.

"Take your shirt off, kid, we need to stick you pretty close to your shoulder," Brennan said with those same smile lines around his eyes. Thane took a deep breath and pulled his hoodie off, then the T-shirt underneath. "If it's any consolation, you know Paka hates doing this more than you do." Turcato grunted. Brennan opened a drawer on their cart and pulled out two syringes, and then three more from the drawer below. After a moment of deliberation, he pulled a final one out of a third and much smaller drawer on the side.

"Six?" Turcato asked. "We're only supposed to give them five."

"Did you see his arm?" Brennan retorted. "He's already showing symptoms and it's been like two hours. I was going to give him an immune booster."

"Fine, I don't care," Turcato glanced at the cart and two disinfecting wipes rose from the tray and flew over to his open hand. He ripped them open and pulled them out, then wiped down Thane's arm on the outside of his bicep.

"Showoff," Brennan muttered, laying the syringes on the top tray and taking some antiseptic wipes himself. He cleaned off Thane's other shoulder and picked up the first syringe. "Do you want us to do them one at a time, so it'll be the least amount of pain but takes the longest, or do you want us to do them at the same time so it'll be much more pain that doesn't last as long?"

"Do them all at once," Thane said without considering, clenching his teeth and trying to prepare himself.

Turcato looked at Brennan with a raised eyebrow. He seemed impressed. Brennan shrugged, and reached for a needle at the same moment one of the six inoculations rose into the air and floated to Turcato.

"Sorry kid," Brennan said, and squeezed Thane's shoulder once. Then they started sliding in the needles.

Hours later Thane's shoulders were still sore. He lay in semi-darkness under white sheets, waiting for it all to be over. There was no way his survival instincts were going to let him sleep in a room full of other people, even if they hadn't all been talking or moaning.

Since there were only three boys and four girls the orderlies had set them up as far apart as possible. Nathiel and the boy Thane didn't know were next to the wall, and he was in the middle bed. The set of beds on either side of the separating curtain were empty, and he didn't know what bed Remi had ended up in and couldn't see through the white cloth to find out.

He was thirsty. Dinner had been brought in two hours ago and most of the students had eaten with good appetite. Thane hadn't been hungry. He still wasn't, but he was hot and dying for a drink. He threw the blankets off and stood up.

Nathiel looked at him. "Bathroom," Thane said, and started towards the door. He only made it three steps before the world spun sideways and he fell, slamming into the foot of an empty bed before collapsing to the floor.

"Hey, are you okay?" Thane could hear Nathiel's voice and he tried to tell that grey skinned intruder to back off, but his mouth felt strange and nothing came out right.

"What's going on?" He heard Remi's voice behind him, and he tried to turn his head to look at her but the movement gave him vertigo and his stomach heaved. He was grateful he hadn't eaten dinner.

"Medic!" Remi shouted, and tried to run to him. Thane saw her come forward and then clutch the foot of his bed with one hand and her stomach with the other. The color drained from her face and she slumped down onto her knees.

"Help!" Nathiel shouted, standing up and opening the door. "We need help in here!"

Thane heard footsteps pounding in the hallway, syncopated against the sudden pounding in his head. His stomach clenched again and he rolled over to dry heave toward the ground.

"Oh kid," he heard Brennan say, right before he gratefully blacked out.

CHAPTER 8

"Losing consciousness is a concern," Thane's fuzzy mind tried to make sense of the words he could hear Haider saying. He tried to open his mouth, but his tongue felt thick and unresponsive and his eyelids were too heavy to lift. "The three of them are getting worse, and with all the new cases coming in, I'm worried we'll need more beds and supplies than we have."

Who was he talking about? Thane considered trying to move his head, but his neck was even more stiff and resisting than his eyelids. He didn't hurt anymore; as he thought about it, he realized he didn't feel anything. He wasn't even aware of any body parts unless he tried to move them. And none of them moved. Even that didn't hurt; it was like trying to push against a mountain. You felt the strain of the exertion, but not pain.

"The Council isn't happy about this," another voice broke in. "I am not happy about this." The anger in the woman's voice was so cold it blistered, and Thane mentally shied away from it. Ms. Yemaja continued. "These Shaelings are under my care, and these three students are more dangerously ill than any of the others. Why." It wasn't an question. It was a demand.

"I don't know," the lion growled, and Thane felt the rough pads of Haider's paw press against the side of his throat. Pumping blood pushed back against them. "Their pulses have slowed even more. I'm glad we didn't administer the darts to the students when they were first cleared for it." Thane felt the paw pull away, and the voices grew distant. "I'm recommending we transfer them to Asclepius immediately."

"I can't allow that," Ms. Yemaja's voice stopped moving away. "I have no jurisdiction there. I won't be able to protect them, and I can't travel underground."

"Neither of us can protect them from what's happening to them now," Haider's voice was heavy with such grief that Thane suddenly felt like crying. Who were these poor dying students everyone was so worried about? Did he know them?

"Do you think Asclepius can do anything for them we can't?" for the first time Ms. Yemaja sounded old, and vulnerable.

"I think it's their best chance," Haider answered, weariness and worry coloring his voice, too. "I'll prepare them for transport and get the files in order..."

As their conversation grew too distant to hear, Thane's attention wavered. With nothing to hold onto, he slipped back into the darkness.

He woke up with a jolt. The bed underneath him bounced and tossed him upwards, and his eyes flew open as his hands gripped the sides of his mattress.

Where was he? The room had gotten much smaller and stretched into a narrow rectangle, and the walls and ceiling were a metallic grey instead of the washed white of before.

"Hey," he heard Brennan shout, following by pounding on the wall, "Watch the bumps, okay? They're not awake yet."

Thane craned his neck around and saw Brennan sitting on a bench that ran all along the small front wall. The floor moved and vibrated underneath them in a way that suggested movement, and Thane looked around again. Were they in the back of a semi? Thane sat up slowly, waiting for the pain and nausea to engulf him again. It was gone. He actually felt pretty good, and ravenous.

"Welcome back to the land of the living," Brennan grinned at him. Thane looked at the man, and then around the rest of the room on wheels. Remi lay on a cot across from him, her face slack and pale.

"Is she all right?" Thane demanded, getting out of bed and trying to cross over to her. His feet were unsteady and the truck hit another bump. Thane lost his balance and flew forward, face planting on Remi's stomach.

"Oof," air rushed out of her mouth and her eyes opened and focused on him. "Thane? What are you doing?" He hurried to get off, but the truck bumped and swerved again and instead of merely standing up he was thrown off and landed on all fours on the floor. "Are you okay?"

He looked up and saw that she'd rolled over to look down at him. He felt his face flush hot. "I'm fine." He carefully pushed himself up and then sat back on his bed before the uneven road could throw him anywhere else. "Are you?"

"I'm hungry." She sat up and looked around. "Are we in a truck?"

"Yep," said Brennan cheerfully. "And out of Sanctum with official paperwork." The truck lurched to the side before straightening. "Twitch is driving, which is the least of our worries."

Thane raised and eyebrow and looked at Brennan. The way he'd said that sounded like there was more he wasn't telling them. "What else?"

"Well, like her," Brennan said, jerking his chin towards the other end of the semi-trailer, towards the doors. Both Thane and Remi's heads swiveled to look.

At the far end of the trailer there was a girl. She sat on the floor in the corner, her back pressed against the wall and leaning up against the doors. Her face was turned away so her long brown hair covered it.

Thane knew her. It was Iselle, the French girl on Omega Team. The one he'd tried to save by shoving a grenade into Rip's mouth, and the one who'd sung that strange lullaby to calm the daemon and save them both. The one who'd brought him food and told him the story about the two blind men who harvested grapes.

That story had been the last time he'd spoken with her, Thane realized. He flashed back to the memory of her holding one of his shaking hands in both of hers, and her soft voice pulling him out of his waking nightmares.

"Iselle?" Thane's question drew a sharp look from Remi.

"You know her?" Remi asked.

"*Oui*, yes," Iselle's quiet voice answered both of them. "I am of Omega Team, like Brennan and Twitch." She brushed her hair back behind her ear as she turned to look at them. Thane was startled. Whatever expression he'd been expecting on her face wasn't the anger that smoldered there now. She directed her ire past Thane to Brennan, who's customary grin was notably absent. "And I strongly suggest that you tell me now what is going on, because clearly we are not going to Asclepius and somehow my comm unit has been disabled." Her eyes narrowed. "You know better to think than you can merely sedate me or dump me somewhere and have me cease to be a problem. Or to think you can lie to me, Mr. Tayler."

Brennan flinched and looked pained, those final words seeming to hurt him more than the others. "Iselle, I didn't mean for you to be here at all," he began. All traces of his sardonic wit were gone, and Thane had never seen the man so serious. Thane felt his chest tighten. How powerful was this girl? "You haven't been briefed, you don't know what's going on--"

"Don't pretend this is a mission," she cut him off. "If this was dangerous or sanctioned in any way, *she* would not be here." Iselle jabbed a finger towards Remi.

This motion finally jolted Remi out of whatever surprise or curiosity had been holding her silent. "What are you doing here? We don't want you. Why did you even have to come?"

"Because General Gage ordered me to," Iselle rose to her feet and held her anger in check, but it was clearly an effort. "My general, who is your father, was worried about you, his only daughter. He reordered the medical rotation so Omega Team would be in the building helping to care for you, so he could get regular updates on your condition. He pulled strings and called in favors to get you admitted to Asclepius immediately, where that highly classified facility is normally reserved for missions, teams, operatives, and assets at such levels that most of Sanctum do not believe they exist."

How closely did Iselle work with General Gage to know all this? Thane glanced at Remi, and saw her jaw clenching and unclenching. Iselle continued, her French accent growing more noticeable as she went on. "He sent me with orders to not leave your side so that I may help and comfort you. That is my directive. And now I find you hijacked, kidnapped by members of my own team who have also disabled my only way to report back and cut me off."

"That isn't fair," Brennan was shouting. "You have no idea what's going on!" Thane pulled away, leaning into the wall so he wouldn't be between them at all. Brennan's face was flushed red from his collarbone to his hair, and a vein in his neck was popping out. Thane glanced at Remi to make sure she was okay but her eyes were narrow, her mouth was set in a snarl, and she breathed heavily through her nose. Thane looked back at Iselle and saw that same furious anger reflected on her face, but he also noticed that her hands were trembling and she inhaled and exhaled through her mouth in irregular patterns. She was afraid, and trying to hide it with anger because she thought anger was safer.

Thane knew better. He spoke in a calm, quiet voice, like he used to talk to Lanie after one of Bert's blow-ups. "Iselle, we're here to do something General Gage can't. You're here for Remi's dad. We're here for her mom."

"What?" her gaze whipped from Brennan to Thane and then Remi, and back again.

"Don't tell her," Remi hissed at him.

"No, you must tell me," Iselle countered, then took a deep and shuddering breath with her eyes closed. Her face relaxed and when she raised her eyelids, she looked tranquil and her arms hung easily at her sides.

Brennan snorted and Thane glanced back. The man was sitting on the bench again, the last traces of his flushed anger fading and acerbic smile subdued, but back. "Iselle could be a big help in the negotiations," he said.

"We don't need her help," Remi insisted, but the anger seemed to be draining out of her as well.

"She's on Omega Team, she's had lots of training," Thane added.

"We don't need her," Remi repeated, casting an irritated look at Thane.

The floor lurched to a halt, and everyone in it was thrown forward with the loss of momentum. "It may not matter," Brennan said, straightening himself up and holding a hand out to Remi. "We're here."

"Where?" Remi asked, ignoring his offer of help and rising to her feet.

A door slammed outside and there was the sound of muffled footsteps outside one of the long walls. Then a clank and the shrill grinding sound of metal against metal, and a white crack of light appeared down the middle of the two doors just behind Iselle. It widened as the door was pulled open, and frigid air burst inward to wrap them all in blankets of air and ice. Goosebumps rose up on both Thane's arms and he saw Remi shiver. Iselle and Brennan seemed unaffected by the weather.

"Anyone who wants to criticize my driving is welcome to stay in the trailer with the door open," Twitch's voice came out of the blinding light beyond the door. Thane stood, wrapping himself in the thin sheet from his bed, and moved forward. He squeezed around the hospital beds, and as his eyes adjusted to the light outside he realized why it was so bright.

In front of him and to either side was an expanse of white snow, pure and crystalline and so cold that the top looked like a sheet of ice. At the end of the snowfield opposite him rose a cliff of shiny black rock, and the sun shone from somewhere behind him. The sunlight bounced off both the snow and the rock so it was like standing inside one of those reflectors that he'd seen photographers use, the kind that eliminate shadows.

Thane shaded his eyes with one gloved hand and looked around. There was a little wooden shack off to one side, leaning precariously into the winter winds that buffeted it. "Move it, Thane," Twitch instructed as he pulled out the ramp from underneath the trailer and latched it in. The tech genius was wearing large goggles that covered his face from forehead to nose as well as a woolen hat and a puffy down coat with sleek leather gloves that had woven patches on his index and middle fingers.

"What, and the rest of us just get to freeze?" Thane asked, half-jokingly as he jumped off the side of the truck while Twitch came up the ramp.

"It's warm in there," Twitch jerked a thumb back over his shoulder towards the shack. Thane looked at it skeptically, but Remi came running down the ramp at that moment and plunged forward into the snow.

"Come on, I'm freezing," she called to him as she ran. Thane shrugged and ran after her, the crunch of snow underfoot familiar and somehow comforting. He glanced back and saw Twitch and Brennan following behind, joking and shoving each other in the snow.

Thane slowed. Iselle was still standing in the back of the trailer, watching Brennan and Twitch with wary eyes. Her shoulders were hunched, and she turned away from them all to walk back into the frigid metal.

"Thane," Remi was holding the door open, waiting.

"Just a second," he turned back and ran towards the semi, dodging around the other two. He slowed as he walked up the ramp, looking into the darkened interior.

Iselle sat on the foot of his cot, arms wrapped around herself and trying not to shiver. Only now with her head bowed and the light pouring in from behind did he notice that her hair was much lighter near the roots then anywhere else.

"Do you dye your hair?" he asked.

"You came back to ask me that?" she didn't look at him, instead shrinking further into a ball to hold in the heat.

"No," Thane moved out of the doorway and sat down on Remi's cot across from Iselle. "I wanted to see if you were okay."

That got a look from her. She glanced up at him and then rolled her eyes sideways, shaking her head. "Why are we here, Thane? Why did Brennan and Twitch kidnap the general's daughter?"

Thane laughed. He couldn't help it. "They didn't kidnap her as much as she hijacked them. This is a rescue mission." Iselle snorted and turned away from him. "You wanted to know what's going on," Thane pointed out, "come inside with us and we'll tell you everything. I promise."

Iselle slowly turned her head until she was gazing straight into Thane's eyes. She held his gaze for a long moment. "I can't tell if you're lying," her voice was so low that Thane almost didn't hear it. "I can't read you at all."

"I don't lie," Thane said. He stood up and held out a hand to her, and saw the black rubber covering his talons. Thane quickly dropped his hand and stood there, self-conscious and hating it.

She looked from his face to his hand and back again. "I don't believe you," she said, but she stood up and tucked her hair behind one ear. "Let's go."

The girl strode past him and into the frigid whiteness outside the trailer. Thane followed after her, pulling off the sheet he'd wrapped around himself for warmth and crumpling it into a ball. "Hey!"

When she looked back he threw it at her. "It's freezing out here," he said, breaking into a run as Iselle caught it and shook it out. He hurried to the shack where the others waited, and he could hear her hurrying to keep up behind him.

Thane burst through the off-kilter door and skidded to a halt. In front of him was a small room, empty except for the old, tattered cot shoved up against the far wall and a footlocker closed and padlocked underneath it. No one was there.

"Move over," Iselle said, elbowing him out of the way so she could come through the door. She shut it and suddenly the two of them were alone. They'd been alone for the last few minutes but something about this felt different to

Thane, alone in a room with a closed door. His stomach felt tight and he didn't know what to say.

"Thane?" Iselle said. He glanced at her. "You're standing on the trap door."

Thane looked down and saw he was standing on a cutout rectangle of wooden floor with a circular metal handle. He fought off a blush and stepped back, reaching down. His rubber gloves gripped the cold iron ring and pulled.

The trap door was surprisingly light, and it sprang upwards. He nearly smacked himself in the face with it, but leaned away in time. Iselle giggled. The warm flush he'd been fighting swept across his cheeks and he was grateful she wasn't still looking at him.

Instead she'd begun descending the hidden staircase underneath the floor. It was steep, but short, only about fifteen stairs before the landing below. There was down there an imposing steel plated door with a keypad and scanner on the wall next to it, but it was propped open with someone's shoe. Thane followed Iselle into the room beyond.

It was a big room and oddly shaped, with walls that slanted away and met at wide angles. The walls were stacked logs and Thane's mind pulled up a long ago memory of camping with Grandpa Whitaker and a skiing lodge in the mountains. There were benches made of split logs making a square in the center of the room, with one side of the square open to a fire that blazed in an opening large enough to fit his Grandpa's old Buick. If he hadn't been looking for Remi he would've missed the flash of anger on her face when she saw Iselle. He would have liked to miss the annoyed glare she focused on him.

"Elle!" Jaeger crowed, and launched himself from next to the huge fireplace on the other end of the room. His leather wings beat twice before he landed on Thane's head. The imp scrambled around Thane's neck, gripping with claws and teeth and tail until he'd maneuvered himself around to facing Iselle. "Hyu haf come to help! This changes all the numbers. We may not all die!" He leaned forward away from Thane and spread out his hands like a baby asking to be held.

Iselle's mouth curved in a smile, and she held her arms out. Jaeger squeaked and jumped to her, cuddling against her. She cradled him and glared at Brennan, who sat on a log bench with one shoe on and rested his elbows on his knees. "Jaeger is involved too?" she asked.

Paka entered the room from one of the doors in the wall nearest the fire. Her tail lashed and her eyes were narrow, and she spoke over her shoulder as she entered. "This is a bad thing. I do not like unknowns in missions already this unsupported," she said to Twitch, who followed behind her. "What are we--" as she breathed in, her head whipped around and she stopped.

Her stop was so abrupt that Twitch nearly ran into her and froze, one foot in the air hovering over the panther woman's tail. Brennan whistled, and Twitch went pale.

Paka didn't notice. "And now you are here?" she asked Iselle. She turned to Brennan. "Does she know? Is she coming?"

"She isn't coming," Remi cut in. "We don't need her."

"But she'd be useful," Brennan argued, "My gut feels better about this whole thing with her on the team."

"She hasn't been inoculated," Twitch brought up, his fingers tapping against his leg, "We have no idea how she'd react to the crossover. She doesn't actually have any Shae blood--"

"She is as much Shae as I am," Paka cut in. "And her training makes her valuable. I am angry that I was not consulted, but pleased she is willing to help."

"How is she Shae?" Remi's snarl was almost as effective as one of Paka's. "I've never seen her do anything."

"Elle, Elle, please come," Jaeger wriggled in her arms. "Aye will protect hyu in Shae."

"Stop telling her where we're going!" Remi shouted.

"Remi, be reasonable," Twitch said, and both Thane and Brennan flinched. "We need all the help we can get. Iselle could make the difference--"

"I don't need her to help recuse my mom from the Shaerealm!" Remi shouted.

Next to Thane, Iselle took a deep breath. He saw her hands tighten around Jaeger and her eyes widen. He hadn't realized he'd taken a small step forward during all the shouting, to stand between Iselle and the rest of the room, but he hurried to move sideways and hoped Remi hadn't noticed.

"So that is why," Iselle spoke in an even, calm tone. She walked forward until she was even with the closest bench and put Jaeger down on the polished wood. As she moved, Brennan's posture relaxed. Paka's tail stopped whipping around. Even Twitch's fingers slowed, the tension draining from his hand. "How do you know she is alive?"

"Aye haf seen her," Jaeger spoke up, waving a hand excitedly. Wooden shavings fell from his claws and Thane saw the imp had scratched numbers and symbols into the bench.

Iselle seemed to accept that and turned back to the group, looking at Remi. "Then we must do whatever it takes to save her," the French girl said. Thane watched Remi's eyes tighten and her jaw clench as she ground her teeth together, but she nodded.

"Well then, it sounds like we need a plan," Brennan rubbed his hands together. "What's our first move?"

"We need to find Ru-" a black blur flashed across Thane's vision as the seat where Paka had been was suddenly empty, and the tips of the panther woman's claws pressed against his cheeks without breaking the skin while the pad of her paw covered his mouth.

"Do not say his name here," she hissed. "Within Sanctum, the dome kept us safe from his prying spells. That is not true here." Her green eyes seemed to glow with the firelight and Thane blinked at her, just once, instead of nodding. Moving his head at all didn't seem like a great idea.

Paka released him as Remi asked, "Don't we want his attention?"

"Not like that," Brennan explained. "We need to meet him in person, and just saying his name doesn't guarantee that."

"Plus, viper birds," Twitch added.

"Who are we finding?" Iselle asked.

"Dragons open ways," said Jaeger, not looking up from his carving. Elaborate equations and strange glyphs covered the bench around the imp. "We must find the dragon to help."

"But how do we find him?" asked Remi, turning to face Twitch and Brennan and therefore turning her back towards Iselle.

Twitch shrugged. "Without knowing his draconic status, Sanctum has been tracking him for centuries. He's always been a high-ranking Shae and placed in positions of power and influence. Until the last century or so, his location was widely known through his aliases, but then shortly after the last world war he disappeared. Theories concerning his identity were proposed but never confirmed. Some thought he'd even returned to Shae, but knowing now that he's a chaos dragon we know that's impossible."

"Wait, why is that impossible? I thought only dragons could open holes on their own; why wouldn't they be able to go home?" Thane interrupted. Twitch paused and looked at him, annoyed.

"Because once a dragon has crossed over they can't go back. It would upset the balance of power between our world and the Shae, and it would break the treaty between the Thunder Alpha and the Guardian Council. We keep the dragons already here on this side, and they won't allow any more to cross over. It's an inviolate law." Twitch sounded like he was trying to explain something extremely simple to a remarkably dimwitted child. Thane wondered if Twitch had any younger siblings.

"Who are we looking for?" Iselle asked again.

Twitch glanced at her. "In our files he was given the code designation Minos."

"Oh." She was standing with her back to Thane so he couldn't see her reaction, but she did sit down. "Oh."

"Thane's father is Minos?" Brennan sat up and glanced at Thane with wide eyes and a furrowed brow, but smoothed out his expression quickly and turned back to Twitch. "Is there a file in Sanctum you haven't read?"

"Yes, the Draconem Codex," Twitch replied with a self-satisfied smirk. His eyes darted to the left and he added, "And the personnel files. Of course," as his face got a little paler.

Brennan snorted. "Of course."

"Who cares," Remi exploded, "we need a plan. How are we going to find--" she shot a glance at Twitch.

"Minos," he supplied.

"Minos," she continued, "when we have no idea where to look."

"He's looking for me," Thane offered. He spoke in such a low tone that only Paka heard him, and so she responded.

"Yes, but we can't very well raise you to the sky and shout to everyone 'here is Thane,' without Sanctum noticing," she wrapped her paw around his arm just above the elbow and led him to the benches and into the discussion.

He sat next to Remi, who seemed to be considering Paka's statement. "What are we telling Sanctum?" she asked. The unspoken question was what lie they were giving her father.

"We have a false connection set up with Sanctum from Asclepius," Twitch answered. "Their lines are too secure to actually break into, so we just changed the connection address for queries about either of you. Sanctum will get regular updates about your treatment and how you're improving for the next two weeks. After that..." he trailed off and shrugged, not bothering to finish the thought. They all knew if they weren't back by then they weren't coming back.

The logs popped and crackled as the fire consumed them, and the group of humans and Shae made no sound but breathing. "Okay, great, but what do we do now?" Remi finally asked. "Minos is already looking for Thane, but how do we get him to find us without Sanctum finding us to?"

"There is one obvious answer," said Brennan. "We need to get Thane somewhere we know his father will look for him."

"Home," Thane spoke. Both Remi and Iselle looked at him, and Remi seemed to hear something in his voice that he'd been trying to hide. She reached out with the hand nearest and rested it on his arm, just above where the glove began.

"Are you sure?" Remi asked.

"Where else would Ru-- would Minos-- know to look? If he knows who I am, then he knows who my family is." That thought made his stomach clench and his chest feel tight. His family.

He hadn't thought about them in weeks, but now their faces filled his mind. Harper, who had never forgiven him. His mom, who'd seemed so sad and broken last time he'd seen her and who had pretended to hate him to protect him from Bert's rage. And Lanie. Little Lanie, who hugged him and missed him and was the only person in the world he was sure loved him. Was Ruan de Argos watching them? Were they safe?

"I have to go home," he said, this time with enough force and conviction that they all heard him. Brennan looked at Thane with a raised eyebrow. "You're right," Thane continued, "Minos can't come to Sanctum, he can't track me, so he has to be watching my family."

"He would have them under surveillance, at least," Twitch agreed. The words "at least" sent a cold shock down Thane's spine and he clenched his hands. Remi noticed, and squeezed his arm.

"All right," Brennan said, straightening up. "Looks like we're going back to Payson."

CHAPTER 9

Winter in Payson was cold, but not as cold as the mountain where the safe house had been. The snow was deep enough to cover Thane's feet past his ankles, He crouched behind a line of bushes, sandwiched between Remi and Brennan, with Iselle and Twitch on Brennan's other side.

"This place is a nightmare," Twitch mumbled, his face pressed hard against a pair of binoculars. Iselle elbowed him, and Twitch shot a quick glance at Thane and Remi. "Logistically, I mean," Twitch added, flushing slightly. "All the houses are so close together it's hard to see anything from far away, and the trees and fences aren't helping. I'm sure it was a nice place to grow up."

Thane blocked the memories before they could surface. There hadn't been much that was nice about his childhood, but now wasn't the time to relive all that. "We're on the wrong side of the city to see much," he responded instead. "If we come at it from the Air Force side, we'd see a lot more."

"Can't risk it," Brennan said. "Too much surveillance over there. Besides, we're not really doing reconnaissance. We're waiting for the recon team to come back." Then he stepped backwards.

As if on cue snow fell off the branches of the tree above them. A mass of snow the size of a backpack fell on the empty space where Brennan had been and another landed on Twitch's head, knocking him onto his backside. Iselle and Remi tried to hide their laughter, giggling into their hands. Thane snorted and turned his face upwards.

Not quite twenty feet above them a black panther perched on a wide branch. Paka's claws dug into the wood and her tail wavered, constantly correcting her balance. The thick branches of the oak tree provided her with cover even when most of the leaves were gone and the few that still clung to the tree were browned and dead. Her green eyes stared into his. She lowered herself down, descending in silence until with only a slight crunch of compacting snow the black cat landed behind them in a crouch.

"There are guards surrounding the house at key points," she said, her voice that somewhere between growl and purr Thane had begun to associate with Paka being excited. "I made six of them, but Jaeger might have more."

"What about my family?" Thane tried to ask, but the words didn't quite come out. Instead he made a grunting noise with a gurgle.

Paka, who knew what being part of a pack meant, understood. "There are no people in the house."

That hard, tight feeling in Thane's chest loosened a little. "What?"

"It is school today," Jaeger's words were the only warning Thane had before the imp landed on his head. Again. "Hyu's sisters are at school. Momma must be out."

"Get off," Thane demanded and tried to grab the imp around the waist.

Jaeger twisted away, the shiny silver plates he wore across his stomach catching the light from the snow and reflecting it into Thane's eyes. "Argh," Thane grunted.

Jaeger had made the plate mail himself from anything he could find at the lodge. Silverware, metal cups, and bakeware had all been scored by the imp's claws. Thane had been impressed how Jaeger sat on the hearth of the fire, molding pieces of metal with one hand and holding a fork or spoon into the fire with the other. Once it started glowing he'd jerk it out and start shaping it into the rest. There was something familiar about the imp's expression. Thane had watched him in fascination until he'd realized it was the same look Lanie had when she shaped things out of clay.

But the result was a chest plate that made Jaeger almost invisible as he flew across the grey skies of Payson. The silver metal blended in with the cloud cover even as the shine reflected the snow below, angled so any flashes of light would disappear in the distance.

"Aye do not like snow on my toes," Jaeger protested, and smacked Thane's hand away with his tail.

Thane flinched reflexively. But there was nothing, no feeling, no sting. The combination of the rubber and the scales made Jaeger's tail ineffective. With a grin, Thane grabbed the imp with both hands and pulled. Jaeger flailed, but Thane prevailed and held the shivering imp inches above the snow.

"No more landing on my head, okay?" Thane said.

"But, but perfekt head--" Jaeger protested, and Thane dropped him another inch towards the snow. "Aye promise!" the imp squeaked.

Thane held him a moment more, then put the shivering Jaeger on the tree trunk.

The imp gripped the bark with his claws and held on, yellow eyes looking at Thane with a mixture of annoyance and admiration. Thane noticed Remi and Iselle were looking at him too, and he fought back the heat that threatened to rise in his cheeks.

During their exchange, Brennan had been discussing the guards with Paka. "All right," he said, pulling everyone else's attention. "There are six guards spread around the house. We need to engage one of them without making noise and convince him that their boss wants to talk to us. There are two Feronin, a Gnorf, two men, and one thrull hidden around--"

"There's a thrull down there?" Twitch jerked the glasses down and to face Brennan. "Where? How?"

"A what?" asked Remi.

"A thrulloxydrum," Twitch said, putting the binoculars back and sweeping the area with them again. "A shade troll."

"You shouldn't use those names," Brennan chided, "it's rude."

"I know, but it's the easiest way to explain it to the songless," Twitch argued. "If I say it's the shade form of the Troglodites, they don't get it. If I say it's a big ugly troll with no morals and a personal agenda, they get that."

"Wait, calling it a troll is rude?" Remi asked.

"It is more like a racial slur," explained Iselle. She glared at Twitch, who wasn't looking at her. "Expedience doesn't make it okay to use."

"None of which explains how it's hiding," Twitch went on. "That thing must be the size of a sedan."

"That is where it hides," Paka explained, pointing down the hill. "Under that thick covering. I could smell it." She wrinkled her nose and squinted. "I cannot seem to stop smelling it."

"Got it," Twitch said. He fiddled with the binoculars, making adjustments. "And I found the Gnorf and both men."

"The Feronin are in the trees," Paka went on. She waved a paw dismissively. "If they were worth anything as hunters, they would have spotted me. They are not a concern."

"And the men are hiding in plain sight on either side of the house," Brennan finished, looking through his own set of binoculars. "One is in disguise as a snow removal service, and the other is pretending to work on a car next door."

"How can you tell he's pretending?" Thane asked.

Brennan lowered his glasses and looked at Thane with a smirk and one raised eyebrow. "Because he clearly knows nothing about cars."

"So what's the plan, here?" Remi asked. She gripped the bottom of her jacket and twisted it back and forth in her hands. "Do we take them out?"

"Shreds, no," Brennan said. "I'll go down there and talk to one of the men. I'll tell them we want to talk to their boss, Minos."

"What if they don't believe you?" Thane felt a hard knot in his stomach. He wasn't sure if it was excitement or fear, and he was glad that his dragon clawed hands didn't sweat the way his human ones had.

"I'll threaten to say his real name. That should shut them up pretty quick. Viper birds aren't picky that way. Pretty much anyone who spoke the name, heard the name, or was with those who did is a target, regardless of who they work for." Brennan raised his binoculars again. "Paka, you come as backup. The rest of you, wait here."

The panther woman nodded and Thane shifted his weight uncomfortably. "Shouldn't I come?"

"You wait here. We don't know what their orders are if they see you. We'll play it safe for now," Brennan placed a hand on Thane's shoulder. "For us, and for your family. Okay, kid?"

Thane tried to swallow past the lump in his throat and jerked his chin up and down in acknowledgement. Brennan squeezed his shoulder once, then let go and gave him the binoculars. "You can watch," he said, then turned and walked toward the road. Paka gave Thane that strange salute, with her fist over her chest and then pushed toward him, before leaping back up into the tree and disappearing.

"They'll be fine," Remi assured him, but on her other side, Iselle looked worried.

"I do not like this," she whispered, "something feels wrong." Twitch glanced at her, then back over his shoulder to where Jaeger hung upside down from the oak tree and spun acorns in his hands. Twitch caught the imp's eye and jerked his head, and Jaeger sprang backwards off the tree and into the air, dropping the little brown nuts as he went.

Thane turned and pressed the glasses to his eyes, watching as Brennan casually strolled down his street towards his house. He tried to find Paka in the trees, but couldn't. Jaeger was a brief shimmer in the sky before disappearing. Beside him, Thane could feel Remi tensing. Thane glanced to his side, and saw Remi clenching her jaw. Next to her, Iselle stood crouched down with her eyes closed and the corners of her mouth turned down, and on the end Twitch was statute still, watching Brennan through the binoculars.

Thane looked back through his and watched as Brennan crossed in front of the house he'd grown up in. "No," Iselle breathed, then she shouted, "Twitch, now!"

The youngest two members of Omega Team and the youngest mercenaries in all of Sanctum burst from their hiding place and ran down the hill straight through the snow and foliage. Thane and Remi locked eyes, then followed them. As they drew closer, the trees and other houses hid Thane's street from view, but a feral scream split the air.

"Paka!" Thane shouted, trying to run faster as the snow pushed back against his legs and dragged down his feet. Remi was lighter, but not faster, and Thane soon left her behind and caught up to Twitch and Iselle. He passed them too, pelting through yards and crossing streets. He flew through the unbroken snow of the house behind his, vaulting into their backyard over the old chain link fence and landed, feet apart and panting, staring at the back of his house.

It was silent, the snow muffling any sound of the others approaching. The scream did not repeat, and there was no sign of Brennan, Paka, or Jaeger. Movement at the window caught his eye and he looked up. Pink curtains drew back and Lanie stood there, looking out the window towards him.

"Lanie?" he whispered, dropping his defensive posture and straightening up. Something jammed into his shoulders and a large weight landed on his back, driving him to the ground and knocking the wind out of him.

"Sanctum dog," a voice growled above him, "I wonder what your blood tastes like." Thane's self-defense training kicked in and twisted, rolling his body sideways. His attacker slid with him, staying on top but now Thane could see the yellowed fangs and dirty white muzzle and belly of what had to be one of the Feronin. It snarled and snapped down at him with its teeth, but Thane jabbed his hand into its armpit and threw his hips upward, forcing the Feronin up and over his head into the snow. It flew off him but Thane felt claws score his shoulder as it went. Thane rolled again, pulling his feet under him and stood in a crouch as the tiger-man did the same.

Thane was desperate to look behind the Feronin to the window where he'd seen Lanie, but knew if the tiger got its claws on him again he wouldn't escape. Instead they circled, arms spread apart.

"You are only a cub," the Feronin hissed. Its voice sounded scraped and growled from its throat, and Thane repressed a shiver. "I will eat your heart and paint my fur with your blood. I-- yeerow!" it yelped and clapped a paw over one eye, stumbling backwards.

Thane looked up one moment before Jaeger dive bombed the Feronin and smacked it full in face with his small red body. "Hyu talk too much," Jaeger announced. "Can hyu even hear it?" and he plunged both hands into the Feronin's ears, shoving acorns inside them.

The Feronin let out a gurgling howl and began to claw at the imp covering his face. Thane flinched as claws shrieked against metal. Jaeger used his tail to pull a steak knife from a hidden sheath in his homemade armor and grabbed it with one clawed hand.

"Stop!" Thane shouted. Jaeger glanced at him, irritation somehow seeming more irritated on his red old man face. "We are not killing anybody in my back yard," Thane demanded.

"Fine," the imp hissed, and tossed the knife away. "Aye don't need to kill the kitty to skin him." Jaeger twisted his head around and bit at the Feronin's exposed neck. Thane closed his eyes and backed away.

"Hyu are still here?" the imp gnashed its teeth at Thane. "Find Brennan. Aye lost track of him."

"I have to get Lanie first," Thane said, running towards the house. Behind him, he heard the tiger yowl again and then felt the imp's claws wrap around his ears.

"There is no one in the house," Jaeger's face appeared upside-down in front of him, filling his field of vision.

"But I saw her," Thane protested, trying to twist free of the imp's grasp.

"He did that," Jaeger said, pulling Thane's face around so they were looking at the raging Feronin. It leapt at Thane, all claws and teeth coming for him.

Jaeger hissed and dove forward, grabbing the lean tiger's head out of the air and driving it into the snow at Thane's feet. "Go now or Aye will let hyu handle him," Jaeger threatened.

Thane nodded and ran around the side of the house, quickly leaving behind the imp and the Feronin to fight it out. He was watching over his shoulder instead of where he was going, and tripped on something warm and squishy.

"Hey!" shouted a voice, and something exploded out of the snow. Thane jumped away, his arms flailing, as a man rose from the ground. At least he thought it was a man. It had arms and legs and a face and was not covered in fur, but there the similarities ended. This creature was a full two feet shorter than Thane and its face reminded Thane of a penny he'd seen that'd been run over by a train, squashed and stretched all out of proportion with long, stringy hair that didn't grow in any singular direction.

"Watch where you're going," it snarled. Thane blinked. The voice sounded like the speaker had stuffed marbles in their mouth, but underneath that it sounded... female. Like a girl. Like not a very old girl. He lowered his fists and took a step backward.

"Surprised, little boy?" the strange girl moved her jaw from side to side with a popping sound and suddenly her mouth swung open, gaping wide enough for Thane's whole head to fit inside. He stared, feeling his own jaw drop.

The edges of her mouth, the parts that almost touched her earlobes, turned up as her eyebrows narrowed. She lunged forward and grabbed him at the elbows, lifting him off the ground. The shock that froze him disappeared and he struggled. Her hands squeezed harder and Thane felt his elbow joints pop and grate. The creature turned him so his hips were in the air and his head was turned down, and began to lower him into her mouth. She was going to eat him.

"No!" Thane redoubled his thrashing, trying to get loose. His fighting didn't seem to phase her at all, but she slowed his descent and kept her eyes locked on his face. Thane smelled terrible breath, like the stench of a hundred different things all kept rotting in a pile. He tried to hold his breath to keep from puking.

He reached out for the Song, the music of the lightning, the Song that used to fill his mind without effort. The Song that had saved he and Remi from Cressa and protected the Shaerealm. The Song that abandoned him and left him feeling only half alive. Thane hadn't been able to hear or feel it for over a month and tried desperately to find it now as he stared down at her gaping maw filled with jagged, rock-like teeth.

Thane jerked to a halt with his nose between her front teeth. He couldn't see anything but the inside of her mouth now, but he felt her body stiffen as though she was turning to stone and then start shaking. The vises around his elbows slackened without warning and Thane fell, her bottom teeth grazing his nose and leaving a cut that stung and bled.

Her body collapsed as Thane landed in the snow on his stomach. He scrambled to his feet while backing away from the she thing that had almost eaten him and spun his head around.

Twitch stood in the snow near him, crouched and holding something out at chest level. Two thin wires extended from it to the thing still twitching and jerking in the snow.

"You tasered it?" Thane gasped.

"Did you want to get eaten?" Twitch said, still holding down the trigger. The she thing made small irregular movements in the snow. "We lost track of Brennan. Find him."

"Right," Thane said, and continued around the front of the house. "Where's Remi?" he called back to Twitch.

"With Iselle, she'll be fine," Twitch said, and Thane caught a glimpse of him opening the side of the taser with one hand and rearranging the wires before the side of the house hid them from view.

Thane was in his front yard now. The house behind him was quiet, and he didn't see anyone on the street around him. The enormous old oak tree in Ms. Knotts' yard rattled and shook, and Thane heard yowls and screeches come from it. Paka and the other Feronin, he guessed. That left the thrull and the two men, which meant the thing that Twitch tasered was probably the Gnorf.

So where were the men? Brennan had said that one was removing snow from walks and driveways and the other had been working on a car. Scanning the street, the house next to Thane had the garage door closed and there was a windowless van across from it with a company logo blazed across the side for "Entropy Home Services."

Thane deliberated for a moment, then ran across the street to the van. There wasn't anyone in the driver's seat to protest so he went to the back and swung open the double doors. Instead of yard equipment, there were computer consoles and tech equipment enough that Twitch might have fainted with joy. There were four video feeds on one monitor and Thane leaned in for a better look. Then he turned and sprinted down the road.

Behind him there was a roar. Thane spun back to see a large canvas, the kind that people cover their cars and trailers with in winter to protect them, burst into shreds two houses away. The pieces fell like strange brown rain around the huge thrull that had been hiding underneath it. Thane stared.

The thrull was the same size and roughly the same shape as a car that had been set on its rear bumper. The bulbous head perched on top was too small for the thick body, and it had a set of fangs that protruded from the slobbering mouth, like the tusks of a walrus.

Thane froze. It had small shiny black eyes that peered around the street, and a large rough brown nose that snuffed and whiffed like a hound. It slouched forward, arms overlong and forearms huge so that it walked on feet and knuckles and Thane got the feeling it couldn't really see him. But it could hear him, and smell him.

With a roar, it locked onto him and started forward in a lumbering sprint. Thane watched in fascination as it drew closer-- could he outrun it? And for how long?

"Hey!" Iselle shouted, and she and Remi burst out from the side of Thane's house. Iselle was waving her arms wildly and Remi threw a snowball. It hit the side of the thrull's head with wicked accuracy. It roared again, a screeching sound that reminded Thane of monsters in old movies, and skidded to a halt on the frozen road.

"Go, Thane, we can handle it," Remi shouted, waving him off.

"No way," Thane began running towards them. He was not going to leave the two girls to fight this beast.

"Brennan is in danger, Thane," Iselle said. That stopped Thane in his tracks, remembering what he'd seen on that video feed. Iselle kept her eyes trained on the thrull that thrashed in the snow in front of her, but strangely wasn't drawing near. "I can do this. Please find him."

Thane hesitated another moment. Iselle wasn't doing anything, just staring at the thrull, but it was thrashing and yowling as though being beaten. Could he really leave them? Would they be all right?

A wet, cold snowball exploded in his face, rocking his head backwards. "Get going!" Remi ordered. She already had a third snowball at the ready. Thane ran.

The image on the screen of Brennan sitting in a chair while a man stood over him with a welder's torch had given Thane their location. It wasn't the garage next to Thane's house; it was a house that had been empty for as long as Thane could remember. It was two blocks over at the back of a dead end street, and Thane knew it because he'd broken in once when he was eight and trying to hide from his dad. The lock on the back door was old and rusted so it'd only taken him a few pushes to get inside. The house itself was musty and falling apart, with rotted floorboards and an awful smell, but the garage had been a safe haven during the very worst times of his life.

Now Brennan was being tortured there. Thane extended his stride, pumping his legs faster. Both men had been in the video, one leaning back against the wall watching while the other had been waving the welding torch. They wouldn't be expecting anyone to arrive from inside the house, but Thane knew from experience that was the fastest and easiest way in.

Thane ignored stealth in favor of speed, running down the road and swinging around the back of the dilapidated two story house on the side opposite the garage. He pelted up the cracked cement back steps and only slowed once he was inside. The floorboards creaked and he skirted the edges of the kitchen, not wanting to fall through the floor into the basement.

Several old appliances sat rusting on the countertops. Thane glanced at them as he placed each foot on the floor, drawing closer to the garage door. He reached out and grabbed a toaster oven, and had to wrench it with both hands to pull it free before tucking it under one arm. He didn't have a plan or a weapon, but he wasn't going in empty handed.

He placed his black-gloved hand on the doorknob and paused, breathing out quietly. He could hear the hiss of the blowtorch and a man's voice. Brennan.

"I told you I want to talk," Brennan was saying. He sounded like he was trying to talk to a particularly dumb friend. "I want to talk to your boss."

"He doesn't want to talk to you," another man responded. The sound of the blowtorch grew louder.

Thane had a rough idea of where each man stood in the room and where Brennan sat. He paused for a moment to solidify the picture in his mind, then burst through the door and chucked the old toaster as hard as he could towards the man holding the torch.

He'd miscalculated. The man was standing closer to Brennan than he'd thought. But the moment the door banged open Brennan kicked out with both feet and caught the man in the chest, driving him backwards, and right into the path of the hurled appliance.

It crashed into the man's shoulder and drove him sideways and back into the concrete. The end of the fuel line for the torch jerked it out of his hands, and the flame snuffed out the moment his finger left the trigger. The other man spun around, lunging for Thane but Thane drove his elbow into the man's face and punched with the other fist, knocking the man off balance and into a rusted bike. Both clattered to the floor.

Thane leapt down into the garage over the concrete stairs and ran the few steps to where Brennan sat with his wrists and ankles bound. The man on the ground was shaking his head and pushing himself up. "Hey kid," Brennan said with an upward nod. "What took so long?"

Thane's fingers, inhibited by the claws and the gloves, scrabbled uselessly against the knots that held Brennan. He could hear the men behind him, getting up, and he growled. Thane risked a glance over his shoulder and saw the two men on their feet, one circling him with a drawn gun and the other retrieving the torch from where it'd fallen. It hissed and popped as he pulled the trigger, and the blue and white flame burst back to life.

"I wouldn't do that," Brennan said. "Minos is gonna be pissed if you damage his son."

"Oh yeah?" the man sneered, taking slow steps forward.

Thane turned to face the men, standing beside Brennan with his feet and hands apart in a defensive crouch. Out of the corner of his eye Thane saw Brennan reach towards his arm. Before he could react, Brennan had ripped the black glove off of Thane's nearest hand and dragged the rope through Thane's claws.

Thane's hand resisted automatically and the rope holding Brennan's wrists bound fell to the ground in shreds. Both enemies froze, staring.

Thane flexed his blue dragon claw self-consciously. The tips of his talons made a clicking noise as they hit each other and Brennan grinned next to him.

"Yeah," he said. "The kid's with me. So do you think your boss will want to talk now?"

CHAPTER 10

Thane had wanted to put his glove back on, but Brennan wouldn't let him. "Take the other one off, kid," he instructed. "Let's keep these schmucks as intimidated as possible."

They were walking back towards Thane's house, with one of the men leading and the other following behind. Brennan and Thane walked side by side between them. Thane kept glancing around, waiting for their enemies to jump him again, but Brennan seemed unconcerned, swinging his arms and even humming as they walked the two blocks back to Thane's street.

As they turned the corner, Thane noticed that the air in front of them seemed fuzzy somehow. Like an image that was just out of focus. He blinked several times, but it didn't help.

Brennan noticed. "Don't worry, kid, it's just Paka," he said. Thane looked at him, the question obvious on his face. "Paka's Song can project images," Brennan explained, "and either she or someone near her can control what the image looks like. Right now I'd say she's hiding the team and their captives in your front yard, which is why your house looks a little fuzzy. It's a big area to cover."

He was right. The moment Thane crossed the sidewalk into his front yard it was like stepping through a curtain and seeing the room beyond. A really weird room.

In the center of his yard sat Paka with her eyes closed, her legs crossed and her tail thrashing from side to side. In an arc around her sat everyone else. Behind her left shoulder lay two Feronin, one of which Thane recognized, and both bound with brightly colored rope that it took Thane a minute to recognize as Harper and Lanie's jump ropes. Jaeger sat on the head of the tiger Thane recognized, looking pleased with himself. Twitch sat on the front porch holding the taser in his lap loosely, while the two long wires that extended from it were still attached to the body of the Gnorf that had tried to eat Thane. Every time she moved, even so much as grinding her teeth, she jumped as if receiving a jolt. She sat mostly still, glaring at Twitch with murder in her eyes.

And finally in his driveway the thrull lay, curled up on its side and whimpering. Every few seconds it would sniff and rub one of its giant forearms across its snotty brown nose. Iselle stood near it, never taking her gaze from it. Remi waited a few feet away with her arms crossed, glaring at Iselle.

"Do you have to keep doing that?" Remi asked. "It's cruel."

"I am not 'urting it," Iselle responded, dropping the "h." Her more noticeable French accent was Thane's only indication of how stressed she was, or how much strain she was under. "I cannot say it would be as kind to us."

"It's cheating," Remi protested, but then she saw Thane. "You found him!"

The man who'd pulled the gun looked around Thane's yard and whistled. "You Sanctum monkeys don't mess around." He walked over to the Feronin and looked them over, then did the same with the Gnorf and the thrull. "Non-lethal damage only, but they're all secure. I'm impressed."

The man who'd held the blowtorch growled, standing in a crouch. The gunman, who was clearly some sort of leader of the group, waved him off. "Don't get all emotional, Linman, the boss is going to be thrilled with us." He looked over his shoulder at Thane with a raised eyebrow. "That is, provided you are who you claim to be."

Thane opened his mouth, and then closed it again, not sure what to say.

"Do you want to check his claws for draconic authenticity?" Brennan offered.

The human who wasn't Linman laughed. "That's above my pay grade. I'll let my employer decide what's going to happen next." He held both hands up, palms out, for the Omega Team members and Remi and Thane to see. "I'm going to reach into my pocket and get my cell phone," the man said.

"Wait, shouldn't someone take his gun away first?" Remi said.

Brennan and the man both looked at her, then at each other. "She's new," Brennan shrugged.

"Hey!" Remi protested.

"If he's any kind of professional, he'll have more than one weapon," Twitch commented. "Getting rid of the gun we can see might only make him more dangerous." Remi's eyes widened and she blinked. The man smirked and reached into his back pocket, pulling out a black rectangle with rounded edges.

He pressed a series of buttons and held the cell phone up to his ear. "Mr. Marcus? I have the kid." His eyes darted around the yard as he spoke, and Thane could tell the man was taking deliberate mental notes. "He wants to talk to the Master. No, he's got a team with him. I'll tell him. You come alone," the man said to Thane, lowering the phone. "We promise you'll be safe, and we'll let your friends go."

Thane snorted. "You'll let them go?" he gestured around with his arm, indicating which team was captive and which wasn't. "No deal. We all go, or none of us go."

"Which includes you." Brennan's voice wasn't threatening, it was certain.

Through this exchange Twitch had pulled out his own cell phone and had been playing with it, adding an attachment and making adjustments Thane didn't understand. Then Twitch put the cell up to his ear.

"This is Twitch O'Malley of Omega Team," he said into the phone. In front of Thane, the man swore and nearly dropped his cell. "We have six of your men captured and the son of your Master is with us. We all go to see him together as guests with right of protection by his oath and Song, or we take these men back to Sanctum now and dragon boy disappears from reach forever."

There were a few moments of silence in the yard, and then the man said, "Verified." Twitch and the man both listened again. "Acknowledged," the man put his phone away and looked up. "It looks like you're all coming with me."

Linman growled again and made a lunging motion towards Thane. Before Thane could react the gunman sliced his arm down and hit Liman on the back of the neck, knocking him to the ground. "I hate these daemon ridden," he sighed. "They're worse than any Shae."

"What?" five heads snapped towards him as the members of Omega Team gaped.

"What did you say?" Iselle breathed.

The man waved them off. "Sorry, not important. Let's get going."

"Going where?" Paka asked.

"All of us?" Twitch asked, glaring at the statue-still Gnorf. Her eyes had never left his face, rage playing across her features.

"Nah, Mr. Marcus won't want these types around the Master. He's volatile enough on his own." The man glanced at Thane. "No offense."

"Who are you?" Thane blurted.

"Finn," the man answered. He glanced at Brennan, who nodded, and Finn walked over to the bound Feronin.

"Excuse me," he said to Jaeger with a small bow. Jaeger eyed him once, and then bobbed his head in return and launched himself upwards. Finn pulled out a knife and grabbed the pink rope.

"Don't--" Thane said, holding out a hand. Finn glanced at him and then back at the rope. The man shrugged, and loosened the rope instead to slide it off the Feronin's wrists.

The tiger man jumped to his feet, snarling. "Stand down," Finn growled back, and it reluctantly relaxed out of a fighting stance. "Take Mr. Fluffy and return to rendezvous point five to wait for your next assignment."

Remi giggled. Finn smiled at her. "The Master has a sense of humor about code names."

The tiger man reached down and deliberately shredded the bright yellow rope that held Mr. Fluffy bound. He threw the plastic handles at Thane. One hit him in the shoulder and landed in the snow with a puff of white, disappearing from view. Both Feronin dropped to all fours and sprinted into the backyard before climbing a tree and disappearing.

Finn knelt down in front of the Gnorf. She ignored him, continuing to glare at Twitch. "Make a move toward him, Princess, and I'll kill you before you finish it," Finn's voice was like Brennan's had been; confident, not angry.

She dragged her cup-sized eyes away from the teenager and focused her hate on the man. Finn held his hand out to Twitch, palm up, and Twitch disengaged the taser. Princess the Gnorf slumped forward, hands shaking and unable to stand. Finn turned his back on her and walked away.

He came to the thrull and stood next to Iselle, looking down at it. "What did you do to him?" Finn asked. Iselle did not respond.

"She made it sad," Remi said, her lip curled in a sneer. "And then when it was too sad to even stand up straight, she made it sadder."

"Huh," Finn looked down at the thrull. Inside, Thane was reconsidering. That was the power of Iselle's Song? She could make things sad? That didn't make any sense. He remembered his first day of Sanctum, and the way General Gage had reprimanded Iselle for leaving her team.

"They need you," he'd said. They hadn't needed her to make them sad.

"Keep him calm, but let him up," Finn instructed. Iselle didn't move. Finn glanced at her, and she looked back with one raised eyebrow. "Please," Finn added.

Iselle nodded, and closed her eyes. The thrull stopped sniffling. Thane tensed. It rolled onto its stomach and heaved itself up onto feet and knuckles.

Thane spread his feet apart and lowered his center of gravity. It whuffed a little, and blinked several times before looking down at Finn.

"Boss," it said, in a voice so deep and low Thane felt the sound reverberate in his ribcage.

Finn nodded. "Go back," he enunciated each word, nearly letter by letter in a loud voice. "Wait for Master."

The thrull nodded, then sniffed and slobbered again, rubbing its eye with one thick paw. It swung the damp forearm down and across, catching Iselle in the stomach and throwing her across the yard. Her spine cracked against a tree trunk and she fell, limp, into the snow.

Thane screamed at the thrull and lunged forward, but Brennan caught him. The thrull bared its teeth at all of them before lumbering into the street. It loped away with surprising speed, disappearing from view before Thane had made it to Iselle.

She was rubbing her back and trying to sit up. "Are you all right?" Thane asked, reaching out a hand to help.

She took his offered dragon claw without hesitation and allowed him to pull her up to standing. "Thank you," she said.

"Sorry about that," Finn shrugged. "They're not the best of followers. But he was calm about it."

Iselle took a step forward and faltered. Thane caught her before she could fall by holding out his arms and letting her fall on them, but one of his claws still tore the edge of her shirt. "Twitch," Thane said, his voice strained. He was torn between helping her and being afraid of causing more damage.

Twitch came over, putting his plethora of tech devices back in pockets or his pack. Together they helped Iselle to the porch steps to sit down. Then Thane straightened and walked back over to where Finn and Brennan were talking. "You," he said, looking at Finn. Finn turned to him, one eyebrow raised.

"If any of my friends are hurt again before we speak to Ru-- to Minos, I am holding you personally responsible."

The anger and fear Thane had been holding inside during the whole fight made his voice shake a little, but his hands were steady. He pointed one blue-black talon at the man. "And I will hold you responsible by making sure you get hurt, too."

Finn raised an eyebrow and exchanged looks with Brennan. "That's the most direct threat I've gotten in years," Finn commented.

Brennan gave a smug half-smile. "What he lacks in subtlety he makes up for in earnestness. Kid's got a thing about lying. Doesn't do it."

"Really?" Finn's eyes traveled up and down Thane appraisingly. "Maybe you are the Master's son after all."

Tightness and heat fought in Thane's chest. What did he mean by that? Was Finn saying his biological father was violent, or that he hated lying as much as Thane did? The pain urged Thane to ask, but he didn't want to talk about it here, in front of everyone. A small voice in the back of his mind asked if he wanted to know at all. Thane shook his head to clear it and asked, "Where are we going?"

"Little place called The Leaf and Dagger. It isn't far, but you'd never know it was there," Finn replied.

Twitch and Remi both burst out laughing. Brennan snorted, and even Thane felt a smile twist across his face. Finn looked slightly startled.

"We may have heard of it," Brennan said. "Do you want to drive or should we?"

Linman started moving and groaning on the ground, before pushing himself up to one knee. "Our van won't hold you all," he said, continuing to rise. His voice had lost all of the viciousness and bloodlust of before. Now he sounded calm. "Sorry about that, Finn," he added.

"Perils of the position," Finn shrugged it off. He did not apologize for knocking Linman unconscious, and Linman didn't seem to expect one.

The drive to The Leaf and Dagger on Main Street in Payson was a short and silent one. Paka, surprisingly trained as a field medic, had looked Iselle over and pronounced her eligible for a healing dart, which Twitch had administered. Thane and Remi sat in the middle seat of the fifteen-passenger van they drove, and Thane's stomach was twisting into knots. He was afraid he might throw up.

The adrenaline of the battle was being replaced by the adrenaline of knowing he was about to meet his biological father. Until only a few months ago Thane had no idea that the abusive Bert Whitaker wasn't his real dad. At the time he had been more relieved about who wasn't his father than curious about who was.

But that hadn't lasted long, and Thane had gone to the other end of the world to learn his father's name. And finding out had almost killed him, and Remi, and Twitch. And then his father, the full blue dragon Ruan de Argos, had blown up a detention facility and killed Thane's chemistry teacher. Who had tried to kill Thane, yes, but it still seemed extreme.

And what if his father thought he was a disappointment? A failure. A nothing, like everyone in school had. Or a problem, like Bert had. Or worst of all, a mistake, like what he was afraid he really was. No one in his whole life had wanted him. Why should his real father be any different?

He felt something warm and small move into his hand. Thane looked down, and saw that Remi's hand was inside his, holding onto him. He turned to watch her face.

"I know this isn't what you wanted," she whispered, looking straight ahead, "and I know you're doing this for me." She squeezed his scaly hand with her soft one. "Thank you."

Thane squeezed back and Remi gasped. Thane looked down. His claws had drawn red lines across the back of her hand, cutting into the skin where they'd grazed her.

He jerked his hand away. "I'm sorry," he said, but she shook her head.

"It's nothing, just scratches. It isn't your fault," she said.

Everything is my fault, he thought to himself as small droplets of blood welled up unevenly through the cuts, and Remi wiped them off on her pants.

"We're here," called Brennan from the front.

Cold fear slammed into Thane's stomach like a fist made from ice. "Look casual," Brennan instructed. He straightened his flat cap and got out. Finn followed, chatting pleasantly with Brennan as they went inside the used bookshop.

Iselle and Twitch followed, she slipping her arm under his and leaning her head on his shoulder as they walked. They were followed by a woman with warm brown skin and spiky black hair who hummed under her breath and held a grumpy baby in her arms, cocooned in a red blanket.

"Who--" Remi started, then blinked. "Wow."

"After you," Linman swept his arm toward the door, and Thane and Remi climbed out. Thane shoved his hands under his coat and Remi went first, opening the door for them both. Linman followed.

The hipster cashier wasn't behind the checkout desk as Thane walked through. Thane could hear him talking among the shelves, arguing about something with Brennan.

Thane quickly made it through the wooden door in the back and immediately the sounds and smells of Raven's pub surrounded him. He couldn't see much, as Iselle, Twitch, Paka, and Remi stood in a wall in front of him just inside the room. Jaeger sat on Paka's shoulder. Linman slipped past them all and went further inside. After a few moments, Brennan came in behind him and shut the heavy door. Thane heard the latch click. Then silence as everyone waited.

"Well," said a smooth tenor voice. "This is quite the entourage. Do you have my son with you, or is this another ill-mannered Sanctum ploy?" The accent was cultured and the tone filled the room without ever seeming loud. Thane's throat tightened and his heartbeat increased.

Everyone else was silent. Even with the mission at stake and quite possibly all their lives in danger, no one wanted to take the moment from him. Thane straightened his spine, following some instinct he didn't know he had.

And he stepped forward. Keeping his chin up and his face calm was the most difficult thing he had done in his life so far, but he did it. Thane moved between Twitch and Remi, and they parted for him.

All the space around the table in the middle of the room had been cleared, and at the table sat a man. There was another man standing behind him and Finn and Linman off to the side, but it was the man sitting that drew Thane's attention.

He had warm skin that could've been a deep tan and a casual perfection of features. Thane understood immediately why women like Cressa would throw themselves at this man, and would stay enthralled. Despite the black hair and tan skin Ruan de Argos had piercing blue eyes that seemed both icily cold and brilliantly hot at the same time.

All this Thane took in the first moment before he saw it. If he hadn't been so familiar with the expression, he would've missed it, but to Thane the disappointment that flickered across his father's face was like being stabbed.

Strangely though, it also felt like the knife cut the bonds that held him back. "Hi dad," Thane said, bitterness coloring his tone. "Where've you been?"

"Looking for you," the man rose, and Thane saw he was wearing an immaculate white linen suit. "If you are my son. What is your name, boy?"

"Thane Whitaker. Yours?"

The man laughed, showing rows of perfect white teeth. "I am Ruan de Argos." He came forward, Finn and Linman flanking him and the other man, olive skinned with curly black hair, following close behind.

Thane could feel the rest of the team stiffen behind him as Ruan grew closer. He felt a surge of protectiveness. "That's enough," Thane said, holding out a hand to stop the dragon from going further.

Ruan didn't merely stop. He froze, staring at Thane's dragon hand, blue scales and nearly black talons held up to halt him. Those blue eyes flicked back and forth between Thane's hand and his face, disbelieving.

"Your eyes and your face are all wrong," Ruan breathed. Thane heard Remi snort behind him and a shuffling movement. "But this..." The dragon man lifted his hand and held it forward to Thane. As it moved, the air around it seemed to ripple and the skin changed from the tan flesh to blue scales. The ends of the fingers peeled back and talons grew from them, so dark they were almost black and curved at the ends with tips so sharp they hurt to look at.

Ruan moved his dragon claw and wrapped it around Thane's. They were an exact match, from the varying shades of blue to the curvature of the talons. Ruan stared at their grasped hands, and Thane felt a bolt of heat travel through his chest. He looked at Ruan's face and saw tears in the man's eyes.

"There are more blue mutt children in this world than any others," the dragon began, still staring at their hands, "but color patterns are hereditary, passed from father to child." Thane felt the grip on his hand tighten, and suddenly he was jerked forward.

"Son," Ruan whispered, wrapping his other arm around Thane in an embrace and trapping their clasped hands between their chests. "You are my son."

The emotion in his voice cracked something inside Thane. That hard place that'd softened when Charlie said Thane was wanted burst open now, being held by his father. Being claimed by his father. Thane's breath shuddered in uneven gasps as he gave in, just for this moment, and hugged his father back.

The room was silent as the two embraced, and Ruan pulled away first, releasing Thane. "Thank you, my friends," Ruan addressed Brennan and the others standing behind Thane. "I cannot repay this kindness, but I will do what I can. Ask anything you like of Marcus, and he will see that you receive it," Ruan indicated the man with the curly black hair. Then he placed both hands on Thane's shoulder, having reverted his dragon claw back. "My son and I have much to discuss, and years to catch up on. Come, Thane," and Ruan tried to lead him away.

Thane resisted. "Um, actually, there is something we wanted to ask you," Thane began. He floundered, not sure what to say next.

"We?" Ruan asked, picking up on the word and stretching it out. He looked down at Thane's claws and then at the others, his eye catching the cuts across Remi's hand. She flexed it and hid it behind her back.

"Of course, your woman can come too," Ruan said, indicating Remi.

"She's not--" Thane began.

"His what?" Remi shrieked.

"Woman is the wrong word? I thought 'pet' would've been too offensive," Ruan smiled, his tone cold and superior.

"Remi is my friend," Thane cut in, stepping in front of her. "My best friend."

"And?" Ruan raised his eyebrow.

Thane cast around for something to say and settled on the simplest version of the truth. "And her mother is trapped in the Shaerealm, and we need your help to save her."

"Ah," was all Ruan de Argos said, but the temperature of the room seemed to drop several degrees with the word. He returned to his seat and steepled his fingers together, his minions arraying themselves behind him. "But I cannot enter the Shaerealm. It is forbidden."

"We know," Thane said, "but you can open a hole so we can go through."

"Out of the question," Ruan made a cutting motion with one hand. "You will not go into the Shaerealm, you are coming with me."

"Even if I don't want to?" Thane's words hung in the air, almost echoing. Finn shook his shoulders to loosen them and Linman lowered himself into a crouch. Somewhere outside, a viper bird screeched.

"Oh," Ruan said, leaning forward and resting his elbows on the table. "I thought you had taken the time to find me because you wanted to come home." His face twisted in an expression Thane couldn't read. "But why would you want to? You don't know anything about me other than what those self-appointed self-righteous idiots at Sanctum would've told you. What your mother would've told you. How is Amelie?" Ruan spoke the name as though it tasted sour.

"Who?" Thane asked.

Ruan's eyebrows rose. "Amelie. Your mother."

"My mom's name is Gwen," Thane answered reflexively, but inside his mind spun. His mother's name had been Amelie. What would that change for her if she knew? Would she remember her life, who she was? Her Song?

"Gwen? You mean that piece of chattel not only stole you from me, but from your mother as well?" Ruan shot to his feet and flipped the table without noticing. He yelled in frustration and picked up a chair, tearing it in half with only his hands. Pieces of wood splintered and flew, and Thane felt Brennan's hand on his shoulder, drawing him away.

Ruan breathed deeply twice, then his face relaxed and he looked mildly sheepish. "I apologize," he said, brushing off the front of his suit. "That display was beneath me. I was overwhelmed." He looked back at Thane and seemed startled to find him standing nearly in the middle of the circle of Omega Team members. "You may call off your empath now, I am in control. I assure you all, you are perfectly safe. You are here under my protection, by my oath and Song. That was our agreement?"

"It was," Brennan answered. "And is." Brennan nodded to Iselle, who took a deep breath. Thane looked at her, how tired she looked again, and fit in the final piece of the puzzle. An empath was someone who could feel other people's emotions; Thane supposed that an empath with Shae blood was someone who could control the emotions of others. He remembered how quickly Omega Team had begun to fight once she'd left. With so many different personalities and struggles, Iselle must be the one who made it possible for them to work together. He stored that away for later.

Ruan nodded. He snapped his fingers and Finn and Linman pulled the broken table out of the way and replaced it with another one, while at the same time Marcus brushed the pieces of the chair away and pulled over another. Ruan sat.

"Please, son, tell me what you and your friends came here to say," Ruan invited, indicating the table. Marcus added an additional chair. Thane glanced at Brennan, who nodded, and Thane walked over to the table and sat down. Thane noticed movement behind the man as Marcus got back into place. A small door, not even as high as Thane's waist, had opened a crack. The sound of the door had been muffled by the rest of the team arranging themselves around Thane, some pulling out chairs.

"You have not been invited to sit--" olive skinned Marcus began, but Ruan waved him away.

"They are guests, Marcus. Now is the time for politeness, at the beginning. Why don't you come and sit as well, my dear," Ruan gestured to Iselle. Marcus reluctantly pulled over a third chair, and Iselle lowered herself into it. "I like to have the empaths where I can watch them. And so," Ruan turned to face

Brennan, who stood at Thane's right shoulder, "Sanctum wants to negotiate with me for the price of my son. How interesting."

"Not Sanctum," Thane spoke up. "Me. I want to negotiate. In fact," he swallowed, debating in his head.

"Kid..." Brennan said in warning.

Thane took the risk. "Sanctum doesn't even know we're here. There's no way they would've let me out to talk to you."

"Truly?" Ruan looked surprised, and laughed with delight. "And this rescue mission, would Sanctum approve?"

"Absolutely not," Brennan answered, after a glance at Thane. "The idea of breeching the Weave to save one person would not only be squashed immediately, but whoever brought it up would be reprimanded." He didn't mention that Remi's mother was a member of the Shaerealm Mercenary Guard or that she had a team with her. Thane hoped his father wouldn't go into that line of questioning.

"How do you know she's there?" Ruan asked instead.

"Aye saw her," Jaeger spoke up. He bounded off Paka's shoulder and landed on the table in front of the dragon. Ruan seemed bemused.

"Yes, you were there most recently," Ruan touched the tips of his fingers together again. Brennan looked as startled as Thane felt. How had Ruan known that? "So you know not only that she is there, but where specifically she is?"

"Aye do," Jaeger nodded solemnly.

"So your plan is not entirely without merit," Ruan allowed. "So again we return to the price of my assistance. You want me to open a way into the Shaerealm through the Weave, and I must assume to also hold it open so you have a way to return?"

Thane blinked. He hadn't thought that far ahead, but yes, he definitely wanted that. He nodded.

"You realize that opening such a way will require a tremendous amount of power," Ruan continued. Thane nodded again. "And that once it is open, it will only be a matter of days before Sanctum arrives to close it and repair the Weave. Even if I were to help you, I cannot commit my men to a fight with Sanctum in which they may lose their lives. I've never understood the idea of losing eight people to rescue one and calling that a success." The dragon shrugged. "What can you offer in exchange for this enormous expense in my Song and manpower, not to mention the risk I assume of Sanctum retaliation?"

Thane gulped. "What do you want?"

"You." Ruan gazed steadily at Thane. Thane tried to keep meeting the dragon's eyes but the expression and intensity of the fierce blue eyes wasn't human, and it was hard not to look away. "It galls me to bargain for what should have always been mine. But, as it has been made clear, you are nearly grown by these human standards, and the choice must be yours. I can force you to come with me," and Thane saw sparks flash in Ruan's eyes. Not imaginary or of emotion; actual electricity danced through the dragon's irises. "But I do not want another captive. I want my son, by my side because he wants to be there. Because he is rightly proud to stand by me. And for that, I will send all these," he waved a hand over the rest of them, "into the Shae. That is my price."

"I'm going with them," Thane said. Ruan's eyes widened, and then narrowed.

"No."

"That's part of the deal," Thane argued. "I'm not sending them there, I'm part of the team. I'm not abandoning them to do this on their own."

"We have had a little practice before you showed up," Twitch muttered. Iselle shushed him.

"I-- hmm." Ruan pursed his lips, considering. "If I let you go, I'm sending some of my men with you to keep you safe. I have only now found you, I refuse to immediately lose you again."

"No deal," Brennan leaned forward over Thane. "This mission is dangerous enough without adding people we can't trust."

"What if they can help?" Ruan ignored Brennan, watching every muscle of Thane's face instead. "What if they're already on the other side, and they can get you where you need to go faster while also minimizing risk?"

"Too many variables," Brennan insisted, "I don't like working with new guys whose motives I can't trust."

"What if I put them under Thane's direction?" Ruan offered. Brennan paused, straightening up. "They would accept his authority as my son. They would be his to command, with my only order being to keep him safe." This time Ruan turned to look Brennan in the eye. "I am doing this to protect my interest in this bargain. This stipulation is non-negotiable."

There was silence for two heartbeats, then Brennan nodded. "I can see that."

"And when you return, you will stay with me," Ruan smiled at Thane.

"What, forever?" Remi spoke up. "No way. He needs to go to school. He needs friends. He doesn't need--"

"Whatever his needs are, I can provide for them," Ruan cut in, glaring at Remi. He looked back at Thane and added, "You would not be a prisoner. In a few years, when I am sure of your loyalty, you would be free to travel and see anyone you like."

"I, um, I can't promise that," Thane tried to sound confident and assured, like Brennan, but it came out weak and small. Ruan cocked his head and waited for Thane to continue. So did everyone else. Thane glanced back at Remi and then to the dragon. "I could go with you willingly, but I can't promise that I'll be, um, I don't know if I'll like..." Thane trailed off. Ruan's forehead furrowed and one of his eyes narrowed, but still he waited for Thane to finish.

Thane sighed. "I don't know if I can really be your son. I'm not good at it," he blurted, then he swallowed around a sudden lump in his throat. "I'm not good at being anyone's son. I can't promise you'll be proud of me. But I'll come, after." He fought against the tears he could feel pricking in his eyes and tried to look less miserable while staring down at his lap.

"No, I changed my mind, I can't ask you to do this," Remi broke in, rising to her feet. "I didn't think he'd want you to give up your life forever--"

"What did you think he would ask for, then?" Iselle cut in, looking at her. "Visiting rights? Alternate weekends? You knew he was shade, you knew he was a dragon, what did you really expect him to ask?"

"I don't know," Remi sounded like she was trying harder not to cry than Thane was. "I didn't think this. I didn't think I'd have to trade Thane for the chance to save my mom. I thought--"

"Now wait, young ladies," Ruan de Argos' warm, calm voice soothed over their budding argument like ice on a burn. "I am not the monster you seem to believe, young empath," he addressed Iselle, "despite how your Sanctum propaganda may have painted me."

He reached out a hand and placed it on Thane's shoulder. "And you are my son, despite whatever brainwashing that soulless wench and her Sanctum rodents tried to give you." Thane shuddered, but didn't pull away.

"How about this," Ruan offered, leaving his hand on Thane's shoulder and opening his other palm. "I will open the hole through the Weave at a point of my choosing. Associates of mine will meet you on the other side with instructions to protect and obey my son. I will keep the way open and hidden for seventy-two hours, the longest I can guarantee a buffer from Sanctum's interference. In exchange Thane Whitaker, my son, will come and enter my service for one year and one month and one day."

Thane jerked his head up and stared at his father, who smiled back at him. "Only a year?"

"And a month and a day. After that, Thane will determine whether he will return to Sanctum as Thane Whitaker, Shaeblooded human, or remain with me as Thane de Argos, my son and my heir. That is my price."

"That is... more than fair," Brennan said. He didn't sound happy about it.

"I am glad you think so, but I am negotiating with my son," Ruan responded, his eyes never leaving Thane's face. "What do you think?"

"I think," Thane swallowed, and held out his right hand, talons apart. "We have a deal."

Ruan de Argos smiled. "Well then, we have much to do," he said, transforming his hand again into the dragon's talon. He gripped Thane's hand, the identical scales making it difficult to tell where Ruan's hand stopped and Thane's began.

CHAPTER 11

"Where are we?" Thane's teeth were chattering so much he almost couldn't yell, and the rhythmic thrumming of the helicopter blades drowned out his words.

"What?" Remi shouted. She sat across from him, belted tightly into the middle of three black seats inside the chopper. Next to her Paka flinched.

"Hang on, we're landing now and can talk outside," Ruan de Argos was the only one not wearing a thick coat and could be heard without effort, even though he hardly raised his voice.

The others nodded, and Thane leaned out to peer out through the open door. Below them was a jagged and broken expanse of white that spread out as far as Thane could see. Strips of dark brown lay like exposed skin across the frozen ground. As the chopper turned he caught a glimpse of a few buildings rising like warts from brown soil and several large wheeled vehicles speeding towards them.

He elbowed Brennan, who was strapped in next to him, and pointed. "Don't worry, those are my men," Ruan said, noticing the exchange.

The helicopter lowered itself slowly and then landed with a gentle thud that made Thane's teeth clack together. The second chopper, the one with Twitch, Iselle, Jaeger, Linman, and Finn, landed moments later a short distance away and four of the all terrain vehicles Thane had noticed skidded to abrupt halts all around them. Brennan and Paka got out, the man stretching and the panther growling at the cold.

Thane fumbled with his straps, the dragon claws making his movements even more awkward. He missed his gloves. He'd gotten used to maneuvering things with them on, but some instinct warned him not to hide his claws in front of Ruan. Thane wasn't sure if it was an instinct of respect or survival, but either way, it seemed the best idea.

Frustrated, he moved too quickly and one of the restraining belts snapped apart, sliced through. Thane flinched and looked at Ruan. Ruan smiled at him. "Not so impatient, my son. Our toys break too easily. Marcus," he spoke louder, not so much a yell as a slightly more intense voice. His servant, who had been sitting in the co-pilot's chair, leapt out of the chopper and ran to Thane's side around the nose of the aircraft. Ruan de Argos waved a hand toward Thane and Marcus quickly undid the straps, and then offered an arm to help Thane disembark.

Embarrassed, Thane mumbled, "Thanks," but jumped out on his own. Once out of the confines of the helicopter, cold air caressed his face and he took a few steps away to look around. Remi came to stand next to him.

"Where are we?" she breathed. The landscape reminded Thane of the desert, but instead of sand the wind blew swirls of snow and ice in whirling patterns. To their left Thane could see a line of bright white glare, like the sunlight reflecting off a huge mirror.

"We're in the McMurdo Dry Valleys in Victoria Land," Finn answered from behind them. Thane saw he was carrying an impressive armload of supplies and gear from the chopper to one of the waiting jeeps. "Only a few more hours to the shores of West Lake Bonney in the Taylor Valley."

"How appropriate," mused Brennan, coming up to stand next to Thane and staring out at the landscape.

"It's O-R, not E-R," Twitch commented, joining them. He was rubbing his left ear distractedly, leaning into his hand and shaking his head.

"Are you all right?" Remi asked.

"You know where we are?" Thane added.

"Antarctica. It is brilliant." Iselle held a shivering mound of blankets in her arms. Jaeger's tail poked out for a second, then jerked back and Thane could hear the imp grumbling and cursing the cold. "I do not even know if we have anyone watching here."

"Satellite tracking," Twitch supplied. "But infrequent. There are only about five thousand people on the Antarctic continent at any time, and anything that comes through from Shae to here would die within hours. Plus..." Twitch trailed off, his eyes widening. "Oh. That's what he's doing! Would that even work?" he rubbed his ear with frantic energy.

"What?" Thane asked.

"Into the jeeps, everyone," Ruan's voice carried even further in the vast Antarctic air. "We're ready to move."

"Where are we going?" Thane asked his father.

Ruan smiled at him. "You'll see."

"Shredding holes," said Brennan, rolling his eyes.

They got into the jeeps in the same groups as they had in the choppers, while those who had ridden in on the ground now climbed up and strapped in for takeoff. The chopper blades spun at the same moment the vehicle engines revved. The sound exploded in the otherwise silent tundra. Ruan didn't explain who the other men were or where they were going, and Thane was too preoccupied to question him.

Or question him about that, at least. "Are we really in Antarctica?" Thane asked, trying to look Ruan in the eye to seem bold and confident, but not quite managing to keep his gaze higher than the dragon's chin. "I thought it would be colder here. I mean, it's cold, but it's not even as cold as Payson right now."

"We're here in the Antarctic summer," Ruan explained. "It feels warmer because it is warmer. It's almost nine degrees out right now."

Thane blinked. "That doesn't sound warmer," Remi argued.

"He's talking Celsius. That would be about forty-eight degrees Fahrenheit," Brennan answered when Ruan did not acknowledge Remi.

Remi narrowed her eyes at the dragon and Thane got the feeling she was trying to resist sticking her tongue out at him. Thane tried to catch her eye and shake his head, but she wouldn't look at him.

The jeeps almost flew over the cold ground, heading towards that bright glare Thane had seen in the distance. As they drew nearer the reflection dimmed and Thane saw it was water. Lake Bonney, Finn had said. The vehicles swerved to follow the edge of the lake and Thane blinked and rubbed his eyes. It was still there. He rubbed his eyes again.

"Do you see that?" Remi shouted. Her voice sounded high-pitched and off balance.

Paka growled deep in her throat and even Brennan looked taken aback. "Are you sure--" Brennan began, and then cut himself off, staring.

"Blood Falls," said Ruan. "Welcome to your gateway."

Ahead of them was a deep cut into the side of the ice cliffs along the lake edge. And the cut was bleeding. Red, seeping liquid flowed from the open wound in the landscape and poured into the floating ice and blue lakewater below. All around the snow was stained with red lines that ran across it like veins over skin, making the white look raw and dirty. It made Thane think of a head wound, the kind that people don't recover from.

The jeeps slowed to a stop on bare dirt near the base of the ice cliffs. Ruan's men scrambled from the last two vehicles while Thane and his friends climbed out more slowly. Thane didn't check the others, but he at least was staring at the blood-red falls with a feeling approaching awe.

"You have a radio tower here!" Twitch sprang out of his seat and ran to Ruan. He looked so happy Thane thought he might hug the dragon but Twitch refrained. Instead the tech genius just grinned and seemed slightly less twitchy.

Ruan raised an eyebrow. "Oh? So your little interface is working again?"

Twitch's face turned an unhealthy shade of grey. "How did you know--" he began.

At the same moment Thane asked, "What interface?"

Twitch glanced around like a trapped animal until he saw the falls. "Whoa. That's... big."

It was. Standing so much closer now, the falls were easily taller than a three-story building. "Set up there," Ruan spoke to his men, and used his finger to indicate a spot along the shore near the falls. The lake itself was only a thin sheet of water over broken ice, and the unnamed employees of Ruan de Argos, the dragon, unloaded the vehicles and moved their cargo efficiently to a spot near the base of the red seepage.

"You have been a student in Sanctum for barely a month now, son." Ruan was looking only at Thane but the dragon had pitched his voice to carry so that everyone on Thane's team could hear him. "How much do you know about the Weave and the Song?"

Thane considered for a moment. He wanted to impress his father and sound smart. "Everything is made up of tiny strings that are woven together. The strings vibrate, and how they vibrate determine what they make. All the strings that vibrate within a specific frequency range create the Weave around one universe, and the sound they make within that vibration range make the Song."

Ruan laid a hand on Thane's shoulder. "Very good. And although the Song of Shae and the Song of Sol are similar, they are not the same."

"Song of Sol?" Thane interrupted.

Ruan didn't seem to mind. "Yes, the Song of this world is named after Earth's galaxy, since the point where the Weaves intertwine is here. And even here, there are places where the Weave is stronger and more separate, or more tangled. This is one such tangled place," Thane's father held out a hand to indicate not just the bleeding falls, but the land around and behind them. "As such, the reality of Earth is both stronger and weaker here, as these falls prove."

"So it really is... blood?" Remi asked in a hushed tone.

Ruan laughed but kept his eyes on Thane. "Blood Falls is named for its color, not its content. There are impressive deposits of ferrous ions trapped underground in the saltwater that oxidize when they come in contact with the air."

"Oxidized ferrous ions... you mean it's rust?" Twitch spoke up. Thane was relieved. He'd had no idea what Ruan was talking about.

The dragon smiled, showing his perfect teeth. "Yes, Mr. O'Malley, essentially the water that seeps from the falls is stained with rust. Hence the red color."

"But that doesn't have anything to do with the Song," Remi argued, "that's just science."

Ruan de Argos turned his full gaze onto Remi and stared, his blue eyes into her brown ones. Thane saw her tighten her jaw at the force of the contact. "Science, little human," Ruan spoke, his voice itself like iron under ice, "is the Song your Earth sings. It would behoove you to pay attention."

He held her gaze for another several heartbeats, and Remi neither looked away nor blinked. The rest of the team kept silent. From the outside, Thane saw Remi's hands clench as she tried to make them stop shaking and how taunt she kept her jaw. As the seconds ticked by, Ruan's expression changed from smooth condescension to curiosity. Whatever he saw in Remi's eyes was making him re-evaluate her.

"So why here?" Thane broke in. Could Ruan see the phoenix soul inside her? That would be an unnecessary complication, and there was no time for those.

Remi blinked, and both she and Ruan looked at Thane. "Here because there is already a weakness," Ruan explained, turning back to the falls. "Here because although your men of science know why the iron makes the water red, it does not know where the iron comes from." The dragon smiled. "It comes from Shae."

"That's impossible," Twitch broke in. "Iron won't pass through the Weave. The frequency is too far outside the range and the strings are too dense."

"True," Ruan acknowledged, "but below this glacier is an underground brine sea, trapped without oxygen. In that sea lives microscopic organisms the like of which are found nowhere else on this earth, for the simple reason they are not from Earth. They are from the Shaerealm, from an identical sea that slips between the Weave in waves and brings its life with it as it crosses over. These little lives thrive in the brine and eat the minerals along the bottom of the water, but they cannot process iron. As they scrub the seafloor, the iron is released. It seeps through cracks and fissures until it finds the oxygen rich surface water, and flows out here. So although the process that creates the Blood Falls is perfectly natural and in accordance with your Song," Ruan locked eyes with Brennan, "the catalyst is not. Science and Shae Song, in harmony, and the perfect place to cross over."

"And all the iron would create a magnetic interference for anyone from Sanctum who might look here," Twitch added.

"It also helps that the Weave is in constant flux here," Ruan conceded. "I see no reason to create work for myself. This benefits you, also." He waved a hand towards where his men worked, erecting small tents and attaching cords and cables to portable generators. "Any other place in the word where I attempted to open a way for you, Sanctum would have a team dispatched within hours. Here I can guarantee two Earth days without interference and hold them off for a third, if needed. Of course, now that I'm using this on your behalf, I expend my advantage." The dragon's eyes glittered as he paused, his eyes moving over Sanctum's mercenaries. "I wonder how much this assistance will be worth in the future."

"Let's wait until we get to the future," Brennan responded, and Paka growled agreement.

Thane was concerned with something else. "What do you mean, Earth days?"

"You haven't explained this?" Ruan's face darkened. "Have you prepared him at all?"

"He's been briefed, and inoculated," Brennan was calm in the face of Ruan's disapproval. They both looked at Thane, and Brennan continued, including Remi in his explanation. "The frequency of Shae's Weave is lower than ours, so time moves more slowly there. We won't notice it once we've crossed over, but this is something else working in our favor. Here he'll have to guard the way for six days, while on the other side we'll have closer to four."

"Relative velocity time dilation in conjunction with gravitational time dilation," Jaeger's muffled voice spoke up from his nest of blankets in Iselle's arms. "Shae not only travels at a different rate, but is larger than Earth. Hyu will weigh more and move more slowly, but so will everyone else, so hyu won't notice."

"Yes, and because of that difference, I have had these made," Ruan said, leading them over to where the people worked. Within the few minutes they'd been conversing Ruan's men had built several small black structures from rectangles attached to generators, all of which made a semi-circle around an intricate looking arch. Cables and wires connected the arch to everything else around it in a delicate weave. On top of each rectangle was a tuning fork, each a different size and facing inward.

"I thought dragons were powerful enough to not need all this extra stuff," Remi said, waving a hand towards the men and their labors.

Ruan ignored her, instead speaking to one of his men. "Boggus, if you please," Ruan de Argos held out a hand, and one of the men scurried up to him and reverently placed a small box on his open palm. The way the man moved made Thane's eyes hurt; it was as though he was moving sideways and forward at the same time, but the thick woolen hat and large goggles he wore hid his face completely so Thane couldn't see any of the man's actual features.

Ruan held the box in front of him and lifted the lid with theatrical deliberation. Inside there were four ordinary looking wristwatches. Thane was more than a little confused, but Jaeger exploded out of his blankets with such force that Iselle had to take a step backwards or fall down.

"Hyu haf solved it?" the imp shouted, shooting towards the box but halting himself with a powerful backstroke. He hovered in the air, grasping claws millimeters from the open box. "How have hyu overcome the observational bias and frequency distortion?" Jaeger's yellow eyes glittered.

A satisfied smile spread across Ruan's face. "There is only one watch, and I will keep it here."

"Ooooh," Jaeger shivered in the air. "How?"

"Blood sings," Ruan shrugged casually, "and cannot be changed. There is a drop of my blood in each to establish the connection, and the true watch remains with me. No matter the space or time involved, they will exist as one, made with the same string."

Finn came over, shouldering a canvas bag and bowed a few feet away. "We're ready, sir," he said.

"Excellent." Ruan pulled the watches out of the box and handed it back to the hovering Boggus. "Mr. Tayler," he held out the first watch. "Guard my son."

Brennan grimaced, but took it.

"My dear empath," Ruan held out the second watch to Iselle. "I trust that you will also protect my son."

Iselle held his gaze with her eyes and opened her hand, but didn't move to take the watch. Ruan smirked and dropped it into her palm. The third watch he tossed to Finn without comment and the man caught it just as silently, and put it on.

"And the fourth watch, my son, is for you as a reminder of our contract," Ruan de Argos held out the small timepiece and placed his other hand on Thane's shoulder. "You will return before this time runs out, regardless of the success or failure of your mission. Regardless of the condition of your compatriots, and with or without them, you must escape the Shaerealm and fill your service to me. This was the oath you made in exchange for the way. Understood?"

"Yes, sir," Thane responded to the authority and confidence of the tone by instinct, and then paused. "I'll do my best, but I'm not very good at leaving people behind."

"You may yet have to learn," Ruan squeezed his shoulder, and Thane felt a corresponding tightening in his chest. Every time he almost forgot, someone else would remind him what a dangerous and stupid idea this was. "Boggus?"

The scuttling man moved from person to person, handing out packs and belts to Iselle, Remi, Twitch, Brennan, and Finn, and larger packs without belts to Paka and Thane. "For those who have little to no Shaeblood," Boggus spoke, the setting sunlight reflecting off the large lenses of his goggles and his voice a strange combination of clicking and slurping behind the regular letter sounds, "these belts have special oxygen masks and filters attached. The atmosphere of Shae holds significantly more moisture than Earth. I wouldn't wear them through the gate, but put them on immediately once you're on the other side. The packs carry supplies as well as locator beacons. They will help you find each other if you get separated. There is also a large beacon in Finn's pack that you should plant near the way on the other side so you can find your way back to the exact spot. These are all made exclusively with Earth tech so no one in Shae will know how to find them or affect their use. Each pack holds one week of rations, one Earth weapon and field medic kits."

"What do Aye get?" Jaeger looked at the watches with covetous eyes.

"This." Ruan pulled a drawstring bag from his pocket. It was crushed blue velvet and smaller than his palm, and he dangled it from his fingertips. Jaeger stiffened at the sight of it. "You know what to do with it?"

"Aye do," Jaeger sighed, and darted in to take the bag.

Brennan frowned. "What was that?"

"None of your business, and can only benefit your mission," Ruan dismissed Brennan's concern.

Brennan would not be dismissed. "Look, there are already too many things about this that I don't like--" he began, but Finn cut him off.

"Sir, the timers have begun," the merc slung his large canvas pack over his shoulders.

"Thank you Finn. Are you all ready? This is your last chance to turn back," Ruan looked over Omega Team, human, Shae, and mixed.

Thane could hear Twitch muttering and heard him say, "Faith," before dropping his voice even lower. Thane hoped Twitch was praying for them all. They were going to need all the help they could get, and as the seconds ticked by he only grew more tense.

"Can we cut the theatrics and get going already?" Remi blurted.

Ruan de Argos, chaos dragon with the authority of the first and one of the seven most powerful beings on the planet, looked at Thane with concern. "Are you sure this is what you want?" he asked. For the first time, his voice wasn't audible to everyone. Even Thane barely heard him. Ruan leaned close and held out one hand. As he moved it toward Thane, it transformed into the mirror image of one of Thane's own claws. "Come back to me, son. Remember your promise."

Ruan blinked, and Thane saw one sparkling tear in the ice blue eyes of the dragon. Had anyone ever cried for him before? Anyone who knew who they were, and who he was?

"Stand here, please," Finn instructed, and the group moved several feet away from the arch. All the workers moved back behind the jeeps. Ruan gripped Thane's hand for a moment longer and then released him.

Thane went to stand between Remi and Paka. He could feel Remi staring at his face and whispered, "He doesn't have to be a bad guy just because he's chaotic."

"I know," Remi whispered back.

"Going to live with him might be a great thing."

"I know," she whispered again. Her voice sounded strained, and strange. "I hope he's the father you deserve."

"I just hope he's as good as your dad," Thane responded. He meant it as a compliment, but her face twisted with pain. Too late Thane remembered they were lying to General Gage, making him believe they were dangerously sick.

"We're doing the right thing," she said, and it sounded more desperate than self-assured.

"I know," Thane reached for her hand, but pulled back before she noticed. The scratches on her hand were still red, bright lines against her pale skin. It matched the lines of iron rust drawn through the snow.

Paka growled. "It is past the point of question, cubs," she spoke to them while keeping her face forward. "Now is the time for action."

A low hum started. Ruan de Argos stood at the peak of the semi-circle with his hands placed on the generators on either side of him. Thane still couldn't hear his Song, but the crackle of electricity was audible to everyone. Each of the black structures came on line with a pop and then that blank hum that always accompanies audio equipment about to be used.

The generators buzzed and thrummed with power as Ruan lifted his hands off of them. The dragon stepped forward, pulling a small silver hammer from the inner breast pocket of his suit and gently tapping it against the nearest tuning fork.

A clear, pure tone sounded over the mechanical buzz of the machines. It sang along the frozen earth and seemed to pound against the red falls, defying the cold and the stillness. The air inside the woven black arch shimmered.

Ruan de Argos struck the second tuning fork with the tiny silver hammer. The second fork was wider and fatter than the first, and the note it sang didn't soar. It sank low and merged with the sound of the working machines, the pulsing generators and the vibrating amplifiers. The subtle sheen in the arch deepened and pulsed. The dragon struck the third fork, so small it made the hammer look large, and it didn't sing so much as fill the light with sound making the fading sunlight dance within the arch. A fourth and a fifth strike completed the chord and it was to Thane like hearing the Song again, flowing through each cell of his being and dancing with the strings inside that made up himself.

Colors swirled beneath the arch like oily rainbows. Each different hue slid across and through the others, and behind it, Ruan produced the last tuning fork. This one wasn't the metallic grey of the others. Despite the purity of their tones and the power that swelled beneath them, they seemed ordinary compared to this. It was only about the size of Ruan's hand, but it looked as though it was made of a single diamond.

Ruan de Argos held the hammer close to the diamond fork and the chord filled the world around them and through them. Then he touched the tip of the hammer to the tip of one crystalline prong.

Thane had been expecting another note, another piece of the Song to make the earth sing. What happened was an explosion of silence. A wave of soundless pressure blossomed from the impact point of the hammer on diamond, smothering every note, every sound, nearly every sensation that Thane could feel. It was the complete opposite of noise and it felt as though the anti-sound cancelled out the vibrations of the strings themselves.

The swirling rainbows within the arch disappeared, bursting outward with flecks of color like droplets from a bubble. Next to Thane, Finn stepped forward and motioned for everyone else to follow. Paka sprang forward, passing the man in her haste, and leapt through the arch at the same moment that Jaeger dive-bombed into the concentrated silence. Iselle and Brennan followed Finn with the kind of calm, measured step that only comes from life-threatening situations being commonplace. Thane felt a hand grasp his, and glanced to his side.

Remi held his hand. He didn't resist her, but didn't grasp her back. She looked at him, her eyes wide and wet, and tried to speak but no sound came out. Or maybe it did and Thane's ears couldn't hear it. Either way, he smiled back to reassure her, and moved forward.

She pulled back on him and pointed. Thane followed her finger to where Twitch stood staring into the void beneath the arch and looking pale. His hands were shaking.

Remi squeezed Thane's hand and let it go. Thane watched her move to Twitch and between his trembling arms. Then she hugged him.

He flinched, then looked at her, then Thane, and finally through the arch. Remi released his torso but grabbed his hand and led him over to Thane. She recaptured Thane's dragon claw in her free hand, and moved forward.

Together the three of them stepped underneath the arch and through the anti-sound barrier, leaving behind everything they knew in the universe.

CHAPTER 12

Thane opened his eyes and grass scratched against his irises. He winced from the pain and jerked his head up from where he lay prone on the ground. The air felt thick and heavy as he blinked and pushed himself up onto his elbows, his claws gouging lines in the wet brown dirt.

It reminded him of the first time he woke up in Sanctum, how the hot air felt wet and weighed on him after the cold dryness of Payson. This felt like that moment quadrupled. The atmosphere was so thick it was difficult for him to draw breath, the air so moist his clothing clung to his skin like he'd been running through sprinklers, and the light was too bright. He lifted himself to hands and knees, shaking his head to dispel the feeling of disorientation.

There was so much color and light it made his eyes sting. He had to blink several times, his eyes burning as they struggled to adjust. Everywhere he looked was differing shades of blue. Was he under water? As his eyes began to adapt to the extra brightness the landscape around him began to resolve into objects his mind could identify. Tall blades of greenish blue grass, still high enough to brush his shoulders while he knelt, waved in the slight breeze.

The sky above him wasn't the pale blue he was used to from earth, but a vivid, neon azure that made his eyes water again just looking at it. He looked back down at his hands. The colored scales that covered them looked almost normal amid the brilliant, flamboyant profusion of blues surrounding them.

A raspy moist sound was repeating itself nearby. Thane looked around for his friends and saw Remi laying on her back on the grass, staring up into the air. She was grasping her neck with both hands and her back was arching sporadically.

It took Thane a moment to process the sight before he leapt forward, not bothering to stand. He sprang on all fours like Paka would, then halted. He needed to get the oxygen mask off her belt and into her mouth without destroying it. Her eyes were unseeing and her movements were getting weaker as he spent precious moments planning each movement.

Gingerly he lay one arm across her lowest ribs and pushed down to hold her still. She resisted, but couldn't fight back. Then he placed the tip of one claw against the plastic zipper and pushed it to release the mask. The pouch opened without resistance and Thane tried to apply pressure to only the strongest parts of the mechanism. He pinched it between his thumb and forefinger's talons and lifted it out.

She was suffocating, her lips losing color, but if he hurried he might destroy the only thing that could save her. Heartbeat by agonizing heartbeat, he pulled the mask free and allowed it to fall into his open palm. Then he pushed it into her gasping mouth and squeezed the edges with the pads of his fingers.

The tube did not inflate, but it made a whooshing sound. Remi's eyes had started to close, but they shot open again and she panicked, trying to push the thing out of her mouth. Thane held her arms down with open palms and pushed his talons into the loose ground.

Her breathing calmed, and gradually reason returned to her eyes. They focused on Thane. The fear in her expression did not dissipate, but the panic drained away as she inhaled deeply through the mask.

"Are you okay?" Thane croaked. His voice was rough and hard, trying to hide how scared he suddenly realized he'd been. His hands shook against her wrists.

She nodded, and there was abruptly enough room in Thane's head to worry about everyone else. Twitch, Iselle, and Brennan had needed the masks too. And Finn. He pushed himself all the way to standing, even through the effort it took nearly knocked him back to his knees.

Paka was only a few feet away, holding Twitch's mask in his mouth while the boy regained consciousness. Brennan was sitting up, holding his own while Jaeger perched on his shoulder stroking the man's red hair and muttering through a frown. Finn was on his feet already, pulling something large and cone-shaped out of his pack. The beacon, Thane assumed.

And Iselle... Thane's head swiveled around. There wasn't anyone left to help her with her oxygen; had it been too long? Where was she?

At first he couldn't find her. The ground cover was thick and several inches tall and had just a little too much blue to be really green. It was similar to grass but each blade was too wide and too tall and looked like some of the bushes Thane had seen growing around Sanctum in their warm, humid climate. "Iselle?" he called. Several of the others looked up at him and he pulled his head back, startled. He hadn't meant to yell, but the sound carried faster and further and his voice seemed distorted.

"Here," she said. She sounded like she was whispering next to him and he spun around. The French girl wasn't near him, and it took him a moment to locate her.

Iselle stood behind them all. The gate stood like a glowing white tear rising from the ground, an incomplete rounded doorway with jagged edges. Iselle was on the other side of it with her back to them, looking away.

Thane pushed himself to his feet after glancing at Remi one more time to make sure her mask was tightly in place. Standing made him feel dizzy, and he forced the thick air into and out of his lungs with effort. Each breath made his body buzz like a string lightly plucked.

"Are you all right? Can you breathe?" he whispered to Iselle. She nodded and turned to face him. Her eyes were a brilliant violet, surprising in their intensity, and once he was past the glowing gateway he could see her body was also luminous, suffused with its own inner gleam. "What... are you?" Thane's words, although spoken softly, carried back to the others and he could hear them coming closer.

He remembered Paka's argument that Iselle was just as much Shae as the panther woman. How Brennan and the others had been relieved when she came. And how both Charlie and Ruan had paid attention to her when they largely ignored other human females.

Iselle was watching him, tight lines around her eyes and her forehead furrowed. "I was born here," she said. She glanced away from him and closed her eyes. Her eyebrows drew down and the light seemed to withdraw inside. Once it was gone, she slumped a little and opened her eyes again, not looking at him. "But they sent me away when I was very young. To a family in France, who didn't know what I was."

"Why?" Thane asked, and she hunched her shoulders and drew her arms in, rubbing them.

"Because they decided there wasn't enough good on Earth, so they infused me with a Djinn spirit and sent me to be a force of peace in that world." She blinked rapidly a few times before turning her face away. "I 'ave not done very well."

"Bah," Paka didn't try to modulate her tone, so the sound burst from her and sped across the open ground in every direction. She had loped over to rise between Thane and Iselle. "You, youngling, have kept Turcato and Loren from killing each other and everyone of us from choking Jaeger for over two years now. In human words, that is no small miracle."

"Keep your voice down," ordered Finn. He'd set up the beacon and drawn some kind of weapon. At least, Thane assumed it was a weapon from the way the man held it. It was about the size of a large handgun and made of something dark grey and shaped roughly like a bullhorn, with a shallow bowl at the front end. "There aren't likely to be many friendlies around here." He put the oxygen mask back in his mouth.

Taking her cue from Finn, Remi pulled hers off to talk. "Do we have to wear these the whole time?" she asked.

"No," Brennan answered. Twitch stood next to him, fidgeting like mad. "Only for a few hours. They will slowly modify the air we're breathing until it matches the air around us. Then we can put them away. But don't try to do anything too crazy or physical," he put his mask back to take a breath before continuing, "the atmosphere here is significantly heavier than our own, as is the pull of gravity. Get used to it first."

"We need to get moving," Finn announced.

Paka's ears twitched at the same moment that Jaeger shot himself into the sky. "Something is coming," Paka announced, "from there."

Every head swiveled to follow her finger to where it pointed away from the gate to Thane's right. In the distance a forest rose up against the expansive meadow they now stood in, the dark line of the trees marking the edge of the clearing. In the sudden silence Thane could hear a faint thumping like the galloping of far away hooves.

The red blur that was Jaeger fell from the sky and landed on Iselle's shoulder. He put a wrinkled red hand on her cheek. "He is armed, and he can move faster than we can," the imp glanced at Paka, seeming to indicate that by "we" he meant the humans. She curled her lip back, baring her fangs. "We must be ready for his attack."

"How long?" Brennan asked.

"Three minutes before he can see us clearly, maybe another two before he's here," Jaeger responded. Paka hissed through her teeth.

"What is it?" Thane asked.

Jaeger shrugged. "Aye could not get a good look through the trees, and if Aye had waited until he was in the open he would have seen me. But he is big. Big as three of him," Jaeger nodded toward Finn.

Brennan muttered something into his mask before pulling it out to speak. "Thane, Remi, Twitch, and Iselle, lay on your stomachs in front of the way. The grass is tall enough that it might not see you, and if it does you can always go back through the hole. Jaeger, Paka, you flank top and back. Finn, you and I will stay low on the sides. It could just be passing through. Do you have another one of those?" Brennan indicated the bullhorn handgun that Finn held.

"You have one in your pack. So does the kitty," Finn answered.

Paka smiled at him. Thane clearly remembered what it felt like to have Paka smile at you. Sometimes he still saw her do that during his nightmares. "Funny human. I may just watch it kill you before I step in."

Finn grinned at her. "And here I thought you Sanctum mercs couldn't have fun."

"Great, we're all crazy together, now let's move," Brennan ordered, and then added, "Where are you going?" to Remi, who was walking away from the gate.

"I'm not going back through," she said, the thumping of the hooves getting louder in the distance. "I'm going to help fight this guy off so we can go get my mom."

In two quick strides Brennan stood in front of her, blocking her way, and leaned down until his eyes were level with hers. "Listen up, little princess," he spoke in a low undertone that carried through the wet air as clearly as if he'd been shouting. "Your daddy may be a commanding officer, but you aren't. You either promise, right now, that you are going to listen and obey my orders without question or I will rip this off and shove you back through the hole before you can even consider having a tantrum." He indicated her oxygen tube and leaned so close into her there almost wasn't enough space between them for her to take the mask out without hitting him with it. The steady footfalls were even louder. "Promise. Now."

Eyes wide, she nodded at him. "Say it," he ordered. "All of it. Out loud, so everyone can hear you."

"I promise to follow orders," she mumbled around the mouthpiece.

"Fine," Brennan nearly cut her off before she could finish. "Now get in place before you get us all killed." The normally easy-going and nonchalant Brennan spun on his heel and stalked away from her, the hoofbeats now thundering in the air.

"Sheesh," Remi muttered, slinking down into the grass next to Thane. "I was just trying to help."

"You help by following orders," Twitch snapped, hidden in the grass on Thane's other side. "You help by being where we expect you to be so that we know what ground to cover in a fight and how far away backup is." His hands were shaking and his voice was strained and strange, as though he was trying to talk without making any sound at all. "You're out of your element here, cut off from everything you're familiar with or good at so just shut up and let us do the job you convinced us was worth dying to finish."

Twitch's whole body was trembling and Thane watched Iselle scoot over in the wet soil until she was lying next to him. She took one of his hands in both of hers and held it. Twitch took a shuddering breath and closed his eyes.

On his other side, Remi's eyes were glistening with more than just the moisture in the air. Thane opened his mouth to reassure her. "Don't--"

Jaeger landed on his head, pushing his mouth down into the dirt. "Either stand up and announce us or stop talking!" the imp hissed before launching himself back into the air.

The pounding hoofbeats slowed, the spaces between the impacts getting larger. Thane resisted the urge to push himself up to see what it was even as his stomach lurched. Whatever it was, it wasn't going to just run by them.

It stopped, silence settling in the clearing all around them and the distortion in the air making it impossible for Thane to tell how far away their assailant waited. His heartbeat thudded in his own ears. It was loud enough he was sure everyone could hear it. The dirt smelled wet and warm less than a finger width away from his nose, and with all other sound suspended he could hear the hiss of the air flowing through the oxygen regulators to either side of him. Blades of grass tickled the sides of his face and he resisted the urge to brush them away.

"What are you doing?" a tiny trilling voice spoke from inside his ear. Thane started and twisted his head to the side, coming eyeball to face with...

He didn't know what it was. Its entire head was the size of a large marble with huge black many-faceted eyes that took up two thirds of its face. Its blue body was roughly human shaped but the proportions were off, the fingers and toes too long and the torso too narrow and straight. Then there were the wings, similar in shape to butterfly wings but translucent and each as large as one of Thane's hands.

Remi was staring at it too, as it hovered between them. "Are you here for the rescue?" it chirped. It sprang higher, up on top of Thane's head where it jumped. He twisted his neck around to watch as it leapfrogged from his head, to Twitch's, to Iselle's, then shot straight up.

"Kith, there are four here in the grass by the shiny light," it called. "And there's a Pantera crouching over there, but she smells all funny."

"Filthy little fairy!" Jaeger shouted as he fell from the sky. The talking bug tried to zip out of Jaeger's reach, but he somersaulted in the air and smacked the fleeing being with his tail.

Thane couldn't see where it fell but he heard its tiny screech of pain, followed by a much louder bellow that shook the ground around them. "Wait!" Thane shouted, pushing himself to his feet and stumbling forward just in time to see an arrow fly through the air at Jaeger's throat.

Paka sprang through the air at the same moment, seizing the projectile in her mouth and snapping it between her fangs. Jaeger dived down and clutched at the ground while Thane spun in the direction the arrow had come from.

The beast roared into the sky, rearing back onto hind legs beating its chest and pawing at the air. It was all brown fur and motion and too many arms and legs. Brennan and Finn rose from their hiding places, training their weapons on the creature as it nocked another arrow.

It was too much. "Stop!" Thane shouted, holding out one dragon-taloned palm in each direction. The word burst outward and somehow got louder, as if each particle of air moved by his voice vibrated with the sound wave instead of pushing against it. The palpable force of the word swept across the combatants. Brennan and Finn lowered their weapons. Paka straightened from her crouch and sheathed a knife Thane hadn't known about. And the beast lowered itself onto four legs and bowed.

"Let it go, Jaeger," Thane ordered. Jaeger glowered at him and hid his hands behind his wings. Thane stared into the imp's yellow eyes and waited.

"Fine," Jaeger sighed, and released the fairy. Or at least he opened his hands. Inside them the tiny blue body cowered, wrapped inside its see-through wings with its arms covering the oval shaped head.

"Are you okay?" Thane asked, holding out his hand. The fairy peeked underneath its arms, the over bright sunlight reflecting off its eye facets. "Don't be scared."

Jaeger yowled as the fairy's head opened wide revealing several rows of needle teeth and bit down on the imp's finger. "Get off, get off," Jaeger flung his hand around trying to dislodge it.

"Let go," Thane said, and the fairy opened its jaw and buzzed away from Jaeger, glaring furiously at the imp the whole while. It hovered over Thane's hand before descending lightly into his open palm. "No biting," Thane instructed, and the fairy giggled.

"I wouldn't bite you! Your scales would break my teeth," it chirped at him.

"Jenariarahl, are you uninjured?" the beast growled.

"Kith, Kith, do you see? We found him! I said we would find him, and you said it would take time but I said it would be right away and we've only been looking for a few hours so I was right and we didn't take long," the fairy called Jenariarahl was so excited her wings buzzed against Thane's fingers and he opened his hand wider to keep his claws away from them.

"What do you mean? You found who? And what rescue did you mean?" Thane asked the being on his palm.

The beast answered. "We found you, my lord. Your father, the mightiest, sent us to assist you in your rescue of a... a... woman," he seemed to stumble over the words and Thane turned to look at him, and for the first time got a really good look at the creature who had been running with such speed.

"Was our master joking?" the beast had four long, narrow legs that ended with split hooves and a body that looked something like a horse. But where the horse's neck would be a shaggy torso rose, covered in thick brown fur with two long arms. He had hands with long fingers that ended in short pointed claws and a thick neck that supported a wedge shaped head, also fur covered, with a small muzzle and curved horns that sprouted upwards. "Have you really come all this way to rescue a songless human?"

Remi had stood and crept closer to Thane after the fairy had landed in his hand. She was standing just behind him, looking over his shoulder at the little creature and glancing up at the beast in turns. At this question, she snorted.

"It's no joke, buffalo face," she said. Thane blinked. He did look like a buffalo.

The beast ignored her and Finn spoke up. "We are here for a rescue. I take it you're Kith?"

"And you must be Finn," Kith glowered down at him. "I am curious to see how well you perform here, without all of your human crutches."

"Science, you mean?" Finn shrugged, tucking his weapon away in a special holster on his belt. "We'll see."

"So you knew he was coming?" Brennan's voice held only a trace of exasperation. "You could have mentioned it."

"The Master only mentioned that his steward Kith would be coming, not when or what he looked like," Finn explained, keeping his eyes on the beast.

"You're my father's steward?" Thane asked. Kith bowed again, a strange combination of bending at the waist and bending his front legs that ended up being somehow both servile and incredibly impressive.

"I am Kith, son of Burth, son of Goron, and direct descendant of Wrenwroth, first steward of the house of Argos," he said, rising from his bow. "And you are the first son and my sworn master."

"And mine!" piped the fairy. She rose from his hand up to the level of his face and bowed. "I am Jenariarahl of the shade and light on the eastern mountains, but you can call me Jena. I help, I'm the helper!"

"And a nuisance," mumbled Kith.

"So you're the ones Ruan has assigned to help us?" asked Twitch.

Kith ignored him. "Yeah, that's not going to work for me," Thane said.

"My lord?" Kith asked.

Thane stepped to one side, so that he was standing in a line with Iselle, Remi, and Twitch. "These are my friends," Thane announced, indicating the other humans and mostly-humans. "You will treat them with the same respect and deference you treat me. Which means you answer them if they speak to you. You protect them as you would me. And," Thane found it much easier to be bold and commanding with Kith, the beast being so impossibly huge he didn't even approach human, "you don't insult them. Ever."

Kith blinked and tossed his head as though something small and annoying was buzzing around it. His foreleg pawed at the ground. "This is not the way," he protested, but Thane cut him off.

"This is my way," he said.

"I can do it!" Jena's entire body nearly vibrated with excitement. "I can talk to them! You're pretty," she flitted over to hover in front of Iselle's face.

"Thank you," Iselle blinked in surprise.

"I don't like pretty humans," Jena continued, and landed on Twitch's face, perched on his nose looking outward. "See, Kith, it's easy!"

"You all talk too much," Paka hissed. She stood at the edge of the group, looking away but keeping the monstrous Kith in her peripheral vision. Thane could tell she was trying to watch everything by the way her ears swiveled. "We have only days to find one human in a realm more than half as big again as Earth, and you stand here out in the open like adolescents at the beginning of mating season. We must move," she emphasized the last word so strongly it almost echoed.

"Paka's right, we can talk as we go," Brennan said, and both Finn and Kith nodded. "Jaeger, which way do we need to go?"

"Where are we?" the imp's head turned side to side. "Aye cannot know where to go unless I know where we start from."

"These are the northwestern plains, near the lands of the Eldergast," Kith supplied.

"That explains the smell," said Paka, hunching her shoulders and shaking out her fur.

"That way," said Jaeger, pointing across the plains in the direction opposite the forest. "The lands of the Sang Evarish are one and a half moons that way."

"Sang lands?" Jena shuddered, still sitting on Twitch's face. He sneezed, and she flew forward several feet before catching herself in the air. "Why there?"

"We're here to rescue her mother," Thane said, pointing at Remi. "Jaeger says she's a captive of some Evarish named Terracatan."

Kith growled something in a language Thane didn't understand. "Terracatan? I know him. I think I may know a way in."

"You know him?" Brennan asked. "That's convenient."

"Not as much as you might think," Kith responded. "The Pantera is correct. We need to move. The Eldergast hunt these plains when the moon rises, and it would be easier if we were not here then. I do not believe they would bother so many of us but it is best to not take risks. Are you prepared to go?"

Finn jogged over to where the beacon lay and straightened it, kicking dirt around the base to keep it stable. "We're good. Let's move."

They turned away from the glowing tear and walked away from the entrance to their world. Thane spared one last thought for home. He hoped that Lanie was all right, and his mom, and even Harper and Bert and that Charlie wouldn't be too mad at him. Now that he was more used to the atmosphere every breath seemed to make him feel more awake and stronger. His eyes had even adjusted to the light so it wasn't painfully bright anymore.

"Do you feel like you've been here before?" Remi whispered next to him. Her voice carried, and Twitch glanced back at her. They were traveling in a loose circle with Thane and Remi in the center. It had just evolved that way, with Jaeger leading the way and Paka scouting for danger up ahead, followed by Kith with an arrow at the ready. Twitch and Iselle both seemed to want to be alone and were walking at the outer edges of the group while Finn and Brennan brought up the rear, both with weapons drawn but down. Jena flitted everywhere.

"What do you mean?" Thane asked. They'd been walking through the grassland for over an hour, Kith insisting he would tell them more about Terracatan once they were out of the open. They were easy to spot here, dark figures against the earth and sky. The bluish green grass still stretched out from them in all directions, but Thane could see hills breaking up the landscape, with bright splotches of color like burst paintballs covering them.

"I don't know," she sighed, rubbing her eyes and taking a deep breath from the oxygen tube. "It's so wet and warm I feel like I'm walking through a hot tub with all my clothes on, but it's familiar. Like something in me remembers feeling like this, being used to it but different. Am I making any sense?"

"No," Thane smiled at her. She made a face and elbowed him.

Jena shot over and pinched Remi on the ear. "Ouch!" Remi squealed. "Hey!"

"Do not attack the son of my lord," Jena squeaked.

"It's okay, Jena, we're friends," Thane tried to wave the tiny shade away.

She buzzed over and cocked her head to the side, hovering in front of his face. "Friends?"

"Yeah," Thane said.

"Only friends?" Jena pressed.

Thane could feel his face getting warm, and not from the heat of the sun. "Wh-what do you mean?"

Jena stared at his cheeks. "Your face is getting red. I have not seen a blue dragon with a red face. You must be ill."

Behind him, Thane heard Brennan and Finn snickering. He ducked his head and stared at his feet, face still burning.

"It is good that you have no romantic entanglements," Kith rumbled. He kept his large head swiveling and two giant hands on his bow with a nocked arrow. "You may not otherwise approve of the plan, and we can do without complications."

"And what plan was that?" Brennan asked.

Kith snorted. "We're almost to the flower hills. We can talk more there."

"Flower hills?" Remi asked. Kith didn't respond at first, and Thane thought the beast must be fighting against Thane's direct order. Before he could say anything the massive Kith shook his head and grumbled.

"The flower hills are hills covered with flowers." If he had to talk to her he was going to make it clear that he didn't have to like it. Thane felt his own embarrassment slip away in the face of Kith's obvious discomfort, and he grinned at his shoes.

"Flowers that eat you!" Jena added cheerfully, and Thane felt a whole lot less like smiling.

CHAPTER 13

The sun looked pale and watery as it lowered towards the horizon. They'd traveled for a few hours longer before coming into the low, rolling foothills and Thane had discovered why they were called the flower hills. Multi-colored blossoms the size of his head grew on stalks taller than he was and spread around them in all directions in a thick forest. The moment they stopped, Jena went zipping out of sight through the tree-sized flowers that had leaves wide and broad enough to lay in like hammocks.

Which was exactly what Kith had prepared, the moment he found a spot he deemed adequate for setting up camp. A group of flowers had grown together in a clump next to a hillock, providing them cover from two sides, with a burbling little stream that was wider than Thane felt he could safely jump across running along the third side.

He couldn't help but notice that the water was a pale green, like Easter grass left too long in the sun. It was only a hint of color in the mostly clear liquid, but it was there. Brennan and Finn knelt next to the stream, scooping water into pots, and Paka, Jaeger, and Jena had disappeared the moment they decided to stop for the night. Kith pulled a curved hook out of a pack and plunged it through the edge of one of the large teal leaves and pulled.

To Thane's surprise, the leaf unrolled like a rug and the creature with the body of a moose, the torso of a hairy man, and the head of the buffalo pulled it out to its full length before using the hook to attach a rope through the hole and tied it off to the stalk of another flower-tree. After it was secured Kith grabbed it with two hairy hands and stretched, then let go. It sprang back and then hung in arc, swaying gently. Kith repeated the process with leaves all around the small clearing until there were six swaying hammocks of various heights ready.

"What if it rains?" Thane asked, wiping the sweat and condensed water from his forehead with his sleeve. Inwardly he thought it probably wouldn't matter; he likely couldn't get wetter, the humidity condensing in his clothes and along his skin.

"Rain?" Kith asked, rolling the word around in his mouth as though it was unfamiliar.

Thane waited, but Kith didn't continue. The silence was getting awkward so Thane added, "Um, rain. Water that falls from the sky."

"Hmm. It doesn't rain," Kith answered with a shake of his massive head. The way he said it made Thane wonder if the beast meant "ever."

"What about you?" Thane asked. Kith looked at him, and it was disconcerting to know that when the wedge-shaped head was turned away was when the creature was watching him. It made sense, as Kith's eyes were on the side of his face like a horse instead of in front like a human, but knowing that didn't make it less strange.

"I wouldn't fit, my lord," Kith grumbled.

Thane flushed. "I know that. I meant, where are you going to sleep?"

"I'll make myself a nest when it's time, but I'll spend most of the night on watch." Thane blinked. A nest? Like a bird? He wanted to ask, but he didn't want to push the beast further or risk offending him. "These are for you two legs," Kith answered, his voice a low rumble. It actually sounded like the stream but several octaves lower, Thane realized. Hearing this, Twitch stumbled over and collapsed into the nearest hammock. Thane saw him curl up into a ball on his side and close his eyes.

There was something wrong there, something more than the thickness of the atmosphere or all the ground they'd traveled today. Thane took a step towards his sometime roommate.

"Do we need a fire?" Iselle spoke, the first words she'd said since before they'd met Kith. Thane paused and looked at Kith.

Either her protracted silence or something about her personally made Kith treat her with significantly less disdain than Remi. "Not unless you need to heat your food," Kith spoke gently, "it will not get cold for several cycles, until Tyrn replaces Agoth."

Remi noticed Kith's courtesy. Thane saw the annoyance twist her features. "Who are Tyrn and Agoth?" she asked, stepping forward and breaking into the conversation. Kith snorted, and pointed upward in a diagonal line across the hills. All the humans looked up except Twitch, and Thane's breath caught.

Hovering about the horizon were moons. Three of them, one larger than the fullest moon Thane had ever seen by at least double and the other two like baby chicks following behind. The biggest was a deep scarlet, so bright that it lent a reddish blush to the darkness. The smaller satellites were only slightly different in size, one a pale blue and the other a deep gold.

"This is the near center of the cycle of Agoth the relentless, when the heat and light blister the ground and the blood moon is closest to Shae. Agoth will grow a few days more and all shadow will gain strength and influence. The peak of their power will be hence three sunsets, and that night the shadow will feast and dance and no one of Shae will be safe from their depravity," Kith's shaggy finger traced a line across the sky. "Then the blood moon will wane, drifting further away into the heavens, and Tyrn the harvester will wax bold to come close immersing all of Shae in his golden, peaceful light. Then all that is good and fae will gain strength that the days will be pleasant and warm and only the deepest nights will cool instead of this furnace now."

The beast's voice was hypnotic, and as he spoke Thane felt he could see the movement of the three moons of Shae floating through space. The way Kith spoke about the moons tickled something in Thane's mind, but it wasn't until Remi spoke that it clicked.

"Kith, are you fae?" she asked. Even in the growing darkness, Thane could see the beast stiffen at the question but the way Kith had spoken about the moons made Thane wonder the same thing.

Everyone else shifted uncomfortably and Thane wondered if Remi even knew how rude that question was. She may not; she hadn't been in Sanctum very long. During the long silence Thane contemplated what he would do if their guide and his father's steward decided to attack his best friend. "I am Dunsinae, and we are the fae of the Centuria," the low rumbling came out of the darkness, and something crackled and spat. Light flared to life, a small round globe of golden flame hanging suspended in Kith's enormous hand and highlighting his face from underneath.

Thane's jaw flopped open. He snapped it shut, glad of the darkness and hoping that no one noticed but inside he felt a surge of hope. Kith was his father's steward, his primary servant and avatar here in the Shaerealm, and Kith was one of the good guys! This was evidence that his father was someone Thane could like or even admire. Even in his own mind he sounded desperate to believe anything positive about Ruan, but he clung to the idea anyway. Why should it be so much easier to have faith in Charlie than in his own father?

Because Charlie didn't abandon you, said a tiny voice in his mind, *Because there was something about your father that made your mother run away.*

He squashed the doubt with force. If his mother left Ruan, why did that automatically make the dragon the bad guy? Maybe it was Ruan that felt abandoned. Hadn't he said that Thane's mother had help getting away? Maybe she was kidnapped. Maybe they were both taken away from Ruan and that's why his mom's memory had been wiped, to hide that secret.

Thane's mind felt caught in a whirlpool, spinning around feelings of loss, fear, and hope. With effort he dragged his attention back to the conversation happening around him, where Remi had asked something else and Kith was answering her.

"...Cormoran the reckless," the Dunisnae was saying. Thane felt better knowing what Kith was. Brennan and the others seemed to be relaxing too, with Kith having admitted to being fae. "The pale blue one is erratic, waxing and waning without pattern. Sometimes he fills the sky along with one of the others, mixing his strength with theirs, and others he departs and can barely be seen. The shade Song sings louder or fades away as his presence does."

"That isn't possible," Twitch's mumble came from his hammock. "There's always a pattern."

"Not in this," Kith asserted. "The Shae have studied the motions of the skydancers for a dragon's lifetime, but none have found the reason behind Cormoran's movements."

"Then they don't know how to look," Twitch answered. Thane was relieved to hear annoyance in the tech genius' tone; it was the first emotion other than fear Twitch had shown since they got here.

Kith gouged the earth with one front hoof. "And a barely calved songless human knows better than generations of the Shae?"

Twitch sat up and glared at Kith, the golden ball of light shining barely enough to see them lock stares. "Maybe I do," Twitch muttered, his fingers tapping together. He turned away from Kith and lay back in his hammock, stretching out to its full length and staring at the night sky, his familiar muttering sounding like a song to Thane.

The conversation broke off then as Kith snorted, and then trotted away into the stalks of flowers. Thane hoped he would come back. He sat down on the springy brown loam of the ground and opened his pack to rummage around for food. He thought he would have to do it by scent and touch in the darkness, but thankfully one of the first things he found was a small flashlight.

"It is good for him to have something to focus on," Iselle's voice was quiet, even in the wet air of Shae. She came to sit next to him, going through her own pack. "He is unusually off balance here, more than I expected."

"It's good he has you," Thane answered, still looking through the bag. "I'm glad you're here too."

"Oh," Iselle said, and her voice sounded strange.

He glanced up at her. "You okay?"

"Yes," she said, suddenly very interested in the contents of her own canvas pack. "Just hungry." Thane's stomach growled at that moment, punctuating her sentence. He flushed and she laughed. "Like you."

"What's going on?" Remi asked, coming over and sitting cross-legged on the ground next to Thane.

"Do you have food in yours?" Thane asked, indicating her pack with his flashlight.

"I don't know, and I don't know if I'd want to eat it anyway," Remi stuck out her tongue. "Who knows what a chaotic dragon thinks is good food?"

"He wouldn't give us something gross," Thane said, stung. "He's trying to help us. Trying to help you."

"I know," Remi snapped, but then stopped herself from saying anything else by taking a deep breath. "I just wish we didn't need so much help." To her credit, she said this without looking at Iselle, but Thane was pretty sure he knew who she was talking about anyway. He was sure Iselle did too.

"Paka and Jaeger are back," Iselle announced. She rose with grace and walked to the other side of the clearing where Brennan and Finn had been next to the stream. Thane stood up and held his arm down to Remi. She glanced at it, then at him, and sighed, grabbing his elbow and pulling herself to her feet.

They crossed together and arrived at the same moment that Paka came leaping out of the shadows from the other side of the water. "We are relatively secure," the panther woman announced. "I have checked for at least a mile around us and there is nothing nearby to threaten. It should be safe for a full camp."

"We are clear from the air as well," Jaeger added, settling down onto Brennan's shoulder.

"Good," Brennan answered. He pulled a cloth from his pack and wiped his face. "I was getting tired of all the red-tinted moonlight. It feels wrong, and makes my eyes hurt." He stood and strung a series of dim lanterns from ropes tied to the tops of the flower stalks, creating a cylinder of yellow light in the center of all the leaf hammocks. Jaeger helped and it only took slightly longer than it would have otherwise.

It was fully dark now, which the light of the glowing red moon seemed to enhance instead of diminish. Thane was silently grateful for the warm yellow glow of the lanterns and he and his companions sat in a circle underneath them, saving only Twitch, who still lay in his hammock gazing upwards, and Kith who had not yet returned. Finn passed out sealed silver packets to everyone.

Paka declined hers, saying, "I have already eaten," with a self-satisfied sounding purr.

"Aye love these!" Jaeger's eyes glittered as he grabbed the proffered rectangle.

"It's food?" Thane asked.

"They're MREs," Remi answered. "Meals Ready to Eat." She'd already taken hers and ripped it open, laying out the individual pieces in front of her after peering at the labels. "Military food rations that travel well," she added, to Thane's blank stare.

"You're had MREs before?" Finn asked her.

"Oh yeah," she rolled her eyes. "My dad has tons of them. He keeps them in case of some kind of national emergency or natural disaster. He says we'll always be ready. Prepare and survive, or something." She opened the nearest packet and took a bite out of whatever was in it. The light wasn't quite bright enough for Thane to make out exactly what it was. "He rotates through them by making us eat the ones that are about to expire about once a week and replacing them with fresh ones."

"You're not quite the princess I thought you were," Finn admitted. "Your dad must be some kind of survivalist nutbag."

"My dad is--" Remi began angrily, but cut herself off before the Omega Team members could. "I don't have to defend him to you."

"Sure, whatever," Finn grinned and shrugged, opening and eating his own food packets.

Thane eyed his skeptically. The others didn't seem to be having any problem, so he pulled the silver covering back and took out the smaller packets inside. The light from the lanterns was dim enough to make reading the small print difficult so he just opened one. He still couldn't tell what it was, so he took a bite. He'd gone to bed hungry often enough that the possibility of it not tasting very good didn't deter him, which turned out to be a very good thing. It wasn't very good, and even after eating it he wasn't entirely sure what it was supposed to be, or even what food group it belonged in.

The others weren't eating with any vigor either, save for Jaeger, who tore into his with much lip smacking and evident enjoyment.

"Kith is returning," Paka announced. She lay on the ground with her feet and hands tucked in with her back against Brennan's. Thane had never seen her look more feline or more feral. Her ears twitched in the direction opposite the stream, and in a few moments Thane could hear the muffled thud of the Dunsinae's cloven hoofs.

The huge Kith emerged from the forest of flower stalks with a bundle under one arm. Finn and Iselle, who were closest to where he approached, slid apart to make room for him in the circle and the great hairy beast bent his front knees gingerly until they touched the ground. His back legs bent and his hindquarters flopped to the side, and Kith sat as part of the group with his head and shoulders significantly higher.

"Here," Kith tossed the bundle forward and it landed with a thump near Thane's feet. "For you, Lord Heir."

"Thank you," Thane responded reflexively. He reached forward and unwrapped the cloth, revealing several pale yellowish objects that were roughly the size and shape of potatoes. Thane stared at them, uncertain.

"They're food," Kith said, crossing his arms in front of his chest. "Are you unfamiliar with food?"

Thane picked one up and sniffed it. It smelled like the wet, loamy dirt. But it was unlikely to taste worse than what he'd already eaten, so he placed it between his teeth and bit down.

His mouth was filled with a sweet juice, and although the outside was almost colorless the inside was a bright purple streaked with pink and tasted like oranges, mangoes, and strawberries all at once.

The look on his face must have shown how unexpected and delicious they were, because Remi immediately grabbed one and took a bite.

"Oooh," she said, "this is amazing."

Thane nodded, his mouth full, and offered the fruit to the others, including throwing one into Twitch's hammock.

"Hey!" an annoyed voice called back.

"Just eat it," Remi ordered.

"Aye am good," Jaeger declined the fruit, instead rummaging through Finn's pack and pulling out a second MRE, which he instantly tore open with his teeth and began devouring the contents.

"Want one?" Finn offered Kith a silver packet with the large block letters.

Kith shuddered. "I'd rather sing with a pack of inugamae."

Brennan and Finn laughed, but Kith's face remained sober. Thane wasn't sure the Dunsinae had any other expression, but he silently agreed with the sentiment. The blocks of pseudo-food may have traveled well, but definitely weren't ready to eat, no matter what they were called.

"So what's this plan of yours, buffalo-face?" Remi asked around a mouthful of the sweet fruit. Kith didn't respond, instead chewing on a rough piece of brown fibrous plant that looked like he was eating a stick.

Thane cleared his throat. Every time he felt he had to speak, he wished there were fewer people around to hear him. "Kith, you need to answer my friends."

"What?" the beast glanced up at him. "It was speaking to me? What is a buffalo?"

Brennan snorted. "Don't worry about it," he said before Remi could respond to being called "it," which response was not going to be positive. "So we're here, we're listening. What do you know about this Sang Terracatan, and how will it help?"

"Terracatan is obsessed with Earth and the songless," Kith began. "He's a collector of all things human, including humans themselves. He's amassed quite the repository and will procure almost anything in trade for goods from the other side of the Weave."

"Well, we certainly have a lot he'll be interested in then," Remi began, starting to rifle through her pack. "Do we need an introduction? He should be thrilled to meet us..." she trailed off, noticing everyone else looking at her. "What?"

"It won't be your things he's most interested in," Brennan said grimly. "Didn't you catch that? He collects humans. Songless. Like us. Like your mother."

"Oh," it wasn't so much a word as the sound of shock. Remi pulled back into herself a little.

"So the question isn't so much how we get in as how we avoid getting added to the collection," Brennan said, turning back to Kith. "Is that the plan you have in mind?"

"Something like that," the Dunsinae rumbled. "I have a long standing trade relationship with Terracatan on behalf of your father," Kith made a little bow towards Thane. "We can enter his lands without arousing suspicion, and you would be a much honored guest. Most of the Sang's best pieces have come from Lord de Argos."

"Wait, your dad trades with the elf that has my mom?" Remi pointed at Thane, her eyebrows drawn down as Paka growled from behind Brennan and Jaeger hissed.

"Can't you control it?" Kith bellowed, jabbing a finger toward Remi and glaring at Thane. "That kind of language is more than offensive, it could get us all killed."

"It again?" Remi's lip curled back in a snarl. "You stupid buffalo. Oh, and a buffalo is a giant wild cow with a tiny brain!"

"Enough," Brennan's calm voice cut through, but Kith overrode it.

"Do you want to know how useful you are here, songless chit?" he snapped. "Humans who end up trapped on Shae generally die within one day. Those who survive are servants, and pathetic ones. They have no power, no song, and no strength. They exist here to amuse us, and once they cease to be amusing they cease to be. If your mother is alive it is because she has found a way to amuse the Sang. Care to guess how?" Kith stared into both Remi's eyes with one of his.

Remi had risen to one knee and was breathing rapidly through her nose with occasional gasps that sounded like sobs. Thane wasn't sure if she was going to attack the Dunsinae with her fingernails or burst into tears. He started to rise, but felt a cool hand on his arm. It was Iselle. Her eyes were closed and she sat with her knees bent and legs crossed.

Kith broke eye contact first. "Bah," he grumbled, shifting his position and shaking his large hairy head uncomfortably. "I dislike this whole thing."

"You dislike it," Remi muttered under her breath, lowering herself back down. She rubbed her arms with her hands, crossing them in front of her and sniffed. Iselle took her hand and its reassuring coolness off of Thane's arm and reached into her pocket.

"Is it not a little too convenient that Ruan de Argos, who sent us here, just happens to have a standing trade arrangement with the very Sang we are here to infiltrate?" Iselle asked quietly. Remi sniffed and gave the other girl a small smile, and Iselle passed something to Remi behind Thane's back while all the others were looking at Kith for an answer.

Kith blinked. "Terracatan pays high prices for anything that comes from Earth. Lord de Argos is currently on Earth, in a position to gather and trade any number of such items. How would they not be aware of each other?" He snorted, shaking his head and taking another bite of his food.

"That makes sense," Brennan conceded. "You're the broker, Thane is the owner, and we're to be the high quality items for barter?"

"Essentially," Kith agreed around a mouthful of food. He swallowed, and nodded deferentially towards Thane. "You'll be invited to stay for several days as an honored guest. Shadow though he may be, Terracatan wouldn't dare insult my Lord de Argos by showing his son any less than the very best hospitality."

"So he won't slit our throats while we sleep," Finn said. It wasn't quite a question.

Kith seemed to ponder that for a moment. "Not unless he feels it would serve his purpose better to do so. We'll need to make sure we're more useful to him alive, or that our deaths would cause too much backlash to be worth it. We should reach the edge of his estate lands in the morning."

"How do you speak English?" Twitch's head popped out from over the edge of his hammock.

"It is the current language of my master," Kith's flat teeth tore another chunk out of the brown plant. He chewed while he added, "all the servants of de Argos have been required to alter their Song enough to speak it. English," and he said the word as though the food in his mouth tasted sour, "is fashionable among the high ranks this century."

"Lucky for us," Brennan murmured.

"Oof," Jaeger fell backwards off Iselle's pack, both his red claws held against his distended tummy. "Aye love a good meal."

"How many did you eat?" Finn demanded, searching through his own pack. Then he cursed. "I have none left!"

Paka chortled, her green eyes appearing over Brennan's shoulder. "If you cannot guard your own food, that is your fault, not his."

"No one sleeps downwind of Jaeger," Brennan ordered before turning back to Kith. "That's a plan to get us in. What's our exit strategy?"

Kith shrugged. "If we find the songless you're looking for we can barter for it- her," he corrected after swinging his head to look at Thane. "I have sent Jena to gather enough of an escort to arrive in a position of power and with additional goods in trade. Unless you were willing to make a direct exchange." He gestured with a hairy paw towards the girls sitting on either side of Thane. "They are young with symmetrical features. One of them would be more than sufficient to trade for a used human female."

"No," Thane spoke quickly, jumping in and holding out a hand to placate Remi without even looking at her.

Kith sighed. "Pity. That would be the simplest."

"I thought you were supposed to be a good guy," the anger was clear, even though Remi's voice was calm. "A fae."

Kith rose to his feet abruptly, his hooves churning up the dirt as his front and back legs straightened independently. He glowered down at Remi. "You believe you are qualified to determine what is *good*, songless?" He spread his arms, indicating all the others as they sat within the circle of pale yellow light, lost in the center of the red darkness. "All these risk their lives, their very existence, because *you* decided your mother's life was more valuable than theirs. Every moment they spend here on Shae will make it harder for them to return to your weak Earth. Many of them may die. The heir of my Lord de Argos and the interests of my Lord here may suffer and servants of both the ancients and the Sang will be punished for misdeeds. So yes, weak and selfish child, I would prefer trading one human life for another. You may be too spoiled to understand, but every choice you make affects every life around you. And I am not ashamed to give you that truth. Bah!" the giant beast made a cutting gesture with his hand. His shaggy head swung back and forth as he turned his back to them. "I will take first watch. I'm too disgusted for sleep.

The Dunsinae stalked away, his cloven hoofs leaving deep prints in the soil. The rest of the group said nothing as he disappeared from sight.

"*Buuuaaarrrrrrrrpp*," Jaeger belched. He patted his tummy and giggled. "The big cow has no idea how to play with humans."

"Dunsinae live lonely lives," Paka's voice purred in the darkness. "They have no pack to run with."

"He's right, though," Remi said. Her voice sounded small, and weaker than the dim light trying to hold the night back. "The rest of you have to go back. I can't ask you--"

"Too late for that," Brennan cut in. "We're already here."

"Why are you here?" Finn asked. "The big fella's right; this is a lot of danger and rule-breaking for you Sanctum mercs. Aren't you more about order and the ultimate good, or some other idealistic idiocy?"

"Idealistic idiocy is our craft and trade," Brennan said with a smile. Thane knew Brennan was lying. He also knew there were other members of Major Gage's team out here, and he remembered what Jaeger had told Brennan about them finding something. Something important.

He opened his mouth to ask about it but Iselle jabbed him in the ribs hard enough to make him grunt. "Are you *fin*-ished?" she asked, pushing her finger against his side again as she over-emphasized the wrong syllable. Thane blinked at her. Behind him, Remi made a surprised sound.

"Yes," Remi answered her, "but I'm thirsty."

"As am I," Iselle said, and rose to her feet. "Brennan, are the purifiers prepared?"

Brennan nodded. "I put enough in the stream to give us water for tonight. After you get your drinks reset them so we have water to fill the canteens tomorrow. Take Thane with you to help carry back enough for everyone else."

"Yes sir," Iselle jerked her chin in a small nod instead of saluting before walking away. Remi rose and followed her.

Thane blinked before jumping to his feet to go after them. He heard Brennan engaging Finn in conversation about tactics and strategies for Terracatan's estate, and hesitated to listen. This could be important.

"Come on!" Remi waved to him impatiently, and when he didn't come fast enough to suit her she went back and grabbed him by the arm.

Iselle was at the stream, taking a deep drink from a thin silver cylinder. Four more flashed under the rushing water as Remi's flashlight skirted across them, and she crouched and took another. She poured some water into her mouth and made a face. "It's bitter."

"The dark moonlight makes it so," Iselle said, swallowing more. "It only affects the taste, though, so it is safe enough."

"I think we should go back, Brennan was starting to plan what exactly we should do when we arrive--" Thane began, but Remi cut him off.

"Brennan is keeping Finn distracted so Iselle can talk to us without him hearing, dummy," Remi whispered. The burbling of the stream was loud enough Thane almost didn't hear her.

"You are right," Iselle smiled a grim smile. "There are things you both need to know, that we are safe to discuss here, on this side of the Weave. Things that have the same kind of protection on them that your father's name carries," she nodded toward Thane. "Those cannot cross the barrier, and so now I can tell you why we agreed to this. Why so many of us came. And why we were willing to accept assistance even from Ruan de Argos, who's goals are so often in opposition with those of Sanctum." The French girl lowered her voice even more and Thane and Remi leaned in to listen.

Thane was momentarily distracted by how very close his face was to the faces of two girls. He breathed in slowly, trying to keep his face from flushing or from doing anything else stupid. His mind wandered a little towards just what stupid things those might be, but he jerked it back harshly.

"Major Gage's mission was classified at the highest levels," Thane forced himself to pay attention to Iselle's words and not that he was close enough to feel her breath on his face when she spoke. "The Council was afraid it would cause panic if it was widely known what they had been sent to retrieve. It was a Ksi team, small and targeted with the best information gatherers and operatives and Major Gage was asked to participate specifically because she was purely human. No one was to know anything about it and their mission was to be pure reconnaissance, information collection only, lasting only a few days. But once they'd crossed over, they never came back." The way she held onto her "r" sounds almost sounded like Paka purring.

"What did they find?" Remi asked. Thane gave himself a mental shake. Remi and Iselle were his friends. He needed to focus. Pay attention, brain.

"The lost shuttle," Iselle said. "The final piece of the Weaver's Loom."

"A shuttle? Like a bus?" Remi asked.

Iselle shook her head. "No, it is named after a part of a loom that weavers will use to make cloth."

"So the Weaver used an actual loom to make the universe?" Thane was confused.

"The name is symbolic. Each of the implements were given a name by the Sylphie when she brought them back from beyond the stars," Iselle explained. "I think she tried to make the concept simpler to explain."

"But what is it?" Thane took another drink of the foul tasting water and regretted it.

"How many pieces are there?" Remi asked at almost the same moment.

"What it is doesn't matter nearly as much as what it does," Iselle glanced around, and lowered her voice even more. "There are nine separate implements in three sets of three. With the proper pieces and enough power, Sanctum could repair the Weave and separate us from the Shae."

Thane rocked back on his heels, shocked. "But we can't do that!" Iselle hissed at him and made a cutting motion with her hand. Thane took a deep breath and tried to speak quietly. "Brennan said that closing the Weave would kill every person with any Shae blood."

"Sanctum doesn't want to use it," Iselle clarified. "But such a thing represents an enormous threat. Because it exists, someone must have it. It would be best if that someone was an organization sworn to prevent it from ever being used and with enough backing to enforce that oath. Don't you agree?"

"You're not just here to rescue my mom, you're on some sort of mission?" Remi seemed both angry and relieved.

"Our lives and our choices here are not your responsibility," Iselle said.

Remi gave a shaky little chuckle. "I don't know whether to be happy that you would've come anyway or mad that you played me. Did you know about this?" she asked, turning to Thane.

"He knew nothing. Every choice and sacrifice he made was only to save Major Gage," Iselle spoke before Thane could. The French girl smiled. "We deliberately kept him in the dark because he is such an awful liar."

"Well now I know," said Thane, exasperated.

"You do," Iselle eyed them both. "Do not let on to anyone that there is more going on here than before. For all we know, Ruan de Argos already knows about the shuttle and is only helping us to retrieve it for himself. Sang like Terracatan would start wars and destroy millions of lives to have such a bargaining chip. Only Major Gage should know of its location. We must find and extract them both."

"You kids done yet?" Finn's voice reached them from the camp clearing, making them all jump. "The rest of us are still thirsty."

"One moment," Iselle called back, and hurried to fill the canteens. She held one out in each hand to Thane and Remi, but did not release them when they grabbed the containers. "They must not know," her eyes flashed with something that reminded Thane of Paka, defiant and a little wild.

"I'm here to rescue my mom. That's it," Remi answered, and Thane nodded. Iselle held them back a moment longer, then dropped her hands. She replaced the purifiers in the stream before picking up the last full canteen and the three returned to the rest of the group.

Finn waggled his eyebrows at Thane. "Well done, kid," he said. "Nice to be the son of the boss, right?"

Thane gave the man a blank look, which only made him laugh and take the water.

"Cut the chatter, we need to rest up," Brennan ordered, and Finn shrugged. "I'll take first watch with Twitch, then Iselle and Jaeger, and Finn and Paka. Kith's out there somewhere but he's going to need some time to cool off so we won't count on him."

"What about us?" Remi asked. Thane nodded.

"You two get some sleep," Brennan ordered. Remi started to protest but he cut her off. "Tomorrow is going to be a long and emotionally charged day, most of all for you two. I need you at your best and I get that by you being rested. And," he stretched out the word, staring down at Remi, "tomorrow we will be in hostile territory among enemy Shae will full access to their Song. I do not need complications and I will not have time to explain myself. This is the last time you get to question an order. Got it?"

Remi scowled, but nodded. Brennan waited, giving her the chance to say something else, but she held her tongue. "Goodnight, everyone. Twitch?"

Thane's roommate rolled himself out of the hammock he'd holed up in. Twitch was still twitcher than Thane had ever seen him, but Brennan immediately began questioning him about the three moons and their cycles and what theories the genius had already come up with. They carried their quiet conversation out passed the small circle of light.

"Brennan is a good leader," Paka noted as she began to extinguish the lanterns. The clearing grew dark. "He does much to understand his pack."

Finn grunted and crawled into a hammock. Thane noted that Paka had maneuvered herself to stand between Ruan's merc and Remi, Iselle, and himself, forcing Finn to sleep in the leaf furthest from theirs. He followed her lead and placed himself in a bed on the other side of the circle, so there would be at least two people between the stranger and the girls.

Paka gave him an approving nod before circling the ground in the center. She stretched and curled up on the soft ground. Jaeger lay in a heap near her, already snoring off his feast of a week's worth of MREs. Iselle and Remi climbed into their beds and were hidden from view by the green edges of the leaves.

Thane pulled himself into his own surprisingly sturdy natural hammock. The air was still oppressively warm and wet so he didn't miss having a blanket, and even though the fibers of the plant were thick and rough it was still more comfortable than sleeping on a single thin mattress on a concrete floor. All things considered, Thane was pretty comfortable. He closed his eyes and tried to not worry about what would happen tomorrow.

There were so many things that could go wrong he didn't have time in one night to worry about them all anyway.

CHAPTER 14

The bright sunlight wasn't what woke him, although it stung his eyes before they were even open. Something was sitting on his nose. He tried to brush it away, but the moment his hand drew close it squeaked.

"Don't kill me!" Jena pleaded, and Thane froze. He opened his eyes and saw that his dragon talons were close enough that the little creature had to lean away from them to keep her wings from being punctured on the tips.

He lowered his hand carefully. "Jena?" He blinked, trying to wake up enough to process. Sleeping in the unfamiliar shape of the hammock had made his back and neck stiff, and he rolled his shoulders to loosen them.

"Yes Lord de Argos, heir of de Argos, I'm back!" she chirped.

"Just Thane," he mumbled, trying to roll over.

The pointed tips of her fingers pricked his nose like tiny thorns as she grabbed it and leaned her face closer, peering into one of his eyes. "Nay, Lord," she whispered, "Here and now you are Lord de Argos, son of the ancient, and I have brought you your army!" She released him on the last word and shot upwards, flinging her arms out.

Thane followed her with his eyes and then sat up.

"Hail Lord de Argos!" a chorus of voices shouted, startling him so much that he fell backwards out of his hammock.

Brennan caught him before he could land on his backside in the dirt. "Hail, mighty Lord," Brennan said, bowing. He straightened and brushed the remaining fingers of his right hand through his red hair. "Apparently your escort has arrived."

Standing just outside the clearing was an assorted array of Shac. Kith stood at their head, front hoof pawing the ground and holding a dark grey spear in one hand and wearing a bright blue sash across his chest. "I apologize, my Lord de Argos, for our tardiness and being so few in number. This was as many as could gather here by first light. More will join us as we progress."

"Um," Thane said, looking at them all and being rendered incoherent by the sheer number of people watching him, waiting for him to say something. There seemed to be thousands of them. He wished for the anonymity of the cold basement in his parents' house.

"We have disappointed our Lord in our weakness," Kith proclaimed, and beat the butt of the spear on the ground. It made a hollow booming noise and the gathered assembly dropped to their knees, or whatever the closest approximation was for each of them.

Thane was torn between staring and finding somewhere to hide. Paka sauntered over to him on all fours and made a deep movement that looked like a cross between a bow and a stretch. "It would be unwise to kill any of them just yet, my liege," she purred, looking up at him. Her back was to the rest of them so only Thane saw her wink. "But my liege is all wise and will determine whether we should break camp and continue or if we may wait here further to dispense punishment."

"Kill the skinny ones!" Jaeger crowed, doing flips in the air and flying over Thane's new entourage. Some of them flinched, and Thane saw they were truly frightened.

That made him angry. "Get up," he said, "I'm not killing anyone, you're fine."

"For now," Paka added. Thane shot her a dirty look.

The assembled Shae were rising to their feet and now that he wasn't so intimidated Thane realized there were only about twenty of them, although it was hard to tell among all the flower stems. "This small token guard will escort us through the lands of Terracatan," Kith explained, bowing deep. "We will break your camp and distribute your supplies if that is your wish, Lord heir."

Thane nodded, not trusting himself to say anything. Twitch and Remi were barely visible coming back on the path from the stream, and her eyes were wide as they took in the assembly gathered before Thane. Twitch barely glanced at them. With a few swift orders the Shae broke apart, gathering up the gear strewn across the ground and hung from ropes and packed with such speed it seemed as though they made the supplies evaporate. Jaeger and Jena played a complicated game of tag in the air above them, and Thane hoped it was a friendly one.

"A word, my liege?" Paka said, her feline form bowing in front of him. Thane nodded and she rose, indicating he should walk in front of her. When they had walked far enough to be out of earshot but still in sight of Thane's brand new pack of minions, Paka rose to her hind legs and stood, her back to the crowd.

Brennan came to join them. "You're doing fine," he assured Thane, also standing so that the servants of de Argos couldn't see his face. "But I suppose you've never taken a public speaking class?"

The bottom dropped out of Thane's stomach. He gulped and shook his head no, and tried to stop his hands from shaking. Crossing into another universe through a dark portal knowing they would probably die was one thing, but having to be in front of all those people was something he didn't think he could face.

"Didn't think so," Brennan said. "It's okay, kid, we'll figure something out."

"You should designate a speaker," Paka suggested. Brennan's smile brightened but Thane was confused and nervous about anything that even indicated speaking.

He couldn't even ask the question, but Brennan came to his rescue. "A speaker is a special and highly favored servant for high ranking individuals," he explained. "People too important to sully themselves by speaking to those below them have a speaker act as their mouthpiece, and do the talking for them."

"So I wouldn't have to say anything?" Thane grasped onto that thought, trying to steady his nerves.

Brennan chuckled. "Right. You'd whisper in their ear and they would talk for you. Although in this case, since you have the least tactical knowledge and field experience, you may just want to fake the whisper and leave the actual decision making to us."

"Great. I'm in. You're the talker," Thane said to Brennan, heaving a sigh of relief so huge he felt like it came from his soul.

Brennan shook his head. "Not me," he said. "They wouldn't accept it." He gestured back towards where the retainers waited patiently, supplies stowed and distributed. "It should be someone who is much more visibly Shae than I am."

A whoop and a cackle sounded overhead. The imp had caught the pixie and was holding her in two hands, shaking her like a pair of dice. "Tell me you don't mean Jaeger," Thane said.

Brennan and Paka laughed. "No, although that would be fun to watch. From a distance," Brennan amended. "I was thinking Paka."

The panther woman bowed from the waist. "Would that be acceptable to you, my liege Lord?" she purred.

"Stop that. Of course it would," Thane said, discomfited by her deference.

She laughed. "Just getting into character. Do not worry, packmate," she grinned at him and gave him that fisted salute over her heart, the one she'd given him when they'd talked about finding a place to belong in what seemed so long ago, "I swear to protect you with fang and claw, with mind and heart, as a brother and a packmate." She twisted her fist and stretched out her arm, opening her fingers right before contact and pressing the pads of her paw on Thane's chest. "By my name, I so swear."

Thane blinked. Even Brennan's eyes widened and he pulled in a sharp breath, which more than the oath or Paka's solemnity told Thane that this was a big deal. Brennan recovered, and started wiggling his mouth. It took Thane several moments before he realized Brennan was trying to tell him something. Thane repeated the words that Brennan fed to him.

"As a brother and a packmate, I," he squinted, and Brennan shaped the word again," acknowledge this covenant and accept your name." Then without prompting, Thane mirrored the gesture that Paka had made.

He gently placed his hand just under the point where her collarbones met, spreading his talons wide so the claw tips wouldn't touch her. She breathed in and so did he, and for the barest hint of a moment Thane thought he heard distant music.

He was so startled he dropped his hand. "Did you hear that?" he demanded of Brennan and Paka. They both shook their heads, but Paka looked smug in the way that only a feline can.

"We are family now," she said, and then gave him a wicked smile full of pointed teeth. "And you just became my little brother."

Brennan snorted. "All right, we've been away long enough. We'll walk back now. Thane, you go first. Wherever we go from now until we get home you go first. Paka will be immediately behind your right shoulder and I will follow you both. We are now your personal escort."

Thane and Paka nodded, and Brennan bowed and gestured back toward the group. Thane swallowed and took one long, slow breath, in through his nose and then back out the way Charlie had taught him. Find your calm, find your center. Everything else will slide off. He squared his shoulders and lifted his chin, doing his best to imitate his grandfather's borderline arrogance. "I can do this," he breathed. He had the dragon inside, the power and the bloodline. He could fake this for a few days.

He started back towards where Kith waited at the head of the Shae. Remi stood with Iselle and the other humans off to one side, and all eyes were on their approach. The closer they drew the harder it was for Thane to maintain his equilibrium. Everyone was watching him.

The air felt heavy and wet all over again, like he had only barely come through the tear. Each breath was a fight, every footstep a struggle, until he physically couldn't move forward any more. Thane stopped, and there was silence.

He felt more than heard Paka move behind him. "I am the speaker of Lord Thane de Argos," she began, and inside Thane's heart thumped. Is that who he was now? "He will speak through me who has been proven loyal by blood, by fire, and by spirit. I am Usiku Paka, and you will hear my voice."

Her formal tone and the weight of her pronouncement landed on the assembled Shae and they bowed underneath it. Only Thane heard Brennan mumble behind him, "Don't overdo it, cat."

"Rise," Paka said, "and form up. We depart for the lands of Terracatan. Hail, de Argos!"

"Hail, de Argos!" the chorus of voices shouted in a cacophony of sound as they rose. Kith held the spear in the air and spun on his back hooves, clumps of dirt flying, and turned the group into a procession. The huge beast led the others forward towards Thane and then around in a wide oval, surrounding he and his friends.

Once they had all turned away and began to make their way through the thick forest Thane's shoulders slumped slightly. "I don't know if I can do this," he mumbled to Paka.

"You'll be fine, little brother," she patted his shoulder, and then pushed it forward. "Now get going. We've got a long way to walk today."

As they passed their former campsite, Remi, Iselle, Twitch, and Finn fell in with them. "I'm liking this servants thing," Remi said, putting the palms of both hands on her lower back and stretching. Thane noticed none of them were carrying any gear except Finn. He kept his canvas bag slung across his back, and he noticed Thane looking at it. He stared back, daring Thane to say anything about it.

Thane did what he did best and stayed quiet. Iselle handed him a piece of fruit from last night and he ate it gratefully while walking, mind spinning with everything that still lay ahead.

By unspoken agreement no one talked for the next several hours as they traveled through the ever-changing shadows of the flower forest. The humid air soaked their clothes within minutes. Thane could feel sweat dripping down the back of his neck and sliding around his eyebrows. Ahead of him, a downward triangle of perspiration darkened the back of Twitch's shirt. The ground swelled under their feet, growing higher and steeper as they climbed the hills where the tall blooms grew and hung heavy in the sunlight. The honor guard of Shae around them made little noise as they traveled, but Thane noticed several of them casting glances his way.

They always lowered their eyes immediately when he glanced at them, some with wide eyes and furrowed brows, others with narrowed glares and curled lips.

"What's with all the death glares?" Remi muttered under her breath. Thane saw her glance around at their escort, narrowing her eyes back and lifting her chin in defiance.

"They dislike humans," Iselle whispered. She was facing straight ahead, but the look in her eyes was unfocused and distant, as though she was looking beyond the horizon. "They blame the songless for all the unease in this world, for the disruption of their Song. And now the son of their long awaited Lord has arrived and instead of embracing them and leading them, he looks like and consorts with the lowest."

"You didn't say you could read minds," Remi accused in a low whisper, darting nervous glances at their escorts.

Iselle sighed. "I can not. Some of them are emoting so strongly it is hard not to figure out why." She breathed in deeply through her nose and exhaled the same way. "Do not let me fall?" she said to Twitch, who nodded and placed a hand on her shoulder.

She closed her eyes and let her arms fall limp at her sides so they barely swung as she continued to walk. Thane couldn't imagine walking through a strange forest with his eyes closed. He'd hit something. Iselle kept her natural grace as she moved, and the edges of her body seemed to shimmer in the watery light.

Remi sighed. Above them, Jaeger's jagged crisscrossing through the sky smoothed into lazy circles. Around them, the angry stares became sullen, then disinterested as the various Shae turned away from Thane and his friends. Some started quiet conversations. Others shifted weapons from at the ready to resting on shoulders. Even Kith, at the head of the column, lowered his silver spear and relaxed his rigid posture. If only a little bit.

Brennan moved up from his position behind Thane to hand Iselle a canteen full of water. "See? Useful," he said to Remi with a little grin. Remi snorted and tossed her hair as she turned away. Brennan chuckled.

Iselle drank deep from the canteen. She didn't open her eyes until she handed it back to Brennan. Thane could see how pale her cheeks were from the side, but when she turned and lifted her lids her eyes were such a bright violet that he flinched away, surprised.

She noticed, and turned away from him, allowing her blond hair to fall over her face as she looked down at her feet. Remi muttered something under her breath that Thane didn't catch. He looked at her, but she shook her head and kept walking.

Thane glanced down at the timer he wore on his wrist, the one Ruan had given him so that he could keep track of how long they had before the tear was repaired. "How much longer until we get there?" he wondered out loud.

Startled glances from around the Shae greeted his words, and too late Thane realized he'd said he wasn't going to talk to them. He started to flush, uncomfortable warmth rising in his face.

Before the silence could get too awkward, Paka sprang forward and ran to Kith. "The heir of de Argos wishes to know how much longer until we reach the lands of Terracatan, the Sang."

Kith's huge wedge shaped head gazed upward for a moment, assessing the landscape or maybe praying for patience, Thane wasn't sure which. "If we continue through the heat of high sun, we will arrive at the portal to his estate to be announced at the evening meal," the beast answered.

"Distribute plenty of water, and an extra ration of food," Paka ordered. "Our liege tires of the endless scenery. We will continue the march."

Kith shouted an order and the Shae burst into a flurry of activity. Without halting their forward progression, they opened packs and unslung bags to pull out food and water. They distributed the supplies amongst themselves and began to eat and drink. The meal seemed to loosen their tongues and calm their anxiety, and the few muted conversations grew into several louder ones.

"My liege," a raspy voice spoke near Thane's elbow. He jerked his head around but didn't see anyone. Until he looked down.

Behind him and on his left was an iguana. An enormous iguana, walking on only its hind legs, and holding out a tray. Thane bit his tongue trying to not scream and instead made a sort of gurgle in the general direction of the lizard, who bowed towards him without breaking stride.

It didn't speak again, but indicated the tray with its long bumpy snout. Thane glanced down and saw that it was bringing him food, as well as a sealed container with what he assumed must be water. He picked up something that looked like dark brown bread and took a bite. It was soft, chewy, and sweet, with the texture of a brownie but with a smooth, nutty flavor.

"This is good," he mumbled, taking a larger bite. "What is it?"

The iguana sucked in a breath between its teeth, making a distressed hissing sound. Thane flinched away involuntarily, and his sudden movement seemed to startle the reptile as it jerked away and wide fins spread out on either side of its head like those small dinosaurs Thane had seen in a movie they'd shown at school.

"Don't spit on me," he stammered. The ones in the movie spat poison.

Between one blink and the next a furry black form interposed itself between Thane and the small Shae. "Be gone, worm," Paka hissed, and cuffed the iguana thing on the side of the head. "You have displeased him."

"What? No," Thane began, but before he could protest further Iselle placed her cool hand on his arm and shook her head, slightly. Thane snapped his mouth shut. Still with fur bristling, Paka thrust her claw out and pointed. The little reptilian Shae fled into the surrounding guard and vanished from view, and all the other beasts and creatures stiffened their posture and adjusted grip on their weapons.

Paka bowed low while still walking, and in a sinuous continued motion dropped to all fours and prowled next to him with her fangs bared and tail lashing. She seemed furious. Thane quashed both the impulse to flinch away from her and the one to pat her on the head, certain that either would get his head bitten off. And he wasn't entirely sure that thought was just a metaphor.

"She is enjoying 'erself," Iselle's whisper barely carried to his ears. Thane glanced aside towards her, but she seemed to be looking around at the sky, the tree flowers, anywhere but towards him. "A little too much, perhaps. But do not be upset with 'er- 'ad she not stepped in, you would 'ave been required to administer punishment." Her soft accent dropped the "h" sounds and her violet eyes made her seem as foreign and strange as Kith or Jena when she glanced at him.

"Why?" he tried to keep his voice as low as hers. She didn't answer, instead breathing in a slow and measured breath as though she was in pain. He opened his mouth to repeat the question, but she shook her head and moved away.

Thane took a step to follow her, but Jaeger's shout cut through the air above. "Aye see it! The gates of Terracatan lie ahead!"

Kith raised a horn to his shaggy head and blew one low note. The Shae around them halted, and the humans casually drew closer together in the center of the circle. Finn loosened his weapons in their sheaths. Brennan rolled his shoulders, and even Twitch raised his head and looked around with measured interest.

The moose centaur with the buffalo head paced back to Thane and bowed. "We will bargain with the guards to open the gates, young lord," his basso rumble enveloped Thane. "It would be best now for you to travel unseen until we arrive at the doors to the house itself. We do not want word of the arrival of the heir to de Argos to travel beyond Terracatan's borders, particularly as far as the thunder lands."

"The thunder lands?" Remi asked. Something strange in her voice made Thane look towards her, concerned. She was pale. Her hands shook. He hadn't heard her speak in what felt like hours and now she sounded tense, almost thin and brittle. Iselle flinched when Remi spoke and the violet eyes closed briefly while Remi's brown ones were wide with dilated pupils.

Kith growled but Paka answered the question before Kith could decide not to. "Where the dragons are, human chit. And from this point on do not speak unless you are addressed directly and you are given permission to answer." The feline's words grew angrier until she spat out the last words as though they were poison.

Thane was startled, but anger flashed across Remi's face and her fists clenched, color flooding back into her cheeks. Surprisingly, though, she did not reply. Iselle let out a long breath and Jaeger backflipped through the air until he landed heavy on Remi's shoulder. "We are not yet to his gates, but four strides more and the tree cover grows thin enough to be seen from the distance."

Kith spoke several phrases in a deep, guttural language that Thane was positive his vocal chords could never reproduce. Four of the larger Shae dropped their packs to the ground. Several smaller creatures swarmed around them, pulling swaths of fabric and flexible poles from inside. Thane saw the iguana that had tried to serve him lunch. The reptile was carefully not looking in his direction and hid from view the moment the Shae had finished.

On the ground in front of Thane was now a strange sort of chair. It had four legs that attached at the bottom to long poles, which lay on the ground like a huge tic-tac-toe board. The chair itself was draped in sheets of blue, silver, and green fabric that hung over the sides and pooled on the grass below. Two more poles with a simple square frame attached at the top were placed behind the chair with fabric hung across them to create a sort of awning.

Behind him, Remi snorted. Thane glanced back over his shoulder at her just in time to see her, eyes still tight with repressed anger, hide her smirk as she eyed the shimmering rich cloth. Even Iselle smiled faintly, although it didn't touch her eyes, and Brennan looked bemused.

Everyone was looking at him, Thane realized. He shrank back and hunched his shoulders unconsciously under their scrutiny until something sharp poked his toe.

"Get in the chair," Paka hissed under her breath, not looking at him. Instead she was glaring around the circle, her slitted pupils expanding and contracting and her feline lips pulled back to expose her fangs. Louder, she announced, "This dretch is hardly worth the notice of the son of chaos. Is this truly the best offering you bring?"

The surrounding Shae flinched, lowering their eyes. That feeling of being watched, being trapped, lifted from Thane as they looked away like ropes loosening from a captive. He took several quick steps towards the chair. He paused in front of it, glancing at Paka, who growled and spat towards his father's servants while behind her back she made a motion for him to sit.

He sat, the chair shifting slightly underneath him. Paka had apparently decided it was dangerous to give him time to change his mind because the moment Thane's weight was off his feet the Pantera gestured to Kith, who gave another command in the language that sounded like far away earthquakes. Four of the largest Shae stepped forward and surrounded him. Thane froze like a sparrow before a cobra, fight or flight instincts screaming at him to flee, attack, disappear, and claw off their faces all at once.

But they turn away almost at the same moment and bent to pick up the poles. Thane was thrown backwards into the billowing fabric. Green and silver filled his vision and loose cloth wrapped around his arms as he struggled to regain his balance and not fall out, which was made immeasurably more difficult as the chair jounced and jerked as the Shae holding him in the air responded to more shouted orders from Kith by raising or lowering the pole ends they held.

There was a thump as several pounds of weight landed on one corner of the awning and the chair tilted nauseatingly. Swaths of fabric were pulled from Thane's arms and suddenly Jaeger's face filled his vision, the red leather skin and wrinkles stretching as the imp's mouth stretched in a grin and exposed quadruple rows of pointed teeth.

"Found hyu, little chaos lordling!" Jaeger chortled.

Thane found himself grinning slightly in return as he swatted the flying devil monkey with his claws. After being in the Shaerealm so long, Jaeger's was at least a familiar strangeness. "Get off my chair," he said.

Jaeger gave a mocking upside-down bow and launched himself upwards, jarring the chair again. "The gates of Terracatan lay before," he crowed. "They open and shut and eat hyu up, and we'll find home no more!"

Thane's grin vanished as his eyes tracked down from where Jaeger flew to the landscape below him. The giant flower trees had thinned enough that he had a clear view for several miles ahead, or he would have if there hadn't been something in the way.

Dark and enormous enough to feel more like a cliff than any wall, the gates of the lands belonging to the shadow Terracatan loomed ahead. The stone they were made of didn't shine in the sunlight; instead their dull gray seemed to pull the light in rather than reflecting it back and the land touching the wall seemed darker than the grassy expanse on the hill.

The entire group of mercenaries and Shae halted as one, even though no order had been given and Kith hadn't looked back at them. There was a low rumbling noise to Thane's right, and he glanced towards it. Paka was growling. The fur on the back of her neck bristled, sticking out in all directions. Beyond her, several of the Shae shifted on their feet and Brennan's hand moved towards his belt. Twitch started blinking and alternately tapping his knee and scratching at his nose.

"Are you all right?" Iselle's whisper brushed Thane's ear, and he leaned forward and craned his neck around to look back to where her hand hovered over Remi's shoulder, not quite touching it. Remi looked pale. Thane could see her hands shaking as she swallowed several times, but she still glared at Iselle.

"I'm fine," Remi answered without moving her teeth and stepped away from the other girl. Iselle immediately dropped her hand.

Finn snorted. "Are we going or not?" he asked, and moved his bag from one shoulder to the other.

Kith shook his shaggy head and bowed back toward Thane. "At your word, lord-son," he said.

Thane sat back inside his curtained chair as he felt all those eyes turn towards him again. No one spoke, not even Paka, although her growl had faded into silence. Through the open rectangle at the front Thane could see Kith, the monstrous wedge shaped head turned to one side so the deep brown eye could watch him. Thane had the random impression that the eye looked sad. But that was impossible- Kith was huge and powerful, and this was his world. He had nothing to fear. It wasn't his mother that was in danger.

It was Remi's. He thought about her pale face and shaking hands. Thane raised his arm and jabbed his index finger out to point at the wall. "Go," he said, and it didn't quite sound like his voice. It sounded just a little deeper, just a little stronger, just a little more like the voice that would match the scaled blue fist and the extended cobalt claw that glittered in the sunlight beyond the edge of his awning.

The assembled Shae let out a wordless shout and lunged forward, moving more quickly through the late afternoon light.

It took most of the next hour to draw close enough to the walls for the sentries to hail them. The heavy stone seemed to suck the light from the air as they drew close. Thane couldn't decide whether it was eating their shadows or turning everything to shadow around them and was staring down at the ground when the challenge came, shattering the relative quiet so abruptly and completely that Thane almost started up through the awning.

So many voices spoke it seemed every stone in the wall screamed at them, but the words were high pitched and shrill. If a thousand chickens and a thousand squirrels got into a shrieking match while chewing aluminum foil Thane thought it might've come close to that sound. He clapped his hands over his ears and squeezed his eyes shut against the agony.

One clear tone cut through the cacophony and silenced it as cleanly as if someone turned off a speaker. Thane opened his eyes slowly, ready to slam them shut again, and saw a multicolored explosion that looked like a tiny rainbow going nuclear. The echoes of the sound faded. The glowing colors popped like a soap bubble and revealed Jena hovering in the air near Kith's head.

"Shreds and shards, what was that?" Twitch hissed.

Paka pushed herself up from the ground, forearms quivering and fur sticking out far enough to triple her size. "The inugamae," she spat. "The gatekeepers. We're arrived at the door."

"And rung the doorbell," Finn observed. "So, anybody home?"

Kith roared. As one all the Shae dropped to their knees, bowing their heads and holding one arm across their foreheads as if protecting their faces. Or hiding their eyes. Even Paka prostrated herself, and Jaeger dove down from the sky.

At almost the same moment the wall directly before Thane began to dissipate. It didn't slide open or part; a section as tall and wide as a two-story house dissolved right in front of him. Thane expected to see an army of monsters with huge and twisted limbs and fangs dripping venom lurching towards them. Or maybe wraiths of mist, formed in darkness and prepared to tear their souls. At the very least he expected packs of those guard dog creatures Paka had seemed afraid of seeing.

What he didn't expect was a panda. A thin panda, or maybe a panther, it was hard to tell, but it was approximately the same height as Remi with white fur and black arms, legs, and ears. The only reason it reminded Thane of a big cat was the long black tail that it carried over one arm like a waiter with a napkin. Lanie would've loved it. Thane had a brief mental image of his youngest sister reacting to this creature, squeaking and throwing herself at it to cuddle it into submission. And probably tying a ribbon on it.

Thane felt his chair vibrating and glanced down. Two of the hulking Shae were trembling, and one other was whimpering. The fourth seemed to be trying to hold perfectly still. They were terrified.

The panda stood and watched them without moving as the last specks of the wall floated away like dust motes in sunlight. What was he waiting for? Was Thane supposed to talk first? Why wasn't Kith doing anything? Thane felt his stomach clench and his face felt hot. More of the Shae surrounding him quivered, including the iguana person who'd tried to serve him lunch. The one who'd thought Thane was going to kill him.

Cold flooded Thane's chest. Who did this teddy bear think he was to just stand there and make the other Shae, Thane's Shae, wait like this in the dirt? Make Thane's friends grovel?

"Get up," Thane growled. The chair bearers below him blinked. The frozen one jerked and looked up at him. But they stayed on the ground.

"GET UP!" Thane screamed so intensely that the words burned his throat on the way out. Kith and his Shae escort stumbled upward like puppets, shoulders and backs leading and heads flopping forward while any of those smaller than the humans scurried away.

"And you," the pole Thane grabbed for balance shattered under his fist as he spoke through his teeth towards the expressionless panda. "Let us in or get out of the way."

The panda raised an eyebrow, then pressed its hands together and bowed low, carefully keeping its long tail from touching the ground. "I beg your pardon, high one," the tenor of its voice made Thane think it must be male. "I am Semubyt, first servant of the highest of the blood, Lord Terracatan prime Sang. I have been sent to bid you welcome and lead you to his halls so that you may take meat at his table and accept the weight of his honors. I meant no disrespect," here he lifted his chin to meet Thane's eyes, but did not straighten his back. The posture made the back of Thane's neck prickle. "I was merely surprised by the... variance in your escort." Semubyt's eyes flicked across the creatures surrounding Thane before coming back to stare at him again.

Thane repressed the urge to glance around, following the same instinct predators have to not look away from other predators. The dragon inside him roared and clawed to get out and Thane relaxed his hold on the leviathan, just a little. Just enough to let it show through his eyes and in the way he pulled back his lips from his teeth in a way that was not a smile; he was tired of bullies. He did not rise to the taunt.

The other predator's posture stiffened and the Semubyt rose from his bow and used the movement to cover dropping his gaze from Thane. "Be welcome, high one, and your people." The first servant's English was flawless, down to a perfect imitation of a British accent, although the effect was somewhat spoiled when Semubyt smiled. All his teeth were pointed, too long and too thin for his round, furry face. Thane held the dragon back from bearing its own fangs in response and instead held his expression in place.

Jena chimed again, not as long or loud as the first that cut through the wall of anger and sound, but enough that everyone could clearly hear. Kith stepped forward with staff held high and the rest of the Shae followed in a staggered circle. Each of the Shae in his entourage pulled closer to Thanes chair as they passed Terracatan's first servant.

"That was mostly well done," whispered a voice near Thane's elbow. Paka strolled next to him, fur smoothed down and gait languid, completely relaxed and unaffected. Thane marveled at her control. His insides felt like oil drops in a hot pan, shaking and threatening to jump out at any moment. She glanced around as they passed by Semubyt and Thane noted how the panther woman made a point of direct eye contact with the panda man for a long moment and then sniffed and looked away.

"Mostly?" Thane mumbled through gritted teeth. He was trying to hold all his organs in place and keep his face from changing expression while also telling his fight or flight response to just shut up. He didn't have a lot of extra focus room for chatting.

Paka's tail lashed, and one of Thane's chair bearers yelped and the seat lurched slightly away from her. "Remember your place," she said, and Thane thought she was talking to the Shae underneath him until she continued. "Remember the power and influence of your father. For all that he has spent centuries as a king and ruler in your word, his word is even greater here. Remember that in the Shaerealm to be a dragon among Shae is to be a god among the ants. And the ants do not talk back."

"And the humans?" Remi asked. Paka froze. The bearers froze. And all the Shae around them became so suddenly and completely still that it felt as though the air itself held its breath in fear.

Kith, still easily the largest Shae in the company by a full head and shoulders, slowly turned and leveled his spear at her face. "The humans," he rumbled, "are dirt that the ants may make use of or remove when it is in the way." There was a streak of light and Remi gasped, holding her hand to her cheek. Jena flitted leisurely back to Kith, making a clearly obscene gesture towards Remi as she did so. Kith raised the head of his spear again and held it upright. "Know your place, dirt."

Before Remi or Thane could react, Iselle had something pressed against Remi's cheek and Brennan had her by the shoulders. Thane was silenced by the expression on Paka's face and by an oily tenor voice speaking uncomfortably close on his other side.

"Your humans are recent acquisitions, I assume?" Semubyt strolled next to his bearers. The Shae nearest the panda man started and shied away in fear, as though none had noticed him there before. Even Paka twitched, moving her head too quickly to look at him. Thane mentally upped the predator rating he'd subconsciously given Semubyt- anything that could surprise Paka was going to be more dangerous than he'd initially assumed.

"Fresh and untouched," Paka responded smoothly with no trace of her momentary unbalance. She stared forward.

"Mmmm," the first servant glanced back appraisingly at Remi and Iselle, then moved his eyes over Twitch, Brennan, and Finn. "The heavy and the girls I understand, but the other two do not seem to have much obvious purpose."

"Mmmm," Paka responded, flavoring the sound with an undertone of smug purring. "They do not, true."

Semubyt's lips pulled back in a pleased expression. "Our masters will have much to discuss. Perhaps we could negotiate in quiet corners, also?"

"Such would be a pleasure, provided all our duties have been properly executed," Paka's smug purr increased in intensity.

Semubyt bowed towards her, and then vanished without sign or sound. Again the Shae around where he had stood flinched, and several of the smaller ones cringed and drew close enough to Thane that he was momentarily concerned his bearers would step on them.

A heartbeat later Paka was back among the humans, tending to Remi and speaking in a low voice with Iselle. Thane was too far away to make out anything but the low murmur of their voices. He felt bad admitting, even to himself, that it was kind of a relief not being able to hear them because he wasn't sure he could handle much more of this trip. What had he gotten them into? Sure, this was Remi's idea, but she was trying to rescue her mom. Getting them to Shae, though? That'd been all Thane. They never would've found a way here if it hadn't been for him, never would've left Sanctum without his big plan to talk to his father the blue dragon. All these lives in his hands- well, his claws- and he couldn't even access his Song to protect them. They were trapped in a different universe traveling towards the house of an enemy, and he had nothing.

There was no way they were getting out of this alive, and it was all Thane's fault.

CHAPTER 15

Thane was standing on a small dais just inside the grand dining hall of the Terracatan estate with Kith and Jena on his right. And he was trying not to gape, or turn and run. If the sanctum cafeteria had been put in a blender with the book Arabian Nights the result would be exactly what Thane was trying not to stare at with his mouth hanging open. He knew it was important to not look like an idiot. The noise, color, and sound would each have been overwhelming by themselves but none held a candle to the variety of creatures that thronged the room, a surprising number of them holding or even wearing flameless candles.

The Sang Evarish, black skinned shadows that Tolkien would've called dark elves but here even a mention of that word would get them all killed, were the fewest but also obviously the most powerful. Their ebony dark skin was marbled with red lines in differing patterns like tiger stripes or veins of blood and they all had hair that fell down past their waists in shining waves of black and red on silver, or silver and black on red, or silver and red on black. They stood in groups of two or three and speaking in low voices with words Thane couldn't understand. No other Shae stood near them or even came close.

Then there were all the others, shadow and shade fae so numerous and varied that in the flickering light and shining colors Thane could barely tell where one creature stopped and the next began, only a constantly moving blur of wings and talons, scales and fangs, fur and tails and things he couldn't identify. And all of them, each of them, were looking at him. Not staring, but eyes from every direction and in every imaginable shape and color glancing at him and sliding away. He felt exposed. He felt sick.

"You stink," whiskers tickled his ear. Fifteen years of practicing invisibility was the only thing that kept him from fainting; he'd no idea Paka was next to him. "Every Shae in the building has the scent of your fear. Knock it off."

"Gee, thanks," Thane's chest was tight and his words came out angrily. The panther woman stood just behind his left shoulder, and he turned his head towards her. "Just the boost of confidence I needed. How do I do that, exactly, and where have you been?"

"Be still," Paka's low voice took on that extra thrum it had that sounded so much like a contented purr.

It annoyed him. "I am standing still," he said, and even he heard how close he was to breaking.

Out of sight of the crowd before them, Paka placed her five-fingered paw against his back on the lower part of his left shoulder blade. Over his heart. The incredible warmth in the pads of her hand came through the thin fabric of the shirt he wore and into his skin, and he could feel the vibrations of that deep sound come through her touch and into him.

"You have always been still on the outside, pack brother," her voice so soft that it seemed as though he heard it through their contact more than his ears. "But inside you have been a storm. In this world, you must be still in here and let the storm blow around you. The smell of your fear is strong, but so is theirs, even through their perfumes and posturing. For all the shadow and shade who wait and watch in this place, you are the only dragon."

Without conscious effort he could feel his heart beating slower and his breath growing deeper to match hers. A flash of music, all drumbeats and wildness and freedom rang through his mind like an echo and he wondered if she were using her song on him but decided he didn't care. He was remembering what Kith had said about dragons being the god among the ants. That didn't feel right to him, but he knew how to be invisible. Maybe he could keep Thane invisible here, and only let these Sang see the dragon they thought he was.

"Better, little brother, much better," Paka lowered her hand, and paused. "Remi and the others are coming. Semubyt had orders to clean us before our presentation to his lord. Don't act surprised."

"Why would I be..." Thane began, and then saw Remi and Iselle coming down the corridor behind her. Some part of his brain might have registered that Jaeger, Twitch, Brennan, and Finn were there too and that Semubyt was leading them all, but that part knew to shut up about it.

Remi and Iselle were barefoot and Thane noticed because their feet were at the ends of their legs, which had been only partly covered by flowing skirts that had slits cut several inches above their knees. Both girls were in dresses that made Thane think of Greek goddesses, with one shoulder bare. Remi's glossy brown hair had been pinned back from her face with ruby colored gems that matched the color of her lips and the fabric of her gown. Iselle's golden hair was wrapped in braids threaded with ribbons that matched both her violet eyes and her dress, but her arms were wrapped in gold filigree from her wrists to her elbows.

"You don't smell like fear now," Paka observed.

Thane felt his neck flush as heat spread through his cheeks. "Shut up, Paka," he said.

He had the small satisfaction of seeing her jaw snap closed but Terracatan's first servant was too close now for her to respond. The fang-toothed panda man made a fluid bow before Thane, but Thane still got the impression the Shae was mocking him. "I am glad you are pleased with our small efforts, high one," Semubyt spoke as he straightened, and that same other part of Thane's noted even when bowing he still kept his tail from touching the ground. "Forgive me for not staying, but I must attend to the First Lord now." Again, he disappeared between one moment and the next as though he had never been standing in front of Thane.

"I don't like that," Brennan said, and then stepped toward Thane. "How are you holding up, kid?"

Thane blinked and pulled his eyes away from Remi and Iselle. It was harder than he expected. "I'm fine." Brennan and the others finally registered in the front part of his brain. "Um, are you?"

Remi and Iselle looked like goddesses. Brennan, Twitch, and Finn looked like a five year old had convinced them to play dress up in a national museum. Brennan had a blue and green tartan kilt with gladiator shoes and a pirate shirt. Twitch had a tuxedo jacket with a half cape and green shorts with red and green suspenders that Thane knew had a name but couldn't remember. Something about the Alps. And Finn was dressed in something that looked like a cross between a samurai and a monk, flowing split robes with pants underneath and tied with a rope for a belt.

"Human fashion is all the rage here," Brennan held his hands out to indicate the three of them. "They just don't have a clear idea of what human fashion is. They tried to put Twitch in the kilt first, but he actually punched the poor guy."

Thane looked at Twitch, who was stretching and closing his fingers gingerly. "My dad's Irish," Twitch shrugged. "He'd've disowned me."

Thane was just glad that Twitch looked more like himself again, curious and conscious and paying attention. He'd been acting dazed and disoriented ever since they came through the gate into Shae; it wasn't until now that Thane realized how worried he'd been about his roommate. Twitch was almost never still. It was how he'd gotten his nickname.

"We should've tried putting you in a skirt days ago," Thane grinned at Twitch.

The tech specialist grinned back. "You're just jealous that Brennan's legs look so good in his dress."

"Yeah," Thane made a very conscious effort to not look at Remi and Iselle again. "That must be it."

"Speaking of legs, though," Twitch started, nodding towards them, "no one's going to be looking at ours anyway."

Thane's face started to flush again as he glanced at Remi, who smirked back at him, and Iselle, who struck a dramatic pose. "I may not do damsel in distress, but I can be very good at damsel as distraction," the blonde girl's soft French accent made the words seem even more suggestive. Thane choked a little.

"You'd better knock it off before his head explodes," Paka's ears swiveled around. "Terracatan's retinue approaches. Get back to your table, Thane. We need to be in place when he arrives."

That felt like a bucket of cold water to the face, washing away Thane's confusion and causing the muscles across his chest to tighten. Storm on the outside, invisible inside. He straightened his shoulders and turned back to the cacophony without blinking. Kith had placed his large bulk between Thane and his friends and the other room so that no one had seen them gather, but now stepped aside and bowed low as Thane re-entered the room and took the place at the center table on the raised dais. The murmur of the Shae around him quieted as Paka and Jaeger took places at his left, and Thane could hear the swish of fabric and soft thud of footsteps as the humans arranged themselves behind him.

All the light in the room vanished. Residual spots of light danced in Thane's vision as he blinked rapidly, trying to adjust to the darkness and be ready, but as he strained his senses against the black he realized it wasn't just his eyes that were useless; he couldn't hear anything either. No sound of cloth moving as people shifted, no murmur of conversation or even breathing. He reached for Paka at his side but couldn't move, couldn't feel.

There was a pain in his chest as his heart spasmed and raced, panic flooding him with adrenaline. For one brief flash the lightning sound burned through his mind like, well, lightning, and he reached out for it with his whole soul. But he was too slow, and it was gone.

And there was light again. Brilliant and red, burning his pupils and making his eyes water. All the other Shae, the ones that were not Sang Evarish, were gone. Instead standing alone in the center of the suddenly smaller room was one figure, black marbled lines shooting through red skin, the only Evarish with red skin Thane had ever seen.

"Welcome to my humble home, heir of de Argos," Lord Terracatan, First Lord of the Sang Evarish, spoke in a mild baritone with a suggestion of a British accent and inclined his head. Thane had expected him to spit and hiss like an animated devil, not speak like the hero in those sappy period romance movies his mom loved to watch. Those drove Thane crazy- he liked cartoons, he liked action. Not those movies where all the actors ever did was pose and talk.

He was dressed in an immaculate black tuxedo, his black and silver hair cut short above his ears and the air around him seemed to shimmer. Every other Sang in the room was on their knees before him. He raised his chin to lock eyes with Thane, and Thane felt a shock run through him down to his feet. This Evarish had perfectly human eyes. Not black on black or red on black like the others but white on the outsides with a circle of colored iris surrounding the black pupil, which widened as Thane stared at his reflection in them.

"They're blue," he said.

"Yes, today," Terracatan smiled and snapped his fingers. Instead of making any noise, light shimmered out from his hand in waves that filled the room, relighting all the candles and returning the other Evarish to their feet. Sound returned to normal as well, making Thane feel like he needed to pop his ears. Semubyt appeared just behind Terracatan as the first of the Sang began moving through the crowd towards Thane.

The black skinned Evarish parted for him, those closest bowing their chins without looking away. Terracatan accepted each nod gracefully, bestowing a word or a gesture to choice individuals like a king passing out food to the starving. Thane, however, had been to high school. He could recognize a show-off. He was also in a position to see what Terracatan didn't; that for every fawning glance towards First Lord's face there were infinitely more venomous glares and calculating sneers following him.

Thane was so busy staring at all the other Sang he almost didn't notice when Terracatan drew near and had to suppress a shudder. The human eyes were creepy to a level Thane hadn't experienced before. They looked normal, familiar, but didn't blink often enough and something about the way they focused was wrong, like the Sang had eaten the person and that dead person was staring out of the Shae at Thane.

Terracatan's eyebrows drew inward, and Thane realized those macabre eyes had him so distracted he'd completely missed whatever the First Lord had said. Great, he was already screwing this up. He'd probably get them all eaten and have their dismembered eyeballs looking out of sinister faces. The visual in his imagination made his stomach squirm.

"Has something displeased you, lordling?" Terracatan asked, and snapped his fingers. Semubyt, who had disappeared in the crowd, appeared next to and slightly behind the Sang. "Whatever disturbs him, unmake it," the First Lord of the Sang ordered, and Semubyt bowed low towards Thane.

This was getting worse. Thane glanced at Paka, who stood in the same place relative to Thane that Semubyt stood to his master. The Felidae bowed smoothly and stepped forward to look down her nose at the panda who could make himself disappear.

"My lord de Argos is unimpressed with your welcome. Was not his father in these halls welcomed by a legion of slaves assigned to answer to his whims? And yet here we see only the bloodless who gape and chatter but offer no obeisance after the sentry of these lands offered us insult at the gate. You think to offer milk to a cub and watch him dance for it, but this is the heir son of Ruan de Argos, beta thunder, Lord of Lightning and Master of Chaos. And now my lord must ponder if we do have business here, or if we should take our trade elsewhere and allow the father to make answer to the insults offered his heir."

If this was what Paka meant by being calm inside and storming outside she could teach classes to hurricanes. And Thane was pretty sure that if they were all killed now at least it wouldn't be his fault. The best he could do now was support her gambit, so he tried to look upset and insulted.

Terracatan's eyes flashed. Literally flashed, vanishing and reappearing so rapidly Thane was unsure it had happened at all, and the Sang bared his fangs in such a way that the hair on Thane's arms began to rise. He instinctively reached to embrace the dragon and he felt more than saw Paka and the others around and behind him crouching low, preparing to fight.

Jaeger jingled. Both Thane and Terracatan blinked and looked upward to where the red imp hung upside-down from the center of the arch that led into the room. In his hand he held a small red bag that was so near his own color that it looked like a growth on his palm. But when Jaeger shook it, it clinked with a metallic sound like coins or small screws.

"You were... offered insult at the gate?" Terracatan's eyes stayed on the bag.

Thane's first instinct was to blow it off, mitigate, anything to avoid confrontation. Then he remembered Semubyt's smugness and the fear in the Shae that accompanied him, and jerked his chin in a nod.

"Drop your tail," the First Lord of the Sang still watched Jaeger's hand. Brennan moved sideways to stand near Iselle and nudged one of the pillows on the floor until it lay behind her.

Semubyt jerked, moving upright and away from his master. "What, my lord?"

Terracatan pulled his eyes from the bag with such obvious effort it almost made a tearing sound. But his voice was calm enough to be monotone. "I will not repeat myself."

The high servant of the First Lord of the Sang Evarish lowered his eyes from his master. He continued to lower them, drawing his head closer to the floor and hunching his shoulders. Semubyt also pivoted until his back was near the closest wall and he could watch the Sang below the dais with his teeth bared. He pulled himself in more tightly and Thane noticed claws emerging from the black paws. Paws that quivered, although with what emotion Thane wasn't sure. Thane followed the Shae's narrowed gaze out into the audience of waiting predators and understood.

Those shaking paws gingerly lowered his black tail to the floor. There was an audible thump when it made contact as though someone had dropped a large rock from a great height, even though the tail touched the stone like a leaf riding a breeze onto still water. The lips of every Sang in the room parted and the anticipation for blood and death in the room was so palpable that it hit Thane like a burst of hot, sticky gas. Behind him, Iselle swayed on her feet and fell into Brennan's waiting arms and was lowered onto the pillow.

Storm on the outside. "What is *wrong* with you people?" he shouted, slamming both dragon-clawed fists down on the table before him. The stone cracked, fault lines radiating out from under the double impacts, the strange air of Shae making the second sounds louder than the first. Several of the Sang pulled their attention from the cowering Semubyt with a flinch.

"Pick up your tail and get her some water," Thane spoke through teeth clenched so tightly his jaw popped as he jabbed a finger back toward where Iselle lay on the floor. Semubyt snatched his tail from the ground and straightened, his pupils constricting and face relaxing before bowing and vanishing in the same movement.

Thane turned to look at the French girl. She was very pale, the color of her dress making her skin look even more bloodless and the violet of her eyes more startling. "Are you all right?" he demanded. She nodded, and Lord de Argos looked to Brennan for confirmation. He nodded also.

"Frail thing, isn't it?" Terracatan observed in the same way someone might have commented on the weather.

If Paka wanted a storm, Thane was fed up enough to give her a hurricane. He sprang over the table and into the Sang's marbled black face. "What is your problem?" he said, and some distant part of his mind noted that instead of screaming his voice had gone flat and quiet. It seemed familiar, but he didn't have time to figure out why. Thane never gave into his anger; rare flashes burst through, but he never let it flow. Not like this. The rush and heat was exciting and made him feel powerful, even without letting the dragon free.

Terracatan had seemed imposing and tall but standing toe to toe with him Thane felt as though he was looming over the Shae. "You think I'm going to be scared of you?" his voice was even quieter now, but tight with anger and even scorn. Somehow more familiar. "I'm not a baby, scared of the boogeyman." For a moment he remembered being afraid and being small, shaking and sobbing in the dark of the basement, shoved down there when they'd brought Harper home from the hospital. "I've already faced the dark, pointy-ears, and it wasn't you."

Bert. It was Bert, his stepfather, the man who'd married his mother and screamed at him and beaten him nearly every day since. His mind replayed a flash of memory, Bert standing at the top of the stairs and telling him to shut up, he was going to wake the baby. Bert's voice starting as a scream, and then going flat and quiet and tight with anger and scorn.

Thane's anger rushed out of him like air from a punctured tire and left him feeling sick and deflated. "I am not like him."

He was so caught up in his own thoughts that he didn't realize he'd spoken out loud until Terracatan answered him. "You are so like your father," the Sang deftly swiveled on one foot so that he could clap Thane on the shoulder and be standing next to him. "Welcome to Lord de Argos, heir of de Argos, wielder of chaos Song, guest in my home for trade and for pleasure." There was a strange echo as he spoke, as though each sound he made was two words, one that Thane understood and one that was the same voice and the same tone but the sound was something Thane felt more than heard and prickled against his spine like tiny needles.

The crowd below spread their hands forward, palms up, and tilted their chins upward as though they were about to pray, or sing, but made no other reply. Terracatan chuckled and squeezed Thane's shoulder hard enough that the joint underneath popped. Thane didn't flinch; he knew better. Terracatan was trying to let Thane and everyone else know even if the dragon boy was welcome, the Sang was still the alpha male, the leader.

"Let the feast begin," Terracatan spoke in that double voice again, and released Thane. Sang Evarish all around the room lowered themselves onto plush colorful pillows and revealed short, round tables placed around the room placed so the Sang could easily reach them while reclining.

Lord Terracatan led Thane around the table behind them and clucked his tongue at the damage to the tabletop. "Dear me, that won't do at all," he said and spread his hand, palm down, and moved it across the cracks and lines. The air shimmered and Thane felt an unpleasant buzzing and pressure in his ears, like a sound trying to come through a barrier. The broken lines withdrew into the impact marks like water being pulled into a drain and then the dents popped up, making the table smooth again. "There," Terracatan's smile at Thane made both his fists and his stomach clench and his fight or flight response start clamoring for control. Thane pulled his lips back from his teeth in answer.

From behind curtained archways on all sides of the room smaller Shae wrapped in cloth slid into view, carrying stone trays covered with shimmering cloth. A small murmur of appreciative noise spread through the Evarish seated before them. Iselle sucked air in sharply through her teeth and Thane glanced at her in time to see Paka squeeze the French girl's arm once and even Remi put her hand on the other girls shoulder.

Looking from them into the room Thane realized every piece of shining fabric that covered the food was the same either purple or red Iselle and Remi were wearing. Remi opened her mouth and Thane knew they were going to die. Brennan caught her arm, and Remi turned her flashing eyes on the not so lucky luck specialist.

And froze, mouth open, eyes wide, for one moment before Brennan helped her sit in the seat he'd pulled up for her and started putting some sort of fruit looking objects on her plate.

Iselle reached across Paka to grab Thane's hand and kissed it between the knuckles and Thane forgot he'd been looking at anything else. "Your consort seems very devoted to you," said Terracatan before taking a small, deliberate bite of something red and squishy he held between two straight pieces of something hard and white and used like chopsticks.

"My... what?" Thane blinked. Next to him he felt more than heard Paka's groan.

"Your consort? Your slave? Concubine? Your..." Terracatan made a rolling gesture with the white sticks as though searching for the word. Red juice flew from his food and spattered onto the bowed head of the servant before him. "Ah. Girlfriend?"

"She isn't--" Iselle's fingernails dug into the underside of his scaled hand, which he barely noticed in time to stop speaking. He swallowed. "I usually just use their names. This is Iselle."

"Mmm." The noise the Sang prince made wasn't insulting, but it made Thane's neck prickle and Iselle's hand go colder. "Your Iselle is lovely, although I tend to favor the dark beauty over the pale. What is the other one?"

Thane suddenly discovered he did not want Terracatan to say Remi's name. "Emily," he heard his mouth say.

Terracatan nodded and took another bite before observing, "It seems delicate. Is it unwell?"

"Um," Thane glanced over at Remi, glad she couldn't hear the Sang Evarish refer to her as an "it," and noticed she really did look like she was about to faint. Brennan was serving her food and trying to get her to take a drink.

"It was a long journey, First Lord, and the humans have not transitioned well to the air of song and life," Paka said, while managing to make a courteous bow from the waist while seated. Iselle pulled her hand away. Thane looked at his companions. Twitch was filling Iselle's plate, but glancing around the room every other moment and muttering in short phrases. Finn was standing with his feet apart and his arms crossed and glaring at no one in particular.

"Yes, the life and song of Shae are typically so overwhelming to humans, I have lost more slaves and whelps to brain sickness than any other cause," Terracatan spoke between bites. "That was one part why I was so agreeable to your father's offer. My third reaches his majority soon, and I wish to have enough gifts and supplies for all my guests and only this moon cycle the Thunder of the Alpha has agreed to come and witness." The way the Sang announced this, casually but clearly watching for a reaction, let Thane know he was expected to be impressed by this. Really he had no clue what his host was talking about.

Paka must have. "The Thunder itself?" Thane could feel her tail twitching madly against his ankle. "They do you much honor," then a short pause, "all of which is well deserved, of course."

Terracatan continued to stare at Remi, food halfway to his lips. "It would eventually adapt and do well here," he mused. Thane didn't know if the Sang was ignoring Paka or really hadn't heard. "Or it may sicken and die and be your burden. Having your pet die in my halls would bring me shame; I suppose I must purchase it to avoid the danger."

Terracatan's too human eyes swiveled to look at Thane. Paka's tail wrapped around his ankle like a cuff and he glanced at her before looking back to his host. "My pet?" Thane repeated, bewildered as to what Terracatan could be referring to- Paka would rip his ears off, Sang lord or no, if he was talking about her. Jaeger looked fine, not like he was going to die at all. The only one who seemed even sick was...

Iselle sucked in a sharp breath through her teeth. "You want to buy R- Emily?" Thane's voice was quiet again. His leg was pulling against Paka's grip now, and if he couldn't feel Iselle's fingernails in his palm earlier he could certainly feel his own claws puncturing the scales he had as skin.

"Or trade, it matters not." Their host finally put the dripping piece of something into his mouth, allowing Thane to see the flash of fangs as they pierced the red flesh.

It wasn't the only red Thane was seeing. "Trade?" he said, something hot and powerful and familiar in his chest begging the Sang to answer.

"Might I sing for you, lord?" a soft voice spoke from Thane's other side. It jarred him enough to let the red clear from his vision, a little.

"What?" he felt stupid as he asked. Iselle's violet eyes seemed to be trying to say something, and he felt even stupider for having no clue what.

"Might I entertain for these, lord, as I have done for guests in your halls? It seemed to please you," she stuttered as she spoke, and hurriedly glanced down and away.

"Yeah, sure," Thane answered without thinking. "You have a great voice."

Iselle actually blushed a little at the praise, and Thane noticed that some color rose in Remi's cheeks as well. Iselle rose in a motion that looked more like water being poured upward than like a girl standing and moved to the front of the table.

"What are you doing?" Thane heard Twitch hiss as Iselle passed by him. She didn't answer. Both Paka and Brennan were trying very hard not to look concerned, but her tail tightened convulsively around his ankle.

"What is this?" Terracatan purred, "you have brought your own entertainment? Was what is to be had in my halls not expected to be glorious enough for the son of de Argos?"

Thane still wasn't sure that the dragon he held back inside wouldn't punch their host in his stupid mouth given the chance, so he didn't answer.

Instead, Iselle answered for all of them.

He remembered hearing her voice before, hearing her sing at the end of the simulation he didn't know was a simulation, when the daemon inside of Rip tried to come out and kill them both. He'd been panicked, broken, sickened, and completely disoriented, and for the first time in his life, ready to hurt someone on purpose. And he really didn't want to.

Then came Iselle's voice, hoarse and weak, but with still enough beauty to calm the daemon that rode the man and allow the man to rise.

That was nothing like this. Here in Shae, where the air felt heavy and thick and surrounded on every hand by creatures whose darkness and evil was so overwhelming it was nearly a physical force, the slim girl embarrassed of her accent closed her eyes and took one deep breath and sang. The sound of it was the first music Thane had heard in months, and as it washed over him water in the desert, or a fire in winter, or a whole list of incredible things that Thane would be mortified to ever say out loud except that it was like life.

Bonne nuit cher trésor,

Ferme tes yeux et dors,

Laisse ta tête s'envoler,

Au creux de ton oreiller,

Un beau rêve passera,

Et tu l'attraperas,

Un beau rêve passera,

Et tu le retiendras.

She sang in French, and even though Thane couldn't understand the words he thought it sounded like another lullaby. Twitch's arm jerked in the corner of his vision, breaking the music's hold on Thane enough to turn his head and look. Twitch was holding his left ear and... crying? Thane blinked. He was crying, a little, a few slow tears leaking through eyes he was squeezing shut. Remi was staring out at the Sang beyond Iselle, and Thane tried to catch her eye to make her notice Twitch. She was oblivious, eyes wide and mouth hanging slightly open with her eyebrows scrunched up.

She was so engrossed Thane turned to look and forgot, for the moment, about Twitch.

He thought he'd had an overly emotional reaction to Iselle singing. He'd barely noticed the music compared to the rest of the hall. Every other eye in the room was riveted upon Iselle as though physically attached to her. Shadow, shade, and fae, every creature in the room was so motionless she wasn't a performer in front of an attentive audience; it was as though she sang alone in a garden of statutes. They didn't even seem to breathe.

And in their excessive and unnatural stillness Thane noticed the other humans for the first time.

They wore the same sort of draped cloth all the Shae slaves wore, hanging on them loosely and hiding the shapes of their bodies and arms. Some had hoods that covered their heads and parts of their faces. In the noise and chaos of before they'd been completely indistinguishable from any other slave but now they moved like people in an unfamiliar museum, both fascinated and horrified by what they saw.

"We have to get out of here," Brennan's low whisper cut through Iselle's song and into Thane's ear. Next to him, Terracatan twitched but did not otherwise move. Brennan stepped closer and spoke more softly so his words would not disturb whatever trance Iselle held the Shae under. "The moment her song is over we need to get out of this hall and to our rooms. They'll be monitored, but they'll be a lot more defensible than this place."

"Why?" Thane whispered back. Paka bared her teeth but did not need to turn her head away from Iselle for Thane to feel the flash of her annoyance.

"Later," Brennan's eyes swept the room, his body tense and crouched.

"Fine. How?" Thane pressed. Both Brennan and Paka grimaced, and Brennan made a hand signal. Twitch rose and motioned to Finn, and both of them helped Remi to her feet and positioned themselves directly behind Thane and in the open archway to the corridor beyond.

"The third," Thane jumped as Jaeger's voice spoke directly above him. The imp was hanging upside-down from the ceiling, but the look on his face sent an icy spike flashing through Thane's sternum and lodged as a pain in his chest. Jaeger wasn't grinning. He looked serious. Jaeger was taking this seriously.

A low growl of a word echoed in Thane's mind, which he instinctively knew was in draconen. And one he knew would get him smacked in the head by his grandfather if he ever said it out loud around a woman. "Tell him it is a present and a surprise for the majority of the third, and that we must withdraw. Then hyu leave. Don't ask permission. Reject the first set of rooms hyu are shown, and the second, and as many as hyu want. Brennan will know when hyu are safe again."

"Okay," Thane said, glancing at Twitch and Brennan's nodding heads.

"She's almost done, this is the last refrain," Brennan stepped to Paka's other side and went around the table to stand near Iselle.

"What about all the people?" Thane hissed after him.

"Later," Brennan said again. "Do it now!"

Iselle's last note was echoing in the air when Brennan swept her behind him with one arm while moving away from the center table and back towards the door.

Thane rose the moment all his friends were behind him. "We are going to our rooms, now," he tried to make his voice sound like steel and ring with authority. He sounded ridiculous.

The Sang in the hall leapt to their feet, slaves scuttling away in every direction, and Terracatan lunged for Iselle with both hands grasping. Without thinking, Thane slammed his shoulder into the First Lord of the Sang and body checked him back several feet. Terracatan snarled at him. Thane noticed the blue human eyes had been replaced by pure black ones that swirled with pinpoints of white light like stars at the edge of a black hole.

"I will have her, manling," Terracatan snarled, and raised one hand.

"She is a gift!" Thane cut off whatever gesture the Sang had been about to make. He didn't want to know what would've happened next.

The First Lord paused. "A... gift?" he spoke as though the word was unfamiliar on his tongue.

Thane felt a flash of inspiration. "Yes, great lord, for the celebration of the majority of your third, Lord de Argos has sent a gift. He knows the Thunder comes, and wants to make you look good. As a favored trading partner, making you look good makes him look good too." He knew Paka's tail was doing everything it could not to thrash around at how bad he was saying all this, but he was sure Terracatan's pride was translating it all just fine. "Tonight was only a sample. An even greater gift awaits for the celebration..." Thane trailed off.

"At the next moonrise," Terracatan supplied.

Thane tried not to gulp. "The next moonrise," he echoed, wondering if that meant in a few hours, which meant they were all going to die, or tomorrow night, which meant they were all only probably going to die. He felt a tug on the back of his shirt and smelled the peculiar leather and hot rocks smell that was Jaeger. "Thanks for dinner," Thane bowed, and walked through the archway behind them.

CHAPTER 16

He heard Terracatan chuckle behind him as Jaeger's claws poked through his clothes over his shoulders and the imp rested against him like a backpack. "Hyu just showed the most powerful and evil thing for two days journey hyu's back after insulting him and leaving his table. Hyu may not be a robot, but hyu has metal balls for sure."

"I didn't really think about it," Thane admitted, looking ahead as the group shuffled around him.

"No wonder hyu's head is perfekt, there's not anything in it to get in the way," Jaeger sprang off his shoulders and into the air, circling them all once before landing in Remi's arms. She cuddled him absently, still lost in thought.

Semubyt appeared in front of them, bowing deeply. "This way, young lord."

Brennan, Finn, Twitch, and Paka formed a rough rectangle around he, Remi, and Iselle as they walked down the hall away from the now ferocious sounds of the feast. Iselle looked drained, her face even paler than usual, and her lips parted as she tried to take deep breaths.

"Are you okay?' Thane asked under his breath. She nodded without answering, but the motion seemed to make her lose her balance and she faltered. Thane caught her around the arm with both of his, remembering at the last moment to be gentle as his blue scaled arms wrapped around her bare skin.

"Thanks," she said, and flashed him a smile. "That took a lot out of me, to hold them still for so long."

"How did you do that?" Thane started to pull his arms back, but she gripped them tighter and placed her other hand against his bicep to restrain him. He complied.

"I am sorry," she said, looking down. "I am not steady on my feet yet."

"Why did you do that?" Thane pressed.

She shook her head. "Later, when there are not so many," she made a vague gesture towards her ears. Thane felt her pull against him as she steadied herself. She'd exhausted herself by making herself a target so that he and the others wouldn't be attacked, and now everyone was acting like they were in more danger than ever. Thane stopped walking.

"What's behind these doors?" he demanded.

Semubyt, surprised, fumbled a moment for words. "Rooms for lower guests, my lord. Your rooms--"

"These will be fine," Thane cut of the first servant of the First Lord of the Sang. "Are there enough for my people?"

"Well, not to stay in much comfort, Lord de Argos," Semubyt tried to regain his composure, but his eyes were getting a little wild. "Some would have to share--"

"That's fine," Thane interrupted again, leading Iselle to the double doors framed by heavy curtains striped with red and gold. He grasped the circular handle and began to pull.

Semubyt appeared between Thane and the entrance. "These rooms are not fit for you," he began, tension in his voice and eyes wide enough to make Thane's own eyes blink in sympathy. "They are not properly furnished. They are in the lower halls. Letting you stay here would do my master dishonor."

"We give him plenty of honor just by being here," Thane was done with this. He wrapped one arm around Iselle's waist to hold her upright and gently but firmly extricated his other arm from hers and gripped the door handle again. "Move, panda man."

"Panda?" Semubyt's brow furrowed for a moment before Thane twisted his wrist and pulled the knob. The door began to open slowly, and rather than be crushed behind it the first servant of the house vanished.

Thane got the impression the door was much bigger and heavier than he realized, because as it moved the curtains stirred and he found he had to plant his feet and strain his muscles against the weight of it. He hadn't had to do that with anything since he'd transformed into a half dragon and been unable to change all of himself back.

It felt *good* to finally use those muscles. Thane grinned and dragged the door open all the way before turning to look back at his friends.

Brennan looked bemused, a half grin lurking on his face. Finn looked impassive the moment after Thane saw the surprise and chagrin in his features. Twitch was looking up and down the hallway while Paka was glaring at Semubyt, who had reappeared behind her. Jaeger was giggling in Remi's arms, and Remi...

Remi looked like she was ready to kill someone. Although she was pointedly not looking at Thane, he flinched and turned around and pulled Iselle into the rooms with him. The others followed.

"My lord," Semubyt began again, but again Thane stopped him.

"We are tired, Semubyt," Thane said. The Shae quivered at the sound of its name. "We are going to sleep now. Get out."

"I am sure you have many other duties to attend to, with the third celebration so soon," Paka purred, not quite touching the other Shae as she escorted him out. He seemed flustered for a moment, and then bared his teeth at them all.

"As you would, my Lord de Argos," the first servant could have been grinning. He could have been holding back on killing them all where they stood. The panda man bowed without lowering his chin in the same posture he'd held at the gate to Terracatan's lands, and vanished.

"Shut the door, Thane," Brennan said. Thane looked at him, surprised by the order. Brennan grinned at him. "I don't think any of the rest of us could move it."

Paka helped Iselle to sit on a cushion while Thane flashed a grin back at the red haired man. Striding to the door, Thane gripped the inner handle and pulled it shut. It moved into place with a satisfying clunk, and suddenly they were plunged into darkness.

"I miss electricity," Twitch's sigh was clear in the darkness, and the familiar clicking sounds of flashlights lit the area immediately around them. "Torches?"

"Aye will do it!" Jaeger crowed, and pushed himself out of Remi's arms and into the room. Red wings and claws flashed through beams of light as the imp moved in and out of the flashlights' illumination. Thane could hear the scraping of claws on stone and fabric tearing and Jaeger's cheerful mutterings echoed from various places overhead. "And the builder said there is light!"

Crystal spheres of amber and white slowly came into view, growing brighter with each moment. They hung from the ceiling and the walls in swatches of translucent fabric or netting, revealing the large chamber around them.

Thane was a little underwhelmed. Semubyt had said these were rooms for lower guests, but considering the wealth and opulence Terracatan had already shown, Thane was expecting more than a stone room the size of half a basketball court with a few rugs and several large cushions on the floor. Each wall was probably two stories tall and covered in more of the draping fabric from floor to ceiling with no distinct pattern.

"Twitch?" Brennan said.

"Done," came the muffled voice. Twitch emerged from behind a large curtain of shiny purple that hung near the door, his glasses askew and hair messed up.

Brennan nodded. "Do it."

Twitch flashed the first small grin Thane felt like he'd seen from the other boy in weeks, and pressed a button on some small device he held in his hand.

Paka, Jaeger, and Thane immediately all pressed their hands against their ears and yelped. It'd felt like getting stabbed in the eardrum with a dagger of sound, but the sensation only lasted a second before fading away.

"I hate that," Paka hissed, then lashed her tail once and studied her claws and tried to look like she didn't care.

"We can talk now," Brennan said, nodding to Thane. Then he grinned. "That was brilliant!"

"Hyu give them advice, and they do whatever they want," Jaeger mumbled from the cushion he'd collapsed into. Then he grinned at Thane too. "Good work, empty perfekt head."

"What exactly did he do that was so great?" Remi snapped. "And why did she," Remi jabbed her finger towards Iselle, "make them attack us by showing off her singing voice?"

"Hey--" Thane jumped in to defend Iselle, who he thought had been quite brave, but Paka cut him off.

"Arguments and name calling are for little cubs and stupid humans," she said. "We have a mission."

Remi, who'd looked ready to go toe to toe with Paka, deflated at the reminder. "Did you see all those people?" she addressed her question to Brennan, but Thane felt like she was talking to him. "Some of them were kids. They wouldn't even look up at us. What have these elves done to them?"

Twitch put his face down in his palm. "Don't use that word," he mumbled through his fingers. "Even in here. You're going to get us horribly murdered."

"Making eye contact with a Sang, or with any of the shadow, is a challenge," Finn spoke up. His voice was uncharacteristically gentle. "You never look up, because their eyes are the last thing you'd ever see. They're smart, those people. They're survivors."

"And how do we get to them? And what happened when Iselle started singing?" Thane felt the questions rising up and couldn't stop them from flooding out. "What do we do now? What did I do right? What is that red bag that Jaeger has? What was that sound that hurt my ears? Who's the third, and the majority of what?" He could feel the panic and adrenaline of the last few hours, really days, surging up as he thought about everything they didn't know and everything that could go wrong. "What do we--"

"Where are Kith and Jena?" Remi interrupted. "They didn't leave dinner with us."

"They'll be quartered with the rest of our entourage near the kitchens and slave quarters," Brennan started, and nodded toward Twitch. The tech genius unslung his bag and rolled out a large white paper across the floor, and then tapped one corner several times.

Black lines spidered outward, moving and turning and connecting until the paper that wasn't paper had an enormous drawing of a building sprawled across it. Thane felt the skin around his eyes stretching and realized he was gaping. He snapped his mouth shut and glanced around to see if anyone noticed; he felt better when he saw Remi and Finn staring at the drawing with the same shock.

"How on earth did you do that?" Finn's words sounded strained, like he was fighting against allowing them out at all. The big man, who still managed to make his samurai-style outfit seem intimidating instead of ridiculous, swallowed and cleared his throat. "Tech doesn't work here."

"Mine does." Thane was impressed that Twitch didn't sound at all smug when he said that; instead, the tech specialist didn't even look up from the map. His eyes traced the lines so intently that Thane tried to see whatever it was that Twitch saw.

Twitch reached forward and double tapped on one part of the map. The picture zoomed in, enlarging that portion and removing the rest.

"It's a touchpad?" Finn nearly sputtered, then grinned. "You Sanctum monkeys hiring?"

"The next recruitment seminar is in two weeks, but you have to have a referral," Twitch paused in his manipulations of the image. "I wouldn't ask anyone who's met you in person."

"Do the other voices in your head think so too?" Finn responded.

Twitch's hand froze. "Other voices?" Thane assumed it was a question; Twitch's voice was a flat monotone, and the tech specialist's chin took several moments to rise enough for his stare to meet Finn's.

But only for a moment, because suddenly the bodyguard Thane's father had sent to protect him from all the dangers of the alternate universe of Shae was lying flat on the stone floor with claws puncturing the front of his robe and a set of bared fangs a whisker's breadth from his eyeballs.

"Mocking our pack is not your right, human," Paka's fur bristled out in all directions. She over-enunciated each word, exaggerating the motions with her lips and tongue. Even though the Felidae spoke with almost no volume, the words carried in the thick air of Shae.

Whether that was the only reason or if the dragon blood was making Thane's hearing stronger, he heard Brennan add, "And our weapons work here, prick."

"That is enough," Iselle's soft words, spoken in a normal tone, sounded like shouting after the tense but almost silent exchange. She rose from her cushion and went to where Twitch was kneeling and pointed at the screen. "Why this? Why here?"

Twitch tore his eyes from Paka and Finn and looked back at the map. "This is where we are," he pointed to the corner furthest from where Thane stood, "and that is the corridor to the feasting hall. Semubyt told us more than he intended when Thane surprised him by picking these rooms; he told us we were near the servant's corridors. The humans will be kept near those, probably in this set of rooms here." His finger rested on the edge of the screen in front of him.

"All of them?" Remi hurried over and crouched down next to Twitch. "How can you know?"

Twitch shared a concerned glance with Jaeger that Remi didn't see. Thane did. "It's... traditional," Twitch hedged.

"It's next to the kitchens and near the stables," Finn spat. Paka growled low in her throat, but Finn only glared. "We don't tell them the truth, either? Humans here are either tools or fodder here, kid. They serve as slaves until they can't, then they're served as food to the beasts. That's how they know."

"That's awful!" Remi's face had gone pale. Thane tried to suppress the urge to punch the prone Finn in his stupid mouth.

"They're evil, princess," Finn's sneer was only protected from Thane's fist because he'd have to punch through Paka's head to get to it. And since Paka's claws were digging further into Finn's chest moving her wasn't going to be easy.

"Someone's coming," Brennan suddenly said. "Places, everyone, and look normal."

Paka shoved her way off Finn, making him grunt in the process. Finn rolled over, not bothering to rise, and pulled a smaller cushion towards himself to rest his head on. Twitch immediately rolled up the screen and shoved it back into his pack before wrapping both arms around it and collapsing down onto the nearest cushion. He closed his eyes.

Iselle and Remi did the same, faking sleep. Jaeger launched himself into the air and extinguished all the globes except one, so there was a soft amber light holding back total darkness. Thane's eyes were adjusting to the darkness while he watched Brennan move away from the door and come to stand next to him.

"You should get some sleep, kid," Brennan said, just loud enough for Thane to hear.

"I want to meet them on my feet," Thane protested. "Present a strong front, not let them catch me off guard."

"They're not coming here," Brennan stopped him. "There's no way they'd interrupt you now- you picked your own rooms without even letting them show you any of the ones they'd prepared. You walked out of a feast. You insulted the most powerful and influential Sang on the planet, and you walk with your claws bare. No one knows what you're going to do next, and they're certainly not going to disrupt you when you're finally off in your own rooms with your doors shut so they can talk about you and modify their plans."

"You told me to stop hiding them," Thane raised his arms in protest. "I wasn't trying--"

"Let's go somewhere else and talk, kid," Brennan placed a hand on Thane's shoulder to cut him off. "You should rest, but clearly you've got too many questions rattling around up there to get any sleep."

"I'm not leaving them," Thane glanced at where Remi and Iselle were faking sleep, then realized they probably weren't pretending any more.

A shadow crossed through the darkness in front of him. "I will watch them," Paka's green eyes glittered, the only truly visible part of her in the dim light. "And I will watch him," she spat the last word toward Finn.

Thane hesitated. "Where else? It's just one big room."

"Try back here," Paka suggested, and tore one of the heavy tapestries from the wall. A door came into view as the fabric flowed toward the floor. Thane blinked as she gathered the yards of cloth into her arms and across her shoulders and even around her tail to carry the whole piece.

"There are six other rooms that join this one without connecting to the hall," Brennan answered Thane's question before he'd had time to ask it. "Each of those have two smaller rooms connected to them. They aren't well furnished, but it is all self contained. That door," Brennan jerked his thumb towards the massive double doors that led to the hallway of the castle, "is meant to be hard for one person to open. It's so Terracatan can trap unwilling guests here without much fuss. This place is meant to be solid; no one gets out or in. The rooms they had planned for you probably had dozens of connected rooms that had doors into several hallways, and likely windows and balconies too. We'd never be able to talk without being overheard. You'd be pampered, served, and obeyed, and Iselle would be kidnapped or killed within the hour. And anytime you asked about her, she'd just be 'in the other room' or 'just stepped out', then it would happen to Remi, and Twitch, and even me." Brennan's face was grim, but then he smiled. "You thwarted that plan. To Terracatan this place may be a prison, but for us, it's a fortress. Nice going, Thane."

"Thanks." The warmth Thane felt was unfamiliar, but he liked it. Brennan was good at saying nice things and diffusing tense situations, but a compliment from him was rare. But the good feeling only lasted until Thane thought through Brennan's words again and remembered all the questions he needed answered. First and foremost now was, "Why is Iselle in so much danger? All she did was sing."

"Come on," Brennan went and opened the door. Thane glanced back over his shoulder and saw that Paka had covered both Remi and Iselle with the huge swath of fabric as a makeshift blanket, and was sitting on the pile of it that remained spilling over at their feet. She was also sharpening her claws with an unfamiliar dagger.

"Where did she get that?" Thane asked.

Brennan chuckled. "I've learned to never ask. Sometimes I think she grows them."

Paka flashed Thane a feral grin, and even from across the room Thane could hear the low rumble of her purr. He smiled back, even though his stomach tightened.

"Every day I'm grateful she's on our side," Brennan said, before opening the much smaller and lighter door to the next room and going in.

"Yeah," Thane agreed, and followed Brennan into the darkness and shut the door quietly.

Brennan's flashlight clicked on, and he handed a second light to Thane. "Why is it so dark in all these rooms?" Thane asked.

"No electricity, and fire isn't safe around all these tapestries, so all of the lighting is controlled by Terracatan's Song or the Song of one of his servants. I'm assuming this lack of light is Semubyt's revenge on us for picking these rooms. If we can't make our own light, we look weak and foolish. If we can, it means we didn't need his help and he didn't offer insult by not giving it."

"This place is great, I'm so glad we decided to come."

"Sarcasm, from you, Thane?" the beams of light were turned outward towards the room, so Thane couldn't see Brennan's face. Before Thane could respond, he felt Brennan's hand on his shoulder again. "Never mind; I keep forgetting you're not used to being on missions. Especially since every time I've seen you someone nearly died, buildings were falling, or we were doing practice missions..."

"Or drugging me, or chasing me, or someone pointing a gun at me," Thane continued. His hands started to shake, and the illumination from his flashlight vibrated and shook with it. He dropped it and sat down on the cool stone floor and put his head in his hands.

For several moments the only sounds were the clicking plastic flashlight case rolling along the stone floor and Thane's disjointed breathing as he tried to get himself under control. What was it about being alone with Brennan that made Thane act like such a baby? He could hold it together in front of everyone else, but get either Brennan or Paka talking to him and suddenly his chest felt tight and his eyeballs started pricking with tears.

"Thane?" Brennan's voice was quiet.

"Sometimes I don't like you very much," Thane mumbled into his hands.

Brennan snorted. "Sometimes I don't like me much either," he said, and Thane could hear him moving around. "Here," the man's voice came from a different part of the room, and Thane felt the whump of air as something landed on the stone near him. Reaching out, he felt another of the large cushions with a fringe dangling around the edges.

"No thanks."

"You'll want it," Brennan pressed. "I think we're going to be here a while." More sounds of movement and pillows and fabric rustling, then another few thumps as more cushions fell near Thane and then finally one of Brennan's knee's creaking as he sat down a short distance away on Thane's left side.

"Iselle is in danger because they've never heard music before," Brennan began without preamble. Thane's head pulled up and he looked at Brennan, who had exchanged his flashlight and it's direct beam for a soft glowing lantern from the pack on the floor next to him.

"How can't they have heard music? The Song is music, they'd have to be surrounded by it here," Thane protested.

"You hear the Song as music, but as far as I know, you're the only one who does," Brennan leaned back against the stack of cushions he'd piled against the wall. "Every other species experiences it differently, either as some sort of visual or even only by instinct."

"But it's called the Song," Thane argued. "Why would it be the Song if no one else can hear the music?"

"That's what Sylphie told us it was called." Brennan shrugged. "Most of what we know about all this started with her. Without her to stop the fighting and provide some answers in those early days, we would have destroyed each other and ourselves millennia ago."

"Why does she care?"

"I don't honestly know," Brennan admitted. "But all the information she gave us was good, and even if we couldn't prove any of her claims we couldn't disprove them either. The only thing she wanted from us was a promise to keep everything stable as we could. That was in our best interests anyway. But that's history. Today the problem was Iselle painted a huge target on herself by showing everyone there that you had something not only that Terracatan didn't, but no one here had ever had before. A magic so strong the Sang and all the Shae were powerless; a song they all could hear and that a human could make." It was the first time Thane could remember Brennan sounding so frustrated it was almost angry. "It isn't like her to do something so stupid and reckless. What happened?"

"Um," Thane tried to think back through everything to the point before Iselle stood up to sing. "Terracatan was talking about trying to buy Remi." Even the memories of that made him clench his fists. "He kept calling her an it."

"Ah," Brennan exhaled. "There it is. Jumping in to save someone by putting herself in danger is exactly like Iselle." He sighed and rubbed his forehead. "Even if it makes everything much harder from here on out. So that's why Iselle is in danger; Terracatan is determined to either own her or destroy her because she makes the Song tangible for everyone and if she isn't his she's a threat to his power. Next question."

"What's the third and why is there a celebration and majority of what?" It wasn't the question most pressing on his mind, but he didn't think Brennan would have a good answer for if they were all going to die here. And Thane didn't want Brennan to think he was a whiner.

"They're throwing a party to celebrate Terracatan's third son is becoming an adult," Brennan tapped a finger against his chin. "I've got a feeling we can use that."

"They're all this excited about somebody's birthday party?" Never having really had one himself or gone to many others, Thane couldn't believe this.

Brennan laughed, but it didn't sound happy. "For the Sang, when the third child reaches his age of majority, the three heirs fight to determine who will be the primary inheritor of the estate and title. It's considered bad form to actually kill one of your siblings, but the contest only ends when two cannot continue. The ones who are maimed or disfigured are kept as trophies, and the winner is healed." Brennan shook his head and made a disgusted noise. "There is fanfare and feasting before and after, as well as an extensive betting pool. Betting on the winner earns a lot of prestige."

Thane didn't want to ask, but he was so tired of going through all this blind. He needed to know the stakes so he could understand how to deal with his host and get out. "What happens if you bet on the loser?"

"You're maimed in the same way, and become a slave to the winner." Brennan grimaced. "They usually don't last long."

Thane hated this place. "What are we going to do?" he tried to keep his hands and voice from shaking, and managed to sound only half as afraid as he was feeling.

"What we always do; whatever it takes." Brennan suddenly sounded both fierce and happy. "That's what we're best at, anyway. You too, Thane."

Brennan's confidence pushed back Thane's fear enough to get him thinking again. "What's in Jaeger's bag? The red one he showed Terracatan?"

"No idea," Brennan said. "Whatever Ruan gave him, he didn't seem surprised by it, but he also didn't tell anyone else about it. I don't think it's relevant to what we're trying to do; Paka can always sniff out if Jaeger is going to cause problems and get him to confess. After his contraption burned two feet of fur off her tail in Mozambique and she wouldn't let him have anything shiny or mechanical until it grew back, I think he's more scared of her than of the Thunder."

"He's scared of thunder?" Thane couldn't believe that.

"Not thunder, the Thunder. A thunder is a group of dragons, like a flock of birds, and the Thunder are the leaders of the dragons."

"And they're coming here?" Thane's voice squeaked on the last word.

"Apparently," Thane was beyond grateful that Brennan did not acknowledge the squeak. "It isn't something Terracatan would brag about lightly. This celebration may be bigger than just the majority of the third."

Brennan stretched, and Thane could hear the vertebrae popping and grimaced. "Anything else?"

"Yes," but then Thane went quiet, thinking. His mind was full but his body was begging to lay down and forget it all for a while, making his thoughts blur and fade. He tried to grab one, tried to chase it down and make it stay...

"Okay, kid, get some rest," Thane's head jerked up at Brennan's voice. He'd fallen asleep and started to dream. Brennan slid down his stack of cushions and put his hands up behind his head and yawned. "I'll wake you in a few hours."

"A few... hours?" Thane's speech slurred and he groped on the floor to find the pillow Brennan had tossed him. "Shouldn't someone keep watch?"

If Brennan answered his question, Thane didn't hear it. He was exhausted, but the moment he gave in to sleep his mind started churning with all of the events of the day mixed in with everything else. Terracatan and Semubyt laughed and mocked him as he tried to take a math test with Ms. Rasmussen shooting at a flying, giggling Jaeger. Ruan de Argos was the teacher, and he shook his head woefully as Thane turned in his test paper. "This is disgraceful. Maybe you're not my son; mine would never be such an idiot. Wake up, Thane. The world is ending, and it's your fault. Who would ever want to be your father?"

Thane woke up with a gasp straight into Jaeger's face. "Oof!" The imp grabbed his nose where Thane's forehead had run into it. "Aye said wake up, the night is ending, not get up and break things. It is time for phase one."

"Phase..." Thane mumbled, disoriented and definitely grumpy from lack of sleep, disturbing dreams, and being so unpleasantly awoken.

Jaeger just cackled and pushed off him, taking the light into the air. Thane could hear the others in the next room, also sounding groggy and annoyed, with Finn even mumbling a few choice curses towards the imp. Thane realized he could hear the others so clearly because the door was open and Brennan was gone.

Thane pushed himself up and stumbled into the large antechamber where the rest of his group was slowly rising and trying to wake up. Jaeger had relit the glowing orbs above so the room was bathed in a warm yellow light. "Twitch won't wake up," Remi said, panic rising in her voice, and Thane hurried over to where she crouched next to the inert form still clutching his bag and sprawled across several large cushions. "I keep trying to get him up, but he won't respond."

Remi took Twitch's shoulder and shook him. It may as well have been a doll for all the reaction she got. She poked him in the side under his ribs, and this time he grunted, but that was it. She tickled his feet, shook him by both shoulders, and even pushed him off the enormous pillows he rested on.

His biggest reaction was to snore, once. "Is he under a spell or drugged or something?" The worry in her voice was getting sharper, and Thane tried to think of something calming and helpful to say. He had no idea what that would be.

"He's Twitch," Brennan's voice came from a different open doorway. The red-haired man strolled into the room and offered a hand to Iselle, who took it and used his help to rise. "You just need to know the right button to push." Brennan walked to the edge of the room and pushed a tapestry to the side, revealing a small, silver object. Now that the heavy curtain wasn't blocking it Thane could hear the small hum it made and guessed it must be part of whatever it was that'd made his ears hurt the day before.

Brennan leaned down to inspect it. "I wonder what happens if I push this button," he mused, not loudly.

"Don't touch my tech," Remi squeaked and jumped backwards as Twitch went from completely asleep to standing and moving toward Brennan. "You'll get your chaos all over it."

"Just curious, that's all, not touching anything," Brennan backed away with his hands up and winked at Remi. She managed a weak smile back. "Now, if everyone's awake, we have some recon to do."

"Phase one," Thane remembered, echoing Jaeger's words from before.

Brennan glanced at him. "Okay, sure, we can call it that. Now we need to get to the slave pens without Terracatan knowing we've been there. It's about two hours before dawn, which is typically when the last of the revelers get to whatever they're sleeping in. It should be pretty quiet around here for the next few hours, except for the endless parade of slaves, servants, and other workers who'll be wandering around getting things done." He glanced at Twitch, who reached into his pack and pulled out the white screen map again. "We need to blend in with those people."

"It will be hard, dressed like this," Iselle waved her hand to indicate both her shimmering gown and Brennan's kilt. "I cannot think of a place anywhere that this would be considered ordinary."

"We'll need disguises," Thane began, but something fell from the ceiling and covered his head. He scrambled to get it off and once his eyes were uncovered, he saw everyone else pulling swaths of fabric off their own faces.

Jaeger giggled from near the ceiling. "Answers from above," he chortled, yellow eye slits vibrating and teeth bared in a weird, wicked grin. "Another benefit of Thane's fortress!"

Thane held the fabric out in front of him and realized it was a robe, crudely made from the most drab pieces of fabric and tapestries that had once covered the now bare stone walls. "This should work," Brennan mused. "None of the servants should look at us too closely for fear they'd interrupt something someone else had ordered, and all of the Sang should be asleep. Good instincts again, kid."

Thane grinned, and started to pull the scratchy material over the too-fancy clothes. Being invisible again for a while sounded fantastic to him. Everyone else did the same except Jaeger, who still flew in loops and circles near the ceiling while giggling and mumbling to himself.

"Imp's gonna get us all killed," mumbled Finn, eyeing Jaeger the way Thane had seen Paka eyeing a little girl who'd called her 'kitty.'

"Jaeger's fine, Finn, focus," Brennan ordered, pointing at the screen. Finn looked down, but Thane saw Brennan's worried glance toward Jaeger, then Paka, before continuing. "All right, we're here." He pointed to the series of rooms that had somehow attained the label "Thane's Fortress." Thane glanced at Twitch, who gave him a bland look back. Iselle grinned at him, actually grinned, and Thane felt heat rising in his cheeks and jerked his chin back down.

Brennan had already continued, dragging his finger along as he spoke. "...this corridor here. We can't all go together without arousing suspicion, so--"

"I'm staying with the kid," Finn stated, his arms crossed and face leaning towards Brennan. "I have orders."

"You're in his group, and you can shut up about your orders." Brennan jabbed his finger out as he spoke. "So is Remi, and Twitch. Paka, Iselle, Jaeger and I are the second group, and we'll need to run interference and provide distraction if necessary. NOT singing," Brennan glared at Iselle.

She shrugged. "Make sure you always have a better plan, then."

"I will," Brennan was not grinding his teeth at her. Almost not, anyway. "Since Thane is the only one who can reliably open or shut the door, his group is second to leave and first to get back. Don't leave us out in the cold, kid."

"I won't," Thane met Brennan's gaze. He would not fail them, or leave them. Especially not with what would happen to Iselle if he did.

Brennan nodded to him. "All right. Twitch and Paka have subsonic transmitters that should stay stable throughout the day-"

"Six hours," Twitch corrected. "My tech works here, but the differences in atmosphere and subatomic vibrations cut the reliable life of any electronic by at least a half, and usually two thirds."

"Six hours," Brennan continued as if he hadn't been interrupted again, "which is plenty long enough because if we're gone more than three, someone is going to notice. Twitch's disruptor should confuse anyone looking for us with their Song and make everyone think we're still in here," Brennan paused and looked at Twitch, who didn't notice and didn't interrupt, "which should prevent any alarms or unwelcome followers as long as no one sees us leave. Any--"

"How will we know if there's anyone in the hall?" Remi asked.

"What are we looking for in the slave pens?" Finn spoke over her.

"What is our cover if we are questioned?" Iselle spoke at the same moment.

"I will kill Semubyt if we encounter him," Paka said.

"Are we using a standard encryption protocol or species specific advanced?" Twitch started speaking after everyone else but still finished first while fiddling with something small and rectangular in his hand.

"--questions?" Brennan sighed. "Twitch, hallway?"

"Readings indicate two Shae within line of sight of our doorway but moving towards the higher levels." He dragged his finger along the edge of the rectangle. "Optimal exit in two minutes."

"Two. Okay. No cover, we are servants of Lord de Argos here, and it isn't their place to question us. Don't let them see Thane unless there's no other option. We're verifying whether all the humans are held in the same place or if special or higher level slaves are kept somewhere else, and where that might be." Brennan glanced at Twitch.

"One minute."

"Thane," Brennan grabbed Thane's shoulder and waited until Thane looked at his face. "Twitch will have a timer. Open the door as little as possible to let us all slip out, and then shut it again as quietly as you can. Jaeger should've taken care of any noise the hinges might make. You have two and a half hours to get to the slave pens, figure out where Major Gage is being kept and if she's here at all, and get back here before we do. Twitch knows the protocols if there's trouble, and remember, Finn is supposed to listen to you. You are in charge, not him. Don't let him boss you around."

Thane could feel Finn glowering at the back of his head, but he nodded.

"Now," Twitch said, and Brennan let go of Thane's shoulder with a gentle nudge.

Thane sprinted to the door as quietly as he could and grabbed the handle. He twisted the large metal ring, grimacing against the remembered creak from before. There wasn't any this time, only a barely audible click as the interior bar retracted.

He threw his shoulder into the heavy wood to shove it forward several inches. After two good pushes Brennan tapped his back and gave him a thumbs up. Thane nodded his understanding and waited as Paka, Finn, Remi, Twitch, Jaeger, Iselle, and Brennan passed by him and into the alcove of the corridor. Thane slid through the opening and immediately put both hands on the door and closed it.

Twitch looked at Paka and moved his mouth silently. She nodded, then swiftly gave Thane her fist over heart salute before lowering her head and shuffling into the hallway, the floppy hood of her robe covering her features. Brennan, Jaeger, and Iselle followed, going back the way they'd come just hours before and looking nearly indistinguishable from each other covered in matching slave clothes.

Twitch stared at his device and seemed to be counting under his breath. Suddenly his head snapped up and he pointed. Remi nodded, pulled up her hood, and started down the hallway in the opposite direction from the others. Thane quickly followed suit, trusting that Twitch and Finn were right behind him.

Remi moved forward at a steady pace, not too quickly but like someone who has somewhere to be and it wouldn't be a good idea to get in their way. Thane knew that walk because he'd used it before to get out of talking to teachers or getting past people in between classes when there wasn't any chance of not being noticed. They went past two intersections before Remi took a left turn, and then past one more before she turned left again.

"How do you know where you're going?" Thane whispered to the back of her hood.

She glanced back to answer. "I was paying attention when Twitch showed us the map, and I'm good with directions. Shut up before someone hears us."

"Someone ahead," Twitch was staring at his hand while he walked, cupping the small device so anyone else would need to be looking straight down at it to see it. "On the edge of the next corridor we have to go through."

"No way around?" Remi asked, slowing down.

There was a short pause while Twitch calculated. "Not without a significant increase in risk. The other two ways to the slave area we could use from here are much more heavily populated."

"Why are we worried about one slave?" Finn demanded. "We'll take him out. Keep moving."

"No," Thane moved in front of the much bigger mercenary before Finn could pass Remi. "We'll go through, but we're not taking anyone out." Finn frowned, and Thane felt like he needed to make it more clear. "That's an... order." The word felt strange in his mouth, the shape of it awkward.

Finn snorted. "Whatever you say, kid."

"Lord de Argos, to you," Remi said without looking back and picking up her pace again. "We're almost there. Move it, meat man."

"I like her better than you," Finn said to Thane, and fell back into line behind Twitch as they continued forward.

"Unknown getting closer," Twitch spoke barely loud enough for Thane to hear. He was sure Remi, who was ahead of him, was too far for the warning.

"Approaching the corner," Twitch updated, lowering his head more and closing his hand around whatever he was holding. "You sure, Thane?"

"Keep going," Thane said to the floor. Remi turned the corner.

"I don't know if--" Twitch started, but Thane couldn't see Remi anymore and cut him off.

"Keep going!" Thane looked back at Twitch to reinforce the sentiment as he turned down the other hall.

And ran into the chest of whoever was coming the other way with enough force that Thane bounced off and landed sitting on the stone floor, hood back, scaled arms exposed.

Finn cursed and ran forward. Remi gasped and covered her mouth, and Twitch started moving his mouth rapidly without making any real noise.

"Ach, ye wee scunner!" Charlie swore, taking two steps away from Thane with shock on his face. "How in all the knotted threads of the Weave didja get here?"

CHAPTER 17

"Charlie?" the word came out of Thane's mouth as a wheeze, as both the surprise and the impact knocked the breath out of him.

"Charlie?!" Remi had no such issues. Both Twitch and Charlie made shushing noises at her and Finn crouched into a ready position, eyes darting up and down the hallway, but Thane thought the red flush rising in Remi's cheeks had nothing to do with embarrassment or fear.

"Hush lass, there's nary a need tae bring the wicked running," Charlie stepped towards them, extending his arm down to Thane as he spoke. Thane glanced at the offered hand, then at Remi's face, and decided it was better to either get up on his own or stay down. He shook his head.

His grandfather either didn't take the hint or didn't care. "Now I was nae asking, boy. Ye'll take m'hand tae get tae yer feet, else I'll drag ye up by yer baws." Thane got up. Once he'd taken Charlie's hand he'd been more jerked upright than helped to stand, and made the mistake of making eye contact with his draconic ancestor.

If Remi looked mad, Charlie's gaze had the kind of irrational towering anger and imminent destruction normally associated with natural disasters. The kind that movies get made about. Even Thane, in his currently Songless burnt out condition, could see the sparks and flashes of lightning pulsing across Charlie's pupils.

They needed to get out of this hallway before Remi's spark of fury ignited Charlie's and the world blew up. "Which way?" Thane asked his grandfather.

Remi spun to protest, but Thane grabbed her arm hard enough that she blinked. Charlie didn't speak, but pointed in the direction they'd been planning to go anyway. Thane moved down the corridor and dragged Remi with him, keeping several steps ahead of Charlie and Finn.   "What do you think you're doing?" Remi hissed at him, pulling against his grip and twisting her arm.

"Finding your mom, or do you want to stop and waste more time being a jerk to my grandfather and get us all killed just so you could have the last word?" Thane shot back.

He had never spoken to her like this, but he was desperate to calm them both down before they blew up at each other and brought guards running. No matter what explanation he could come up with, at a minimum their cover would be blown and they'd be thrown out without ever finding Remi's mom. Well, he'd be thrown out. Remi and Iselle would be kept as slaves, and slavery would be the best Twitch and the others could hope for. Thane glared at her to save her life.

It must've been a pretty good glare. Remi's eyes widened for a moment, then she wordlessly brushed past him. He let her go.

"You're one of us, now," Twitch said as he walked past Thane too.

Thane hurried to catch up. "What do you mean? One of who? You're not part Shae."

"Omega team." Twitch's hand fluttered up towards his left ear in half a motion before jerking his hand away as if burned.

Thane decided to ask that question later. "Why?"

"Didn't Jaeger tell you what Omega team was for?" Twitch asked. Thane tried to think back, but couldn't remember anything Jaeger had said other than something about more than two billion people on Earth being at least part Shae and dying if the Weaves were ever separated. He shook his head.

"The Council sends in Alpha Team when the objective must be achieved with the smallest disruption possible." Twitch smiled cheerfully at Thane. "Omega Team is called when the objective must be achieved no matter what the collateral damage."

"Collateral... damage?" Thane repeated.

"Collateral damage can refer to the unintentional or incidental killing or wounding of non-combatants and/or destruction to non-combatant property during attacks on legitimate enemy targets." Twitch looked grim for a moment, then shrugged. "Gage once said we were the squad who would destroy the world to save the universe."

"I know what collateral damage means..." Thane trailed off, trying to wrap his head around the rest of what Twitch had said. It didn't work very well.

"Left there," Charlie instructed from behind them, and they followed after Remi around a corner.

"What?" Thane heard Remi's surprise and glanced up. Not far ahead of them was a stone wall, with no other entrances or exits to the passageway. Charlie had taken them to a dead end.

"Dinnae be losin' faith so fast, lass," Charlie wove his way through the group to the wall, somehow not touching any of them in the confined space. "Ye giant in the bathrobe, is anyone in the hall behind?"

Finn leaned back around the corner for a long moment before coming back and shaking his head. "None within sight, sir."

Thane glanced up at the use of the honorific. Finn was standing with his body turned at a slight angle away from Charlie so that a bit of the mercenary's back was showing, and he kept his chin down and eyes lowered.

"Yer worth a bit of salt then," Charlie nodded once, then turned towards the wall and placed two hands on a round stone near the center just above his waist. Pressing the stone with his palms, Charlie began to hum.

Twitch stepped closer and peered down, the fingers of his left hand tapping his thumb spasmodically. Charlie's hum grew louder, but it also seemed to come from all directions as though surround sound speakers were hidden all around the small corridor.

"Resonance?" Twitch flattened his palm against the stones nearest him.

Instead of answering, Charlie began to twist the piece of wall he pressed. At first it resisted, then with a barely audible click it began to turn under his hand and the solid rock and mortar surrounding it wobbled. Like a very thick liquid or a very soft solid the wall jiggled and then began to shimmer and flow in a spiral, draining into that center stone.

"Gan through, there's naught inside t' feart," Charlie motioned with his head. "I'll release the keystone when yer all on t'other end. Portals of this sort cannae be found but by lookin'."

Thane reached his hand forward to touch the darkness that swirled with bits of liquid stone before him. It reminded him of watching motes of dust floating in sunlight, but in reverse, and he opened his hand to feel it coursing past.

For just a moment, a millisecond in his mind, he felt it like the swirling of all the planets and stars and galaxies in a universe, moving and thrumming along to once central, resonant sound.

Then somebody's shoulder hit him in the back and he went sprawling through the sock motes and into the darkness behind it and onto his face with something heavy on his back while something else bounced off his leg.

Thane heard a moan and felt movement, and realized the thing on his back was Remi. She pushed herself up to a sitting position in the dark and spat out a curse word her dad would be mortified to learn that she knew.

"Why, Finn?" Twitch's voice came from somewhere by Thane's feet, and he realized the thing that'd hit his leg was probably Twitch's face.

"Someone was coming and you were taking too long. He said get in, I got you in," Finn's answer came from much higher in the dark, proving to Thane that at least his bodyguard hadn't been knocked through the opening like a bowling pin.

"And why, exactly, are you taking orders from Charlie?" Twitch asked, his voice rising and the pressure lifting from Thane's shin.

"You don't piss off a dragon, kid, especially one that seems to know you." Finn snorted. "I thought you had missions training."

"How do you know he's a dragon?" Remi asked, and then squeaked and jumped up as Thane moved underneath her.

"Shut yer gobs and put oan yer naps," a warm yellow orb appeared in the palm of Charlie's hand, the glimmer of it expanding outward to fill the room with honey colored light. It would have been pleasant, if the first thing it revealed hadn't been the twisted lips and partly bared teeth of Charlie's scowl. The chaotic blue dragon was angrier than Thane had ever seen him and even the leviathan inside cowed and shrank within itself. That had never happened. Not facing guns or lunatics or the end of the world; each of those times the dragon had fought to be free, to take over.

"Self control is naught a thing I ken much," Charlie managed to carefully enunciate each word without parting his teeth, and the muscles along his jaw flexed and quivered with each word. "An so I ask ye oncet- an it better be a belter of a reason- whit in the name of awl the Song possessed ye tae whist away tae the bawl end of the universe wan I tol' ye specifically gonnae no dae that?"

There was an endless silence in which Thane prayed that anyone other than himself would answer and therefore become the focal point of Charlie's wrath. Even Remi; she was the only one who wasn't shrinking in the face of the dragon's ire. In fact it was strange that she wasn't saying anything; no one else was.

Because no one else had any idea what Charlie had said. Mentally, Thane smacked himself in his face with his palm. But the only sound he made was a small exhalation before squaring his shoulders. "We're rescuing Remi's mom. You told us you wouldn't help, so we found a way to do it without you."

"I never said I would not help," the Scottish dialect dropped with the timbre of the voice, and the hairs on Thane's head and upper arms tingled as electricity shot through the air of the room.

"Charlie, not here!" Twitch's voice broke in loosening panic. His hair was standing on end and he stood with hands and legs held away from his body, his eyes wide.

"Do not presume, meat," Charlie's glare swung toward the tech specialist and he took a step closer.

"The Thunder is coming, here, tomorrow," the tremor in Twitch's voice was gone, replaced by an authority and determination Thane hadn't heard from him before.

Whether it was the words or the attitude, it had the effect Twitch wanted. Charlie instantly deflated, predatory posture slumping, and the current in the room drained away leaving the air feeling stale and empty.

"Aye, lad, I know." Thane suddenly felt that he could see the weight of centuries pressing down on his several-greats grandfather. Charlie passed a hand over his face. He continued speaking with his eyes covered, "I didnae say I wouldnae help, I said I would niver allow her tae be in such danger as surrounds her here."

"I don't need to be protected!" Remi didn't sound angry as much as desperate, even exasperated as she threw up her hands. "What are you even doing here?"

"Finding yer mum, ye numpty!" Charlie looked away and took a slow, deep breath.

"I-- what?" Remi blinked.

Thane understood. "He didn't say he wouldn't find Major Quinn, he said he wouldn't help us do it," he remembered the odd look on Charlie's face now, when they'd asked him to open a gateway into the Shaerealm for them.

"Why?" Remi's face wasn't changing expression, as though she couldn't quite process what was going on around her.

Charlie's lips twisted in a smile at her so filled with pain and sorrow that Thane felt tears pricking in the corner of his own eyes. "It was the only thing I kenned would keep ye safe, an get ye happy again."

"Why?" Twitch's face was a startling match to Remi's, showing shock too deep to move through. "You'd risk the compact- the alliance- the integrity of the shredding Weave itself," his voice had become more unintelligible with each word until Twitch was only making strange noises, sounding like a terrible cell phone connection where only every other or third syllable could be heard.

"Wait, you came here from Earth?" even Finn couldn't quite sound deferential while sounding so incredulous. "You..." Finn gulped before continuing, "*passed through* the Weave, just to try and find some Sanctum whore because some mouthy b--"

He cut off with a gurgle as Charlie's hand closed around his throat and made a significant dent in his windpipe. "I see ye dinnae ken whit yer sayin', an bein' as yer tasked wit guardin' my grander, I'll leave ye wit yer tongue, but dinnae speak ill of this lass or her kin again else I'll pull oot yer windpipe through yer lugs an tie a lovely bow fer yer nob wit it. Ye ken?" Charlie didn't look or sound angry in the least, which chilled Thane even more than the threat. Finn, too, was very affected, and bobbed his head up and down with as much enthusiasm as he could with the iron grip around his throat and only his toes still touching the floor.

"Guid awn ye, then," Charlie released Finn immediately, and slapped him on the back as the mercenary slumped forward, gasping. "An naught a word more from ye awn it taether," Charlie looked firmly at Twitch.

Twitch glanced at Finn, who was still struggling to breathe, and back at Charlie with a shrug. "Damage is done, for now," he said, but added, "as far as I can tell. I'll need to study it further, and we may have to talk again then."

It was Charlie's turn to shrug. "That's as may be, I ken tis yer job an ye'll only be doin' it well. Tadpole an messell are goin' tae be havin' a verra long talk as well oncet this is past. In the meanwhile," Charlie turned to face Remi and held out one hand toward her, bowing slightly, "would ye like tae go an see her?"

"Who?" Remi asked, still bewildered.

"You did it?" Twitch's head snapped up again from poking at his little rectangle.

"Major Gage, a certain Ms. Meagan Quinn, an more 'n two thirds of her team intact," Charlie said, still bowed and holding out his hand. Remi gasped, all the rest of the angry red flush draining from her face and neck and leaving her pale and wide-eyed. Charlie continued, his voice low and gentle. "She's naught save a few minutes more a walkin', an iffin I brought ye this near an naught the whole way she'd give such a lashin' as would make yer da proud."

The mention of her father seemed to stiffen Remi's spine, and she straightened up. "Yes, lead on, please," she said, her face resolute although still without much color. Thane thought about how he'd felt- not even a week before, he was shocked to realize- when he'd been about to meet his father for the first time. It wasn't quite the same, but it was a closer experience than any of the others had.

He moved next to her and squeezed her shoulder carefully, with his palm more than his clawed fingertips. "She's going to be so proud of you," he said, knowing it was the one thing he'd wanted more than anything for someone to say to him. No one had.

But the smile, the real smile, Remi gave him and the blush creeping back into her cheeks drove any remaining guilt or doubt from him. "Thanks," she mouthed, and turned back to Charlie.

"What are you standing around for, dinosaur man?" she quipped. "Move it. We've got a timetable to keep."

Charlie grinned back at her. "Aye, yer majesty," and he bowed low while dropping his hand. Only Thane was watching him closely enough to see the flash of disappointment and grief while his hand fell away, rejected. Charlie turned smartly on one heel as well as any trained Sanctum soldier on parade, and marched through the back wall.

The light vanished with him. "Um, Charlie?" Thane called.

The dragon's handsome face appeared along with the light he held. "Yer supposed tae come wit me, ye great lumps. It's nae really a wall iffin ye care tae follow," and with a snort, he disappeared again.

Thane felt Remi's hand slide into his, her human skin soft, fragile, and warm against his hardened scales. He both heard and felt her inhale and pause, then exhale deeply.

"I can push you again," Finn offered, voice still weak and croaking.

"I could have him kill you," Remi offered back, her tone light and blithe.

"I'm already walking through," Twitch's voice came from in front of them in the darkness, with the ending of the last word cut off to mark where he'd passed through.

Thane felt his arm moved forward as Remi began walking, and started to move with her. He braced himself for impact with the wall until he heard Remi giggle, and realized his eyes were closed.

"We're, um, we're through," Twitch was looking at him, his mouth twitching, when Thane opened his eyes. They were standing high on one edge of a bowl-shaped, well-lit room. A large room, full of people. All were staring at them, some frowning, some openly gaping, and four or five on their knees and groveling while still others hurried children out of the room. Thane's head kept turning, taking in the enormity of the room with straw strewn thin across the floor and stacked in piles at regular intervals. He guessed the whole space was about the size of his high school gymnasium, with three archways each on the walls to his left and right and one large barred door directly in front of them.

And the humans. They were everywhere! The arrival of Thane's group should've taken them by surprise in the middle of the night, but instead of sleeping what must be nearly a hundred of them had only paused their labors to stare. Thane saw people weaving cloth, more of those hanging tapestries that were everywhere being made by human hands. People mending clothing. People grinding wheat. People raking straw, stirring pots over low fires, peeling vegetables with sharpened stones, and a multitude of other tasks that his modern mind couldn't identify.

"What in seven shredding hells of Shae is this, Niall?" a woman's voice carried across the room without echoing against the cavernous walls. Thane's eye was drawn to a small crowd that moved towards them from one of the furthest archways. Three women and two men strode across the straw floor, and Thane guessed the woman at the front of the group was the one who had spoken.

She had dark hair and a familiar face, although she couldn't be much older than Brennan. Remi wasn't reacting to her, so Thane thought it couldn't have been Major Gage. She spoke again, leading her party and drawing nearer with every step. Thane was startled to see the humans coming at them each held stone knives low in their hands.

"You have been continually unstable, which we thought was just the result of your recent capture, but to bring outsiders here unasked, and through the back passage!" She raised her knife in a threatening gesture and jabbed it towards Charlie. "This is the last straw, Niall. We're going to have to take you into custody."

"No, please," Thane held up his hand in protest. The sleeve from his robes slid back and revealed his cobalt scales and indigo claws, which reflected firelight like dark jewels.

Everyone in the room had frozen as completely as if turned to stone by the sight of his arm, and now as one they collapsed, prostrate, to the floor. Thane could see the looks on their faces as they fell, each one a variant of fury or horror. He jerked his offending hand and arm back underneath his loose robes.

His stomach twisted with shame. "No, I, please get up," he mumbled, trying to gesture without using his arms. "I'm not, I mean," he gulped against the knot in his throat and the burning sensation growing there, looking at the tops of their heads and remembering their faces. He didn't want to be the monster of their nightmares.

He felt a steady hand on his shoulder. Warm, calloused, and strong, it rested there in support and his grandfather voice rang loud in the vacuum of terrified silence. "Git up, ye boggin cakey bampots! D'ye ken I'd nivver sell ye oot tae the likes of the Sang? I'll have tae fergive most of ye, but Meagan, ye of all should ken better. Now git yer face oot the dirt an come tae meet this quine of yer own."

"My... what?" the woman Thane thought had looked familiar lifted her face and stared at them before rising uncertainly to her feet.

"Mo-Megan?" Remi stammered, tightening her grip on Thane's other hand. She was squinting and straining to see better in what Thane suddenly realized was a huge room half lit by campfires. He'd forgotten entirely that here, on Shae, his eyesight would be much better than hers because of his inherited Shae blood, and dragon blood besides. Remi wouldn't have been able to see the woman at all yet.

Twitch stepped forward and gave a sharp salute. "Major Quinn, I am Sergeant Timothy O'Malley, specialist in tech, Omega Team of Sanctum. We are one third of the reconnaissance and rescue group sent to free you. And-" here Twitch's military training seemed to desert him and he faltered, the hand against his eyebrow shaking a little, "um, and we brought your daughter with us. She insisted," he added quickly.

"Remi?" Major Meagan Quinn Gage, decorated officer of the most elite military force in two universes, did not sound pleased. "You brought my daughter, Remi, *here?*"

"Ah," Twitch did not exactly hide behind Finn's taller and broader bulk, but it was suddenly much more difficult to see him.

"Mom?" Remi spoke again, louder, and let go of Thane's hand to start pelting down their side of the bowl. "Mom!"

Meagan Gage sprang to her feet and started running. Thane saw one of the men from her group try to grab her ankle and hiss something up at her, but she kicked him in the face and pulled away.

Remi stumbled and fell on her hands and knees, skidding several inches before picking herself up again. She tried to jump and weave over the humans, many of whom were getting up in confusion. She knocked into at least two more, tripping again and careening off the other.

"Clear a path!" Major Gage shouted. Her military authority and the natural force of her personality caused people to scramble away on their bellies or knees. "Remi!" Thane could see her eyes shining with tears she would not shed. He knew Remi's face would look the same.

"Mom!" Remi pushed through a set of people too slow to get out of her way and threw herself at the woman in front of her.

Meagan Gage caught Remi with arms wide and the force of their impact spun them both sideways, tipping them off balance and onto their knees. They clutched at each other, Remi's face buried in her mother's shoulder and shaking, Meagan making soothing shush noises and cradling the back of Remi's head with one hand while keeping the other wrapped around her daughter's waist like the belt of a life-preserver.

The rectangle in Twitch's hand vibrated audibly. Finn, Charlie, and Thane all turned to look at it, then at him.

"Time's up, we've got to get back," Twitch said. "Go get Remi."

The other three gaped at him, Thane feeling horror rising in his belly.

"I'd think back on that, lad," Charlie's voice was not, quite, a growl.

"But the others--" Twitch began in protest, but Thane cut him off.

"The others will die if I don't get back. The rest of you can stay here and protect Remi and explain what we're doing here to all these people." Thane said, but Finn and Twitch both argued immediately.

"I'm not leaving you." Finn's arms were crossed and his face set.

"Not all of us coming back is just as suspicious as none of us coming back!" Twitch glared at Thane through his glasses, which reflected the firelight oddly.

"Ye'll nae be takin' her from her mum," Charlie didn't need to cross his arms to look irresolute and dangerous. "The three of ye'll git, an I'll stand watch over the Gage wimmin."

"Because we need watching, Niall?" said a warm voice. Thane spun around to see Remi and her mother, both faces shining with tears and smiling so wide it must've hurt, standing behind him.

"Charlie, ma'am," and the dragon bowed dramatically and with flourish before her.

"Charlie?" Meagan Gage blinked once, and then with clenched teeth repeated, "CHARLIE?" with enough chill anger to freeze a star.

Charlie grinned and winked at her. "In the flesh, such as it be."

"Of all the idiotic..." Remi's mom visibly calmed herself. "This will be dealt with later. At length." She glared at Charlie, but managed to include all the other males in their party as well. "In the meantime, Sergeant O'Malley--"

"Twitch, mom," Remi corrected. "We all call him Twitch."

"Explanations later, pup," and the word seemed to affect her, as her eyes misted again and the arm around Remi's shoulders tightened. "Now I would like to know what the plan is. You do have one, I presume?"

"Ma'am, at the moment we need to rendezvous with the rest of our party outside our rooms before we are missed." Twitch saluted again. "All of us," he added, Thane thought completely unnecessarily.

"Oh." Meagan Gage's eyes glistened again, but her back was straight and it was the Major who answered. "I understand."

"I don't," Remi looked imploringly at Thane, "Now? I have to right now?"

"The others, um..." Twitch stammered and halted when both Gage women turned their eyes on him, one set of fire and one of steel and both trying not to cry. The rectangle in his hand vibrated again, louder and more insistent, and the center began to glow with a pale, greenish light.

Twitch snapped his fingers. "You're sick," he announced, pointing to Remi. "You were ill at the feast, everyone saw how awful and pale you were, even Terracatan commented. You're sick."

"Awful and pale?" Remi repeated, and Twitch flushed.

"Can you hide her here?" Thane asked Major Gage.

Her eyes flicked down to where his arms were hidden in the robes and then back up to meet his. They were not friendly. "I can," she replied, with the same level of coldness she'd had for Charlie.

Thane flinched. "Charlie, keep an eye on them?"

"We don't need any of his help." Major Gage's arm tightened again around Remi and she began to lead her daughter away from the dragons and men. "Sergeant O'Malley, I will await further communications from you. And a full read in." At this she paused, and turned to stare at Twitch until he made eye contact with her. "I will not operate in the dark again."

"Yes ma'am," Twitch saluted again, almost a nervous tic itself now, and took a deep breath. "Neither will I, ma'am."

"I beg your pardon?" Major Gage did not look like she had ever begged for anything from anyone ever.

Twitch gulped, but pressed on. "I'll need to report to my commanding officer, ma'am, and he's going to have one question. Did you find it?"

Major Gage's eyes narrowed and her hand, the one away from Remi, moved. Thane saw the sharpened stone knife as the light of the nearest fire glinted along its edge, saw that she held it by pinching the end of the blade. The way Charlie had said professional throwers held it. "I don't care who you style yourself to be, boy," her voice was low, and deadly. The only voice Thane could compare it to was the one and only time he'd heard the daemon that rode inside Rip speak, and that exchange still haunted his nightmares. "There is only one person I will speak to about that, and you. Are. Not. Him."

The green light in Twitch's hand had begun to turn yellow, and Thane wasn't sure if the color of Twitch's face was because of that light or Major Gage's answer. But they had to hurry, regardless. "Charlie, can you take us back through?" Thane asked.

"Aye, tadpole, back through the wall," and Charlie stepped again through the stone wall and vanished. Twitch and Finn followed suit. Thane cast one last look back at Remi, who seemed completely oblivious to anything other than her mother, and followed them into the storeroom beyond.

"How will we contact you?" he asked his grandfather, as Charlie spun the stone wall into mist again. Twitch was staring at his device, making sure the hallway beyond stayed empty.

"These shadow will sleep for an hoor or more, then be up an aboot tae bother ye," Charlie said, finishing the spell to open the portal.

"The majority of the third celebration is tonight," Twitch added. "We need a plan in place before then." He cut off speaking but continued to move his jaw and throat in a curious manner, looking both worried and exasperated. "Paka says they're nearly back and they're getting anxious. I told them we're on our way with lots to report." He closed his eyes. "I know she knows how incredibly loud and distracting it is when she growls in her throat, and-" here he cut off speaking out loud and instead began to make those strange movements and mouthing that indicated sub-vocal speech.

"The Sang will come for ye tae show off more, an expect ye'll be starvin' but he'll nae feed ye until afternoon tae make ye crabby and off yer game,"

Charlie ruffled Thane's hair under his hood. "That blaggart has nary a clue whit he's tanglin' wit. Stay strong, taddypole, an' I'll be findin' ye a bell after the noon meal. I'll see aboot bringin' back Remi then, iffin I can manage it."

Thane nodded. "Clear now, two halls if we hurry," Twitch said, and bolted through the motes of swirling stone into the hallway beyond. Thane clasped hands with Charlie, then followed, with Finn close at his heels.

Servants thronged the third hall, scurrying in both directions and carrying platters, bundles, and all manner of objects. Thane watched as two short servants going opposite ways collided. Their bundles burst and their hoods fell back, revealing two of the small lizard men Thane remembered from his entourage that Kith had gathered.

They squeaked and clawed at each other while scrabbling around on the floor trying to gather their things back again. Other hurried and harried servants tried to move around them, most with success.

"Follow my lead," Thane mouthed to the two with him and then stuck his foot out beyond the corner. Instantly a tall, gangly Shae fell forward and ran into the two servant slaves ahead of him. All three went down in a tangle, and Thane slipped into the corridor in the mass of confusion. He grabbed at a loose bundle on the floor and began walking away with it back toward his rooms.

The squabbling behind him grew louder instead of quieter as he drew away, but he did not risk glancing back to see what was happening. He did pause, twice, waiting for Twitch and Finn to catch up, but Twitch glared at him for it.

"We'll draw too much notice- none of the others are moving in groups," Twitch said in a hurried undertone. "We all know where to go. Move!" The other servants were emptying the hallway, trying to run from the noise and the notice it would draw, and Thane followed their example for the next two turns and into the hallway where his rooms were.

And stopped as Terracatan and Semubyt were standing in front of the massive double doors he was supposed to open for his friends before anyone else discovered them.

CHAPTER 18

Thane froze, surprise and dismay overwhelming him and holding him captive as he stared at the First Lord of the Sang and his first servant. But only for a quick heartbeat; years of hard won instinct had him moving again, head down and steady, before either of the beasts before him could notice.

Terracatan was not pleased. "This is a second failure in the turning of the same moon, Semubyt," he would not condescend to sound angry. It was unnecessary, as his fury emanated from him in almost palpable waves. Thane stayed stone still behind the heavy curtains opposite. He could feel the blood in his veins pulsing so hard that it rang in his ears as he watched the master of the house evaluating just how much of his fury he could take out on his servant.

Thane felt a strong sense of deja vu, a forceful sense of familiarity. Outside of his species, of his planet, and even of his universe here he was again, hiding behind the curtains from the wrath of someone who held all the power. It was the same. He was still small and cowering, hoping that if he tried hard enough to be invisible no one could find him to hurt him. Thane's chest burned, and it was painful to breathe around the hard lump in his throat. He could never escape. Nothing had changed.

A red flash further down the hall caught his eye. Terracatan and Semubyt were standing inside the alcove at the large doors and wouldn't be able to see from where they were, but from Thane's vantage across the hall he saw Jaeger grinning and clambering across the tops of the tapestries like a drunken monkey. When the imp saw him looking, Jaeger gripped the cloth with his tail and hung upside-down, pointing below with both hands.

Thane's eyes followed the line set by the red claws until he saw Paka's face glowering at him from between the folds of indigo and scarlet. Even as far apart and obscured by robes and their hiding places as they were, Thane could still clearly see her silently mouth, "Late," at him and snarl.

A few things may have changed. He grinned at her. He couldn't help it; he drew an easy, deep breath before nodding to her and then gliding with the stealth developed over a lifetime. Music was a talent, and a passion. Getting around without drawing attention was a finely honed survival skill. It was a matter of minutes to move far enough down the corridor to be out of Semubyt or Terracatan's line of sight and then move across the open space with the flinching, shuffling step of the perpetually terrified before sliding back behind the hanging tapestries of the opposite side.

But he didn't join the others. Instead, he looked up to Jaeger, the imp's head curiously tilted and still upside down, and then jerked his head to the side and slid away from the others and turned down the next hall. Moving further, he found an empty alcove covered by the hanging fabric and invisible from the corridor.

It was a dead end similar to the one Charlie had led them into, and Thane crouched down in the furthest corner to reduce the chances of being seen. He started going over a recent piece of music from his study of the Song class to keep himself calm. That turned out to be a mistake; even only two phrases into the music he was so wrapped up in it he jumped when Paka slid into the alcove next to him.

"Where have you been?" she hissed at him in an undertone. Brennan and Iselle came in right on her heels and crowded around him in silence. Brennan's glance around the small niche for Twitch and Finn. When he did not see them, he raised an eyebrow at Thane.

"We split up..." Thane began, but stopped when Brennan covered his face with his hand. It was the right one, short two and a half fingers, and a disturbing sight when Brennan opened his eye and looked straight at Thane without lowering his hand.

"Split up? Have not any of you ever seen a horror movie?" this statement seemed as incongruous coming from Iselle as it would have from Paka. More, really; Thane thought Paka probably liked horror movies. She could see things from the hunter's perspective.

Thane shook his head to clear it. Why was he getting so easily distracted? "Twitch said we'd be less noticeable that way, and it was only a few minutes ago," Thane defended himself and his friend, and asked what he thought was the more important question. "Why is Terracatan here?"

"He sent Semubyt to spy on us last night, but that blinker couldn't get past the disruption perimeter Twitch set up," Brennan answered.

"He was very angry, and lost much face," Paka looked smug. Only cats could look that smug. "All his Song and his spies say we must still be in there, because only Twitch can make tech to work here and so they are completely blinded. The eel Sang thought to wake us early after bumbling around in the dark and take us surprised and unbalanced and restore his own supremacy, but instead finds his first servant weak and mewling outside our door and no one to answer when he knocks." She blinked, and her feline pupils dilated and retracted again in surprise. "If you hadn't been late we wouldn't have seen him so dishonored. I am glad you were late," she grinned at him with her feral fangs sharp points of reflected light in the dimness behind the drapes and ruffled his hair.

"That is all well and good, I am sure, but what do we do now?" Iselle asked.

"Too much meat sack for a perfekt head, Aye suppose," Jaeger said in tones of regret as Finn ducked into the alcove from the hallway with the imp riding on his shoulders like a small child at a parade. "Aye found him not far."

"What about Twitch?" Thane asked, but Brennan held a finger up in a signal to wait. He seemed to be listening for something.

They all fell silent, modulating their breathing to be more shallow and create less sound. One slow moment passed. Then muttering could be heard in

281

the hallway, and as it drew nearer Thane heard, "Just about here," and Twitch, staring down at his rectangle, walked into the middle of them.

And bumped into Iselle. "Oh," he said, jerking his head up. Twitch colored slightly as Iselle regarded him.

"What's just about here, Twitch?" Brennan asked as the tech specialist mumbled something like an apology to the French girl. "And where's Remi? She wasn't with Thane, so I thought for sure she'd be with you."

"Remi's with her mom, and Charlie," Twitch began. "Now if I'm reading this right you've already found--"

"You found Major Gage?" Brennan demanded, and then blinked. "Wait, Charlie? That isn't possible. Must've been a shape shifter. We're compromised. Jaeger-"

"It was Charlie," Thane protested. "He knew who we were, who Remi was, and why we were here!"

"Not so loud," Twitch raised both hands. "We aren't secure here, let's go back inside the disruption perimeter to talk."

"Terracatan is at the doors," Finn protested as Twitch pushed through the others to the far wall. "How do you suggest we get past him? And if you say anything about a distraction I'll hurl you at the Lord Sang to make one."

Twitch didn't seem to hear the threat, already engrossed in his rectangle and staring at the wall. "Resonance," he said, and then, "Thane? Come and help?"

"What?" Thane moved closer to Twitch, but it was hard to focus. His mind kept drifting off in different directions, constantly distracted by, "It's humming!"

"Hm? Oh, the wall. Yes. I need you to make a matching resonant pitch," Twitch said, putting his device in his pocket and placing two hands on the center stone. Just like Charlie had.

"It's another portal?" Thane asked.

"If I say yes and promise to explain once were inside, will you please hum?" Twitch said with a short glare back.

Thane hummed. The pitch was easy to pick out; the air and the walls around him were already vibrating with it. Twitch's hands twisted on the circular keystone and the wall surrounding it started to spin and melt inwards.

Finn didn't wait to be told. The big mercenary pushed one finger into the swirling motes, then walked through after his probe met no resistance with the imp still riding on his shoulders. Paka bounded through after while Iselle and Brennan glided through.

"Do I go first or you?" Twitch said, although it wasn't clear if he was talking to Thane or not. Thane shrugged in reply anyway.

The rectangle in Twitch's pocket buzzed once, the sound and the vibration disrupting the resonance of the stone. It began to harden again and both Thane and Twitch grabbed the other's shoulder and lunged forward, each pulling the other through.

This completely offset both of their balance and they sprawled on the floor and over the cushions of the room where Thane had gotten those few hours of sleep what seemed weeks ago.

The rectangle buzzed again. "What does it want?" Thane asked in annoyance, letting go of his friend and pushing himself to his feet.

"Proximity warning," Twitch said, standing himself and pulling the rectangle out. "Semubyt is right..." he turned around and pointed at the wall they'd just fallen through. "There."

Thane did not gulp. The momentary tightness in his chest and lump in his throat made gulping impossible.

Brennan was not so affected. "I expect to be fully briefed, and I am not happy you disobeyed orders and left Remi behind, no matter what the reason," he cut off Thane's protest before it could be spoken with a slash of his arm. "There will be an accounting for that later. Now we need to go open the doors before our host decides to bring an army to tear them down. We will tell them that she is sick," Brennan answered Iselle's question as she only began to open her mouth. "They all saw her last night at the feast, and besides, you are the greater prize now. Meat sack and I will answer the door as guards. Twitch, Paka, and Iselle make yourselves look presentable while Jaeger fixes up our lordling here. Whatever happens today, you four stick with him. Not you," Brennan jabbed half a finger at Finn. "I let you do that once and you lost a quarter of your party. Suck it up and fill me in while we do more recon, because you're going to make it up to me by taking me back to where you left Remi. Not a request."

Finn glared sullenly at Brennan. "You're not the boss of me."

Jaeger was pulling the servant robes off of Thane by grabbing a corner and flying straight up, jerking off the fabric and knocking Thane off balance again. "Just do it," Thane rubbed his jaw where his own arm, pulled by a sleeve coming off, had whacked him in the face.

Finn looked grim, but nodded. The two walked out of the smaller room to the great antechamber while Twitch scrambled out of his own scratchy servant robes and dashed out after them. Jaeger dipped and flashed about Thane, who felt his limbs and torso pushed and pulled around and sometimes even his hair being tugged. "Now hyu are lord of the perfekt heads," Jaeger announced. Thane cringed inwardly. How bad that could be, he didn't dare imagine.

"You 'ave done well, Jaeger," Iselle complimented. Her French accent was noticeably stronger, a sign Thane knew meant she was under stress. He turned to try and say something nice to her and lost conscious train of thought.

Underneath the shapeless and grey brown of the servant robes he'd forgotten she was wearing that violet dress with one bare shoulder. She'd managed to fix her hair up while he'd been under Jaeger's ungentle makeover, and she once again looked like a goddess from a Greek play.

"Hyu should know, hyu haf an open mouth," Jaeger commented. Thane snapped his mouth closed and blushed. "Here they come," Jaeger added, and Thane became conscious of a loud grating sound, like someone dragging a heavy log.

The doors. They were opening the doors. Thane stepped out of the smaller chamber in time to see Terracatan's grand entrance, flanked by five large servants on each side who were throwing their shoulders into the enormous and heavy portals. Brennan and Finn stood stoically before them at attention. The Sang's eyes flicked over the room in rapid succession, and Thane saw him take note of the glowing amber orbs hung high in the fabric near the ceiling, the cushions that somehow had been organized into neat arrays throughout the room with comfortable and rich blankets folded tidily around them, and then Thane himself emerging from a side chamber and followed by Iselle.

Terracatan gave Thane a pleased and knowing smile, drawing his eyes back from Iselle to look at Thane again. Instead of feeling embarrassed Thane felt a little smug himself, noting the tightness in the Sang's jaw and knowing that Terracatan had been unable to enter these rooms or even send a spy until Twitch had turned off the disruptive perimeter. Whatever that was.

Thane smiled back at the Sang, all confidence and no warmth. Terracatan's smile slipped a little but he bowed, all graciousness. "I hope we have not wakened you too early, Lord de Argos?" In all the tension of the hours before, Thane had forgotten how oily Terracatan could be. But again, years of survival skills in hiding his own feelings made it easy for Thane to hold his expression.

"My lord has awakened only when he wanted to," Paka purred, moving like liquid on all fours until she stretched, and then rose to her hind legs next to Thane. Thane took a great deal of private satisfaction at seeing the flash of anger in Terracatan's once again too human blue eyes at the clear acknowledgement they had heard them knocking and chose to ignore it until convenient.

But a flash was all it was. If Thane hadn't known what to look for, been waiting for it, he wouldn't have noticed. Terracatan strolled past Thane to Iselle and reached out his hand to touch her hair with all the confidence of ownership.

"I am pleased with the gift you have brought, de Argos, but I think I will keep her for myself instead of presenting her at the ascension of the heir," the Sang said. "She can only blossom best here with me."

It was Thane's turn to see red. His teeth ground together with such force the sound of it echoed in his skull, but before he could do anything potentially lethal to his party and his purpose, Iselle moved away from Terracatan. Like a dancer switching partners at the correct moment in the music she ducked from under his touch and hid behind Thane's right shoulder and ducked her head against him.

The contact and her preference for him gratified his anger in an instant. "She isn't the gift, Terracatan," Thane matched the Sang's smug informality. For a moment.

"Then I insist you show me what is!" Terracatan's teeth shimmered in the amber light, the tips of his fangs exposed in the wideness of his smile.

"It's a surprise?" Thane hated sounding uncertain, all the more because he could see Terracatan enjoying his weakness.

"From the third, surely, but I am to make all the necessary preparations for this night, and for that I must be let in on the secret. Especially if it is as spectacular as you've said." Terracatan's eyes flicked around the room again, searching. "Where is the other? Emily. The red and brown one," he said.

"She's sick," Thane said, and with a sudden mental realization added, "she may not survive the transition." He waved a hand to indicate the other rooms, and added, "We may leave her here when we go, if her disposal wouldn't inconvenience you too much," as though she were a torn shirt, or luggage with a broken zipper.

"No, not at all," Terracatan gave a hint of a shrug. Thane smiled back, trying to appear grateful. Well, actually trying to appear less grateful than he felt that the gambit worked; if Remi wasn't valuable and even a detriment, Terracatan might ignore her. That was all Thane could've wanted right now.

"So where is this magnificent gift you have for my child?" Terracatan pressed.

And a plan. Thane wanted Remi ignored and a plan. He glanced at Brennan, and then Finn because he was standing next to Brennan, before looking blankly back at their Sang host.

Which Terracatan misinterpreted completely. "Ah," he said, "let us walk, then, and I will give you a tour of my treasures where we can talk in more security."

Terracatan thought Thane didn't want to talk in front of Brennan. That was something. "Sure," Thane answered, and then drew Iselle's arm through his. He didn't need Brennan glaring at him to know it was a bad idea to leave her here with all of Terracatan's servants and guards and thought she would be safest if he kept her close. He still hoped he was too important for the Sang to confront him directly.

"Jaeger, will you also join us?" Terracatan's trick of making his voice carry without speaking louder made it seem as though he spoke from everywhere in the room. Thane paused; he hadn't expected Jaeger to be invited.

Well, his turn again then. "Twitch, you too?" Thane said. Twitch bowed, and came to stand behind and to the other side of Iselle. Thane approved.

Terracatan did not. He looked down at Twitch as though noticing an unpleasant bug, and then glanced toward where Semubyt had waited, silent, near the entrance throughout the exchange. The Sang almost spoke before glancing at Paka and closing his lips again. Thane could almost hear him thinking if he commanded Semubyt to join him Thane would bring Paka, Something about that prospect did not appeal to him at all. "Semubyt," Terracatan began, and before the name was finished the creature appeared at his master's side with a low bow. "Take Lord de Argos's steward with you and see to their needs? I'm sure she can inform you on whatever they lack."

Whatever Paka and Semubyt privately felt about this directive, they each acquiesced although Paka added, "With my Lord's permission," to Thane. He nodded. Thane didn't know what else to do, and he didn't dare look at Brennan again.

"Well then," Terracatan held out his arm like a man calling back a falcon and Jaeger flew down and landed on it. "Off we go," and he turned and walked out the door again.

Thane followed, leading Iselle and Twitch following close behind. Paka and Semubyt came immediately after and departed down a long corridor, at first walking, then quickly walking, until they were both sprinting away. The double line of guards pulled closed the giant doors with a long creak and an ominous boom. Five of them then stood at attention in the doorway, and the other five followed Terracatan, Thane, and the others.

Now they were outnumbered again. Any sense of comfort Thane had been holding, thinking it was four against one, shattered as five fully armed guards of a sort of lumpy, grey creatures stalked behind him. Ahead Terracatan and Jaeger spoke in low tones, too quiet for Thane to make out even with his dragon enhanced hearing. He didn't even dare say anything to Twitch or Iselle for fear of what the guards would overhear and so it was a long, awkward, quiet march through long corridors where the heavy tapestries gave way to silk hangings and the dark stone walls were gradually changed into a shining tile mosaic.

"This, I believe, you will find of a most spectacular interest," Terracatan said, stopping after they crossed another corridor.

Thane and his friends came up to stand next to the Sang and turned to look in the massive alcove. It was enormous, a perfect half circle tall enough for a dinosaur to walk in without bumping its head. Each wall was made of tile that looked like sea-colored glass and polished to a mirror brightness so the light from the windows opposite in the hallway glittered and danced with prismatic rainbows. And at the center of all this was a door.

The most boring, ordinary, dull brown front door that Thane could imagine. It wouldn't be out of place on any of the homes in his neighborhood. It wouldn't be noteworthy as the entrance to any lower-middle class American household anywhere in the nation, with its flat wooden finish and slightly chipped brass knob and deadbolt.

But it was here, a universe away, in a castle owned by an evil alien who was frozen in place by lullabies.

The look on Thane's face was must've been stuck in some form of shock and incredulity, because Terracatan chuckled. "This is the entryway to my museum. The study of Sol is a little hobby of mine, Earth most particularly." He threw his right arm upward, causing Jaeger to launch into the air, before moving closer to the door. Terracatan took long moments to languidly wrap each finger around the handle in something more than a mere caress; enough more to make Thane look away and feel uncomfortable.

So he wasn't looking when he heard a piece of music in his head, only two or three dissonant notes not quite resolving into a minor chord, and then a very audible click passed through his eardrums and knocked the song out.

The Sang opened the door and two of the guards dashed in first, weapons at the ready, and darted off in opposite directions once inside. Terracatan didn't seem to notice, but stepped in while inhaling in a luxurious manner.

"Welcome home, young Lord de Argos of Earth," the First Lord of the Sang Evarish said.

Thane went through the door. He had to let go of Iselle's arm, because the doorway wasn't wide enough for them to pass through together, but he kept her hand held gently in his scaled one. And stopped. He was so shocked that he gasped, and began coughing in the dry, thin air.

Iselle leaned over him with an expression of great concern. "My Lord?" she said, and her lower lip quivered. In a tone both quieter and more firm she added, "Breathe in more often and more deeply; there is not as much oxygen or water in this air, and you need to adapt quickly. He is watching."

He jerked his head up and down in a quick nod and inhaled as much air as his lungs could hold, and then exhaled quickly and repeated the process. It did help; although the air was thin and dry, Thane didn't feel so dizzy anymore.

"Shredding holes," observed Twitch as he came through the doorway behind them, and altered his own breathing to compensate.

The room they were in had a faded hound's-tooth couch resting on a dark orange shag rug. There was a television with crooked antennae in the corner on a small stand, incongruously attached to two full stack speakers that towered over it. The wall opposite was dominated by a china cabinet filled with ceramic figurines of all kinds, puppies and kittens and clowns and children playing with multicolored balloons interspersed with chess pieces, action figures, and rubber toys Thane would've guessed were meant for pets.

"What." It wasn't a question as much as a vocal pause while Thane struggled to wrap his mind around this room. Other than the clutter and the mismatched decor there wasn't anything spectacular about the... parlor? Living room? Thane wasn't sure what to call it. But the visual of the First Lord of the Sang in his immaculate dress and red skin marbled with black veins reclining on the definitely-somebody's-grandmother's-couch struck him as hilarious. And Jaeger, curled up next to him on the couch and staring with visible yearning at the rubber balls with bells inside was not helping.

Terracatan spoke and his voice was not as resonant or powerful in the thinner atmosphere. "This is only the antechamber, please, continue," and he waved a languid hand towards a beaded curtain hanging between the couch and the curios.

Thane could feel his face contorting into strange expressions as he struggled not to laugh and saw Terracatan raise an eyebrow. He hurried through the beads before his host could ask him any more questions, and was again startled by the bizarre contradictions around him as each thing he could see was familiar, but all the context was wrong.

He couldn't tell whether the room was supposed to represent something indoors or outdoors. Taxidermic birds hung suspended in the air and short fake trees lined a sidewalk made of colored tile that led to a canopied bed with a nightstand next to it. There was a lamp and a jewelry box on top of the stand, as well as a universal remote and four different game controllers. A bear skin rug lay sideways under the bed so the head and one claw poked out. The walls and the ceiling were rounded and painted blue with irregular smears of white, but the blue had too much green in it and felt like being under water instead of in open air.

Even though the room was the size of a classroom the effect as a whole was suffocating. Terracatan was speaking to them, going on about this piece or that and how he'd acquired it and seemed especially pleased with the bear rug as he kept referring to it with fond tones, but Thane could not pay attention. Besides all the visual discordance there was a sound. Dissonant and upset, like the humming of angry bees and the scraping of metal on chalkboard, the tones close enough to grind against each other but not close enough to blend together. It filled his head until it ached. They continued through more rooms filled with so many things Thane couldn't process them all but instead saw them in strange flashes.

A football helmet holding fake fruit and a statue of a man with an elephant's head. A marble statue with too many arms holding a music box. A Christmas tree with a shining star on top and hung with broken cell phones and barbed wire. A display of children's toys and guns and rusted knives and hypodermic needles and office supplies. Each of the million billion things on

Earth shaken in a mixing bowl and spewed into another universe and put on display by someone without context or understanding. All displaced, and all screaming in voiceless despair that grated against Thane's eyes and inside his skull until he wanted nothing more than a safe place to be noisily sick.

He squeezed his eyes shut against the incoherent visuals around him and tried to silence the discord within. A cool, soft hand pressed against his cheek and he heard Iselle's murmuring voice close to his ear, but the harsh rasping stole her words so he could not understand them.

She didn't press him or speak again. Instead she held his arm more firmly and kept him moving, kept him turning so Terracatan's voice was always somewhere behind. Thane could feel Iselle holding him up, standing next to him and exuding her calm to wrap him in it so he could fight the battle of sound within. He didn't understand why this was having such an effect on him. All these were just things, objects, lifeless, and he was still burnt out of his own Song. How could they all be screaming with such rage and pain and fear, and how could he hear it? And why so clearly? And why now?

He reached his other hand across his body and gripped Iselle's hand where he could feel it on his bicep. She continued to steer him through as he could feel the texture of the floor change under his shoes, soft and yielding like grass to a rubbery asphalt consistency and from there to hard and smooth similar to wood before returning to the tile of the outer hallway. He focused on those surfaces, trying with an increase in desperation to ignore the shriek of agonized Song until it began to fade.

"It is beautiful," Iselle breathed, and it was the first thing Thane could hear in an eternity. Her voice was beautiful. With great caution and no small hesitation Thane squinted through his eyelids, prepared to slam them closed again. But he didn't need to; she was right. They had emerged from the museum of horrors into a corridor beyond, where the air had returned to the heavy, wet atmosphere of Shae and filling the wall before them was a piece of art that felt whole, balanced. Terracatan paused in his conversation with Jaeger to smile back at her.

"I had it commissioned from a human artist, and have been told it is very good likeness. Is it similar?" Terracatan inquired.

"What?" Thane looked at the wall again. He'd thought it was just another piece of art, like the tapestries, but he'd been so distracted by the glory of the colors and the miraculous and cleansing feeling of harmony he hadn't looked to see what the picture actually was.

"Versailles, isn't it? From the main courtyard?" Twitch stepped closer. "Late summer, mid-morning..." Twitch paused, and blinked. "This is before the 1814 restoration by King Louis the thirteenth. The man who did this for you, he'd seen pictures of it?"

Terracatan glanced at Thane. "I cannot decide whether it is juvenile or endearing that you allow your slaves to speak so freely." He waved his hand to forestall Thane's answer. "From memory. The human said he'd grown up there, although for what purpose they would allow those caterwauling useless pests in such a palace I cannot fathom. Perhaps your science Song has a way of making them mute?" Thane shook his head in response. Terracatan sighed. "Pity. I cannot find a way to do so here that does not permanently maim them. I thought perhaps your science would have a better solution; having a way to keep them silent until you wish them able to speak would be a most useful ability. You seem to be quite good at it, if your lackeys aren't."

Thane thought most of his teachers would agree. Terracatan turned forward again and continued walking, his low conversation with Jaeger resuming as though it had never been paused. The feeling of nausea and vertigo still hadn't left him, and he was more grateful than he could articulate for Iselle's steady presence next to him.

"Focus on the mission, Timothy," Iselle spoke with almost no sound so the guards following behind could not hear. "You are making it difficult for me to

get past you. It is all I can do to keep Thane from vomiting on all our shoes."
Thane blanched.

"He was raised there?" Twitch was thinking about the painted mosaic. "And then brought here, and was able to recreate that from memory- no easy task, and not a short one either- and the paint isn't faded at all. We have reliable intel on the lifespan of the Sang Evarish, and that would fall well outside the established range unless," his voice cut off, and Thane looked back at his friend to see him standing stone still in the hallway, mouth open, before one of the grey creatures shoved him with the butt of its spear. Twitch stumbled forward enough to come within a breath of bumping into Thane and Iselle.

"We got it wrong, the time dilation we got it wrong. The effects are even slower here than we thought which means that the time outside on Earth is passing faster than we expected and we don't have five days, we have four. If we don't leave tonight we won't make it back to the way in time," the brilliant tech specialist said in a rapid burst while he was close enough for Thane and Iselle to hear and far enough from the guards for them to not.

It was all too fast and too much for Thane to process, but it must've been something bad because the red flush in Iselle's cheeks faded and turned greyish. "No, no, that cannot be right," she protested, but it was weak.

"What can't be right?" Thane's frustration made his words carry further than a whisper. He flinched.

Jaeger's voice rose ahead of them and Thane caught a few words, "energy storage," and "semi-permanent," but Terracatan lengthened his pace to draw further ahead of them. Their voices returned to inaudible murmurings.

"Check your watch," Twitch demanded. Thane looked at him blankly for a moment before remembering the watch Ruan de Argos, his father, had given him before they stepped through the portal. He'd forgotten about it. He tried to move his sleeve and glance down at it without attracting the notice of the guards or of the Sang. He needn't have worried; no one else was paying attention to him anyway. It was a lucky thing, too, since once he looked at the watch face his jaw dropped and he managed to trip on his own feet and Iselle had to keep him from falling.

They were supposed to have four days in the Shaerealm, which would take six days back on earth. It was midmorning when they arrived, a day and a half of travel and half a day here in the fortress of the Lord of the Sang. Thane and his friends had used two days. The watch hands should've been split, one straight up and one straight down signifying half of their time used. Six o'clock on a twelve-hour clock.

Not just before nine. Not two thirds of the way done. Not missing a full day of planning and time to escape. He swallowed, hard, and the lump traveled down his throat with a burning pain. A day and a half of travel. If they left now, this moment, just grabbed them all and ran, they still wouldn't make it. And they didn't even have a plan.

"I think I have a plan," Twitch said. "But I'll need Jaeger to steal it, first, and we'll have to break back into the Sol Museum."

Thane vomited all over the tile, and his feet, and Iselle's feet, and saw Terracatan recoiling in aristocratic horror. His knees went weak and he felt himself falling, but knew he could not let go of Iselle or they would take her. He locked one arm around her waist. Guards rushed at him but he swung his claws at them with his draining strength and growled. Blackness crowded the edge of his vision and he heard Terracatan's voice, annoyed and disgusted, commanding servants and slaves. Thane fought to grasp at the last pinpoint of light until he heard Paka hissing and shouting and then saw her dark furry face staring down at him.

She would protect Iselle. He could trust his packmate and let the blackness take him and finally, finally silence those voices that screamed to him in pain.

CHAPTER 19

"Dinnae fash yerself, tadpole, yer nae the first bairn tae swoon aboot a monster beneath yer bed," Charlie's voice dragged Thane's consciousness upward through the swimming darkness and into the light of the amber globes. He blinked, trying to pull together some memories of the recent past. It was so hard to think. His grandfather was hovering over him, trying to hide concern with a smirk and not doing it very well.

The state of his mouth penetrated his consciousness and he groaned, exhaling. "Oh, gross. Your breath smells like something died," Remi said.

"Tastes like it too," Thane said, rolling his head to look at her. She smiled down at him, her face glowing and happier than Thane could ever remember seeing her. "Wait, you're here?"

"We all are," said another voice, less familiar but not foreign, and Thane pushed himself up on one elbow to look at Meagan Gage kneeling next to him and wringing out a clean cloth in a bucket of water.

Even in her flat brown slave robes she held herself like someone who mattered. If Thane had never known Remi, he still would've moved to obey any order or directive Major Gage issued because she expected to be heeded. It was the opposite of being invisible; she commanded such a presence in the room it was impossible not to see her. Thane had seen glimmers of that in Remi, but he'd thought it was a result of always being new in every school. Then he thought it'd been a part of being a phoenix. Seeing her mother leaning toward him and feeling her using the rough cloth to wipe the stale sweat from his face he thought he understood better. That presence was a part of her. It was genetic, encoded into her DNA. It, like so many other things about her, made her Remi.

"How's au wit ye, lad? Yer seemin' a mite flushed," Charlie said. Thane realized he was staring at Major Gage with his mouth open, not quite gaping, but not quite not gaping, either. He felt his cheeks burning.

"Can I have some water?" he mumbled and tried to pretend he had not been staring at his best friend's long lost mother, or even if he was it was no big deal.

Major Gage nodded, but it was Brennan who brought over an empty cup and a second bucket. "Swish first, kid. Rinse it out as many times as it takes," he instructed, handing Thane the empty cup and setting down the bucket next to him. Major Gage slid over the clean water so Thane could reach it easily, and then slid her arm behind his shoulders to help him sit up further.

He could feel the flush from his cheeks spreading down his neck. Why was Remi's mom so young? And why did she keep looking at him like that, her eyebrows scrunched together and her mouth not smiling, but not unhappy? Her expression made his stomach get a strange, fluttery feeling, not like he was going to be sick but not like he wasn't, either.

"What happened?' he asked, before filling the cup with water and sloshing it around in his mouth. The grit and bile loosened and he spat the mess into the empty bucket.

"Hyu hurled like a volcano," Jaeger's gleeful assessment sounded a little distracted, but he couldn't see the imp. Thane could hear the jingle of bells coming from a direction near Jaeger's voice. "Vesuvius in vomit, all over the floor and walls. Terracatan told his guards to pick hyu up and take hyu to the healer, but hyu wouldn't let them get close. Hyu fell and dragged Iselle down to puke town with hyu, yelling not to touch her. Terracatan shouted for Semubyt, and he and Paka came. Aye think Terracatan would have just killed hyu, but he couldn't get close without stepping in the messy. He made the grey men carry hyu and Iselle back once hyu had gone under and sent for the human healer to tend hyu."

Jaeger's head shot up from between the floor cushions, much closer than Thane expected. He had the cat toy in the corner of his mouth; the rubber one with the jingle bell inside Thane remembered from the first room of that unsettling museum. "It was not the best plan but a good one; we escaped from the shadow to plan and Paka made it so the healer must bring both her assistants and here we are all together to reverse the stomach flow and bind the wounds before we make our plan to go."

This rather long and mumbled monologue made the rubber ball shoot out of Jaeger's mouth and bounce away, jangling obnoxiously as it went. Jaeger bounded after it, his tail lashing and claws out while giggling.

"You did this on purpose? Wow, that worked really well. How did you know my mom was the healer?" Remi asked, then added, "What would have made it the best?"

"Blowing stuff up," Brennan and Twitch said in unison while Jaeger catapulted straight up the wall behind them.

Something else was bothering Thane. "Bind up what wounds?" he asked, struggling to sit up more and ducking sideways out of Major Gage's attempted assistance. "Where are Iselle and Paka?"

"Paka is in the bathing chamber, washing again," Iselle's soft voice came from behind him, and he twisted his torso around to look at her. "She was... displeased at the mess you made of her fur. I do not think she would like to stand near you for many days."

He dropped the cup with a clatter and started toward her before getting dizzy. She was sitting on a cushion and leaning up against the wall. One hand was bandaged from the tips of her fingers to her elbow with rough cloth, and even more was wound about her waist. Breathing seemed difficult; there was a slight rasping sound with every shallow inhalation. Her normally pale face was almost completely devoid of any color but an ashen grey under her cheeks.

"What did they do to you?" Thane demanded. "I'm so sorry, I wasn't going to let them take you away, I'm so sorry they hurt you," he held his hands out to her, both in apology and trying to find something he could do to ease the pain or help at all.

She didn't answer his question, but said, "It is not so bad, I have had much worse. Once, even, in your previous company, when you also tried to save me from a monster." The smile she gave him was serene and warm, if weak. He smiled back at her, one blue-scaled hand still half reaching out.

"They didn't even do it," Remi's voice cut in through their shared memory. "You did."

"What?" Thane rocked back on his heels. He felt sick again.

"Remi," Major Gage frowned at her daughter with her eyebrows furrowed.

"She isn't telling him the truth," Remi shot back. Some of that happy glow from earlier had gone. Not all of it; even scowling at her mom there was still more in her face of joy and wonder than argument. "Shouldn't he be more careful with those things?"

Thane recoiled, her words feeling like a stinging slap in the center of his chest. Those things were his hands, or used to be. Remi saw the look on his face now and faltered. "No, I-"

"Every word I spoke was true," Iselle cut Remi off, the French accent coming out thickly through her set jaw and narrowed eyes. "I 'ave 'ad much worse, even from members of my own team. I am not so weak as you would like, and as I am the one bearing the wounds I think I should 'ave been the one to determine who would bear the guilt of them." She used her good hand to push against the wall and rose to her feet, casting a warning glance at Charlie when he moved to help her.

"I am glad we 'ave found you, Major," Iselle said, with a little bow in lieu of a salute. "Twitch 'as already discussed 'is plan with me as you cared for Thane. I believe it will work, and I will gladly perform the role it requires of me. For the moment, I must go and rest in order to heal." She looked at Remi with a raised eyebrow, then looked down at a where Thane sat, slumped and miserable. "I would gratefully exchange a few cuts for not being a slave in this evil place. Thank you for allowing me to be strong enough to make that choice. *À bientôt!*" She left the room at a measured pace, steady but slow.

There was a beat of silence before a jingling blur of rubber smacked Charlie in the side of the head. "Ah, ya bawbag!"

"That was French," Jaeger stated while flipping through the air. He ended up ahead of the ball and smacked it with the end of his leathery tail.

"I know," said Remi, ducking out of the way as the rubber whizzed past.

"It means see hyu later," Jaeger continued, positioning himself to kick the ball from where it bounced off the wall.

"I know!" Remi scrambled backward on hands and feet as the hard red rubber thwacked against the floor where she'd been.

"Enough," Major Gage didn't yell. Yelling would only have diminished the authority with which she spoke. Jaeger grabbed the ball with both hands and curled himself around it, halting both forward momentums and tumbling to a cushion.

His head popped up and he looked at Remi, slitted eyes whirling and mouth working.

"Don't," warned the major.

"And her accent is worse when she is angry," the imp blurted and did a backward somersault onto the floor and under a stack of pillows.

Major Gage sighed. Remi had the grace to look embarrassed and guilty instead of angry, and Thane just wanted this whole thing to be over. "So there's a plan?" he asked. He was watching Remi from the corner of his eye and saw

301

her look of gratitude. Thane wasn't mad. He was way too tired for mad. Sad seemed to fit snugly inside exhausted and would take work to evict so he let that one stay, bone heavy despair and bone deep weariness indistinguishable. And his mouth still tasted awful.

"Yeah, the plan," Twitch was staring down at his palm. Thane wasn't sure he'd looked up once during the entire previous confrontation conversation. He was engrossed in the little rectangle he held, tapping it so quickly it sounded like tiny rain until he slid it out on the ground. It poured out of his hand like white liquid and expanded on the floor until it became that same tech Thane remembered from earlier, the map that was also a touch screen.

"I haven't seen this form of Song before; what is it?" Major Gage asked Twitch, looking down at the backlit screen.

"Not Song, technology," Twitch corrected, and then added a belated, "ma'am," when she didn't answer.

But she wasn't waiting for protocol. Major Gage was staring at him with her eyes wide and her eyebrows furrowed. She opened her mouth, paused, shut it again, looked down at the rendering map, and back up at Twitch. The second time she tried to speak her voice sounded thin and strained, and she addressed Brennan. "You got tech to work here?"

"Only his," Brennan jerked a thumb at Twitch, "And only when he uses it."

"That's amazing," Major Gage looked back at Twitch. "What is his bloodline?"

"Human, nothing else," Twitch answered for himself. "Plan now?"

"Wait," Brennan said, and took something out of his pocket. It was small and round and shaped roughly like a walnut. He put it to his mouth and blew once, then returned it to his pocket.

Paka came into the room, followed a few paces after by a sullen faced Finn. Paka was scrubbing the fur on the back of her head and neck with a towel. She paused and glanced at Brennan to comment, "Iselle is resting and says she has already been briefed," in a way that was not quite a question. The slight hissing she always made when pronouncing the letter "s" was more wild, more alien here, and the look she gave Thane was definitely feral. He shivered, unable to repress the chill that ran down his spine.

Brennan nodded to her and she sat down, cross-legged, on a pillow near the door. Finn leaned against the wall without comment but as far away from the Pantera as he could be and still be in the room.

"Nae time like the present, lad, get jabberin'," Charlie's cheerful criticism broke the mounting tension by being universally obnoxious. Every adult in the room glared at him while Jaeger chortled, causing his pile of cushions to shake, and Remi rolled her eyes.

"Okay, so here's what we know," Twitch began, moving to the screen and using his fingers to manipulate the map. "We've established those resonance portals are here and here," glowing green dots lit up on the wall outside the room they were in, and in the smallest storeroom adjacent to the human area.

Major Gage moved forward, and it was only as she did that Thane noticed she and Remi were holding hands. His throat suddenly felt hot and tight and his eyes burned. He blinked and tried to swallow while Remi's mom interjected while pointing to the map.

"Resonance ways are also here to the kitchens," she pointed to the wall outside a large room, "here and here," a room and a hallway Thane was unfamiliar with, "here, near the main bathing chamber, and in these final three locations."

Twitch was following her movements with his own, and green lights lit up in all of the places the Major had indicated. The tech specialist grew more agitated with each new door until Thane wasn't sure if Twitch was going vibrate through a wall all by himself.

"You're sure, you're absolutely sure all of these are accurate and undiscovered by the Sang?" Twitch demanded, leaning towards her until his nose was inches from hers. "All of them? Each of them? That one?" He jabbed his finger backwards at the map while moving his face so close Thane couldn't tell if they were touching. One of the lights started to blink.

"Sergeant Tayler?" Major Gage made his name sound like an order and a reprimand.

"Ease off, Twitch," Brennan said, but also added, "now answer the man's question, Major."

"Yes, I am sure of all the ways," she replied once Twitch had leaned back. "We patrol and check them regularly, and only humans," she paused to glower at Charlie, "or someone who can sing can use them." She looked back at Brennan. "I heard you got a front row seat for how most of the full blooded Shae react to music."

"Exactly!" Twitch punched his hand at the map and stuck out his finger at the last moment. The blinking light illuminated the tip of his fingernail with each flash. "If her intel is correct, this just got minimally less likely to fail. We can move faster and get out sooner and get further away before they release the inugamae and we die. This is excellent!"

"I'm getting mixed signals, here," Remi whispered to Thane.

He tried to smile to reassure her, but it was hard to do. Thane felt so tired, and heavy, and he tried not to stare at Remi's fingers where they were twined with her mother's. He should be happy for them. He felt a warm hand fall on his own shoulder. "Yer nae s' guid at tellin' stories, yer great twitchy lump," Charlie interjected. "We dinnae have long. Cut tae the meat of it." Charlie squeezed Thane's shoulder. "We heroes have a might of stuff tae do afore the nether moon."

"Right, right," Twitch shook his head to clear it. "The plan is in four parts. One, we need to break into the Sol museum and bring back these things." He brought up several images on the screen with items highlighted. "We need to distract Terracatan so he won't catch us, and also so he won't go back to the museum before tonight. Two, we need to get all the Sang and most of the Shae into the same place, preferably somewhere large with good acoustics like that feasting hall. Three, we need to get a signal to Kith and Jena so they know when and were to meet us with the rest of the Shae we brought so we can get back to the soundgate, which will hopefully still be there."

"How far is the soundgate? How will you get it open again?" Major Gage asked.

"It took us a full day to get here, but we stopped for the night," Brennan answered. He ignored her second question. "So we need two teams working in tandem with set rendezvous times. Of necessity Thane and Iselle will be on the first team, but we'll need Paka and Finn with them this time for backup and muscle. Twitch, Jaeger and I will be the retrieval team for the items in the Sol museum." Thane was embarrassed at how relieved he felt at not being on the team who had to go back into that mad place. "Charlie, you take Major Gage to her rooms so she can gather up any possessions she feels it important come with us," Brennan said that so nonchalantly he could have lit sparklers and hung a banner that said GET US WHAT WE CAME FOR and been more subtle.

"And prepare the others," Major Gage added.

Brennan paused. "What... others?"

"All the other humans we're taking with us," she said.

Twitch, Paka, and Brennan exchanged glances. "How many others?" Brennan asked again.

"I'm sorry, I must have phrased that badly." Major Gage stared Brennan down. "We're taking all the other humans with us." She waited for a beat with one eyebrow raised, then added, "otherwise I see no reason to leave at all."

"What?" Remi sounded like she'd had the breath knocked out of her, like she'd said that word instead of ouch.

Major Gage immediately turned to her and grabbed her other hand. "Remi, I'm so proud of you, and I'm so grateful I get to see you, even if these idiots should never have brought you." Remi's mom held both the girl's hands in one of her own, and used the other to brush back the hair that fell into Remi's face. "It's such a shock to see you, and how much you've grown up," Meagan Gage swallowed, and her voice quavered, "even more than I realized. I've thought about you every day, prayed that you were safe and happy, and hoped you missed me. Not enough to make you sad, just enough to know I really loved you. Love you." She laughed and gasped at the same time, wrapping her arms around her daughter and pulling her in close. "I am going to kill Andrus for letting you do this."

"He doesn't know," Remi mumbled into her mother's neck. She couldn't see Major Gage's face, but Thane could. He saw shock, then confusion, and then anger move across her features like emotional flashcards before settling into a neutral sort of blankness that Thane instinctively feared.

Slowly she released Remi from the hug and put her hands on Remi's shoulders. "What do you mean, he doesn't know? You have tech support, and a trained team," Major Gage indicated Brennan as representative of them all. "Who authorized this?"

"That's what you're worried about?" Remi's voice broke somewhere between anger and disbelief. "We lied to dad, mom. We broke out of Sanctum. I made them do it, because I told them I was going with or without help, and when they said I'd die without their help I told them I knew that! Dad already broke the rules; he sent Jaeger here to find you through a rift my science teacher created. That's how I knew where you were!"

"What?" Meagan Gage looked around. "Jaeger!" No response.

At least, not from the imp. "It isn't Jaeger's fault, mom," Remi protested, lifting her arms to shake off her mother's restraining hands. "I made him tell me. I made them all come. For you. Because I wasn't going home without you, even though you left us. You left me. And now you're not coming home because of all these random people?"

"Remi, puppy, listen," she tried to recapture Remi's hand, and Remi let her hold one in both of her own. Thane couldn't see Remi's face, but he saw her flinch at the pet name and could see her shoulders shaking and her hunched back. He knew she was crying, and he felt like someone had punched him in the stomach. "When I left on this mission, I knew I was coming back. It wasn't supposed to even make it as far as the Shaerealm; it was reconnaissance only, and some extraordinary events gave us once shot to save the world. We talked about it, about the risks, and we took it together. All of us. They had families too, people they'd left who were waiting for them. It was nearly impossible to walk out our door without you and Andrus, even expecting to come back. How could I abandon all these people, who I've worked with and fought with and survived with here for years, knowing no one will ever be back to save them? Knowing," and here she pulled up Remi's chin and made her daughter face her, "Terracatan will be furious and take it out on them. We don't leave people behind, puppy, you know that."

"I do," Remi sniffed and wiped her nose on her shirtsleeve before glaring at Charlie. "We don't leave people behind. Of course we're bringing them all."

"Of course we are!" Twitch threw his arms up in the air, the words exploding out of him. "Why shouldn't we? Why couldn't we? Oh yeah, because there are old people and baby people and sick people and we're trying to outrun a shredding shadow army. And not just out of his lands, but across the hills and back to a hunting meadow full of predators where there may or may not be a functioning gate to take us home!" This last exclamation seemed to drain all his remaining energy, and he plopped down on the cushion behind him and put his head in his hands. He mumbled into them, and Thane could make out the words, "too quiet without you" in the middle.

"He makes an important point," Brennan said, pushing himself up from the wall he'd been leaning against and turning to face Major Gage directly. "You say if you leave without them, which I know you're not willing to do," he held up a hand to forestall her protest, "Terracatan will punish them. May even kill some of them. If we take them with us some will die, and perhaps all of them. We have no guarantee of safety, nor of passage, nor even the way we came will still be open. We have the bones of a plan and a hope that some of us will make it back to Earth still alive and every additional person we take increases the odds of someone else dying." He broke eye contact with Major Gage then and glanced at Remi, then back at her mother. The implication was obvious- for every extra person they brought, the odds that Remi would be one of the ones who didn't make it back got higher. "Even if that is a risk you are willing to take it is not your place to make that decision for anyone else. We are not taking everyone with us."

An immediate cry met this pronouncement, some in agreement and clearly some adamantly opposed, but Brennan cut it short with a shrill whistle. "Instead," his voice was quiet, barely loud enough to make it from one edge of the chamber to another, "we are going to give them the choice. Anyone who wants to risk coming and dying, can, and anyone who wants to risk staying and dying can do that too. We can't undo coming, so we can't take away their risk. I will not take away their choice."

"What if one of them tells?" Finn's voice broke into the conversation for the first time. He still looked sullen, but his eyes were hard and Thane couldn't tell if he was angry or terrified. Thane wished Iselle would come back; his head hurt and he wanted to apologize again, but out loud this time. "How do we know one of them won't go scurrying off to their master to tattle just to get a pat on the head?" He shook his own back and forth. "No way. I know you self-righteous piss pots don't care if I have an opinion, but I'm getting my boss his son back and I'm going to do it with you or through you." He narrowed his eyes and his nostrils flared as he glowered at Brennan. "Unless you think that Lord Ruan de Argos, First Lord of Chaos and the Shae beyond the Stars sent his only heir to a place outside his control without a backup plan? Or three?"

"What backup plan?" Thane asked, but his question was completely drowned out by Major Gage's reaction to Finn.

"Ruan de Argos?" she shrieked. So quickly it seemed between one blink and the next Thane saw Major Gage sitting on the floor next to Remi and then the major was standing over a prone Finn and holding a long rifle aimed at his throat. Finn's rifle, Thane realized.

Other people had moved during that one blink. Charlie had placed himself between Remi and everyone else, and Paka had a long dagger in each hand and was crouched and tense next to Major Gage and Finn, one weapon primed for each target.

"What is this scum talking about, Tayler?" Major Gage demanded. "What does de Argos have to do with any of this?" Her jaw tightened so hard Thane heard it pop. "Are you traitors? What did he offer you? It won't happen, I guarantee it."

"Mom, no!" Remi tried to push past Charlie, but he wouldn't allow it. She growled in obvious frustration. "We aren't traitors to anybody, mom, calm down. Only Finn works for de Argos, and he had to come. It was part of the deal."

Major Gage and Brennan wore identical expressions of mouths pressed together in thin lines with eyebrows furrowed, and Thane heard Brennan's soft groan of resignation. "What deal," Major Gage demanded. It was clearly an order, not a question.

"My deal," Thane said, trying to push himself to his feet and finding it surprisingly difficult. He wanted to get between the others and the danger, but it was getting harder to think. "It was the only way to get here."

"I want to hear this from you, Tayler," without moving the rifle from Finn's throat, Major Gage managed to include Brennan in the threat.

"Have you ever met your daughter?" Brennan answer seemed to surprise her, because she flicked her eyes away from Finn to glance at Brennan, and then

Remi, and then back. "I know you've been gone a while, but I can't imagine her personality is something that developed after you left. Remi is your child, Major, yours and the general's. What would you have done if you found out she was alive but trapped in the Shae? What about Andrus, what would he have done? Take those two responses and add them together. That's her," he finished, pointing at Remi.

Major Meagan Gage snorted. "That was the only reason I haven't already killed you for bringing her. Meeting Andrus was like being caught in a windstorm. Remi has always had the determination of a force of nature. I was living with the immovable object and the unstoppable force, but they were *mine*. But none of that explains the snake de Argos."

"He opened the gateway to get us here." Brennan's statement hung in the air, echoing in the silence it created.

"Why?" Major Gage glanced at Charlie. "I thought you'd done it."

"Nae, lass," Charlie's voice was unexpectedly soft. It felt gentle, with echoes of loss and sorrow over centuries. "Nothing in all the Weaves and Ways couldae enticed me tae throw yer daughter intae this bear trap. I came so she wouldnae have tae."

"But you didn't tell me that!" Remi exploded. She pushed him aside with both hands, and he allowed her to. "Dad wouldn't help, dragon-brain here wouldn't help, Thane was the only one who had a plan that might work so we snuck out and went to see de Argos! And the only way he would let us come is if we brought Finn to guard Thane."

"Shut up," Finn growled from the floor.

Major Gage pushed the muzzle of his rifle into his Adam's apple. "Don't. Speak. To my daughter," she shoved each word through gritted teeth.

"You were the stupid human who brought it up," Paka growled. She straightened out of her fighting stance and stretched, knives disappearing. "I think she can kill you if she wants. I don't like you."

"You did bring it up," Major Gage mused. "What did you mean?" She blinked several times, and Thane could see her mouthing the words Finn had spoken, more than just his father's name penetrating her thoughts. The edge of the rifle relaxed on Finn's neck, although her grip on the weapon remained firm. She stepped backwards to allow the man to sit up without giving him any opportunity to regain his firearm and looked at Brennan again. "Why did de Argos help you?" her words seemed strained, like it was hard to get enough air for them. "What did he mean, his only heir?"

Thane suddenly didn't want her to know, didn't want to see the way she looked at him change from whatever it had been to disgust or fear. Considering her reaction to his father's name he could only imagine how she would feel to find out Remi's best friend- were they still best friends?- was the son of a dragon she so visibly loathed. Everyone was looking at him. He shook his head in negation, holding up both hands in protest and then seeing them, dark blue dragon limbs, and he jerked them back. He was so tired.

"Consider it a surprise," Finn answered. He pushed himself to his feet, sneering at them all unpleasantly. "And now it's about time for Thane and I to be going, before the Sang appears with his minions to kill us all."

Remi snorted, and Finn raised an eyebrow at her. "Don't believe me? Where's Jaeger?"

"He's over there," Remi pointed to the pile of pillows Jaeger had hidden under, to avoid Major Gage's reprimand.

"Is he?" Finn's face was unpleasant in a familiar way that made Thane's stomach clench. Memories flashed of faces, Bert in his most vindictive moods and bullies throughout school, were both dizzying and distracting. Finn moved forward and brushed aside the pillows with a broad sweep of his arm. Jaeger was not beneath them.

"Twitch?" Brennan's voice wasn't worried. In fact, it was so not worried Thane knew there was definitely something to be very worried about.

Twitch bent over the screen on the floor, tapping and moving pieces of the visible images. Then he went to the wall and moved aside a curtain to reveal another small device that looked like a small silver egg on a little cup. It had a flashing light on one side.

"He isn't in our rooms," Twitch confirmed. "Location unknown. We aren't getting a signal from his biotag."

Brennan closed his eyes and breathed in for several beats. "Please tell Iselle we will be joining her soon," he said to Paka. She left the room as a black ripple, silent and smooth as ink being poured into a jar. "Twitch, gather your equipment and take it into the main hall. Major?" he said, and she nodded and rose, pulling Remi up to standing with her.

The two Gage women started towards the door, but Major Gage paused and looked Brennan in the eye. "You're sure you can handle this?"

Brennan chortled. "Me? No. But I don't need to." Brennan nodded to something behind Thane. Major Gage turned to look and her eyes widened.

"Oh," was her only comment, then she too left, pulling Remi with her. Remi had seen whatever her mother had seen also, and was gaping.

"C'mon, kid," Brennan said, reaching down to slide his arms under Thane's armpits and help him rise.

"Leave th' lad," a familiar voice spoke. A familiar, deep voice. A voice so large and resonant that the stones underneath him vibrated with it. Brennan lowered Thane again, but squeezed his shoulder once in a comforting way before leaving the room and shutting the door behind him.

"Yer stayin'." Charlie was speaking to Finn, somehow using his full dragon voice without changing shape or losing his accent like every other time Thane had heard it.

Finn paused in his striding to the door mid-step, then lowered his foot to the ground.

"Feast yer eyes this'a way," Charlie instructed, and Finn turned to face him.

"There's things ye ought tae be lairnin' naow," Thane could hear Charlie's muffled footsteps as he drew nearer to where Finn was motionless, standing between Thane and the door.

His grandfather came into view, then, much closer than Thane realized. He was barefoot, which Thane noticed because his head felt so heavy that he could not hold it up anymore. Charlie's feet looked strange, weirdly elongated and blue at the edges and fuzzy. Thane blinked. Everything looked fuzzy. His mouth still tasted awful, and his head felt like it was made of thick stone someone kept trying to hammer a wedge through.

Charlie's hand came to rest on his shoulder, the same one Brennan had squeezed. "Ye should ken that this lad isnae only Ruan's child, he's my grander. The single offspring of my loins that I've heard tell of in the last half century."

Thane couldn't lift his head enough to see Finn's expression, but he did hear the hiss of air Finn sucked through his teeth. "An mebbe yer in the dark aboot it, but a dragon always kens when one of his own has been poisoned."

Thane blinked. Poisoned? He tried to pull his thoughts together, but they wouldn't come. It required an effort to keep enough attention on the room around him to hear Charlie's words and he had nothing left over for thinking.

"An ye mebbe dinnae ken I myownself has made a bit o' studyin' on the topic, as me first love passed from th' bite of a poison." Charlie's hand tightened on Thane's shoulder painfully, but Thane didn't have enough energy left to protest or even wince as Charlie raised him in the air. "An I fancy yer naught a bad sort, an it's like yer actin' on orders, an mayhaps yer even tryin' tae save me tadpole from hisself and the Sang, an this is naught but a backup plan from yer boss, as ye say. But here's th' part most pertinent tae ye."

An electric current crackled around Charlie's hand, the one gripping Thane's shoulder. It jumped from Charlie and through Thane, bouncing against the non-conductive stone under his feet and back again. As Thane's heart stuttered and jumped back into motion, forcing his sluggish blood to move,

Charlie's voice echoed in his ears and his mind. "I dinnae give a boggin rat's clag-tail. Ye mucked aboot wit me grander, an hurt him."

Charlie released Thane, and his feet found solid ground underneath. The dancing power of the lightning absorbed inward, strengthening his back and straightening his spine before rising up his gorge. He felt the urge to spit. He did, into the bucket where he'd spit the water before, and glob of thick and sticky blackness like mucus and tar sank into the filth.

"Huh." Thane watched it sink before looking at Finn, who did not seem either as tall or as imposing as Thane remembered. "Why? What would it have done?"

"He'd've been a weight tae carry all that long way," Charlie observed. "Ye wouldnae've made it tae the fence wit him."

Finn tried to swallow, and Thane watched as the man's Adam's apple jostled up and down his throat in the struggle. "Kith," he finally managed.

"Ah, which means ye have a way tae contact the hairy mess an his wee pixie." Charlie smiled, and Thane felt a small flash of pity for Finn. A very small flash. "I'm feelin' a mite generous, seein' as ye only tried tae put the lad intae a long sleep, unpleasant as the fallin' is. I'll give ye one chance tae tell me of yer ownself. How d'ye call the bug?"

"None of your-"

"I was hopin' that'd be yer feelin' on the matter," Charlie cut him off, his smile wider with more teeth. "What d'ye ken around me?"

"You go by Charlie, you're a blue dragon, you've worked both for and against Sanctum in the past, and never managed to amass anything for yourself," the pattern of Finn's voice suggested repeating something he'd read, or perhaps been briefed on.

"Aye, meatling, aught else?" Charlie prompted.

Finn swallowed again. "There are rumors that you've had more contact with The Sylphie than any other mortal, and you are in love with a phoenix soul who you relentlessly pursue until you find her."

Charlie's smile vanished and his eyebrows drew together. "Relentlessly is a bit harsh, dinnae ye think, tadpole?" Thane shrugged, declining to comment. Charlie made a face at him. "Regardless, the rest is true enough. So noaw, morsel meat, what d'ye imagine I'd do tae the man who threatened the safety of my phoenix?"

"Why would that matter?" Finn asked. Charlie stared at him without speaking. Finn glanced at Thane, and Thane raised his eyebrow and made a slight up and down motion with his chin.

Finn went red, then pale and sweaty. His hands flew into his pockets and he dug around, frantic and shaking, before pulling out a slender piece of wood with a small crystal embedded in one end about the size of a large sewing needle. He held it out to Charlie, but his hands were trembling so much he dropped it at Thane's feet.

Thane bent down and pinched it between two fingers and stood back up, looking at Finn. "R-rub the crystal and say her name," he said, his eyes wide.

"Excellent, ye toley roaster," Charlie took the stick and placed it in a hidden pocket Thane couldn't see. "Mayhaps I'll manage tae refrain placing yer sorry sack inside a large bulb an pretendin' tae be Thomas Edison. He said it took him a thousand tries tae get it right- I wager I could make that twice wi'oot breakin' a sweat. An ye should ken," Charlie's face and voice lost all pretense of playfulness or banter, and he stepped forward so Thane knew the two men stood close enough together for Finn to see the lightning spark in Charlie's too-blue eyes, "if ye further attempt tae threaten or impede this lad, be it by standin' or actin', I own yer life." The blue dragon man dropped his voice to a bare whisper. "An if ye endanger the girl, even in yer wee brain, I'll take yer soul. Ye ken?"

Thane couldn't see Finn's expression through Charlie, but he was sure it wasn't happy. "Past time tae join th' rest of th' team, eh, tadpole lad?" Charlie spoke to Thane without taking his eyes off Finn.

"No, grandpa," Thane heard his own voice coming out of his mouth without thinking it through. And kept talking. "Ruan de Argos sent Finn with me, so he's my responsibility. Did my father tell you to poison me?"

Charlie didn't step aside and Finn would not move, so Thane still couldn't see the man's face. But he could hear his voice. "No."

"Because it's a drug, not a poison, right?" Thane had dealt with Harper, his younger sister, for years, and ever since she could talk she would say anything to keep from getting in trouble. Or to get him in trouble. She didn't have any scruples against lying itself, but it was a favorite game of hers to see how much she could mislead someone without actually saying something that wasn't true. Especially when Thane would protest, and his mother would ask if Harper was lying.

If Harper could only see him now. Thane stepped forward and to one side to see Finn's face. "Did he make sure you had the drug with you and knew how to use it?"

There was a long pause when Finn didn't answer. "Tell truth, ye great sod," Charlie muttered, and made as if to grab his arm.

"Yes," the word came pushed through Finn's clenched teeth. "For your safety, and only if those SMG zealots decided to go haring off to do something stupid."

"For the record, Finn, if you'd taken me away and my friends were left behind to die, or worse, the moment we got back I would've asked my father to drug you and throw you back through the portal to find them. Or die trying."

"That's too much of a balance," Charlie protested. "Ye cannae be so pithy an' judgy an' being most of a blue."

"If his plan worked, you would've gotten them home anyway, so he'd be stuck here," Thane said. He was shoulder to shoulder with Charlie now, glaring at Finn, who looked more worried than terrified. That annoyed Thane. "So here's the new deal, Finn. If I die, my father will kill you. If Remi dies, Charlie will kill you. But if you don't swear to me, right now, you'll do everything in your power to get my team and the other people home to Earth there won't be enough of your soul left to piece together beyond the shattered stars." He leaned in, staring the other man straight in the eyes. "I will end you, forever."

The only thing that matched the level of shock on both Finn and Charlie's faces was how surprised Thane was to realize he meant it. He inspected the feeling and found it solid and whole, heavy and hard in his chest like a stone. He was going to get them home no matter what he had to do to make it happen.

"Y-yes sir," Finn saluted.

"Swear," Charlie ordered.

Finn nodded, and swallowed. "I swear. I'll help get them back."

"All of them," Thane demanded.

"All," Finn agreed.

"Git tae the others," Charlie ordered. He thrust the bucket of clean water into Finn's hands and spun him around by the shoulder. "An' give the lady Iselle a drink." Charlie shoved the man none too gently forward, and Finn stumbled, water sloshing, before gaining his footing and going out the door. It shut behind him with a click.

"Well enough, tadpole," Charlie clapped Thane on the back and grinned at him. "Yer being a grander of my own, surely. I'm proud of ye, lad."

Thane was a little ashamed of the satisfaction he felt hearing that. "But there's still Jaeger- are we in trouble? Where did he go? Ow!" He gripped his wrist over the watch his father had given him, wincing and sucking air in through his teeth.

Charlie was next to him and removing his hand finger by finger in a manner that did not quite hurt but was also non-optional. Thane didn't mind because his wrist felt like it was being branded with an iron hot enough to push through steel, but he could not move his other hand off by his own power. For a brief moment he was intensely grateful he had scales instead of skin- the cobalt blue of them didn't seem to be damaged in the heat even though he could still feel it. Delicate human skin would've been destroyed so thoroughly there wouldn't have been anything left.

His grandfather lifted the last finger off Thane's wrist and held it in place so Thane couldn't cover the wound again. Which was a good thing; his hand jerked and twitched convulsively trying to get back and protect the place that hurt so badly. The place where the watch his father had given him was trying to burn a hole through to his bone.

The hands on the watch had entered the final section of the countdown, pointing just past what would on a normal clock be minutes after nine. The entire watch face glowed with a blue white heat and a trickle of something not quite smoke and not quite steam rose into the air around it. Thane's nose was tickled with a faint metallic odor.

"Huh," Charlie seemed non-pulsed. "Gift from yer da?"

Thane nodded and swallowed, not trusting himself to speak. "That's blood metal," Charlie observed, his voice even and calm. "An' made inta a watch. Wit a timin' trigger. Songs and shreds, lad, I dinnae ken how yer standin' on yer own feet. Yer touchin' enough boilin' blood metal tae light Vesuvius, an' all yer doin' is tremblin' a mite. Didja put it on yer own self, by yer own hand?" Thane nodded. Charlie sighed. "So I cannae break compulsion. An' I cannae take it from ye, as yer a father's son an' blood will call to blood. Well then, lad, seein' as yer da has borrowed this arm from ye, I'll be needin' a loan of the other."

The pain was getting worse, and Thane was shaking too much to pay attention to what Charlie was saying anymore. His eyes were riveted on the glowing watch and the metallic smelling not smoke. He barely registered any movement as Charlie lifted the clawed finger he still held and moved it over Thane's burning wrist. Charlie mumbled something that sounded like, "Well, a nod's as guid as a wink tae a blind horse," and moved Thane's other hand in one sharp motion.

Something wet and thick and red fell into Thane's field of vision and splashed on the watch. It spat and hissed and sizzled on the watch face but did not evaporate. Instead it seemed to fight back, congealing instead of dispersing, and another large drop followed. The two merged, and seemed to start leeching away the heat from the watch and the pain from Thane.

Another drop fell, and another, and as they covered the watch face they hid the dials and the ticking countdown. The moment Thane could no longer see the watch he gasped, pulling air into his lungs as though emerging from the bottom of the ocean into the sky. "What-" he began, then stopped, staring.

There was blood on his finger, on the edge of his talon, and on the hand Charlie still held. Underneath it was Charlie's other arm where bright drops of ruby blood from the narrow but deep gash cut into it welled up and rolled off. As they fell, the drops touched and converged on the watch, wrapping it in something like a scab so it was separated from direct contact with Thane's arm. It still hurt; Thane had been pushed down staircases that hadn't hurt this much, but it was so much less than it was he could almost ignore it.

"What did you do?" It wasn't the first question he'd tried to ask, but it was suddenly much more important.

Charlie's face was covered in a sheen of sweat and his usually handsome and vibrant face was pale and a little drawn. "Blood calls tae blood, lad," he let go of Thane's hand and patted it. "An though yer father's bond is closer an more like, yer still a hatchling of mine. I cannae stop it, but I can protect ye from th' meanest of it."

"How do we get rid of it?" Thane asked. He wanted to tear it off but was too afraid to touch it, and either way, Charlie's forearm was bleeding now. He grabbed the nearest of the wall hangings and used his talons to cut a long piece of the fabric and started wrapping the laceration on his grandfather's arm.

"The one whose blood infused the metal can open the lock; it's the only way tae get it off fer sure," Thane did not like hearing Charlie's voice so weak and unsteady. It was the opposite of everything Thane knew about Charlie. "Yer da's a clever one, I'll grant him that. He's goin' tae make sure yer comin' back tae him one way or t'other, even if ye have tae suffer tae make ye git back."

"But we don't have time for this," Thane's emotions were all knotted up inside; fear, pain, and anger tumbling over each other and tangled together. Thane grabbed anger and yanked it out. "There's no way we're going to get this done, and get everyone out, and all we're doing is taking more time so even if we get out of here we won't have anywhere to go!" He slammed his fist into the wall as hard as he could, something he hadn't done since that day so long ago where Brennan had pushed him over the edge at the hospital in Payson.

He'd broken his knuckles, then, and cracked the cinderblock wall. This time the stone didn't crack. Instead it dissolved before him and inertia carried him forward, stumbling, into the hallway beyond.

Hands emerged through the wall behind him and jerked him back into the room as the stone solidified behind him again. Charlie gripped his shoulders and holding him up until he got his feet underneath him again. "What," he began, then stopped as his feet hit something. He looked down.

Jaeger was sitting cross-legged on the floor amid a pile of wires, gears, boxes, and pieces of cell phones, speakers, wireless video game controllers, and a beautifully lacquered brown wooden box. "Hyu have the same problem as all humans," Jaeger said without looking up at him. "Hyu talk too much. Don't hyu know we are already out of time?"

CHAPTER 20

Everyone was back in the small room, watching as Jaeger sorted through the stacks and pieces of gadgets and separated them into piles. Thane couldn't tell what the imp was looking for, because as the vertical slit's of Jaeger's eyes whirled with the intense study of each piece of Earth he would place it carefully in one of the four piles before him. But there were no discernible similarities between the objects in any one pile.

Twitch had tried to inspect what Jaeger brought back as well, but every time the tech specialist tried to reach for anything the imp brushed the hand away with a leathery red wing or a smack from his tail. "Are you sure you got everything?" Twitch asked for the tenth or twentieth time, rubbing a welt that ran across his knuckles.

"Aye am sure; hyu had a good plan, but Aye have a better," Jaeger said. "Hyu need to stop thinking so small. There is more than just escape to consider here."

"But how did you do it? Are we compromised? How will we keep Terracatan's minions from reporting the theft?" Major Gage seemed more than merely tense. Her eyes darted from Remi to Jaeger to the main door, and then back and forth from Charlie to Thane. Something about the way she stared at him made him uncomfortable and he hunched his shoulders a bit, subconsciously trying to appear smaller.

"Theft?" Jaeger looked up at her, blinking. "Aye committed no theft. That would be terribly rude. No, Aye was given these things by Terracatan himself. He thinks he barters well, but Aye am much better." Jaeger's grin spread wide, unnerving Thane as it always did. If a person grins ear to ear it means they are smiling as largely as they can; for the imp it was a literal statement, since the opening of his mouth actually ran all the way around his jaw. Thane had once asked Haider, the doctor from Sanctum who looked like an enormous golden lion, how Jaeger's jaw worked. Haider had shuddered and said he'd rather not talk about it.

"What did you trade, you little red beastie?" Iselle asked. She sounded more curious than insulting, and Thane got the impression it was more of an endearment than otherwise.

"Only what Aye had been given, and then not all of it," Jaeger turned back to his sorting, but his tail wrapped around something and tossed it into the air towards Iselle.

Paka caught it, snatching it from the air not quite halfway to where the French girl reclined, still resting. The Pantera opened her fist to show the others the small red bag Jaeger had carried, the one Ruan de Argos had given him, although there was barely anything in it now where it had been full before. Paka used the tips of her claws to pinch the bottom of the bag and upend the remaining contents into the center pad of her paw.

"Batteries?" Remi's voice hovered somewhere between confused and accusatory. "You traveled to a different universe and your special secret mission from a potentially dangerous dragon was to deliver a nine volt and some double A's?"

Jaeger chuckled, trying to speak. "And he doesn't even know he needed the size C!" The red Shae seemed overcome, falling backwards and laughing with his clawed feet in the air. Thane and Remi shared bewildered glances while Brennan covered his face with his hand.

"So while we were all planning, you went to Terracatan to barter for the stuff we needed, changed the plan, got different stuff, and played a prank on the First Lord of the Sang?" Brennan spoke without uncovering his face.

"Yer a canny wee nyaff," Charlie cocked his head sideways to look at Jaeger. "D'ye play at cards?"

"No!" Twitch, Iselle, and Brennan all shouted, Twitch taking a step forward and Iselle reaching out a protesting hand while Jaeger's head snapped to look at the dragon man with interest.

"He makes the cards explode," Twitch answered the confused looks of the rest of the room. "And not just the ones that he's holding. The ones you're holding. One from the middle of the deck. The entire Sanctum headquarters is banned from playing Texas Hold 'Em because of three separate incidences with the river card, powder burns, Adam Gold's footlocker and Delta Team's customized programmable wrist comms."

"That took months to clean up," Brennan lowered his hand and looked at Jaeger.

"Shuman's comm still makes him sound like a five year old girl whenever he tries to order his team into action," Iselle commented. "He's ordered three new ones, but it doesn't get fixed."

"Five," Twitch corrected, "he's ordered five, but whenever it gets synced with his DNA profile for the biolock it change the voice, and he can't use an unlocked one because it can't communicate with the others. He's been fuming about it for years now."

"I may've seriously underestimated the fun we could have," Charlie observed to Jaeger.

"You have," agreed Paka.

"Can we please focus?" Major Gage was visibly agitated now. "I need to know what's going on so I can go and get my people ready. You said you had a better plan," she looked down at Jaeger, her voice and posture in full command mode. "Well? What is that plan?"

Brennan and Paka shared a glance, Brennan wincing and Paka looking smug. "Aye will not tell hyu," Jaeger said without looking up. "Hyu will talk and talk and talk like all the humans do and we will all die of being too old before anything happens. Hyu will know what hyu need to do, and all the pieces will work together."

Major Gage was going to kill someone; Thane could see it on her face. "You will tell me and you will tell me now, imp-" she started, but Jaeger cut her off by pushing himself into the air and flapping his wings to hover in front of her face.

"Hyu want to bring out all the people. Hyu will not tell us the one question we ask. Hyu have made all the demands and asked all the questions and have not said thank you to this girl for risking us to save hyu. Hyu have kept all the people alive and safe from the Sang, good for hyu. Now shut up and let us do what we do." Jaeger snapped his wings shut and dropped back to the floor, going back to his sorting.

Everyone took a small step backward, away from Major Meagan Quinn Gage. She looked like a bomb about to burst, with shaking hands and a jaw so tight the muscles twitched. Then she burst out laughing.

"I finally understand why you insane misfits have always been Andrus' favorites," she said, wiping away a tear with the back of one hand. "I'm sorry, I'm sorry. It's been so long, and so much," she inhaled a slow, shuddering sigh. "You're right, I'm sorry. Remi," she turned to her daughter and held out her arms. Remi ran into them. "Remi, puppy, I'm so sorry, I'm so sorry! It just- it feels like a bad dream, having you here and not knowing what's going to happen but knowing all the bad things that could happen, like I only get to see you now so they can take you away again. I've missed you so much but I knew I could, I was, still keeping you safe by being here, by keeping it away and yes," she responded to Brennan's grunt and Iselle's small gasp, "the intel was good and it should be enough to keep you all from getting sent to the deepest reaches of the Sanctum dungeons if we can get it back to the council. If we all survive and get out of here." She was speaking to them all through Remi's dark hair, her head pressed down against her daughter's and her arms wrapped tight. Thane could see the tear streaks on her face, see drops falling from her nose onto Remi's scalp.

His throat hurt suddenly, constricting around a lump that burned. Meagan Gage's eyes met his, and she held out a hand to him. He blinked. "Thank you for being my daughter's friend, Thane," she whispered, and left her hand out, waiting. Gingerly he reached forward and held his own hand, claws and scales, within reach of hers.

She took it and gripped it. Remi twisted her head to smile at him, tears in her eyes too. Something hot wrapped itself around the iron resolve he still carried in his chest. Burning like molten lava it encased his determination to get them all home, like the superheated core of the earth itself.

"I need to get back, and make sure everyone is ready," Meagan Gage said, dropping Thane's hand and wiping her eyes. "Come with me, Remi?" she asked, not releasing her daughter but holding her out by both shoulders to look her in the face.

Remi grinned. "Of course! They think I'm your healing assistant now, anyway, as long as I keep my hood up."

Major Gage looked at Brennan for confirmation, and he nodded. "Iselle, you should come too, so I can replace your bandages." Remi looked decidedly less happy about this, but Brennan helped Iselle to her feet and brought her over.

There was a huge boom, followed by a second, and a third, before they could all hear a familiar and unpleasant voice shouting from the main door. "Open for the Lord Terracatan, First of the Sang, Prince of Shadow and Son of Agoth the Bloodfire Moon!" Semubyt's words were clear and loud, echoing in the smaller room as though he stood with them.

"Running out of time," Jaeger muttered.

Despite their fortifications they could hear the door creaking, and then a crack so sharp and huge Thane glanced at the rifle Major Gage still held, wondering if it had gone off. "Stay here," Brennan instructed to Thane. He jerked his chin towards Paka and they both hurried out of the room to intercept Terracatan.

"I cannae be in here," Charlie moved toward the back wall. "I may be confined tae this handsome self, but Sang'll still ken what I am if he's close enough." He gave a gallant formal bow to Remi and her mother. "I'll find ye in the caves, m'lady." He turned to Thane. "Stand tall, lad. Sang's a shark- he'll pounce if he smells blood in the water. Ye held off a gaggle of his guards yerownself whilst sick tae near dyin'- he didnae see ye weak, he saw ye strong an' mad. Hold on tae that."

With a flourish, he hummed himself through the back wall.

Remi and her mother huddled near Iselle and tried to make no noise at all. Twitch hurried to Jaeger and the two began a rapid mumbling conversation about wires and gears Thane couldn't follow at all. Thane could hear raised voices in the main chamber, excessively polite but loud, and Iselle sucked in air through her teeth like she'd been punched.

"It is not going well," she breathed, with just enough volume to hear her. "Terracatan is angry, and he brought many soldiers with him. They are restless, and excited. They are hungry." She shuddered. "A dark hunger."

"Out of time," Jaeger murmured. Thane took a step toward the door but Finn blocked him.

"Stay in here, idiot!" the mercenary hissed.

Thane paused, looking the man up and down. Then he grinned.

Thane could see the surprised looks on all the faces in the room before him, including Terracatan's, when he kicked open the door and bodily threw Finn out onto the stone floor. Striding into the chamber he grabbed Finn's collar and dragged the man forward, leaving him in a heap on the ground before the Sang's perfectly polished shoes.

Dragon strength was useful sometimes, and it felt awesome. He flexed his muscles in glee, and spoke before the startled Terracatan could gather himself. "Great Lord, please accept my most sincere apologies for the unfortunate incident this afternoon," Thane bowed with the same gallantry and flourish he'd just seen Charlie use. He ignored the panicked thumping of his heart by picturing Remi in the room behind him and wrapped all his fears and doubts into something much smaller than his determination. No matter what it takes.

"Yes, that made quite a mess in my upper hall and seriously injured several of my guardsmen," Terracatan's voice sounded like a masterful mix of irritation and concern, which they both knew was a lie. Thane had heard it before, every day on the bus for years when Harper and her mean girl posse tortured the other girls in her grade and the grades below, managing to make them feel small and make them feel like it was their own fault.

Thane had felt small. Thane had felt invisible. Thane had felt like his very existence was offensive and something he should be blamed for, and spent every day apologizing for and trying to make up.

In this moment, his existence was keeping his friends alive. "Guardsman," Thane said the word derisively, making a dismissing gesture with one hand like throwing away trash. "And as for the mess, it seems the hospitality of your table is not all it has been rumored to be." Semubyt made a hissing sound at the insult, but Terracatan cut him off with a curt wave.

"What could you mean, de Argos?" the lack of honorific was notable, but the Sang seemed more curious than angry.

"The factions of my father's house are many, and some have not been pleased to have so visible an heir," Thane was dragging every piece of terrible plot and manner of speaking he could remember from those daytime dramas and stupid romantic movies his mom loved to watch. He could always hear the dialogue from his basement since the air conditioning vent was right under the TV. Inwardly he grimaced, remembering how hard he'd worked and saved to get his first cell phone, mostly so he could put in headphones and listen to the music that he loved instead of those awful shows. "This betrayer had poisoned me."

"Truly?" Terracatan looked down at Finn, who must have decided to lay still and see how this played out. "And because this internal strife played out inside my walls you would lay its blame at my feet?"

"Perhaps," Thane paused, seeming to consider. "My father would be most displeased. He isn't good at controlling his temper, you know."

Some memory or emotion flashed behind Terracatan's creepy fake human eyes. He jerked his hand towards Finn, and a set of guards detached themselves from the rest and came forward, reaching out for him.

"No," Thane said, holding up a firm hand to forestall them. "The offense was against me and this dirt is in my father's employ. I will let my father handle it."

"You doubt my ability to make him regret his actions?" For the first time today Thane sensed Terracatan was actually offended. "I could make him weep blood and beg-"

"I have heard your threats before, Terry," Thane cut in. Terracatan's eyes widened and his mouth twitched. Something huge and dark, like black thunder, boomed in the far boundaries of Thane's hearing, and inwardly he smirked. Watching Harper had been more useful than he'd realized. "But I have seen my father's work. I have yet to see yours."

Every person standing near Thane and Terracatan shrank back and away. Even Semubyt and Paka tried to seem smaller and less noticeable. The black thunder sound grew louder, music like the scream of tympani drums and out of tune violins in minor keys. Was this... Terracatan's Song? Could Thane hear it again?

He reached for his Song with his mind, that beautiful music of lightning and wild dancing of electricity. Nothing. Thane stretched further, trying to push his senses out to find his Song and regain that piece of him left dark and empty. Almost, almost he thought he could hear it, or an echo of it. A sound at the edge of his universe, his Song calling back to him.

But he couldn't grasp it, and it was gone. The black thunder sound was gone too, and Thane realized he'd been staring at Terracatan for a long time without blinking or moving.

The Sang shifted his weight. He was... uncomfortable? That couldn't be it. Thane mentally shook his head and pulled his focus back.

"A compromise, then," Terracatan offered, and there was no trace of anything but courtesy and confidence in his voice. "When Agoth rises tonight the celebration of majority will begin. I personally have trained all my children in their Song and art and they have centuries of study left to equal me in talent, although none may ever achieve my creativity." Terracatan's lips pulled back in an approximation of a smile. Thane nodded for him to continue. "If you are impressed, I will take charge of this slave and his punishment in exchange for the blood of my guards. If not, you may offer something else and take him home to Lord de Argos."

"Seems fair," Thane said. "How long until moonrise?"

"Your marking of time is not the same as ours," Terracatan pursed his lips, thinking. "Five, perhaps six hours?"

No time. That was not enough time to get everything ready, and they needed to leave before the ceremony started or there would be too many other dark Shae here. And they needed a head start, too.

"Excellent." Thane smiled. "Are all the preparations going well?"

"Quite," Terracatan waved a lazy hand. "Last minute details, here and there, but now mostly we're just waiting."

Thane's mind raced. "Perhaps a diversion, then, to ease the boredom?" he offered. Terracatan raised an eyebrow. "You have been most patient and accommodating regarding the gift I have brought. Would you like a preview?"

A hungry glitter appeared in Terracatan's eyes. "When?"

"Three hours, by my time?" Thane tried to appear nonchalant. "For you and all your guests already arrived? Assuming you have a space large enough to hold them all, outside the celebration chamber. And can have it ready in time."

The subtle insult hit its mark. "Easily done," Terracatan waved to a now tense Semubyt. "See to it."

"Yes, great one," Semubyt bowed and vanished.

"Is there anything you require, Lord de Argos, that my servants may provide?" Terracatan was all consideration and politeness.

"If I think of something, I'll let you know," Thane said dismissively. "Was there anything else, Terry?"

"I have only the best interests of us both at heart," Terracatan bowed, but the nickname was getting to him. Thane could see his cheek twitching.

"Thanks, Terry," Thane glanced at Paka and Brennan, standing to his right. "Take him somewhere safe and drop something heavy on him so he can't move." Brennan and Paka bowed low, and dragged Finn away towards the smaller rooms by holding him under his arms. "See you in three hours."

"I will send my steward to escort you and your party," the First Lord of the most evil race on Shae smiled at Thane. "I wouldn't want any of them to miss it."

Thane smiled back, ignoring how his stomach tightened at the threat. "No one should miss this, Terry. Not anyone you want to impress, anyway."

Thane could tell he'd pushed the Sang as far as he could. He bowed, more of a dip of his chin and shoulders than any gesture of respect, then turned his back to his host and walked away.

Behind him he could hear Terracatan snarling at the guards in a language that was definitely not English, and then footsteps going back into the hallway. Thane opened the nearest door and stepped inside the darkness. He waited until even the echoes of the footsteps had died away before coming back out and closing the enormous doors to their rooms again.

Or trying to. Before he'd even gotten them halfway shut Kith came galloping into view down the hallway. He slowed to a stop and bowed low, pawing the stone with one front hoof.

"We're here, Lord de Argos!" Jena's voice squeaked and her light zipped and flashed around his head.

"We came immediately upon your summons, my Lord," Kith raised his head and set his staff firmly on the floor. "What do you wish?"

Thane glanced down the hall in both directions before backing up. "Come in," he said, and they both entered. Thane started pushing the door again and to his surprise it swung shut easily.

Kith stood next to him, helping push. "I will do the other, Lord, if it please you," the giant Shae rumbled, and moved to do it without waiting for Thane's response.

"What have you been doing?" Jena's constant movement was making Thane a little dizzy, and he held out his hand for her to land on. She perched daintily at the end of one taloned finger and placed her fists on her hips. "This whole place is turned upside down. Everyone is rushing around like they're all going to die if they stop moving, and they're all talking about some amazing present you brought for Terracatan. I've seen all your stuff and we already traded everything we brought and none of it is very impressive."

"You traded?" Thane asked. "What did you trade?"

"All the stuff Lord de Argos has been sending for the past few months. He's going to be really happy- we got twice as many of those shiny rocks he likes to decorate Earth with and all the other stuff from his list to send back with you through the gate but we were supposed to leave this morning but you made everything messy and Terracatan is so mad and now we won't get back in time and half our slaves already had to leave to make other trade runs so we don't even have enough Shae to carry everything!" She stamped her foot and glared at him. "You aren't very good at this, are you."

Kith growled his disapproval at her and she stuck her tongue out at him. "It's true," she argued with Kith's frown. "It's like he doesn't even care about making a good trade. Now Lord de Argos is going to be mad at us because we can't get him his stuff back!"

"And no one wants to make him angry," Thane mused. "Not even Terracatan."

"Even the First Lord of the Sang would ponder long and hard about upsetting your father," Kith agreed in his deep bass.

"I have an idea," a smile crept across Thane's face. "Kith, Terracatan just told me to ask for anything I needed. Well, I need slaves to bring the goods back to Earth for my father. Only humans, though, no Shae. And they need to leave immediately. You will lead them."

"My Lord, the Sang will protest this use of his humans," Kith warned.

"Tell him it's a personal peculiarity of mine, or tell him I like to watch humans grovel because it makes me feel powerful or something," Thane instructed. "Do it. Make it work. Use as many of the humans as you can, especially the kids and the old people. Split loads into smaller and smaller loads so they all have something to carry. Get them organized and get them moving now." A flash of pain shot through his wrist, and he could feel the heat getting more intense even through the barrier Charlie had made. He grimaced. "We're running out of time."

"If we are only requesting the most useless of his slaves, he might not argue too badly," Kith mused. "But the journey will be harder on them. They will not perform as well as the healthy and those in their prime- are you certain, Lord, you do not want fewer but only the best?"

"I am positive. Once you've reached the humans, find a man named Niall. He'll help you pick the ones I want," Thane said.

"I know him!" Jena bounced up and down on his finger. "He's the one who called me and sent us to find you!"

That made sense. Thane was intensely grateful Charlie was here, too. "Okay, great. Get going; this is important." He looked at Kith's face and realized he was starting to be able to read the large Shae's expressions. Kith was disapproving, of course, but he also looked worried. "Trust me," Thane added.

Kith stiffened. "That is not a phrase to use among us," he replied. "This request will make him believe you do enjoy watching the humans suffer. He may allow it on those grounds alone."

"Fine, whatever, just get it done and get it done now," Thane directed, pointing at the door.

Kith bowed again, but neither as deeply or as fluidly this time. "As you say, Lord de Argos," the buffalo head dipped and the steward put stronger emphasis on the name. He turned and began to pull one door open enough to pass through into the corridor beyond.

"Come back and tell me when you get going?" Thane asked Jena, who still stood on his finger.

She jerked her chin up and down in affirmation. "Don't worry about Kith," she confided, stepping closer to Thane's face. "He's just concerned about your human blood making you too evil. But not me!" She burst into light and zipped around his head once before fluttering in front of his eyes. "I don't mind at all!"

She gave him a half bow, half curtsey in midair and then shot through the closing door after Kith. There was a beat of silence after the door boomed shut and then Thane could hear feet running behind him.

He turned around and Remi threw herself into his arms. "That was brilliant!" she shouted, squeezing him around the waist.

He grinned and blushed and tried to hug her back without using his hands. It was awkward. Major Gage came into the large room next, one of Iselle's arms draped over her shoulder to help the injured girl walk.

"That was impressive thinking, kid, good job," Brennan added as he, Paka, and Finn also returned to the main room.

"And it'll guarantee the rest of the slaves stay quiet, once we have their loved ones hostage. That was a nice touch," Finn added.

No one acknowledged him, but no one could quite deny what he said, either. "Now I really have to get back," Major Gage said, holding out her free arm to Remi. "I have to get everyone else ready and keep them from panicking because your Shae are taking their children."

"They'll have at least a three hour head start on the rest of us," Thane said. "The rest of us can't go until we've trapped all the Shae."

"How are we going to do that? And what present do we have?" Remi asked. Everyone looked at her, and she blushed. "Well, it seems like everybody knows but me. What did I miss?"

A blast of sound rolled out of the chamber where Jaeger and Twitch were still working, and was abruptly cut off. "Almost there!" Jaeger yelled. "Just a bit more."

"It still has to be portable," Twitch could be heard protesting. "We can't make it too complex or we won't be able to move it."

"The sound must be a wall, to bind before breaking," Jaeger argued. "Bigger!"

"Bigger doesn't always mean more sound. Besides, we don't have enough power for bigger." Twitch's words were interspersed with crackles and fizzing noises.

"We have power aplenty," Jaeger was giggling again. "We have dragons. Aye have made desserts explode. This will be a sonic boom!"

"Never mind," Remi said, turning away from their argument. "I don't want to know. I'll just be ready."

"Come on, puppy," Remi's mom took her hand. "Let's go back."

"Wait, Major, you had training as a field medic, correct?" Brennan stepped forward before they could get back into that small room again to pass through the secret gateway in the back wall.

"I did," she said, looking at him. "That's why I'm the main healer, here."

"Given time, and rest, would Iselle's injuries heal without further care?" Brennan asked.

Major Gage stared hard at him for a moment. "Yes, they would. Given lots of time. Do you need her for this?"

"We need everyone for this, but yes, especially her," Brennan confirmed.

Major Gage nodded. "I'll leave her to you, then." She saluted, and Brennan returned the gesture. Thane had seen Brennan salute before, but this was the first time it felt truly sincere, without a trace of mockery or condescension.

"Be careful, okay?" Thane said, starting after them and reaching out a hand before quickly lowering it again.

"We will," Remi winked. "See you in three hours."

"See you," Thane watched them walk into the back room and head towards the furthest wall until he couldn't see them anymore. He turned back and saw Brennan holding a familiar looking tiny dart in his hand while Paka braced Iselle.

"Healing dart?" Thane asked. Brennan nodded.

"We need to sit her down, first," Paka advised.

"Yes, please," Iselle breathed, still pale and visibly weak. Brennan and Paka walked her back into one of the other rooms, letting the door click shut after them.

"What about the guards?" Finn said.

Thane blinked, looking around. He and his assigned bodyguard were the only ones left in the main room. "What guards?" he asked.

Finn snorted. "Terracatan's not going to just let your people walk away with half his slaves; he's going to send guards with them to make sure they come back. What about them?"

Thane sighed. "We'll figure that out after we get out of here. At least I got them on the road and moving in the right direction."

"If Terry even lets them go," Finn mused. "Look kid, I respect what you're trying to do here, be the hero and save everyone and all, but at some point it's going to come down to either you or them. I tried to push that once already, but it was clearly a bad idea." He held up his hands in a gesture of submission to that argument. "I don't think you've thought it all through, and I think you should. When we run it's going to be for hours and they're going to come after us. When they do, not if, but when, are you prepared to do what it takes to keep your promise to your father?"

"Are you prepared to keep your promise to me?" Thane snapped back. He was going to get them all home.

"I will do my best, for all of them, I swear. I just don't think you've thought enough about the consequences of all this." Finn sighed and took a deep breath. "I've been watching you; you go along with whatever plan is in motion, reacting to things as they happen. You don't step up to lead or take control, they have to make you do it. You're spending all your time trying to get through the next half hour. Sometimes that's great- you can't live inside your own head too much. But mostly it means you won't get to pick where you end up because you're not the one driving."

"Shut up, Finn," Thane said, rubbing his head with his open palm. From the other room they heard Iselle's muffled scream of pain, and Jaeger and Twitch's arguing was a continuous undercurrent of sound broken only when they had clearly connected something to something else and music blared through the chamber for half a beat.

"All I'm saying is you have a little time right now to really go and think about what it is you want and what you're willing to do. You should use that time." Finn moved to a side of the room where cushions had been stacked in a loose pile. "I am going to sleep. Always need a nap before a fight to the death." He dropped down on the pillows and in moments was snoring.

Thane started at the man's back for several moments. Finn had been threatened, thrown around, partially beaten, and tromped through a dangerous alien mansion for the better part of a day and he fell asleep like it was no big deal. What was his life normally like? Like this?

Twitch and Jaeger's arguing caught his attention and he wandered in to the room where they worked. "How's it going?" he asked.

"About like you'd expect with five generations of tech and no appropriate workshop and the plans and schematics in the brain of an insane devil monkey," Twitch responded without looking up.

"So..." Thane trailed off, unsure what to say.

"Fantastic!" Jaeger crowed. "Half an hour more and we will have a working prototype!"

"That's good news," Thane said.

"It is," Twitch said. "And if the prototype doesn't fall apart, blow up, break, get jostled, get wet, or short circuit, we might even be able to generate enough power to make it work once, until the power source runs out."

"Or moves," Jaeger added.

"Right," Twitch said.

"What?" Thane asked.

Twitch glanced left before looking up at Thane. "What we are making is technology, not magic. It needs power to run. We have a few batteries and whatever we could scavenge from the cell phones and controllers, but it isn't enough. Jaeger wants to use Charlie as a power source, which would work," he quickly added when Jaeger started to jump in, "but the moment Charlie walked away the power dies. Boom. Spell broken, game over."

"Science, not spells," Jaeger muttered.

"So to make it work as long as we need it to work, Charlie has to stay here?" Thane asked.

"Pretty much, yeah," Twitch turned back to his work.

"Which he will, to save her," Jaeger added.

"True enough," Twitch shrugged.

"But then once we're away he can leave and catch up to us, right?" Thane's mind was trying to grapple too many problems at once. Why couldn't any of this just be easy?

Twitch and Jaeger exchanged glances. "Sure," Twitch said, shrugging.

Thane could tell that wasn't all of it. "But," he prompted.

"The Alpha Thunder will almost be there by then, and the dragons will sense him," Twitch began.

"If they haven't already," Jaeger interjected.

"And kill him. He won't be able to escape them," Twitch finished.

Thane froze, his spinning thoughts grinding to a halt. "Why would they kill him?"

"Because dragons can't cross the Weave, it's in the contract. Their Song is too powerful, affects too wide of an area. Every time a dragon even comes close to a tear in the Weave the whole thing gets a little less stable." Twitch shook his head. "It's why Charlie won't change into his dragon form; or, at least, he shouldn't. He's trying to keep his Song firmly tapped down so it doesn't affect things as much as it's supposed to. If he transformed he'd be spilling his Song all over Shae, and no matter how far away they were the Alpha Thunder would come hunting."

"Won't using his Song to power the device do the same thing?" Thane asked.

Twitch blinked and sat back on his heels. "Huh," he said.

"Definitely yes," Jaeger responded without slowing down.

"Wait," Thane said, searching around. He'd brought his bag in here, he was sure of it, but so many of the cushions had been pushed around it took him several minutes to find it. Once he'd located it he sat down and rummaged through it until nearly at the bottom he found what he was looking for.

"Would this work?" he asked, handing Twitch something silver and cylinder shaped.

"You brought this?" Twitch looked up at him and blinked, adjusting his glasses.

"I always carry it around, just in case. Even here." Thane shrugged. "Habit, I guess."

"It is perfekt, perfekt head" Jaeger cheered.

It was the battery Twitch had made for him, not even that long ago. He'd wanted a safe repository for extra power, somewhere he could safely store his lightning without anyone getting hurt. Twitch had built this at Charlie's request.

"This will supply hours of electricity," Twitch grinned.

"Excellent! How do hyu charge it?" Jaeger asked.

They both looked at Thane.

He dropped his face into his hands.

Why couldn't this ever be easy?

CHAPTER 21

"There is no possible way this is working," Thane knew he'd already said this three or four times, but what he was doing still felt impossible. He, Jaeger, and Twitch were sitting in a circle around the battery cell Twitch had made for him, each spinning a simple device made from cardboard, wire, magnets, and a nail in their hands to generate electricity to charge it.

And it was working.

Thane had been prepared to undergo painful and imaginative experiments from Jaeger to force his Song to charge the battery. Jaeger had laughed at him.

"Hyu have a perfekt head, but an empty one," Jaeger flipped in the air. "Song isn't science, and can't be forced, only felt. Ha!" The imp pounced on Twitch, clutching the boy's ears with both his clawed hands and planting his feet on Twitch's chest to stare at him face to face. "Electromagnetic induction!"

Twitch didn't seem surprised or uncomfortable. In fact, Thane got the impression this was part of their normal method of working together. "Where will we get the varying magnetic field?" Twitch asked. Jaeger pulled himself upward in a backflip onto Twitch's head, using the ears he held for momentum, and then turned Twitch's head to one of the piles of electronics. "Ah. And those will have open box solenoids!"

"Aye have nails," Jaeger launched himself upwards and then dove into a different pile.

"Cardboard?" Twitch asked.

Jaeger seemed stumped. "Aye don't have that."

"Huh," Twitch said.

Thane looked at them both, slumped and dejected, and walked back to where his pack lay on the floor. "What about this?" he asked, holding up the box containing one of his MREs.

Jaeger blinked. "Perfekt head is empty, but stomach thinks just fine." He grinned, his whole face splitting wide and showing rows upon rows of sharp white teeth. "We do this."

They had gone to work in a blur, pulling coppery wire out in yards and wrapping it around the cardboard and pulling magnets out of the speaker cabs. Thane tried not to flinch when they'd taken the speakers apart. They'd driven the nails through the open ended cardboard and attached the magnets to the nails on the inside, and then stripped the other end of the wire and connected those to the battery cell.

"Spin the nail," Twitch instructed, handing one of the devices to Thane.

He had, feeling foolish and not sure if they were making him the butt of a joke or not. But they had made more of them, enough for Twitch to have one and Jaeger to have two. The imp held one in each foot and spun the nails with his hands.

And the battery was charging. It was taking forever and Thane's hands were starting to cramp, but it was working. "Very clever," Brennan commented, as he came in the room with Paka and Iselle on his heels.

"Iselle," Thane tried to stand up, but one of his legs had fallen asleep and instead he wobbled and fell over. He felt the heat rising in his cheeks and knew he was blushing, but he kept talking anyway. "How are you feeling?"

"I am much better, thank you," she said, eyeing them all curiously. "What is this you are doing?"

"Electromagnetic induction," Twitch answered her question without looking up. "Whenever a circle of wire surrounds a magnetic field, and if the magnetic field then changes, a voltage appears. The faster the magnetic field changes, the larger the voltage becomes. This circular voltage tries to force the movable charges inside the wire to rotate around the circle. It makes an electric current. The more wire is wrapped around the bigger the current. We wrapped these about six hundred times."

"How long will the charge last?" Brennan asked. The underlying question he didn't say was how long they would have before the Sang started chasing them.

"Aye haf taken all the residual power from every other cell phone, controller, remote control and battery here, in addition to this," Jaeger said. "Aye would calculate it will haf about two hours before being too drained to continue."

Brennan pressed his lips together. "With what margin of error?"

Jaeger shrugged. "Half an hour."

"Ah," Brennan grimaced.

Thane glanced at Twitch. "What does that mean?" he whispered.

"It means he has no shredding idea," Twitch answered.

"Oh," Thane blinked, and began to spin his nail faster.

Brennan, Paka, and Iselle each took turns spinning the nails to give the others a chance to rest. "Don't pack," Brennan warned. "Don't have anything with you."

"Right, because we want to look like we're planning on staying for the celebration," Thane agreed.

Brennan shrugged. "Sure, but more because we have a long way to run and I don't want to be carrying any extra weight."

Thane swallowed. "Right. Okay. Um, how far is it again? To run the whole way?"

Brennan smiled at him. "Don't worry too much, kid. The running is the easy part. I know it took us a long time to get here, but we took it slow to allow everyone time to adjust to the change in atmosphere and gravity. Too slow, it turns out." Brennan sighed, and shrugged. "I didn't think we'd be cutting it so close. But then, when haven't we?"

"Dubai, two years ago, Paka was designated leader, we had two weeks to accomplish the objective and we were done in two days," Twitch commented without looking up from his work.

"She sold Jaeger into slavery to make the deal," Iselle protested. "She broke six policies and two international trade agreements."

"They only kept him for a week and then paid us to keep him away," Paka's feline face was smug in ways only Paka's face could be. "You are upset because you were in hiding from your fate-"

"To answer your question, Thane," Brennan jumped in, glaring at Paka, "we took a day and a half to get here because we were moving slow and waiting for the rest of the Shae Kith had gathered. Now we've been here for a while and everyone's adjusted, and the air and Song of Shae has more moisture and is more nutrient rich without pollutants so even though it's been stressful here, we should all be healthier. Stronger."

"Faster, if you'd like to race again, cub," Paka's teeth gleamed white.

"If we move as quickly as we can, and you've ensured we'll only have the most healthy and able humans with us," Brennan gave Thane an approving nod, "barring any other roadblocks I'd stay we could make it back to that meadow in five hours, maybe six."

"So, moonrise?" Thane asked, thinking back to what Terracatan had said about the celebration tonight.

"Moonrise is six hours from now, but yeah, we should hit the meadow around the same time the second moon rises." Something about that seemed to make Brennan uneasy, because as he spoke his forehead wrinkled and he frowned. "The first moon will be up for about half the run."

Iselle raised her head from her work and looked and the red haired man. "We will be able to tell if danger is coming from a far distance," she said.

Brennan nodded to her, but it didn't smooth out any of the creases of worry on his face.

"The power of the Shae wax and wane with the moons," Brennan mused. "Having Agoth, the shadow moon, rise first, doesn't feel like a good thing."

Paka blinked at him. "It is not a good thing. Agoth is the protector of blood and fire and shadow and the weapons of our enemies will fly more true and straight while ours falter and fall. Hearts of courage will feel fear and those who fight and flee for love and life will lay broken and water the soil of Shae with their blood. This night not only the shadow, but the sky itself is against us and will rejoice to see us die."

This pronouncement was followed by silence from everyone but Jaeger, who had been humming tunelessly for hours. Thane stared at Paka with his mouth hanging open and his hands dropped motionless in his lap. Even Twitch and Brennan looked somewhat taken aback.

Iselle sighed. "Paka? Remember the talk we had about being positive around the Sanctum students?"

"Hmm?" Paka glanced around. "There are no- ah," she said, her eyes falling on Thane. "I forget that you are still a cub in truth and not only in jest." She pulled her lips back to expose all her fangs and leaned towards him. "I am sure we will be fine and not all the weak humans will be slaughtered."

She was trying to smile reassuringly at him. The realization made him snap his mouth shut.

"Paka," Iselle said, shaking her head and returning to her nail spinning.

Thane burst out laughing. He couldn't help it; the situation had gotten beyond absurd and Paka's attempt at comforting him pushed it over the edge. If the best she could do was to say not everybody might die, then there wasn't any point in being afraid anymore. He'd done what he could, and now he had to trust it would be enough.

Paka's tail lashed and she gave Iselle a self-satisfied smirk, all without pausing in her spinning.

There was a humming sound from the back wall and Thane turned in time to see Charlie push through, leading Remi. He winked at Thane and threw a mock salute toward Brennan before stepping back through the invisible gateway into the hall.

She came over to them and stared. "What are you doing?"

"Generating electricity. Long story. I thought you were going to stay with your mom?" Thane answered quickly, wanting to ask the question before anyone else could speak.

"Charlie said it would look suspicious if I wasn't with you, and mom agreed but I don't think she liked it." Remi paused for a long moment, her gaze turned inwards. "I think I owe Charlie an apology for being such a jerk to him."

"Yeah, good," Thane said, trying to feel happy about that. He should be glad Remi was willing to be nicer to his grandfather, but there was a pit in his stomach that was definitely not pleased with the idea of Remi and Charlie getting along. He shoved that thought aside to deal with later.

"Get ready," Brennan advised. Remi nodded and stepped out to change back into the dress Terracatan had supplied her with.

Finn appeared in the doorway of the room. Surprisingly none of the members of the SMG seemed to be angry with him, despite everything he'd done so far against them. Thane wasn't sure if it was an extension of professional courtesy, if it just wasn't worth the effort, or if they'd really decided Finn was Thane's problem and they'd all dropped it. Whatever the reason, Thane was grateful for the lack of animosity all around.

"Footsteps in the hallway," Finn announced. "Lots of them, so I could hear them coming from a distance. I think it's show time."

Brennan nodded and rose. "Let's get it done."

Thane rose too, and went with Paka, Brennan, and Iselle, into the main chamber and Remi joined them there. Iselle and Remi were again dressed in those goddess style gowns, and Jaeger had managed to fix Thane's shirt and make it look presentable again. To Thane's initial surprise Jaeger had removed the sleeves to expose Thane's arms up to the shoulder, but once he put it back on he realized it made his dragon arms stand out even more. Subtle show of force and power, again.

The footsteps were loud enough Thane could tell they were almost to the door, and he didn't wait for them to knock. Instead he reached forward and breathed in, thinking about what Brennan had said about being stronger here. He grabbed each door handle in one dragon grip and placing his body in the centered position he remembered from the kata Charlie had taught him. He breathed out, and in again. Using every muscle from the bottom of his feet through his torso and his arms he heaved backwards and the massive doors flew open with a boom that reverberated down the corridor in both directions.

Guards and soldiers in the hallway jumped and some raised their weapons. Semubyt stood in the center of the doorway with one paw raised as if to knock on the doors that were no longer there. He blinked once, then recovered and bowed deeply, still keeping his tail carefully away from the stone floor.

"My Lord and Master wishes me to escort you to the hall of audience," Semubyt's voice carried smoothly into the room past Thane, bouncing off the walls and echoing. "He desires all of your party to be in attendance." He straightened and the steward's gaze flickered over Remi and Iselle, deliberately skipping Paka and dismissing Brennan. "Shall I retrieve the lagging three?"

"No," Paka said, stepping smoothly in front of Thane and bowing with even more fluidity and grace than the panda man had. "My Lord de Argos has commanded them to bring the gift, and any interference in this would be rude in the extreme."

Thane couldn't wait to get out of here and talk like a normal person again. He nodded stiffly, more of a small head jerk, grateful Remi had returned, and Semubyt bowed again. "As you wish. We shall present you with all honor."

He clapped, the pads of his paws making the sound strange and muffled, and the guards behind him swarmed into the room. And kept coming. Shae, all of them, and full-blooded as far as Thane could tell, and easily more than a hundred sent to bring the seven of them to wherever Terracatan waited.

He felt like his palms should be sweaty but they weren't, dragon scales being non-porous unlike human skin. Thane wiped them against his pants anyway as he, Remi, the Omega Team, and Finn all lined up to be brought before the First Lord of the Sang. The iron and lava resolve still held firm in his chest but it was surrounded by quivering human.

He felt a cool hand take one of his, the skin silken soft against his scales. Iselle smiled at him. "Breathe," she mouthed, without making any sound.

He tried to smile at her, but the facial expression he managed felt twisted and weak. Something warm and strong gripped his other hand, and he looked at Remi on his other side.

"Let's go kick that smug elf in the teeth," she whispered.

Thane grinned. Paka's ears twitched in their direction and she grinned too, glancing toward Semubyt to see if he'd heard the slur against his master. There was such feral joy in her smile that the three guards nearest her leaned away, trying to escape without actually moving their feet.

He must not have heard because the steward gave no reaction, moving instead around the guards to ensure that everyone of Thane's party was well accounted for and heavily surrounded. Twitch and Finn held the device, covered in a swath of gold fabric, between them in the air while Jaeger flitted around it, hissing at any guard who came too close or appeared too curious.

"What is it?" Semubyt asked. His tone was neutral but his eyes were narrow.

"The gift for the celebration of the majority," Paka answered, stepping between him and the hidden device. "If we would not divulge the secret to your Lord it would be a slight on his honor if we told you."

Semubyt's jaw tightened, and one lip rose and curled backward in a snarl. "You may think me blind, or ignorant as to the ways of your Earth, but I have seen what your soldiers do when they arrive. Black powder and their Song of Physics and claiming they come to talk and then slaughtering thousands of Shae with metal and lightning." He spat on the stone near Thane's feet, and Thane saw spots of red mixed in with the spittle. The steward had bitten his own tongue. "I will not let you destroy this house with one of your weapons, no matter how fascinating my master finds your Earth scat."

"I won't hurt him," Thane heard his voice talking, but didn't remember deciding to say anything. "He wants this, I promise."

Semubyt stared at Thane, not bowing or scraping or making any pretense of servility at all. "It is truly a gift? You swear?"

It's music, Thane thought. *We're giving him music.* "It's the most valuable thing I can think to give anyone," Thane answered simply. Semubyt seemed surprised at the passion in the response and stepped back, glancing at the covering fabric again.

"Then I thank you," the steward bowed low, even turning his face to the ground instead of keeping his eyes on Thane or his party. "My master is waiting."

"What just happened?" Thane whispered to Paka as they moved their slow and careful way through the corridors of the fortress.

"Semubyt is shade," she answered. "His master is evil, but it does not follow he must also be."

"What was all that about soldiers coming with physics songs?"

Paka snorted. "Not all humans are kind. The Shae did not understand humans could choose good or evil or levels of each. Humans exploit, and what they do not exploit, they destroy." Her tail bristled and the passing light shimmered on her black fur, revealing again faint patterns of darker and lighter gray throughout her coat. In that momentary flash the shading looked deliberate, almost like a picture. Or a glyph.

Jaeger thumped down on his shoulder, throwing off his balance and making him stumble. "It may hurt a little," Jaeger confided in Thane's ear, speaking so closely that Thane could feel the saliva from Jaeger's teeth dripping onto his earlobe.

"What?" Thane flinched away.

Which was pointless, because Jaeger was sitting on him. The imp grabbed his head and pulled his ear even closer so the edges of fangs slid along Thane's skin. "When the music stops. Aye fixed it to the best plan."

"The best..." Thane closed his eyes. "Jaeger, I promised."

"No, hyu said it was something he wanted. Hyu promised it was valuable and that hyu would not hurt the Sang. Hyu spoke truth." Thane pushed the imp off his shoulder, wiping his ear with his arm. Jaeger wiggled his eyebrows at Thane before flying back to circle the device and keeping the curious guards at bay.

"What was that?" Remi whispered.

Thane glanced at her, then looked forward. "Jaeger made it the best."

"What?" Remi was silent for a moment, then grinned. "Sometimes he's my favorite."

"You two have a lot in common," Thane said, thinking that if Remi had a Shae ancestor, it would've been a chaotic one. Thinking of Remi as a Shae reminded him of what Brennan said. "How are you feeling?"

She glanced at him, one eyebrow raised. "I actually feel really good. Mom says it's the air here, it makes people healthier because there's no pollution and something about the ways the atmosphere is different. But it's more than just healthy, I feel... strong. Bigger on the inside, somehow." She flexed her hand, looking down at it. "Sometimes Shae seems familiar, like I should remember it or dreamed about it. Sometimes breathing the air feels like breathing fire, but in a good way. Does that make sense?"

It did, more than she knew. The phoenix soul inside her was responding to being back on Shae, but what effect that would have on Remi Thane didn't know. He wished Charlie was here so he could ask his grandfather about Remi and if anything like this had happened to her before. If anyone knew, it would be Charlie. His grandfather.

He gulped. "Are you all right?" Remi asked, placing her hand on his arm. "You suddenly went quiet and pale. Did I say something wrong?"

"No, no," he stuttered. Iselle looked at him sideways and placed a hand on his upper arm, in the place where the scales faded and his skin started again. Remi glared at her and Thane shook his head.

It wasn't Remi that suddenly bothered him. Well, it was, but not anything she'd said. He'd suddenly realized something and felt like an idiot for not making the connection sooner. Remi was a phoenix. She was Charlie's phoenix love, the one person he pursued and married over and over throughout the centuries. Charlie was his grandfather.

So Remi was his grandmother.

It was both more complicated and more distant than that, because it was many generations back and it wasn't actually Remi it was only her immortal soul, but still, there it was.

"My Lord, are you ill?" Iselle's concerned whisper broke into his spiraling thoughts and halted them. He did feel like puking again, but this time he couldn't blame it on poison or inanimate screaming objects with broken Songs. Remi was his grandma.

"I'm fine," he breathed, and slowly kept inhaling and exhaling. He needed to focus. They were all going to die when the moon rose, and he was upset because his best friend was married to his great great great great great grandfather who happened also to be a giant reptile.

"Lord Terracatan, your guests have arrived," Semubyt's voice cut through Thane's attempts to calm down. Before him Terracatan strode in his perfect tuxedo, coming to a stop well away and surveying their party.

"I'd forgotten how small your entourage is," Terracatan began, both his voice and his bow conveying polite condescension. "Allow me to introduce you to mine."

The wall behind the First Lord dissolved to reveal hundreds, if not thousands, of Sang Evarish seated in the rows of a grand amphitheater. The light in the room was brighter near the front and going dim as the sea of eyes, claws, and fangs faded into elevated far away darkness so it was impossible to tell how many there were. All staring. All waiting. And all so hungry for blood and violence that Thane could feel it emanating from them and Iselle's hand on his arm went from reassuring to holding on for dear life.

The murmur of the crowd came from behind him as well, and Thane turned around to see all of the walls of the corridor had dissolved, exposing row after row of dark Shae staring down at them. It wasn't an amphitheater; it was an arena, and they were standing in the center.

"I'm sorry," Remi's tremulous whisper came from the other side of him. Thane couldn't tear his eyes away from the horde before them, but he felt Remi's hand trembling in his own. "This is my fault, I'm sorry."

"Bow!" Paka spat at them in an undertone, stepping in front of them and bending low. "Hide your faces, you stink of fear."

Once their eyes were lowered and the Sang could no longer see their mouths, Paka continued. "It's a mirage, an image Song. I don't know who's doing it because it isn't a Sang ability, but there are only about four rows of them."

"How can you tell?" Remi asked, turning her head very slightly toward Paka.

"This is a skill of my Song," she answered, and straightened to her feet. Thane and the others did likewise.

"Great Lord Terracatan, First of the Sang, this is a grand welcome," Paka announced with a voice that boomed and echoed as she moved forward from the others. "May I present to all the children of Agoth Lord Thanos Medici de Argos, heir of Ruan de Argos, Alpha of Earth, son of Cormoran the wanderer, He Who Breaks The Pattern. My Lord de Argos, these are the children of Agoth!"

There was a roar from the crowd, but there were also gasps of surprise. Thane stood in the center of the stone floor and looked out at the imaginary Sang. He could now tell where the fake ones began, because after the first few rows the individuals repeated in a pattern as far as he could see. But the way they were staring at him, some with wide eyes and open mouths and others with narrow glares and bared teeth, was not what he expected.

"Are you doing that?" Remi whispered to him from his left.

He glanced at her, and then up and behind him where she was staring. In the place where his shadow would be stood instead the transparent form of an enormous blue dragon, claws extended and crackling blue energy jumping between them. A faint song, joyful and wild, murmured through his thoughts and he glanced at Paka. She held herself in a formal bow towards him and the monstrous glowing shadow behind him, but tilted her chin up enough so he could see her wink.

Thane could play with this. He held his hand up and imaginary lightning played through his fingers like otters in a pond. A smile pulled at his lips, but then his chest constricted and his stomach clenched. He fiercely, painfully missed his Song. He hadn't had it very long and had even resented and feared it, but being without it made him feel as though he was missing a limb, or an organ. He wasn't complete.

Self pity later, escape plan now. "Children of Agoth," he spoke in a normal tone, and either the acoustics of the room or the Song of the Pantera carried his words throughout the chamber, "I bring you a gift from my father, Ruan de Argos, to honor the house of Terracatan and this celebration of majority."

The crowd roared in eager approval, bloated with bloodlust. Thane held up his hand and the Sang quieted, but not completely. "Before I present to Lord Terracatan the most valuable possession known to man," at this description Terracatan, who had taken a seat in the center of the front row, leaned forward with lips parted and breath coming quickly, "What if you could trap a Song from someone else, and then use it whenever you like?"

"Impossible," came a growl from the crowd. There were murmurs of agreement. "You can destroy their Song, burn it from their souls, but you can't capture it."

The way the Sang spoke gave Thane the impression he was speaking from the long experience of experimentation. He repressed a shudder and went on. "Perhaps you cannot, son of Agoth," he said, "because your Song is limited to only what the Shaerealm has given. Mine is not."

The dragon image behind him roared and a shower of sparks burst like fireworks over the crowd, startling Thane and exposing the roof several stories overhead. He spared a brief glare at Paka, who was clearly enjoying herself, and then turned back to the waiting audience. "Here is a Song more powerful than any you've experienced," he held a hand back towards Iselle, and she shyly came forward to stand next to him, casting fearful glances toward his dragon shadow. Her acting was superb; Thane himself was fooled until he saw Remi rolling her eyes behind Iselle.

"She will demonstrate her Song for all, and in so doing, will have it taken away by this, our gift to Lord Terracatan!" Thane held his arms out and

Brennan pulled the fabric off the device with a flourish, like a magician unveiling his greatest trick.

There was silence in the audience. Thane glanced at Terracatan, who had leaned back into his chair with a furrowed brow. The other Sang stared at the stage in mingled confusion and disgust, with wrinkled noses and sneers. Thane couldn't really blame them; it wasn't a pretty machine. It lacked balance or symmetry, and the speakers and wires were irregularly placed. Most of the internal workings were visible and they hadn't bothered to polish or shine any of it. The hadn't had time.

But it worked. They'd tested it twice in the chamber, but only briefly so as not to use up the battery. Twitch had modified the comm units so the one Iselle wore was attached to the device as a microphone and would also record once activated, and the background track would play once she began singing.

With piles of spare parts and wiring, speakers and magnets, Jaeger and Twitch had built the perfect weapon to overcome the most evil, vicious, and sadistic race in all of the Shaerealm. A karaoke machine.

Not really, but it was the same general idea. It played music, but it was modified so that as Iselle sang it would record both her voice and the music as it played. Twitch had found a song she knew on one of the cell phones from the museum and modified it so the recorded vocals couldn't be heard. "Beauty and power do not always go hand in hand," Thane said, drawing the audience's attention back, "But results are unmistakable."

He signaled to Jaeger, who launched himself into the air and dimmed what lights there were so only Iselle and the device were visible. The amber light shone off her dress and her hair, making her seem bathed in gold.

There was an unnatural stillness in the air as the tens of thousands of Sang watching, both real and projected, held their breath. Iselle opened her mouth, and began to sing.

"Go!" hissed Brennan, grabbing Remi by the arm and shoving her towards Finn. All around them Terracatan's guards were frozen in place, held fast by Iselle's voice, her Song made manifest. "Don't bump anyone," he added as Finn took Remi by the arm and led her to where Jaeger waited, the single green light of Twitch's rectangle bouncing up and down to mark the imp's location in the darkness.

Thane waited, watching. Twitch and Paka remained with him, Paka for show and Twitch in case anything went wrong with the tech. Brennan, Jaeger, Finn, and Remi would deal with any remaining Shae in the hallway, which considering the size of the guard Semubyt had brought with him, shouldn't be many. Major Gage and Charlie should already have the human slaves on the move and the gate at the edge of Terracatan's lands would already be down to let out Kith, Jena, and the trade convoy who'd left hours before. Remi and the others would meet up with Major Gage and the slaves, and they would be on their way.

The song Iselle sang was slightly longer than four minutes in length. She sang it through twice without stopping, the modified speakers carrying her voice to every part of the chamber and echoing off the roof. The Shae were spellbound, unmoving and barely breathing if the guards that stood around them were any guide. Thane followed the song in his mind, counting down to the last notes of the final phrase of music and knowing that when the Sang woke, it would be with a vengeance. It was critical for him to get their attention before they went completely berserk and tore Iselle apart.

One measure left. Thane motioned to Twitch and Paka, and the three of them surrounded the French girl as her voice faded on the last note. The moment before the music was gone from the air, Twitch threw the golden fabric over Iselle while Thane and Paka stood between them and Terracatan. Iselle hunched over and jumped backwards, out of the light and into Twitch's waiting arms where he spun her around and placed her inside a speaker cab on the machine. They'd deliberately left it empty to hide her there. After the reaction of one room to Iselle's singing, Thane didn't want her visible at all once an entire army of Shae woke from her voice.

But Iselle was still standing exactly where she'd been. The Sang Evarish awoke from her song and there was momentary pandemonium as hundreds of crazed Shae tried to claw over each other to reach where she stood.

"Enough!" Terracatan's voice was harsh and his eyes were blood red, the fake blue irises gone. The First Lord of the Sang panted and licked his lips as the stone all around him cracked and heaved, blocking the paths of the other predators. "She is mine."

"No," Thane said, "she is nothing." He plunged the knife Paka had given him into Iselle's back between her spine and left shoulder blade. She squeaked, a weak sound of pain and fear, before crumpling to the broken stone beneath her. Blood pooled and overflowed from her back to the floor, the dripping sound it made as it fell into the crevices of rock the only sound in the shocked silence.

Paka was a genius with these projected images; Thane could even smell the blood and viscera from the body on the floor. The Sang could smell it too. Several of them were licking their lips with flaring nostrils, glancing back and forth between the fresh kill and the First Lord.

Terracatan's facade of perfect civility and control was showing as many cracks now as the stone floor. "That was a *waste*," he growled, and the stones underfoot cracked again. "Impure filth, your father cannot save you here. I will spill your abomination of blood and let the Inugamae drink the marrow from your bones. Your very existence is anathema to Shae, to Song, and to me." Terracatan leapt over the broken stone at Thane, his fangs and talons elongated and eyes blazing.

Thane stood immobilized by those eyes. His brain screamed for him to move, but his muscles wouldn't react. He heard Paka yelling but couldn't process the words. He could only stare as those burning red orbs grew larger in his vision.

Something slammed into him from the side and he was thrown to the ground, the side of this head bouncing off the stone. Iselle's voice came bursting over him, cutting through the ringing in his ears and singing somehow even more sweet sounding. Thane's mind blearily wondered if Twitch had managed to make the device auto tune as well as record and play.

He pushed himself up on one elbow and looked around. Terracatan lay frozen on the ground, one of Paka's very real knives sticking through his leg, and a silvery black liquid oozed out of the wound. Paka herself was crouched on the ground near the Sang, hovering over a bleeding human body. Thane thought it must be the projected image of Iselle, but the shape was wrong. He blinked several times to clear his vision.

It wasn't Iselle.

It was Twitch.

CHAPTER 22

"Twitch!" Thane shouted, pushing himself to his feet and stumbling forward. His roommate lay in a widening pool of blood, his face pale and his body shaking. As Thane drew close he could see where the blood was coming from.

Twitch's right arm was missing.

Thane spun around and threw up noisily, splashing blood with vomit and seeing it spatter over Terracatan's prone form. Iselle came running from her hiding place and gasped, covering her mouth with both hands briefly before bending over Twitch's prone body and placing her hands on his skin, one on his forehead and the other on his neck.

"Twitch is going into shock," she said, her voice calm and even. She looked at Paka and then up at Thane, her violet eyes even more brilliant with pain and worry. "We 'ave to move 'im."

"He'll die if we move him!" Thane protested, remembering some half piece of information from a first aid class.

"We will all die if we do not," she snapped back. "Give me your shirt."

Thane immediately pulled it off and handed it to her. "And your belt," she ordered Paka, who removed her leather waist tie and handed it over. Iselle folded the shirt several times until it made a pad slightly larger than Twitch's shoulder socket and used the belt to tie it securely in place. "I will need something 'ot to cauterize the wound quickly so the artery does not bleed out," she said, grabbing the golden fabric, "but there is not anything in 'ere. 'elp me."

Despite the evenness of her tone, her accent was so thick it was difficult to understand her. Paka braced Twitch under the shoulders and lifted while Iselle slid the fabric underneath them and that gave Thane enough to know to lift his legs so she could get Twitch all the way on the makeshift gurney.

Even with the music playing Thane could hear murmurings and see small twitches of movement from the surrounding Shae. Apparently the recording was not as powerful as the live singing. Thane wordlessly cursed and struggled to carry Twitch on the blanket with Paka and Iselle, all trying to jostle him as little as possible.

"How soon do you need to cauterize the wound?" Thane panted as they half walked, half ran down the empty corridor.

Iselle glanced down at Twitch. "The moment it 'appened. The blood loss is very severe. Even now." She was right; his folded shirt was a sodden mass of blood with more seeping out onto the fabric they used to carry him.

"What do you need to do it?" Thane's heart was pounding so hard he could feel the blood rushing in his ears. This wasn't happening, this couldn't be happening.

"Something very 'ot, or silver nitrate or liquid nitrogen, or a stable electric current and a grounding pad," she listed.

Thane's feet froze. Twitch was thrown hard in the fabric as his sudden halt jerked the others to a stop from where they gripped the temporary blanket. "I can't," Thane stuttered, his eyes wide and panicked. "I'm still burned out- I can't find my song-"

Iselle let go with one hand and slapped him across the face. "I am not asking, I am answering your question, now move!" she ordered.

Thane lurched forward and the three of them moved along again until Thane saw something familiar. "Wait," he cried, pulling back on the cloth to stop them.

Iselle spun to face him, her eyes dark with fury. "If you are 'aving a crisis-"

"No, I have an answer, this way," Thane responded, and pulled them into the nearest alcove.

"Put him down for a second," Thane said, and once Twitch was on the floor Thane spun around and grabbed a stone in the center of the wall. He started to hum.

"What are you-" Iselle began, but Paka shushed her and grabbed a corner of the stretcher, ready.

The stone spun and swirled before them, and Thane didn't even wait for it to complete the pattern before lifting Twitch again and pushing forward into the dark storeroom. This time he didn't put Twitch down, merely reached forward with one hand and already humming deep in his throat. The wall made its invisible opening and Thane pushed through, dragging Paka, Iselle, and the unconscious form of Twitch with him.

Before them spread the bowl shaped ground of the human caves. They were empty now, instead of bustling and busy like last time, but Thane wasn't looking for people. He was looking for something else he remembered, something near the largest cave openings.

"There!" he screamed, pelting down the hill with Paka and Iselle, all of them fighting together to keep Twitch level. He ran toward the cooking fires, most of them put out but the largest still with a heavy clay pot and smoldering coals.

They laid Twitch alongside the fire, his injured shoulder as near to the coals as they could. "Now what?" asked Thane.

"Remove the pad," a dagger appeared in Paka's hand and she sliced through the leather before Iselle could finish speaking the thought, "and 'old 'im still. Zis will 'urt, even unconscious."

Paka lay across Twitch's chest and braced his leg down with her knee. Iselle reached for the fire.

"What are you doing?" Thane pushed her hands away from the glowing coals.

"We do not 'ave time to find something to lift them with," Iselle spat. "Get out of my way."

"No," Thane plunged both his scaled hands into the pit, grabbing for a large stone at the center.

He wanted to scream. He could feel his scales burning, their edges turning black and flaking away, but he held on and lifted it out, watching Iselle.

She had tears in her eyes. "Place it against the wound, as flat as you can," she instructed. Thane did, using the bottom of the stone for the increased heat. Flesh sizzled and the smell of scorching skin and muscle filled the air around them, mixed with a metallic smell like iron and far away rain.

Twitch's body jerked and flopped beneath Paka, who tried to hold him still without injuring him further. Thane kept pressing the stone into the wounded and broken flesh until Iselle laid her hand on his arm. "It is not 'elping any more; the 'eat is gone from the stone."

Thane released the rock where he held it, and it hit the ground next to Twitch with a muffled whump. Scales and pieces of scales flaked off with it, falling over the stone like a drifting black snow. Thane's fingers curled inward and he shuddered uncontrollably, the pain so intense it crept up his arms and across his shoulders until it met in the middle.

Paka looked at him. "You are not immune to fire, Thane dragon-son," she said in a neutral tone.

"I know," his whisper was hoarse and shaky. He swallowed.

Paka shook her head. "We have not even left this giant stone dungeon, and already two are injured past moving." She growled.

"We are the last," Iselle noted. Her hands were laying on Twitch again, one on his forehead and one on his neck. "The rearguard is always the first to die."

"But I am not," Paka pulled open her pack and put in her paw. She drew it back out, fist closed around something she'd been carrying. "These were supposed to be for much later," she grumbled before holding them out.

Four tiny needles attached to small balloon shaped pouches. "Healing darts?" Thane asked.

Paka gave him a look that said she would not dignify that with a response, and tossed one to him. He couldn't make his injured hands even try to grab it. Iselle reached over, picked it up, and stuck it in his arm.

"Hey, ow!" Thane squeaked.

Paka chuckled. "Fireheart stone gets nothing, and one tiny needle makes you say ow?"

"It isn't the needle," Thane protested through gritted teeth, "It's the healing. It-" he cut off as he stared down at his hands. Where the scales had flaked of and all underneath had been blackened and burned, pink human flesh was now appearing. It spread up his fingers and across his palms, lines and creases where he remembered them. The nails were still dark cobalt talons, and the backs of his hands and forearms were still covered in shaded blue overlapping scales, but everywhere the fire had touched was healing human.

"Huh," he said, showing his palms. "I wonder-"

"Not now you don't," Paka cut him off. "Before imminent battle is not the time to experiment with fire and losing your claws!"

He shook his head. "You're right, but what about Twitch?" he asked.

Iselle's face twisted, pain and indecision plain in her features. "I do not know. Cauterized skin is ripe for infection, and 'e 'as lost so much blood..." she trailed off, dropping her head into her hands. "If I give Twitch the dart 'e may die."

"If you don't he will," Thane echoed her words from the arena back to her.

She shuddered. Then she brushed Twitch's hair back from his face and straightened his glasses. "We do not 'ave time to wait for 'im to 'eal," she said, holding out her hand to Paka. Paka gave her the three remaining darts. Without hesitation, the moment they touched her hand Iselle drove all three needles into the freshly burned flesh and squeezed. Whatever miracle was in the darts was pushed under Twitch's skin. Then she grabbed the corner of the soiled cloth and lifted, looking into Thane's eyes. "Lead us out," Iselle said to him.

Thane nodded, lifting down near Twitch's knees. Paka grabbed the side opposite at his torso, and the three began to run.

Back through the storeroom and into the corridor, Thane could still hear the recording of Iselle's voice singing from the arena. Whatever spell music caused here was still holding, since the hallway was blessedly empty. He turned down the only way he knew for sure, back past their rooms and towards the main dining hall where they'd had dinner only the night before. It felt like years ago. A few Shae slaves scattered from them as they pelted through, down the raised dais and over the main seating area to the front doors.

They were open, unconscious guards slumped on both sides and on the steps before them. Anyone of authority or importance should've been in that arena, so they encountered no resistance as they dashed across the courtyard and into the fields beyond.

The gate should've been coming into sight at any moment when Twitch's body began to writhe. It wasn't until that moment Thane realized how close Twitch must have been to dying- every time he'd been shot with the darts it had affected him immediately, pain wracking through him from top to bottom until he was healed. If so much of Twitch had to be repaired that he couldn't even respond to the pain of it... Thane shoved that thought out of his mind. Now was not the time.

"He's falling off!" Paka shouted, and Thane turned just in time to get a knee to the face as Twitch moaned and flailed. Thane went down and Twitch landed on top of him. Either the impact or the pain or both was too much, and Twitch vomited on Thane.

It wasn't very much, but it was still unpleasant. "I owed you that," Twitch said weakly, opening his eyes.

"No you didn't," Thane protested. He was grinning, though. Twitch was alive.

"It was for Iselle, then," Twitch rolled on his back, body still trembling and his face both pale and sweating. "Did we make it?"

"No, and we won't if you don't get your lazy butt up," Thane stood and held out his hand to his friend.

Twitch stared at him. "What happened to your hand?"

"Ask questions later, get up now," Thane ordered.

Twitch made a strange sideways movement before his eyes widened. "Where's my arm?" his voice was shrill, and Thane realized Twitch had been trying to reach up to take his hand. "Where's my arm, where's my arm?!"

Paka reached down and grabbed Twitch by the front of his shirt, heaving him to his feet. "Terracatan took it off when you pushed Thane out of the way. You saved his life. You may have saved all of us. But unless you want us to die now you have to get moving. We are still in Terracatan's lands. We have maybe two hours before they start coming after us. They will be mounted; we are not." She spun him around by grabbing his bad shoulder and pushing without letting go. "Now run!"

Twitch was still disoriented and dizzy, and they could not move as quickly as they wanted while he was still healing. His balance was off and he kept stumbling until Paka came next to him. She drew his remaining arm around her shoulders and they ran together.

"Stop," Iselle commanded. The others staggered to a halt around her, panting lightly and looking at her quizzically.

"There are Sang ahead of us," she said, pointing to the wall. "Along with other Shae. They are coming through the gate. We need to hide."

In the distance Thane could make out a few small figures coming into view near the opening in the barrier. They were dark, and rode something with many legs that were definitely not horses.

"We need to keep moving, we're running out of time, especially if they're heading to Terracatan's castle," Thane argued. "We don't know if they'll be trapped or not. The music will be slowing down soon, and those Shae could break the karaoke machine."

"If we get any closer they will see us," Iselle glanced around. "They should already be suspicious because Semubyt is not waiting to greet them."

Paka's lips pulled back, showing every one of her sharpened fangs. "You're right, he should be there. He welcomes every guest. Get down," she made a sharp gesture with one paw.

Twitch collapsed to the ground without protest, and Iselle laid herself flat. Thane looked at Paka and she winked at him, holding her fist to her chest in salute. He held his own fist over his heart in response and laid down on his stomach in the tall grass as she loped away.

"What is she planning?" Iselle whispered.

Thane shrugged, and found it awkward to do while laying on the ground. "I don't know, but with Paka it could be anything." He wriggled forward. "Let's move down off this hill and away from the path to the main house."

Iselle responded by pulling herself forward in an army crawl, being careful to disturb the plants around her as little as possible. In the distance ahead, they could hear sudden angry voices and then the pounding of heavy running animals.

"Get further away!" he hissed to the others, and they rolled down the hill perpendicular to the road the riders were on.

The coterie of Sang and Shae pounded past them, not slowing at all, angry voices calling to each other in words Thane didn't understand. The language made his skin crawl. And he nearly jumped out of it when Paka appeared next to him, chuckling to herself and exuding self-satisfaction.

"They will be out of sight beyond us in a moment," she murmured, and her lashing tail brushed against Thane's leg as she chuckled again.

"What did you do?" Thane asked.

Her feral smile flashed. "Semubyt met them near the gate, but he may have had some less than flattering things to say about the second born child of his master before vanishing." Her throaty chuckle was so pleased it was almost a purr. "I believe they will spend no small amount of time searching for the steward before seeking Terracatan himself. And he will not be pleased when they find him."

"That should buy us a little more time," Iselle said. She rose to her feet. "They are far enough away now. We move."

Paka grabbed Twitch again and wrapped his arm over her again. They ran to the gate and Thane could hear the echoes of the screams and howls from the inugamae as they passed beyond the unending blackness that separated the land of the Sang from the rest of the Shaerealm. Then they were through and into the lands beyond, with the flower hills before them.

It was getting dark. "How much longer until moonrise?" Thane panted.

Paka glanced skyward. "Agoth should rise just after we reach the hills. The flower forest will provide some shelter from his face."

Thane glanced back to her, his stomach churning in an unsteady way. "You don't mean he can see us, right? It's just a rock in space."

"Our moon is just a rock in space, orbiting our planet and controlling the magnetic flux of the oceans and stabilizing the Earth's axis so we don't have dramatic climate change," Twitch's voice seemed out of sync with the rest of him, like he was only spouting facts and not taking conscious part in the conversation.

"Agoth changes our Song," Paka said after a worried look at Twitch. "The Song of the shadow is not only more powerful, shade and fae Song becomes weak. Strength is drained, hope is dampened."

"So we need to run faster now," Thane said, belaying his words by slowing down until he was even with Twitch and Paka. He wrapped one arm around the injured boy's waist and leaned into him to help him stabilize. Twitch's head was hanging low and Thane met Paka's eyes. They ran faster, moving in unison and carrying Twitch between them. Iselle scouted ahead, her violet eyes and inner senses spread wide in the deepening dark.

The flower hills stretched out before them, enormous petaled heads bobbing in the warm evening breeze. It looked peaceful, like a child's daydream. Thane's heart was thudding in his chest and Twitch's breath was rasping in his ear and they slowed to a jog as they entered the trees. Glancing back Thane could see a reddish light creeping across the ground toward them, rising like a poisoned gas.

It felt childish, irrational to be afraid of moonlight, but Thane suddenly didn't want that red glow to touch him. "Go, get in deeper," he cried, and the tension in his voice got the others moving again.

Running uphill was difficult, especially as they had to weave through the trunks and avoid rocks and roots on the ground. None of them could afford a twisted ankle now. Iselle's head snapped up and she paused, listening.

"I hear the stream," she announced, pointing. "There."

"Can we get some water?" Twitch rasped.

Iselle glanced at Thane, who nodded. He and Paka carried Twitch to the stream and set him down. He collapsed, face forward, into the water and slurped, gulping mouthfuls down until he had to come up sputtering for air.

"How far ahead are the others?" Thane asked, breathing hard and resting his hands on his knees. Racing Paka was one thing, but running uphill while carrying someone the same size he was drained him.

Iselle closed her eyes and went still in a manner Thane was starting to recognize as her using her Song. "Kith and the traders are still too distant for me to sense, but the group Brennan and Finn are leading are not far away." Her eyes snapped open and she looked up. "We need a light."

Paka and Thane glanced at each other. They weren't carrying anything; they'd left all their supplies behind on purpose. But Twitch pushed himself up out of the stream and tried to reach in his left pocket with his remaining right arm. It didn't work very well.

Instead of allowing him to continue to struggle or waiting for him to ask for help, Paka thrust her paw into his pocket and pulled out a small white rectangle. She handed it to Iselle while speaking to Twitch over her shoulder. "How many of these do you have?"

Twitch shrugged. The motion unbalanced him for a moment. "How many daggers did you bring?" he said, working to steady himself.

Paka chuckled. Iselle pressed the center of the small piece of tech and a white light shone directly upward, like a tiny but powerful flashlight. She held it in one open hand, and used her other one to cover the beam, then let it shine, and passed her hand through in three quick movements.

"What are you doing?" Thane whispered.

Something large and heavy landed on his head. "Calling to me!" Jaeger's upside-down face filled his vision, black and yellow eyes gleaming and the leathery skin of the imp's nose pressing into Thane's. "Aye found hyu!"

"Jaeger," Iselle sounded like a stranded sailor finally finding land. "Twitch is injured. We need to move 'im."

"Aye will get a cookie," Jaeger chuckled. "Remi said Aye will get a cookie if Aye find hyu." He shot into the air, using Thane's head as a launching platform. "Aye will get two cookies for bringing help!"

Large chunks of torn petals drifted down, torn from the path of Jaeger's flight and touching the surface of the stream before floating with the current like colored boats. Red light filtered through the opening and glinted on the water. Paka hissed. "Agoth."

A booming sound echoed in the distance behind them, followed by a roar. Thane felt chills shiver along every vertebrae of his spine and goose bumps rise on his skin. "The best plan," Twitch muttered, pushing himself up to standing. He wobbled and over-corrected and started to fall, but Paka grabbed the back of his shirt near the collar and held it until his feet were firm beneath him. "We have to go."

Iselle's face screwed up in protest, but she didn't speak. Paka released his shirt and tried to pull his arm across her shoulders again but he resisted. "I'm slowing you down. Just go, and I'll keep up," Twitch said.

"If you start slowing me down I will drop you on your head like a birthing giraffe and leave you as a chew toy for the inugamae," Paka answered. "For now, suck it up and run."

Twitch's face twisted in the ghost of a smile and he allowed her to arrange his arm as she liked. The four of them moved across the stream, careful to avoid the open patch of moonlight on the water, and began running through the waving stalks again. Thane stayed close to Paka and Twitch in case the latter needed more balance. Iselle took her place in the lead. She darted like a shadow through the woods, never misplacing her feet or seeming to lose her way in the darkness.

Thane caught a glimpse of the sullen red moon above through a break in the foliage. It seemed to glare back down at him, and he could've sworn he felt malice emanating outward, carried by its reddish glow. "Yeah, well, I don't like you either," he muttered under his breath. He lowered his chin and ran.

The warm breeze turned into a night wind. It blew at their backs, pushing flower heads into their path and making it more difficult for Iselle to see. Thane could see her trying to brush the hair out of her eyes over and over. Something the size of a dinner plate blew past his head and he tripped trying to dodge it before realizing it was only one of the enormous petals.

"Argh," he breathed, pushing himself back up and wiping dirt and plant matter off his hands by rubbing them on his pants as he ran.

"Stop playing with the flowers, cub!" Paka chided him over her shoulder.

"Brennan!" Iselle shouted. Thane and the others increased their speed as they followed her into a small valley between two of the hills. The tree-flowers thinned out here, and moonlight bathed the small clearing in thin red light as Brennan emerged from the forest on the other side. He raised his hand in greeting, the one missing the fingers.

Iselle froze mid-step and sucked in a breath. Both her head and Paka's swiveled to stare up the valley at the same moment as a huge shadow detached itself from the ground and came lumbering forward toward Brennan.

The light was too dim and the beast moved too quickly for Thane to get any kind of clear view. All he had was an impression of many legs and something the size of an elephant with mottled fur with patches of bright colors and dark spots- camouflage, he realized, for the flower petals- bearing down on a waiting Brennan.

Who was standing now at the edge of the line of plant stalks and watching. The first member of the Shaerealm Mercenary Guard Thane had ever met wasn't doing anything to try and escape or prepare to fight the behemoth bearing down on him. He was just there, his feet slightly apart and hands now thrust in his pockets.

"We don't have time for this," Thane could barely make out Brennan's words over the distance and the noise of the attack, but he saw clearly enough as the man took something out of his pocket, aimed, and fired.

It wasn't a gun. Thane heard a noise that sounded like a cross between a rapidly ticking clock and a steady buzz, and two tiny sparks of blue light flickered in unison from the monster's head. The gigantic creature went rigid for several moments and then collapsed and lay twitching on the ground, filling almost the entire space between Brennan and where Iselle, Paka, Twitch, and Thane stood.

Iselle pushed her hair back out of her face again. "Really, Brennan?"

Brennan shrugged, detaching the wires and returning the weapon to his pocket. "We're in a hurry."

Paka snorted at him and started forward with Twitch. "Cheater," she said. Brennan smiled at her and wrapped an arm around Twitch's waist, helping ease some of the weight off Paka and moving back into the cover of the overhanging leaves.

Thane stood there blinking for a moment as the four of them started to fade into the forest. "Wait, you had a taser this whole time?" he yelled, and broke into a run to catch up. "Why hadn't you used it yet? Does anybody else have one?"

"I was waiting for the right moment," Brennan said. Thane noticed he did not answer the second question.

"How far are the others?" Twitch asked, his voice strained from exertion. He was still so pale that even the red light of Agoth couldn't hide how sallow his skin looked.

"Not sure," Brennan answered. "Jaeger found me first because I was lagging behind on purpose. I thought you guys might need a hand." Thane glanced over in time to see both Brennan and Twitch flinch at the poor choice of words.

"Lucky us," Twitch mumbled. "At least you can't wiggle your fingers at me and tell me it could be worse anymore."

"I've never said that," Brennan protested.

"Yes you have," Paka, Iselle, and Thane all answered together.

Brennan grinned at them. "Not in so many words, and at least I wasn't wrong. We weren't doing this last time."

"Can we not do this next time?" asked Twitch.

"That depends on how good Thane is at learning a lesson." Brennan poked him in the shoulder with his free hand as they ran. "Thane, what do you do next time a pretty girl asks you to do something stupid?"

"Make sure Ms. Yemaja sees me putting glue on Ms. Tagore's keyboard," he answered after thinking it over.

Brennan stumbled, pulling Twitch and Paka off balance with him and making all three struggle to regain their footing. "Whoa, kid, I don't know if I'd go that far," Brennan said, once his feet were back under him and moving.

They'd crossed another hill without meeting any resistance, but the wind was getting stronger again. It buffeted them with leaves and petals and other bits of forest small or light enough to move. Dirt swirled in Thane's face and stung his eyes, making them water. He kept running anyway. Brennan was just ahead of him with Twitch and Paka, and Thane reached out a hand and gripped the man's shoulder so he wouldn't lost his way or run into anything while he tried to blink and clear his vision.

There was a crack and a deafening boom, and the ground trembled beneath their feet with enough force they were thrown down and slid into tall flower stalks and thick underbrush. "Everyone okay?" Brennan called as Thane rolled over to push himself to standing again.

"I am all right," Iselle called. Paka growled and Twitch groaned in response as she wrapped her paws around his torso and heaved him upwards.

Ahead of them, screams rose into the air, human voices crying out in terror and fear.

Behind them the eerie howls of predators catching a scent floated toward them in the fierce wind.

"Move!" Brennan grabbed Twitch and started sprinting. Paka dropped to all fours to catch up and pushed back to hind legs, catching Twitch's arm with her neck as she rose. "The inugamae have been released!" Other sounds, screeches and shrieks and unearthly roars rang in the far distance. The Sang were free.

Thane was certain they were also very, very angry.

"Aye think hyu should run faster," Jaeger swooped down, cutting through the branches and leaves behind them and landing on Twitch's back.

"That would be easier without carrying you, you rodent with wings!" Paka spat at him.

"Aye am helping," Jaeger said, climbing higher and twisting around so he faced away from them. He gripped Twitch's shoulders with the claws on his feet and opened his wings wide. The wind caught them like sails and the force carried Jaeger like a kite.

Thane could see the weight being lifted from both Brennan and Paka as their shoulders straightened and they picked up speed. They moved so much more quickly they passed Iselle, no longer needing her to lead them to everyone else. They could just follow the screaming.

Willing his legs to move, Thane's feet pounded into the dirt and he fought to keep up. He'd been fast before, but here, after spending days in the Shaerealm where his dragon blood coursed through him and his burned out mind could still almost hear the Song, he could nearly fly. Thane reached out his hand and grabbed Iselle's as he moved past her to keep her from being left behind.

The five of them burst out of the other end of the flower forest, their speed continuing to increase as they raced down the final hill. The acres of meadow appeared before them. The blood moon Agoth had continued to rise during their time in the hills, and its red light was bright enough to illuminate the field.

A battle had already started. Crates and boxes were strewn and shattered, contents spilling out into the long grass, remnants of the trade items that hadn't made it through. Interspersed with them were bodies, some Shae, some human, tossed and broken with their internal cargo spilling out just as carelessly as the damaged goods.

But all that was background to the trees. Standing more than twice the height of Kith, who Thane saw charging through the melee swinging his staff in one hand and spear in the other, creatures that looked like twisted and gnarled trees stomped through the ground, swinging wide branch arms that knocked the combatants into the air and throwing them for several feet.

"The Eldergast," Paka's voice was closer to a whimper than any other sound Thane had heard her make. Ever.

"They shouldn't be awake," Iselle's hand, still holding Thane's, spasmed and gripped him tighter. "This is not their time or their season."

There were only two of them, but with their massive size and long reach they kept every attacker at bay and swept through the humans with ease as they stood guarding the gate. The arch behind them was still glowing, but the shining oil and water looked less bright than he remembered. Every time someone tried to escape they were either crushed or swatted away. Thane saw a spark of multicolored light zipping and darting through the dark and screamed so intensely his throat burned. "Jena!"

The glow paused, and then shot towards him. The little fairy appeared in his vision, bobbing and flitting as though it were impossible to hold still.

"You made it, my lord!" she squeaked.

"What is going on?" he said.

Her light blinked. "The Eldergast are attacking your humans."

"I can see that!"

"Then why did you ask?" he saw her head cock sideways, and she dashed in a zigzag pattern between he and the scene before them.

"I wanted specifics," Thane closed his eyes for a moment to think. "Where are Remi and Major Gage? And Charlie?"

"Your girl is over there with the bossy lady, and I don't know who the other one is," Jena answered, flying in a line to indicate the part of the field away from the gate and on the other side of all the people.

"What? Oh, Niall," Thane corrected, his eyes straining to see Remi in the red dark.

"Oh, him," she gave a twitch of her wings that managed to be both condescending and dismissive. "He's over there too."

Iselle, Paka, and Brennan, who'd been listening, all looked at each other. Paka and Brennan lowered Twitch to a sitting position on the ground and started running toward Major Gage's position. "Stay with Twitch and keep him there!" Brennan ordered over his shoulder.

Jaeger saluted, and then sat on Twitch's head and removed his glasses. Twitch slumped down in visible exhaustion and resignation.

"What about everybody else? There were a lot more people than this," Thane pressed, trying to keep the fairy's attention. "What about all the ones you brought?"

"The guards killed some of them when they were too slow or too whiny," she said, staring at Jaeger with wary attention. The imp was wearing Twitch's glasses, the lenses making his eyes large and disproportionate. "Kith killed the guards who killed the slaves. The other guards got mad and started fighting Kith and our Shae. Kith got rid of most the guards, and some ran away. I killed the grumpy one," she did a backflip midair and curtsied.

"Great job," Thane said, hoping fervently the grumpy one was one of Terracatan's guards and not an elderly human. Jena could've taken out either. "Then what?"

"Kith made everyone hurry and picked up some of the small ones. They dripped and made terrible noises," she covered her ears at the memory, "and then Kith put some *on his back.* Four of them! He picked up two more in his arms and ran all the way to the gate and then ran back to get more. He kept doing it until all the tiny stinky gooey ones and the wrinkly smelly dry ones were here. Then Agoth rose and there was that cracking noise and Kith started shoving them through the gate if they hadn't already gone. The other humans came out of the hills at the same time the Eldergast reached the gate and Kith said a *really* naughty thing," her eyes were huge in her tiny face and she covered her mouth with both hands and stared at Thane. "I didn't know a fae could even say that out loud without their Song hurting!"

The screams and impacts from the battle with the Eldergast were so loud Thane had forgotten the inugamae and the other screeches and sounds on the wind until Jena shrieked a shrill little scream. "Gryll!"

"What?" Thane shouted at her to be heard over all the other noise. But she had already fled back toward Kith. He looked back to see what had frightened her and immediately wished that he hadn't. He ran toward Jaeger and Twitch and gripped his roommate around his torso, throwing him up on his feet. "Move!"

"No, stay here," Jaeger reached for Thane's arms, but instead Thane grabbed the imp by the waist and spun him around. "Yeah, okay, run," Jaeger agreed, wrapping his arms around Twitch's head and twining his clawed feet through the boy's shirt. He flapped and strained, and Jaeger, Twitch, and Thane ran toward the huge murderous trees with as much speed as their drained bodies could manage.

Behind them the sky was filling with dark shapes and hundreds of pale grey animals with dripping fangs and eyes like dying coals surged out of the tall flowers and into the open field.

The Sang Evarish had caught up to them.

CHAPTER 23

"We have to get you through the gate," Thane yelled. Jaeger nodded but Twitch frowned.

"I can help! You're outnumbered and there are a lot more people than just me to worry about; let me go," he tried to twist out of Thane's grip.

"Help by getting us reinforcements!" Thane held on harder, fighting against Twitch now instead of them running together like before.

Twitch fought harder. "No one will come!" he had to shout to be heard over the noise as they drew closer to where the Eldergast guarded the gateway back to Earth. "Every time someone passes through the Weave gets weaker and we've done a ton of damage already! If I go through and then come back with more people and then we all try to go back again we might as well just cut the Weave and end the worlds ourselves!"

"I don't care!" Thane yelled, but he knew it was a lie. The humans suddenly redoubled their screams. They'd seen the inugamae coming and the Sang flying on animals that looked like black griffons. With the Eldergast between them and the gateway, they were surrounded. Trapped.

"I have to go find Remi," Thane shouted, trying to get the words past the tightness in his throat. Paka's words from before, that maybe not all the humans would be slaughtered, suddenly seemed ridiculously optimistic. "Do whatever you can to get people through those trees."

Jaeger's ears perked up. "Are hyu in charge, now?" he asked. It didn't feel like a challenge. Instead it seemed hopeful.

"Sure. Yeah, I'm in charge," Thane said. What did it matter now?

"And hyu say Aye must do anything Aye can to get the peoples through the hole?" The imp's eyes were swirling faster.

Thane was already running, heading in the direction Jena had said Remi was with her mother and Charlie. "Yes!" he shouted back, diving into the battle and dodging both people and Shae as he worked his way to the other side. He could swear he heard Jaeger giggling as he left the two of them behind. He could only pray he would see them again when this was over.

"We need to get these people organized!" Thane could hear Brennan shouting, and changed direction to follow the sound. "If we don't have a line of defense it's over!"

"An' what makes ye think it isnnae already over?" Hearing Charlie's voice gave Thane another burst of speed, and he dove through a final cluster of terrified people before skidding to a halt.

He was immediately tackled. "Thane!" Remi yelled, diving into him and wrapping her arms around him. He hugged her back, pressing her into his chest before letting go. "Where have you been? What are those?" she pointed to the sky.

"Gryll," Brennan answered. "They are what the Sang keep in their stables. One of the things, anyway. The Sang enslaved their minds centuries ago and crushed their free will--"

"Stories later, Tayler, right now we need a plan!" Major Gage snapped.

"We need a miracle," Iselle murmured, her eyelids squeezed shut hard enough that the lines in her skin extended well past her eyebrows. The red light that illuminated her started to turn violet. Thane stared at her, half a thought rising in his mind as all the moonlight began to change, blue filtering in through the red.

"Sing," he whispered, and then grabbed Remi by both her shoulders. "Sing! We need to get everyone singing!"

Her eyes went wide, and she opened her mouth. Nothing came out and she snapped it shut again. "Sing what?"

"It doesn't matter, something that everyone would know," he wracked his brain for something simple, something that many different people would know that might buy them some time.

"A, B, C, D, E, F, G..." Brennan's voice scratched out of his throat, notes a little flat and strained. Remi and Thane dove in and sang with as much force and volume as they could muster while Iselle looked at them, bewildered.

"I... I do not know this song," she stammered.

Thane shrugged at her but did not stop. The group of humans closest to them stared, but when the inugamae slowed as they drew close, more ragged voices joined in. The Sang circled overhead but did not attack. Thane didn't know why and didn't care yet; he was grateful for the reprieve, slight as it was, and as he stared upward he saw the blue moon rising from the horizon line. Cormoran had joined Agoth in the night sky.

More and more voices joined in as they repeated the song. It seemed not everyone knew it, and something about either the simplicity of the melody or lack of emotion kept the Shae from freezing as completely as they had before, but it kept the inugamae back and the Eldergast moved now with slow, sluggish gestures.

Nearer the gate there was a human scream. Thane couldn't see what happened, but could not investigate right now. His voice was getting weaker and hoarse, the exertion of the last few days drowning what was left of his breath. What he wouldn't give for a bass guitar right now.

"Oh Danny boy..." a voice rang out from somewhere near the gate. It sounded familiar, although Thane knew he'd never heard this voice sing before. It was louder and more pure than any other song on the field, and all the others fell silent.

Twitch stood on a pile of crates, singing into the small end of a large cone he must have thrown together out of the various things strewn on the ground around him. He'd built a stage and a megaphone.

Another human screamed, and this time since he was already looking in the direction of the gate Thane saw someone flying through the air and directly into the swirling colors. Their body flew in a low arc, the pinnacle being a few feet higher than the top of the archway. The Eldergast swung at the human but they were still entranced by the sound and moved in slow motion.

Thane spun to find Paka. She was crouching on all fours, teeth bared and claws out, starting at the front edge of the inugamae pack. "Go help Jaeger," he ordered. The panther woman glanced at him, then back at the snarling ghost wolves. "Please," he added. Paka sighed, then spun away and disappeared into the grass.

"We need to move, now!" Major Gage snapped, starting to herd the rest of the almost freed slaves into motion. "That boy's voice isn't going to last forever. Get going or die!"

Agoth's red light grew brighter as the blood moon rose toward its peak and something like a long black cloud moved in front of Cormoran, not hiding the orb but certainly blocking its glow. The people started to move toward the gateway, but the Eldergast were still too large and too much in the way. Only a few more humans were near enough to pass through the portal between universes before the malicious trees bent over, completely blocking the swirling light coming from the arch.

Thane heard a click and a thud, and a ball of misshapen cloth and shiny metal flew through the air and hit one of the Eldergast in the center of its trunk. It stuck there, hanging like a velcro ball thrown at a fuzzy target. The tree-man ignored it. It took the space of four heartbeats before it started to smoke and burn, and Thane could hear a ticking, sizzling sound from the inside of it.

It had to be from Jaeger, and that meant... "Get back," Thane shouted, pulling Remi away and shoving her behind him. "Everybody get away!"

Startled humans saw the smoke and did as he said, but not fast enough. The burning ball exploded, shooting bits of wood, bark, and sap in every direction as the Eldergast snapped under the pressure, top half toppling on one side of the gate and the bottom falling the other way. Sticky pieces of burning tree-man insides flew through the air and hit like darts on the panicked humans. One of the large branch arms spun through the air and crashed into the makeshift stage Twitch was on, and Twitch was thrown off backwards into the dark.

Thane heard Brennan grunt and cry out and turned around. The inugamae had attacked, and Brennan was trying to fend them off with two short pieces of broken wood. While two of the spectral grey forms lay unmoving at Brennan's feet, more circled him and a long gash showed dark blood soaking into his pant leg on one thigh. All around more of the inugamae dove forward, slashing with tooth and claw at the helpless humans. Some tried to flee but had nowhere to run. Others were being dragged into the darkness by two or three of the vicious creatures, all resistance gone.

"Charlie!" It was Remi's voice, and Thane spun frantically around trying to find her. He started running in the direction he thought he'd heard her, but the in the darkness and confusion he couldn't make out anything. He didn't know where any of his team were now; Twitch had fallen, Brennan was surrounded, Jaeger was somewhere with Paka throwing people at the arch, and Remi, Charlie, Major Gage, and Finn were out in the dark.

"Light," he muttered. There were only shadows around him, the stretched grey bodies of the inugamae and dull glowing eyes blending in to Agoth's angry illumination. "We need more light," he shouted. Remi screamed again, the sound wrapping around him in the wind so he couldn't guess which way it came from. The blood moon shone down, and Thane could swear he felt both its animosity and amusement toward the little speck of mud having a tantrum.

That iron ball of determination he'd been holding in his chest burst. His whole body filled with heat and power, and he threw back his head and roared, a wordless cry of defiance and fury. It surged outward from him like a physical wave of force, canceling all other sound to silence. "You!" he bellowed, thrusting a talon out to point at the moon of chaos. "You're supposed to be on my side. Do something useful!"

The black cloud that stood between Thane and the moon Cormoran changed direction and picked up speed. Cormoran had continued to rise, and now the bottom of the orb cleared the horizon and pale blue light flowed outward to wash over Thane and embrace the field. Another lopsided sphere sailed toward the other Eldergast, who swung one massive arm like a baseball bat and hit it with a dull thwack. It burst with the impact and shrapnel scattered through the air, glinting and shining in the shifting moonlight. Gemstones and weapons fell among the people below.

"That's where they are!" roared Kith, his hooves pounding against the ground as he dashed past Thane. The Dunsinae's fur was matted with blood and dirt. He still held his spear and his staff, bashing or impaling inugamae as he charged. The giant half buffalo half moose warrior threw his spear straight into the air and bent down, scooping something out of the grass and tossing it to Thane before pivoting on his back two cloven hooves and catching his spear midair, swinging it around to break the jaw of a lunging predator.

His hands came up reflexively and Thane caught the small weapon flat between his palms. It was like a short knife, but instead of a metal blade it had a shaft of black stone as long as his forearm with sharp green colored stones lined on one side and the handle stuck out at the wrong angle. It certainly looked flashy, but he wasn't sure it would be very functional.

Until his vision was filled with a lunging inugamae, open muzzle so close he could smell its breath. Thane reeled back. He jerked his arm up to protect his face and the colored stones moved through the narrow head with as little resistance as waving his hand through a shadow. The ghost wolf screamed with a sound like nails on a chalkboard and faded out of existence, leaving nothing.

Thane was holding the blade so the stone shaft pressed along his arm almost to his elbow and the handle he gripped pointed up. He looked at it for a moment, and then lifted his chin. He yelled, "Remi!"

"Thane!" she shouted back. In Cormoran's blue light he could see where she was, standing back to back to back in a triangle with her mom and Charlie. Either Kith had gotten there also or they'd armed themselves with more of the gemstone weapons holding two apiece. They were closer to the gate than he was, and more inugamae surrounded them, lunging forward and snarling or snapping and being driven back. But Thane could tell the circle was getting tighter, and he was very far away with an entire battlefield between them.

A cluster of the weapons shot into the air, aimed at the remaining Eldergast who still guarded the archway. The gems glittered and sparkled in the mixing moonlight. Thane's eye followed the path of the projectile backward, trying to see where all these flying humans and exploding textiles were coming from. He knew the who was Jaeger, but he didn't know how.

A catapult. Jaeger had built a catapult, a full on dark-ages style trebuchet that launched anything and everything he stuck in the split box at the top end of the arm. Thane could see the imp dancing along the top of it while Finn cranked the gear that brought it back to readiness until it clicked into place.

Thane's feet were moving before his brain caught up to the decision he'd already made. He didn't have time to wonder if it was smart- it wasn't. But it might work.

"Jaeger!" he shouted, swinging his arm around to slice open the neck of an inugamae who was lunging toward a screaming woman and sliding underneath a second one leaping at his head. He held the weapon above him and allowed the momentum of the creature's jump to drag its stomach along the gems, gritting his teeth against the screeching noise of it fading away. "Jaeger!"

"Perfekt head, hyu said whatever Aye could do-" Thane cut Jaeger's protest short by vaulting himself up into the payload area at the end of the throwing arm.

"See Remi?" Thane pointed, not thinking about what was going to happen next. The circle of inugamae around them was getting tighter. "Aim."

Jaeger's eyes widened, and his face split into a grin. He clapped. "Meat man! Help aim!" he ordered, and Finn grunted in response. The imp and the mercenary pulled the front of the ballistic machine until Thane's feet were pointed straight at Remi. He saw snapping teeth close over her foot.

"Go!" he screamed, and Jaeger jerked hard at a rope and Thane was suddenly flying through the empty space between the battle below and the mounted Sang watching above. The air stung at his eyes but he wouldn't close them, instead focusing of Remi and the exact moment he needed to duck and roll. Falling down staircases so often growing up had its uses.

He came up a little short of Remi. He pulled his arms in and tucked his head so the first thing to hit was the rounded outside part of his shoulder and rolled with the inertia instead of fighting it. Thane kept the gem blade on the outside of his torso facing away so as he slammed through one side of the inugamae like a bowling ball several of the creatures vanished with their awful sound as the weapon sliced through them.

Even prepared as he was it still hurt. The wind was knocked out of him and he lay in the torn grass feeling more like a giant bruise than a person. Thane struggled to roll over and tried to call out for Remi again, but something powerful yanked him up from behind and something else round and hard was driven into his stomach repeatedly as he was bounced around.

"If ye liked tae fly, I'd say tae use yer wings, tadpole," Charlie's arm held Thane in a firm grip over the dragon man's shoulder as they ran, and Thane could see Remi and Major Gage holding hands and following close behind.

"Remi-" Thane tried to speak again, but Charlie's shoulder kept punching him in the abdomen and driving his breath away before he could catch it.

"We need a rally point," Major Gage was shouting. "Everyone needs to get together so we can have one strong front. We're getting slaughtered out here."

"Jena-" Charlie's motion forced the air out of him again and he pounded against Charlie's back for attention.

Charlie slowed for a moment to put Thane on his feet, but they didn't stop. Even in that short pause Major Gage killed two inugamae and three more appeared at their heels, and Thane allowed Charlie to keep an arm around his waist so they could still move quickly while Thane got his breath back.

"That was brilliant," Remi said, coming up on his other side.

"That was stupid, but it worked," Major Gage corrected, dispatching another attacker.

"Are you okay? I saw one bite your foot right before I, um," Thane made a whooshing motion with his hand.

"It did?" Remi looked down at her foot and grimaced. "Huh. I didn't feel it."

There was a loud boom and all their heads jerked toward the archway to see what happened. The second Eldergast had fallen, hitting the ground full length and still trying to brush away the people who swarmed over it with drawn weapons, both taking the opportunity to destroy it and using it as a vantage point against the inugamae.

Charlie and Major Gage looked at each other. "Do it," the major said, and Charlie nodded. He started moving faster, dragging Thane away and Thane reached out at the same moment Remi did. The gripped each other's hand, and his best friend and her mother were pulled along in Charlie's wake.

His grandfather didn't have any visible weapons, but he didn't seem to need any. Even with one free arm he cleared a path through the hordes of grey skinned hunters, breaking bones and tearing flesh as he went. Thane had dropped his gem blade to get Remi but still managed to punch a leaping shadow in the face. He was grateful for the scales and claws; they were nearly as effective as the green stones had been.

They reached the side of the now still Eldergast, and Charlie let go of Thane to grab Remi and boost her up. She was thrown high enough to almost reach the top without having to scramble at all, and turned back to reach out a hand to help catch her mother, who was the next up. "On we go, lad," Charlie said, intertwining his fingers and bending down to make a step for Thane.

Thane stepped up into it and felt Charlie's immense strength as he was again shot into the air, but not nearly as far. He grabbed the rough bark with his claws and found the sideways tree an easy climb. Remi and her mother waited at the top, and Charlie was next to him almost before he was fully standing again.

"Get everyone here," Major Gage ordered. The opaque gateway back to Earth and home stood on the other side of the tree, easily visible from where they now stood. Major Gage glanced around, some of the despair easing out of the lines in her face and leaving only tension. "This tree is blocking the most direct access to the gate. If we can get everyone up here, we can send down fighters to guard the sides and funnel everyone through while only needing to defend a small area."

"That's great, mom!" Remi put her fingers in her mouth and whistled. It was loud and shrill, and it carried over the screams and shrieks of the fighting.

A multicolored light zigzagged through the moonlight and stopped near Remi's face. "How did you do that?" Jena chirped, glaring at Remi. "I'm supposed to be the only one who can make that noise. Not you. Give it back."

"We need everyone here, on this tree," Remi said.

Jena stamped her foot. "It is not a stupid tree, it's a dead Eldergast and I don't have to listen to you stupid pretty human who steals my noise!"

"At least we are both pretty," Iselle's voice was weak as she appeared at the edge of the tree. She was climbing with only one hand, holding the other arm at an angle across her chest and Charlie rushed over. He lifted her by the waist and gently placed her on the rough bark near Thane.

"I didn't steal anything," Remi protested. "It's called a whistle."

"Bring everyone to the dead Eldergast," Thane broke in. "Tell Kith to start gathering as many as he can and tell everyone else. Have Jaeger help you."

She winced. "There aren't that many left, I don't think he needs to help," she said, and zipped away before Thane could argue or add anything else.

There was movement in the dark by the gate below, large and fast. Thane tensed and pointed when a shadow on all fours started moving up the side of the tree and readied himself for another attack.

Iselle rested a hand on Thane's shoulder. "It's Paka," she said.

No it wasn't, Thane wanted to argue. The motion wasn't right... but the Pantera stood as she neared the flat summit of the corpse they waited on. It was Paka, but it wasn't. There was a stiffness to the way she moved, but she didn't have any injury he could see. The way she walked toward him was unsteady and her eyes were flat and her ears laid back.

"Paka..." he said, "are you..." He swallowed as he realized what the wrongness about her was. Why she couldn't walk well, why her fangs were bared and her balance was off.

Her tail was gone.

She didn't speak, but she did lock eyes with Thane and glared as if daring him to speak again.

"We're going to start moving the people over the Eldergast and through the gateway so we can protect them from the inugamae," Remi said, keeping her voice neutral. "That way we only need to fight them off on the sides."

Paka jerked her head up and down in a nod, not breaking her stare with Thane. He didn't look away, didn't acknowledge the shame he felt from her or let go of the pain he saw hiding behind the anger in her eyes. He held it with her.

"I dropped my knife while we were running," he said. "Can I have one of yours?"

She blinked. "Stupid cub. You never drop your weapon in battle." She lifted a paw from her waist, her movement stiff and slow. He opened his hand and she dropped a long dagger with a jagged edge into it.

"I will try to learn better, packmate," he said. Paka suddenly grinned at him fiercely, pain just as strong but no longer holding her powerless.

"You will have to try very hard, I think, Thane cub," she said.

Kith came galloping over, two gravely injured people laying across his back and one more running next to him. Charlie climbed halfway down and together with Thane and Major Gage they got all three up on top before Kith surged away again. More people were coming now, some running toward the tree and many acting as a rearguard, holding the remaining inugamae back with the weapons the Dunsinae had smuggled.

The seemingly unending pack of ghost wolves had dwindled down to only a few- Thane thought there must be less than twenty still harassing them. It was harder to tell how many of the people had made it. All had sustained wounds, many of those very severe. The last few stragglers were making their painful way up when Thane saw Brennan again.

His leg was roughly bandaged with cloth wound around it and tied in place. Judging by the sallowness of his skin and how slow he was moving he'd lost a lot of blood, but he was here and he was alive. Finn and Jaeger had already showed up. They were with Remi and Charlie discussing the next step with Major Gage. That only left one.

"Where's Twitch?" Brennan asked, his eyes roaming over the gathered people. "Jaeger!" Thane turned around. There was no sign of the caffeine addicted tech specialist anywhere as the imp flew over and landed on Thane's head. "Where is Twitch?"

"Aye only know where he is not, and he is not here," Jaeger answered.

"Find him," Brennan did not sound worried. He sounded like he did not have the energy left to be worried. Or to hope.

"Twitch is all right," Paka said. She came over to where they stood, walking on all four legs for better balance.

Brennan's face screwed up and his whole body flinched as if he'd been punched somewhere already painfully tender. "Oh Paka," he said, and ran his hand through his hair, the one with the missing fingers.

"If Turcato loses a leg in our next mission, Aye will haf Bingo," Jaeger said to Thane in a loud whisper.

"You flying rat," Paka hissed, but there wasn't any malice in it.

Brennan chuckled with a wheezing sound to it. "How do you know he's okay, Paka?"

She shrugged. "He was unconscious from the fall. I shoved him through the gate when no one was looking. Kith said all the old and the cubs were already there, so they can take care of him until he wakes up."

"Good move," Brennan almost smiled. "Now if we can get the rest of us down and out of here I'm going to sleep for a month."

Black shadows dove from overhead, and Brennan grunted and collapsed. All around the tree people screamed and cowered in fear as the Sang on their dark mounts flew through them, herding them like sheep with the beaks, maws, and talons of the gryll. They landed, heavy claws making deep score marks in the flesh of the tree and surrounding Thane and his friends in a loose circle.

Terracatan sat on an enormous winged beast directly in front of Thane. His shoulder was covered in heavy bandages and he was hunched forward, posture uneven and face twisted in a feral snarl. "Hail, Lord de Argos," he spat. The wet spittle hit the tree near Thane's feet. "Are you enjoying your little adventure?" Thane stared back, not sure what to say. His hands were trembling and he balled them into fists, willing them to be still. "What, no brave speeches now? No promises of gifts or riches? I'm disappointed."

The First Lord of the Sang made his gryll take two steps toward Thane, so the giant beak could snap out and take his head at any moment. "Now I admire a good traitor," Terracatan went on in a conversational tone, "Lying in the name of self service I completely understand. Reaching out and taking what you want, regardless of whose hand is holding it is the kind of initiative I encourage in my children." The Sang spared a glance to the other side of the waiting circle. Thane didn't follow the look. "But do you know what I can not abide?"

The Sang paused, waiting. If he was waiting to force Thane to answer, he was going to wait a long time. Thane clenched his jaw.

"Waste." Terracatan whispered the word. If there hadn't been silence from everyone else, even the wind, Thane wouldn't have heard him. The Sang kneed his mount and it moved forward again, forcing Thane to back up or be trampled. "You ridiculous humans, you can trap your Song and make it so any idiot child can repeat it and you throw it away. Your world is in desperate need of leadership and control and you destroy it in the name of fairness and humanity," he twisted the word in his mouth, making it sound foul and loathsome.

"Charlie," Thane could hear Remi speaking low behind him. "Can't you, you know, and scare them away?"

"Can't, lass, it'd be the end of all of us," he muttered back.

"And you," Terracatan was going on with his rant, "you are the worst waste of all. It makes me sick to think a dragon- a dragon! The only word in both the realms you simpletons got right, because even your puny comprehension couldn't miss their power- and he made you, disgusting, worthless you, mixed breed mutt who is more useless as a dragon than you even are as human. Look at you. You couldn't even get out of the Shaerealm with an open gate waiting for you." He sneered.

"Charlie," Remi hissed.

"Tisnae worth it, girl, we'd all die an' the Weave itself may come apart," Charlie's whisper caught as he spoke as though he was drowning.

"So here's how it's going to go," Terracatan's beast lunged, knocking Thane aside and to his knees. The Sang leaned down and snatched Major Gage, lifting her by the throat so her legs kicked as she dangled from his hand. Remi jumped for her mother, trying to help her get free, but Terracatan lashed out with his boot, striking her in the face. Charlie caught her before she hit the tree, but she pushed him away.

"Mom!" cried Remi.

"I am going to take back what's mine, starting with this one, the healer." Terracatan moved his hand so her head swung around to face him, both her hands clutching at where he was crushing her neck. "Yes, pretty little toy, you have made plans and acted against me many times. I let it slide, because you were never a danger and all the others worked so much better when you kept feeding them those hopeful lies." He drew a stone knife and laid it across her cheek by the sharp edge, drawing a fine line of blood down her face.

"Meagan?" Thane's heart constricted as he heard that voice. He scrambled back to his feet so he could see the arch, the glowing and open gateway back home.

In it stood General Andrus Gage, leader of the Omega Team and one of the most powerful and competent men Thane had ever heard of. "Dad!" Remi yelled.

Major Gage tried to crane her head around to see him, but Terracatan's grip was too tight. "Andrus!" she tried to yell, her constricted windpipe making her voice a hoarse croak, "Catch!"

She pulled something out of a hidden holster inside her clothes and threw it towards the sound of his voice. It was long and thin and unremarkable looking, except that the Song bursting out of it was so loud and so great it made the inside of Thane's head ring like a bell with a single note.

Terracatan plunged the knife into her chest and she gasped, a weak, startled sound. Her body dangled limply as her arms twitched and her face spasmed, once.

There was a sharp crack and Terracatan slumped, Major Gage collapsing to the ground as his hand went slack. The gryll shied away and the body of the First Lord of the Sang dropped like a weighted sack and landed on top of Remi's mom.

"No!" Remi rushed to her mother's side and Thane followed, helping her push the body of the Shae off the edge of the tree. There was pandemonium all around them, and a crackling sound followed by a roar so loud it made the tree shake with people, Sang, and gryll screaming and the sounds of more fighting.

All of that was background to Remi clutching her mother's hand as Meagan Quinn Gage fought to breathe. The knife in her chest rattled with every inhalation, and Thane was sure it had punctured a lung and made it collapse.

"Shh, shh, puppy, your daddy's here now," Meagan tried to reach up, but her hand only flopped feebly next to her. "He'll make it all right again."

"Mom, mom, you can't die now, we have to get you through the portal and they'll save you, the doctors, they can do it," Remi was babbling, and trying to pull her mother up to sitting by the one hand she held in both of hers and fighting back tears. Something about the moonlight made Remi's hands seem to glow, but Thane thought that must be his own eyes blurring. He swallowed and blinked rapidly.

"No, I wouldn't survive the trip, no, honey, shh," she tried to smile at Remi, then her eyes slowly moved in short, jerking motions until they focused on Thane.

"Did you know I held you when you were a baby?" her voice was so quiet and weak Thane was certain he'd heard that wrong. She smiled at the look on his face. "Really. I did. Amelie was so brave, trying to hold on so you could be born. I was barely pregnant with you then, puppy," her eyes wandered to Remi and back to Thane.

"Amelie?" Thane repeated. "But my mom's name is Gwen…" his protest was weak.

"We'd been running from de Argos for days," she continued as though she hadn't heard him. "Amelie was so tired and scared, and then you came out all blue and scaly and not breathing." The word seemed to remind her of the action, and she tried to draw another painful breath, closing her eyes against the effort.

"I saved you," Meagan Gage whispered. Her chest was barely moving at all, and both Thane and Remi had to lean close to hear. "You couldn't breathe, and I saved you." Her eyes opened, bright and clear and staring into Thane's. "You owe me, dragon boy. The Sylph herself worked to save you from de Argos, but I made you live." She looked again at Remi. "Keep her alive."

"Mom," Remi was crying so much the tears dripped from her face and fell on her mother's hand, running down the skin and soaking into the cloth of her sleeves.

"Meagan!" Andrus Gage was shouting into the melee around them, trying to get to them through a wall of Sang and gryll. "Remi!"

"Andrus," Major Meagan Quinn Gage breathed out his name like a prayer, and was still.

Remi crumpled forward over the body of her mother and sobbed.

Thane rocked back on his heels, shocked and hurting. He saw Jaeger snatched out of the air by a gryll and his rider, and Finn grappling with a Sang and deflecting a blow from a claw so it sank into his arm instead of his face. Paka screamed in rage and pain as her torso over her ribs was slashed open by a glancing blow, and another of the Sang Evarish was creeping up behind Remi with a curved dagger raised high.

"No!" like before, the roar burst out from him with such force it was a physical thing, throwing those closest to him off balance. Unlike before, this time he exploded outward with it. His body stretched and grew, scales and talons rising out of his skin to cover him as though it had always been there. And it wasn't only his shape; the leviathan inside him, the monster he'd tried so long to push down and hold back expanded within and became him, clicking into the place it always should have been.

He was not his father. Not the one who shared his DNA or the one who raised him. Not Lord de Argos and not Bert's punching bag, not Harper's whipping boy or Ms. Rasmussen's ticket or Jaeger's science experiment or the invisible boy in the hall no one noticed.

He was Thane, and he was going to get Remi home.

He opened his senses to Shae, and the Song of lightning flooded through him. The Sang who threatened Remi was thrown into the sky with a bolt of pure electricity and landed somewhere far enough away he wouldn't be a threat again. The now riderless gryll fled in terror and Thane ignored it. He stepped across Remi to where General Gage grappled with another Sang and grabbed the Shae by the back of the neck and the seat of its pants and heaved it into the air so it flew, arms and legs spinning, until crashing face first into the blood soaked meadow.

More of the Sang, hundreds more, poured out of the darkened sky in a rain of beaks, claws, fangs, swords and knives. Thane roared out at them and the waves from the sound became visible as they rippled through the eagle like wings of the flying creatures. Sang were thrown off their mounts as gryll were thrown sideways or backward. Panicked, the gryll began to slash and bite at each other, trying to drive the falling ones away and clear their own paths. Dark feathers drifted like snow as the black and silver Shae tried to regain control and return to the attack.

Thane didn't want to wait. Crouching down, he launched himself into the air with his talons outstretched and caught the foreleg of the nearest flying gryll. It shrieked and snapped at him but he'd already pulled himself on its back, grabbing the previous rider and throwing him off backwards. Thane threw his leg over the back of the animal and grabbed the reins, hauling its head around before kicking into its sides and driving it straight into a cluster of Sang who were preparing a diving attack.

The gryll plowed into the formation and Thane let go, jumping up and backwards so as he fell he still faced them. He opened both hands and shot bright blue lightning into them with wild music singing in his head and through his blood, and he watched as the electricity arced and sizzled through his enemies. He landed on all fours on top of another Sang who was charging at General Gage and Remi with a drawn sword. The impact knocked the Shae unconscious, and Thane kicked the body off the tree.

General Gage's eyes were dark and angry. Remi's father stepped past him and stood, staring down at the broken body of his wife and his weeping daughter.

"I will not allow this," Thane heard General Gage's flat, toneless words.

A roar split the sky as if in answer. It was like Thane's; sound so powerful it wasn't heard as much as felt, but it was so much more, exponentially more, like a mountain is more than a pebble.

On the other end of the tree, a dragon lifted his head and looked skyward. In his foreclaw he held a motionless Brennan with Iselle hunched over him, and Paka, Jaeger, and Finn all crowded near the shelter Charlie's immense body offered.

"Time to go," Charlie's dragon voice held the same relentless quality that General Gage's just had.

Between the two dragons the Sang were quickly driven away and all the humans placed at the arch. They entered by twos and threes, sometimes helping to steady or even carrying their wounded as Thane and Charlie stood a silent vigil.

General Gage was one of the last to go back through. He held the body of his wife in his arms, ignoring the blood that still trickled from the wound and stained his uniform. Remi, shaking, was standing next to Thane.

The mountain-sized roar came again, and this time Thane could hear words in it. "Charlieeeee!"

His grandfather shrank back, folding in on himself until he was back in his familiar human form. Thane watched him, and looked at the sky. "Who is that?"

"Not the time," Charlie was curt. "Naow get yerself down so we can go."

"How?" Thane asked.

Golden light spilled onto the battle torn meadow from the opposite end of the sky as the third and final moon finally appeared. Tyrn had risen. It seemed smaller than Thane remembered it, and he turned back to look at the other two moons to compare.

The black cloud he'd seen was much larger now and moving fast, blocking part of his view of red Agoth. The blood moon was still by far the largest but Cormoran had doubled in size from the last time Thane had seen it in the night sky. Tyrn was still small and far away.

"There's something wrong with that cloud," Thane commented, entranced by its movement and finding it hard to pull his gaze away.

"There are no clouds in the Shaerealm, boy!" the frantic fear in Charlie's voice cut whatever spell held Thane, and he jerked his head down.

"How do I change back?"

"Ye just do! Take control of yerself," Charlie looked at Remi. "Get through, lass, we'll guard the back of ye."

She ignored him as though she hadn't even heard him. "Remember what it feels like to be Thane," Remi said, placing her warm hand against his leg. He turned towards her and saw double, Remi's body standing there touching him overlaid with the phoenix soul she was, the glowing fire of her center white hot. "Remember Payson. Remember being in class. Remember sitting on the swings in the park, and talking in my room." She blushed a little, the skin on her cheeks flushing red and the head of the phoenix burning brighter.

He remembered. He pulled up all those memories she'd listed, along with more. Lanie getting her monkey. His mother sneaking him soup when he was sick. Running with Paka and yelling at the sky, feeling free and whole for the first time. Thane knew the Song of lightning but somewhere in his mind he found the echoes of other music, a melody of getting back up every time he was knocked down, of his love of the bass guitar, his need to be loved and part of a family. It was simple, but strong and complete unto itself. It was hope.

It was Thane, just as much as the dragon and lightning was. He realized he'd been closing his eyes and he opened them again, seeing Remi's face. They were eye to eye and she was still crying, but holding his hand now.

"Your eyes are blue, now," she said.

Charlie's groan came from somewhere so deep inside him it seemed to echo from the ground. Thane looked at his grandfather and saw that centuries old sorrow etched in the lines of the man's face again, the same way he'd seen when Charlie had spoken the first time about his lost phoenix love.

"CHARLIE!" the thunderous boom was so close now it knocked them off their feet.

"Go through!" Charlie screamed from the ground, and Remi and Thane crawled to the gate.

Thane pushed Remi through first and reached back to help his grandfather. Behind Charlie, the black cloud was so close now it blotted out the sky and the light of all three moons. Except it wasn't a cloud.

It was a flight of dragons. Beasts so huge Thane's mind reeled away from trying to comprehend their enormity and numbers. But there was no doubting their anger, rage pure and elemental and in the darkness, Thane couldn't see what color the lead dragons were.

He could see their fangs as they opened their giant maws to attack, and even though they were still far enough away Thane didn't think they could even see him, he knew their Song would kill them.

He grabbed Charlie by the shoulders and rolled through the gate. Thane's last image of the Shaerealm was blue fire and molten lava eradicating the meadow where the bodies of the fallen had been left behind.

CHAPTER 24

The ground his face was pushed into was frigid and rocky, and he gasped for breath but couldn't seem to get any. The air was too thin, too dry, and too cold. It burned his lungs and made his head feel light and dizzy. He started coughing, but the spasmodic gasps of air he sucked in only made him feel like he was losing more air, suffocating as if he were in space. Rough hands rolled him over and held a hard plastic thing against his face. Thane tried to open his eyes, but the chill of the air stung them immediately shut again.

"Shh, shh, now lad," the warm mellow voice sounded familiar, and with the glimpse of golden fuzzy blur Thane had gotten he thought it must be Haider, the lion man doctor from Sanctum. But what was here doing here? "Be still, the shock of the change is rough, like going from sea level to La Riconada with nothing in between."

"La... what?" Thane's voice sounded all wrong, too weak and hoarse and high pitched.

He felt the deep rumble of Haider's chuckle. "It's a city in Peru, the highest in the world by elevation. But you'll have time for geography lessons later. Rest, and breathe."

Thane focused all his effort on pulling air in and pushing it out of his lungs without fainting from the exertion. There were questions he should be asking, people he should find, but his mind was too tired to hold on to any one thought, and they drifted away. The smell of the oxygen was sweet and a little cloying. It seemed to pull him down towards darkness, and he had nothing left to fight it.

When he woke up he felt like he might actually live, even if he might not enjoy it. His face was swollen and painfully pushed down against something hard and squarish. Both eyes were gritty, but when he tried to move his hand to rub them it would only move a few inches, and the other arm jerked with it. There was a sound, a motor running, and the way his body was jostled he realized he must be in the backseat of a car or truck.

"Ye wakin' up, boy?" It was Charlie's voice, but it didn't sound like him. There was nothing of the teasing warmth or underlying confidence Thane had come to associate with his grandfather.

Thane opened his eyes and stared at a silver door handle for a moment. His body slumped sideways and his head was resting against the passenger door. The fake leather stuck and pulled at his skin with a tearing sound when he used his elbows to push himself up to a sitting position and look around.

He was in the backseat of a truck, high off the ground with two soldiers in Sanctum military uniform in the front seat. The one driving glanced at him in the rearview mirror. "Welcome back," he said, but his tone wasn't kind.

Moving his arms around uncomfortably behind himself Thane decided he must be handcuffed. He had been put into a thick warm coat so he couldn't feel the metal on his skin, but the way the restrains clinked and had no give or stretch indicated it wasn't rope or zip ties. His feet were bound too, but looking down he saw those weren't cuffed, but instead individually bound with chain and attached to bars under his seat.

"Um, what's going on?" Thane asked.

"You're under arrest," said the soldier who'd spoken before. The guard in the passenger seat frowned at the driver but didn't say anything.

"Oh," Thane sat back against the seat, his back arched awkwardly over his arms. "Why?"

"Because we rescued nigh over five score of people wi'oot askin' fer Sanctum's by yer leave an' dinnae break th' right rules at the right times so these clag-tails'll lock us somewhere deep and dark 'til they ken we're a long time deid." The venom in Charlie's voice shocked Thane. His grandfather was in the backseat near him, and presumably bound in the same manner, which would be easy for the dragon to break. But he sat slumped over, as though in addition to the chains and cuffs he was held down by an invisible weight much larger than he was.

"Shut up," the soldier in the passenger seat growled at Charlie, lifting a rifle so Charlie and Thane could both see it, "or I'll make you."

Thane could only manage to stay silent for a few seconds. "What about the others?" he burst out. "Did Brennan make it? What about Twitch? Is Remi-" he swallowed, memories of those last moments in Shae flashing through his mind, "is she okay?"

The angry soldier raised his gun again, but the one driving made a curt gesture with one hand to stand down. He glanced at Thane again in the rearview mirror. "Tayler is going to be fine, even though he lost a lot of blood. He'll spend a few days on lockdown in the infirmary before he joins the others. So will Twitch and Paka, based on the severity of their injuries."

"Shut up, man, we're not supposed to talk to them," the other guard was not happy.

The driving soldier shrugged and looked back at Thane. "Iselle and Jaeger came through with only minor wounds, and they'll be confined to quarters until the others are healed so they can all stand trial together."

"Stand trial? For what?" Thane sat up straighter at this news and glared at the angry soldier who started to protest again.

"For treason, kidnapping, passing through the Weave outside proper channels, consorting with the enemy, endangering civilians, leading non-combatants into battle, and a list of other broken regulations." The soldier signaled and made a left turn, causing Thane to slide against the door and smack his elbow painfully.

The offenses bewildered Thane. They swirled through his mind as he tried to make sense of them all. Most he could at least make sense of, but some... "Kidnapping?" he asked.

The soldier nodded. "You, Remi Quinn, and one other student, Nathiel Grey."

"What?" It felt like months since Thane had even remembered Nathiel, the student who had escaped with them. Where had he gone? Thane couldn't remember. "But it was our idea."

"So? You're still minors, placed in Sanctum's care. Members of the Mercenary Guard took you away from that. Whether you choose it or not is irrelevant."

"You need to shut up now. Our orders were not to talk to them or let them speak to each other!" The soldier in the passenger seat looked around as the truck pulled off to the side of the road and the other soldier put it in park. "What are you doing?"

"Those were your orders," the driver corrected. He held up a pistol with an irregular muzzle and fired.

For a moment, the soldier looked shocked as a dart quivered where it had struck in the center of his chest. Then he fell, bonelessly sliding off the seat and onto the floor mat of the truck.

"What?" Thane felt like that was the only word he remembered how to say. The edges of the soldier behind the wheel went fuzzy and made Thane's head hurt to look at. He blinked and looked away, and when he looked back Nathiel sat in the front seat looking back at him.

"Hey Thane," he said. "How was the Shaerealm?"

"Wh-" Thane made an effort to stop himself from saying "what" again. Instead he tried, "Where have you been? You were with us and we were talking, but it was like suddenly you'd never been there at all and we just kept going. I hadn't thought about it until right now."

The expression Nathiel made was technically a smile, but there was no feeling behind it. "Yeah, I'm good at that. It's my skill, that and shapeshifting. It's nice to not always have to be me, you know?" Thane's nod was a reflex, not really an agreement.

"So, are we going to rescue the others?" Thane was groping for ground, here. Too much had happened in too short of a time again, and his mind was reeling.

Nathiel snorted. "No, I'm not here for that. I'm here for you."

"Me?" Thane blinked.

"Yeah, your dad sent me to get you. A year and a month and a day, right?" Nathiel opened the door and climbed out of the truck, then opened Thane's door and pulled himself up again. The boy with the grey skin pulled keys from his shirt pocket and unlocked the handcuffs first, then bent down to undo the padlocks holding the chains around Thane's feet. "You can ride up front with me, if you want."

"Um, okay, yeah," Thane felt like an idiot, unable to keep up. "My dad sent you? You work for him?"

"For a while now." Nathiel shrugged as Thane rubbed feeling back into his wrists. "He's a pretty good boss as long as you get it done for him. Better than my last two." With that remark he climbed out again and got back into the driver's seat.

"What about Charlie?" Thane asked. His grandfather's silence through all this worried him. Was he hurt? Did something happen Thane hadn't seen?

Nathiel chuckled, but there was no humor in it. "Charlie is free to go, of course. Ruan says he's stirred up enough trouble to keep him more than busy for the next few millennia."

"Look, no offense, and thanks for keeping me out of Sanctum jail and all, but I'm sick of people giving me mysterious non-answers to questions." Thane folded his arms across his chest. "What are you talking about?"

Surprise flicked across Nathiel's eyes but did not change his expression. "Charlie crossed the Weave," he said, in a measured tone Thane recognized as being like the one is math teacher used when explaining something very simple to a student who just wasn't getting it. Thane gritted his teeth. He remembered that he didn't like Nathiel much. "Dragons don't pass through the Weave- it was part of the compact The Sylph made with the Thunder Alpha and the original Guardian Council. They have too much changeable mass and Song, no matter how small their form is at that moment, and the Weave... snags on them. It unravels, and the area they passed through gets unstable. Things around it get blurred, and start leaking out. Not just back and forth between Earth and Shae, but outside both. It disappears because there's nothing to hold it, no reality to make it real. A void." He glared at Charlie, tone changing to something dark and angry. "That's what this idiot was doing. He risked pulling us all into the void, getting both of our whole universes unmade. And the Alpha Thunder know."

The memory of the black cloud in the Shaerealm sent a cold chill through Thane. That last moment where earth, fire, and sky all seemed to combine to try and destroy them... that was for Charlie. And for what Charlie did, or tried to do, for Remi.

"Look, there's more to it than that, you don't know the whole story-" Thane began, but Nathiel's joyless laughter cut him off.

"Do you think I care? That anyone does? There won't be any mercy, any forgiveness for that." Nathiel turned away.

"I dinnae need mercy," Charlie mumbled. "I lost her. She'll not forgive me, not ever, nor ken why I was too late..." he trailed off, and Thane felt his heart crack. Anguish and despair were dramatic words, but they seemed small and weak compared to Charlie's faint whisper. He was suddenly very glad Charlie was bound, because what Charlie would do if he was free, Thane didn't want to contemplate.

Nathiel grunted and got out of the truck again, this time walking around to Charlie's door and yanking it open. "Ruan doesn't want you, doesn't even want to see you," he said, unlocking Charlie's restraints efficiently. "I understand dragon, even if I can't speak it, and the nicest name he called you was dangerously useless." Thane's grandfather neither answered nor reacted to the loosening of his bonds, hands not even changing position as the handcuffs were removed. It didn't seem to matter to him.

"Out," Nathiel ordered. Charlie didn't move, didn't acknowledge anything had changed about his situation.

"Charlie," Thane began, then swallowed. "Grandpa..."

His grandfather lifted his chin barely enough to meet Thane's eyes. Thane flinched, that look feeling harsher and more violent than anything he'd experienced so far. "Dinnae fash yerself, lad," Charlie's words were in direct contrast to his face, "I cannae flee forever. Even the ancient run out of time." He moved stiffly, as though every bone and joint were going to shatter unless he was obsessively careful.

He fell more than climbed out of the truck, landing on the frozen ground in a heap. "Charlie," Thane called again, moving to go after him.

"Stay in the truck, Thane," Nathiel wasn't going to let him argue. "There isn't anything you can do for him."

"But he's my grandpa," Thane protested anyway, and started to get out to go help Charlie.

"Lad, dinnae take one step more," Charlie stood, brushing the dirt from his pants. He turned his back on Thane and strode into the bleak and empty landscape of Antarctica without looking back. "Leave me be, boy."

Thane stood dumbly, one foot out of the truck and one hand holding the roll bar as he watched his grandfather walk away from him. It hurt. Not like being punched or beaten or shot or burned; it was a much deeper aching, with a pain he could neither explain nor compare.

He heard Nathiel moving around, grunting a little. In his peripheral vision Thane saw the body of the unconscious soldier roll out of the truck and onto the ground. The grey boy followed after and dragged the Sanctum guard out of Thane's sight, and then the driver's side door clicked open and shut.

"Come on," Nathiel said. Thane heard the click of his seatbelt buckle.

"You can wait," he said back. Charlie's shape grew small, the flatness of the landscape making distances distorted. Thane kept his gaze locked on his grandfather until he couldn't see him anymore, feeling convinced this was wrong but unable to articulate why.

The shapeshifter was silent. Once Thane was positive no matter how he strained he couldn't see Charlie anymore, he swung himself into the front seat and slammed the door shut. He slouched against it, as far away from Nathiel as possible, and crossed his arms.

They didn't move. "Drive," Thane said. Nathiel glanced at him, looking at the unfastened seatbelt and back. Thane pretended not to notice.

"You don't deserve all this, you know," Nathiel shifted the truck into drive and pulled back out onto the road, making a three point turn and heading off in the opposite direction. Thane continued to ignore him, not wanting sympathy or kindness right now. Remi had liked Nathiel; Thane had even liked him the first time they met, that morning in the locker room. For those reasons he didn't just tell the guy to shut up, and sat without speaking.

Apparently Nathiel didn't need a response. "Everyone is treating you like a spoiled prince, and all you do is mope like a pansy." Thane'd been wrong about the sympathy, too. "Your father literally moves heaven and earth to break some pretty fundamental rules to get you where you want and you don't even ask about him, your grandfather gets a death sentence for helping you, and you're mad at him for leaving. Gage treats you like a son and you get his wife killed in front of his daughter. Who, by the way, is also the girlfriend who is way too good for you that you just left behind without even making me answer your question about her."

"She isn't my girlfriend!" Thane's shout had more than a little growl in it, and electricity jolted through his hand and into the dashboard. Static blasted through the radio at top volume and the car alarm blared. Nathiel jerked the wheel in surprise and the truck went into a skid on the icy road, sliding sideways and fishtailing back and forth until he got it back under control.

"Are you trying to kill us?" Nathiel's tone screamed the "you idiot" part he hadn't actually said.

"Remi isn't my girlfriend, and you're right, she is too good for me," Thane kept his voice deliberately quiet, not lashing out with his Song and frying this guy until his eyeballs burst. Nathiel snorted, and Thane clenched his jaw to hold back. "Do you know about Charlie, my grandfather?" Thane put venom into those last words, the threat of all the violence he was not doing. The other boy lifted his chin in a nod, watching the road and seeming unimpressed. "Remi is a phoenix. *Charlie's* phoenix."

That got Nathiel's attention. The quick look he gave Thane was wide eyed, with a slightly open mouth. "She's... whoa. So that's why..." he trailed off, shaking his head. "Your own grandmother? Dude, that's sick."

Thane's hands were shaking with exhaustion, with anger, disgust, residual fear, and so many more emotions swirling and fighting for dominance he couldn't even tell them apart. They clawed at his insides and weighted him down. He wanted to blast the truck into pieces, followed by the whole world so he could put the pieces back together in a way that made sense and no one was going to jail or in love with the wrong person or wandering off alone.

Sparks danced along his fingers and he closed them into fists. They were human hands again; pink flesh and short dirty fingernails and calloused pads on his left hand from his bass guitar. He needed to get it together before he did something else stupid.

"Just," his voice creaked and broke. Thane swallowed and tried again. "Just tell me what happened on this side. How did you get here? Where's my father? How did Sanctum get here? Why did General Gage to through the gateway to the Shaerealm?" He took a deep breath and stopped there, holding the rest back for now.

Nathiel was quiet, as if deciding whether or not to speak. Before Thane could either scream or start punching the answers out of him, the grey boy opened his mouth. "When you all decided I wasn't going with you, I left a Song of suggestion behind so none of you would remember to think about me and I went back to de Argos. He always knew you getting into the Sanctum school was a possibility, so he placed me there early so I would be a few years ahead of you if you showed up. Even though my cover wasn't blown I wasn't going to be useful there anymore so I went to report."

Thane leaned forward and rested his head on his fists. It seemed like everyone he'd ever met was leading a double life, spying on him or lying about their motives or their name or their memories. He remembered General Gage's words about the darkest lie ever told are that we're alone, but he sure felt alone.

"After he found out you were going to Payson he went and set up an operational base there to meet you." Thane could feel the truck accelerating as Nathiel resumed his story. "He was pleased with how easily you got through his guards and since you'd already decided I wasn't going, he assigned Finn to stay with you. Finn isn't the brightest banana in the bunch, so the watches were a backup." He stopped speaking, and Thane turned his head enough to see. Nathiel was looking at his wrist. He couldn't see the watch underneath the think outer coat but he would know it was there.

Thane sighed but didn't comment. The other boy waited a few moments more, then went on. "So you left for Shae and de Argos stayed to keep the gate open. Since I wasn't at Sanctum anymore, I'm not sure what tipped them off or got them started looking, but after two days there were helicopters in the sky and a golden dragon bearing down on us."

"Adam," Thane commented. "Adam Gold. He leads Alpha Team."

When Thane didn't offer more, Nathiel kept going. "They didn't let the dragon get too close because of the way their Song impacts any openings in the Weave, but he was obviously there to show us there was no way to run. But de Argos was smarter than that; he went to the Shadeleaf Mercenary Guard under a white flag and asked to talk to General Gage. When they told him Gage was busy, he asked if the general would be interested in knowing where his daughter was."

That got a reaction. Thane flinched with his whole body, stomach going tight and pushing his clenched fists harder into his forehead. They'd tricked General Gage into thinking Remi was seriously sick, and then run away. First he'd thought she was dying, then she was gone. What would he have thought then, getting that message from Ruan de Argos?

"The SMG got the message back to stand down and wait, don't engage, but don't let anybody go, either. Gage was on his way. He was there in less than two hours, and he and de Argos went off to one side to talk, alone." Thane could feel the truck changing direction again and speed up, the road underneath becoming rougher as he was jostled into the door again. "Both sides were forbidden to use listening devices, so no one knows what they said. But when they came back de Argos and all his people were allowed to leave without restraint, and Gage ordered the archway be protected and kept open at all costs. I was ordered to stay behind and retrieve you when you came back through."

There was more noise outside the truck, the sounds of large engines and people shouting, and the road smoothed out so Thane wasn't getting thrown around anymore. He still didn't look up, waiting for Nathiel to finish.

"They'd waited almost a day and a half before anything happened. Gage stayed right by the gateway the whole time, even having his cot and desk set facing from his open tent. But he didn't sleep or work, just sat and watched. I'm not sure he blinked until the old people and the kids started coming through. They just kept coming, and they'd fall over and start coughing or faint and a lion in a lab coat started shouting orders. Medics set up extra tents and they carried all the people into them. The guard even recognized some of the old people and started crying." More shouting and the truck slowed and stopped, engine running, and Thane glanced up enough to see a large chain link gate being pulled open.

The truck started moving again. "It was way past the time de Argos had told you to get back, but I didn't know if any of the Sanctum guys knew that. I think Gage did, because he was looking really gaunt and sick, staring into the arch with his hands clasped together. He may even have been praying. Then Twitch came rolling through and knocked over his chair and they both fell down."

He snorted as if the memory were funny. "That lion doctor guy got up and grabbed Twitch and stuck an oxygen mask on him before rolling him onto a stretcher. He tried to take him away to a medical tent but Gage wouldn't let them. Gage kept screaming about Remi and Meagan and when the doctor tried to hold him back Gage shoved him so hard he landed in the dirt and dropped the oxygen."

General Gage's panic and fear were too easy to picture. Thane had seen only a small glimpse of what General Gage was like after Remi had been in danger, and it'd been both terrifying and endearing. Haider was lucky General Gage hadn't broken the lion's jaw for getting in the way.

"Gage grabbed Twitch by the shirt and ordered him to talk. He gasped out something about a battle and the Sang and Major Gage before passing out. Gage grabbed a sidearm and dove through the gate while everyone else started yelling, but no one would follow him." The truck made a hard turn and started moving upward. It leveled out and stopped, Thane hearing the gears shift and the engine go quiet as the keys clicked. The bench seat moved as Nathiel relaxed and leaned back, breathing a sigh. "When you all came back through Haider took charge, getting them all acclimated and stable again, and stitching up Brennan. He was really pissed at whoever fixed Twitch's arm- apparently there was a way to get it to grow back, but not now."

Thane absorbed that and added it to the list of things he'd done wrong and people he'd hurt without thinking. There were so many. It was getting so long he was afraid there would be no way to atone for it all.

"What about Remi?" Thane forced the words out. He needed to hear, even if he didn't want to. He'd gotten her home but she'd rescued him more than anything he'd done. Major Meagan Quinn Gage had been there when he was born and saved his life, if what she'd said was true, but Thane had failed to save her. And now he'd broken his only promise to Remi; he'd left without saying goodbye, and she'd never know what'd happened to him.

Nathiel hadn't answered him yet. Thane raised his head to stare at the other boy, who looked uncomfortable for the first time. He shifted in his seat and wouldn't meet Thane's eyes. "Nathiel." Thane didn't think he'd said the boy's name out loud before, and the grey boy twitched when he spoke it.

"Physically she's fine, or she was," he started, fiddling with the truck keys and not looking up. Thane didn't rise to the bait, only waiting and starting. Nathiel sighed again, heavy and resigned. "I don't know. We didn't stay long after you showed up; Haider got you stable but Gage ordered your and Charlie's arrests immediately, and the isolation of the Omega guards. He was still holding Major Gage's body in his arms. He wouldn't let anyone take her. Remi was furious and trying to scream at him but she couldn't get enough air in her lungs. Instead she dove at the guards that tried to take you away, clawing at their faces with her fingernails. She kept saying it was all her fault for making you all go, and his fault for lying her whole life. She called him a coward and said she... hated him."

Nathiel's voice had grown softer, and he shuddered. "Everybody around them stopped talking. She went pale and tried to get close to him, but he wouldn't let her. Gage asked the doctor really quietly if he would come help lay out the body of his wife. Remi fell down crying. Charlie was already on the ground, not moving much, so the Sanctum guards took you two and put you in a truck to take to a holding facility. I took one of their places when they stopped to fill the tank before leaving the base." He finally turned his face so his grey eyes met Thane's. "That's all I know."

Thane closed his eyes, then thought about Remi and opened them again, pulling down the visor and looking in the mirror. They were blue, vividly blue like crayons but with flecks of gold. She'd known what color his eyes were and noticed when they'd changed. What did this mean, now?

He heard the door click open and saw Nathiel getting out of the truck. For the first time Thane looked around and realized they'd driven into the cargo bay of an airplane. Their truck was small compared to the space around it, which was full of crates and boxes and three other vehicles.

The plane engine thrummed to life, the body of the plane vibrating under Thane's feet. "Where are we going?" he asked Nathiel.

The grey boy shrugged. "Don't know. You'd have to ask the pilot." He pointed with one hand toward the front of the plane and a ladder that led to an upper deck. "I've got to go check in."

He turned around and walked off, disappearing between stacks of cargo. Thane took one hesitant step after him, and stopped. He didn't want to follow anymore. Instead Thane walked around the stacks of unmarked freight to the ladder and pulled himself up.

The engine noise was growing louder and the plane lurched, starting to move. Thane stumbled into the bulkhead and hit his elbow before catching his balance again. He saw someone ahead of him and called, "Hey!"

It moved away strangely, seeming to scuttle rather than walk and move sideways and backward at the same time. Thane had seen it before. He thought for a moment, trying to pull the name from memory that seemed long ago and far away. "Um, Boggus?"

It stopped, and then turned to face him. At least Thane assumed it was the face, since this side of its head was wearing thick goggles. It bobbed, waiting.

"Where's the pilot?" Thane asked. Boggus lifted an arm and pointed to a narrow door that was closed.

"In there?" Thane looked at the door and then back. Boggus made an up and down motion, almost like a curtsey, and pointed at the door again.

"Can I go in?" Thane took a step forward and reached a hand to the handle. Boggus made that same curtsey and pointed again, more insistently. Thane grabbed the handle and twisted. The door clicked and opened.

The thing in the goggles started moving away. "Boggus?" Thane called. It paused, turning slightly. "Thank you."

It ducked and sidestepped, then scurried off. Thane finished opening the door and entered the cockpit of the enormous plane. The view through the windshield showed a long runway with a tower on one side with blank Antarctic landscape on the other, the plane picking up speed as he watched. The only person in the small room was the pilot, thick headset on and both hands on the controls while the co-pilot's chair sat empty.

The pilot looked up at Thane and smiled with real warmth. "Welcome back, son," Ruan de Argos had to speak over the sound of the engine, but the relief and happiness in his voice was louder than the plane. "Have a seat. We can fly this thing together."

Thane sat, numb with shock and strain. Ruan smiled at him again and reached out to grip his shoulder for a moment. "I'm so glad- I've worried about you every day. Strap in, we're about to lift off."

That stupid lump in his throat was back, the one that burned and made it hard to swallow. There was something wet in his eyes too that he tried to blink away before Ruan noticed. He turned to face forward in the chair and pulled the belts across his chest, making them secure. "Where are we going?" he managed to say without sounding too weak.

Ruan pulled back on the handles and the nose of the plane lifted so all Thane could see was the open blue sky. "We're going home, son," Ruan answered. "I'm finally taking you home."

The word broke something in Thane's chest, and he started to cry.

EPILOGUE

"Twitch, wake up," the voice in his ear was as familiar as his own, and at first he didn't realize what a miracle it was. He groaned and tried to roll over.

It didn't work. He felt resistance in two places across his chest and on his thighs, ankles, and wrist. The other arm was free, though, and he tried to use it to fix his glasses. Nothing happened.

"Twitch, you shade-cursed shadow-blighted idiot, wake *up*," Faith was shouting, and she never shouted. "There are some serious knots going down, and you're finally back and you won't wake up!"

His eyelids were so heavy. He made an effort to lift them, but it was hard. He could hear Faith moving around the room, machines beeping and the blood pressure cuff on his arm activating. She was mumbling to herself like she usually did. "Vitals look good, blood pressure stable, blood work... ah-hah!"

There was a sound of clicking keys, although none of the machines that monitored him should've had a keyboard. More beeping and a click. She hummed as she worked, snatches of songs Twitch didn't recognize. "There, and... there," she said, then moved back to his ear.

"In two minutes an orderly is going to come and give you a shot Haider ordered to be rushed. It'll take forty-five seconds to move through your bloodstream enough to counteract the mild anesthesia they've kept in your system. Then we'll have five minutes to talk." She made a nervous humming sound. "I hope that's enough. This is big."

One hundred seconds later a door latched clicked and Twitch could hear footsteps. Someone was mumbling and getting closer. There was a clatter as the pad was dropped on the table and the wood on wood scraping sound of

416

drawers being open and shut. A warm hand gripped his forearm and rubbed. Next there was a tear and a swipe of cold liquid. Then the sharp prick of a needle piercing his skin and a burning feeling as medicine was pressed into a vein. Syringe extracted, then the clink and thunk of a trash lid being open and shut. A pause, then the footsteps receded and the door clicked shut again.

"Wake up wake up wake up," Faith was muttering in his ear. The burning had changed to a dull warmth spreading through his arm, and then a cold shock flashed through him, bringing him back to full consciousness.

Twitch's eyes flew open. "What's going on?" he muttered to the darkness. He tried to move, but there were thick leather straps across his forehead and chest, both legs and one arm. He groaned as memories came flooding back in, clenching his teeth. He was not going to cry. He hadn't cried once since meeting Faith. He wasn't going to break down now, not when they could finally talk again.

"Twitch!" The joy and relief in her voice eased his mental anguish. He could hear her again. "Did you miss me? What was it like? Did I help at all? Never mind, I need to talk and we don't have much time. But still tell me if you missed me."

He grinned. "Yeah, maybe a little. It was nice not having someone harping on me all the time."

"Whatever, you were lost without me," she said. She sounded pleased with herself. "You don't get to leave me again, by the way. It sucked not having anyone who could hear me."

"Nah, I bet you loved going anywhere you wanted without being tethered to the comm," Twitch argued, but he was secretly pleased she'd missed him. It'd been torture without her. He hadn't realized how dependent on her always ready help he'd become. Saying she was his other half was ridiculously cheesy and something he would never say, but that didn't change it from being the truth.

"I stayed in Antarctica the whole time," she said.

He paused. "What? Why? There isn't even that much tech there to support you. You must've been bored out of your mind."

"I was worried." He could hear the shrug in her voice. "Besides, de Argos had all kinds of toys he wasn't showing you. We have tons of new specs to go over. There was even a piece that we could modify to solve that problem with the mapping system..." she trailed off for a moment, then came right back. "Later. Twitch, something's wrong. Something big. And I need to tell you because I can't do anything with this and they're trying to court martial you but that can't happen."

"Court martial?" Twitch blinked. He knew it'd been a possibility, but then they'd saved so many captured humans and they'd brought it back... at least, he thought they had. Major Gage said she had it and she wouldn't lie about something like that. What would be the point? He thought they'd be heroes, bringing back a lost team and achieving their objective, plus rescuing the general's wife and giving him his family back.

As usual, she'd monitored his brainwaves to follow along with his thoughts. "Oh," she said, "oh, oh dear. That's right, you came back first, you wouldn't know, you were unconscious. Um." Faith stopped, giving the impression she was taking a deep breath.

"What. Happened." Twitch both spoke and thought the words as hard as he could.

He felt her flinch. "Major Gage died," she said. He went rigid. "And less than half the humans made it through."

"Remi? Brennan? Paka?" he asked, allowing his mind to think the rest of the names.

"They all made it, Iselle and Jaeger too. They were all hurt bad, Paka lost her tail and Brennan nearly died but Moirai came and wouldn't let them touch him. She's scary." Twitch silently agreed. "Thane and Charlie were arrested but intel came in that they got away, although there was some chatter about them splitting up. The Guardian Council is furious because Charlie passed through twice. The Weave near Blood Falls was so unstable they had to send a team to use the shuttle."

Twitch bolted upright. Or he tried to, but the straps held him firm and he ended up just flopping a little. "We got it? And they used it?!"

"They had to, there was seepage." He could feel Faith's shudder and hear the fear in her voice. "Not just Shaerealm- there was a void event."

"What?" The restraints kept him down again, but this jerked him so hard he nearly knocked the bed over. The nothing of the void, the unmaking of existence was the only thing that truly frightened Faith. Twitch was afraid of several things, but the void was top of the list.

"Shut up, shut up, stop talking so much, you're sidetracking me," in his imagination he could see her shaking a finger at him in admonishment. "None of that is the point, none of that matters and you have to listen!"

He obediently tried to quiet his mind. He'd had to practice this a lot when he'd first met Faith because she'd run away, accusing him of interrupting and ignoring her because he just couldn't stop thinking. She caught and interpreted every electric synapse firing and receiving as words. Only with him, he was pretty sure, because of the implant he had inserted behind his left ear after he'd found her so they could talk more easily. But no bluetooth or wireless signal was strong enough to cross universes.

"Still talking," she warned. He stopped thinking about it and waited, his mind as blank as he could make it. "Better," her voice was mollified. "This is going to need a lot of room."

Twitch could feel her taking a deep breath. "When the SMG surrounded de Argos in Antarctica, he sent General Gage a message asking if he wanted to know where his daughter was. Nope!" she stomped on the thought that shot from hearing this, "Still my turn. I went with the signal to see how the general would react. He used many bad words and his face turned purple. Then he used the doors to get to South America and took a plane to Antarctica."

Faith paused, letting all that sink in, and Twitch focused on keeping quiet and paying attention. "Ruan wanted to talk to General Gage alone, so they went far away and turned off all their comm stuff. Of course they didn't know about me, so I tagged along and turned them back on without connecting them to the network. I made their two comm units a closed system so I could hear them both well. Twitch," her voice took on a hollow quality, like it was echoing from an underground cave. "General Gage made a deal with de Argos. And he sold us out."

"How?" Twitch asked, not finding it hard at all to stay completely focused now.

"That dragon told him Remi took you all to find his wife, and that Major Gage had the shuttle in her possession. The general asked him how he knew, and de Argos just said he had mysterious sources." Twitch's mind could see her wiggling her fingers and making a face at the word "mysterious." "Then de Argos told him he knew Jaeger had been there and found his wife and that was how Remi knew. General Gage went pale and his heart rate almost doubled but he tried to stay calm and asked why de Argos was sharing."

"That seems like a good question," Twitch interjected, starting to think of possible reasons and her imaginary self stomped her foot.

"Shut up, we're almost out of time!" Twitch snapped his jaw shut and cleared his mind again. "Ruan said he wanted to leave in peace but General Gage had to keep the gate open and if you came back," she strained the word "if", "General Gage needed to make sure you were all kicked out of Sanctum forever. He didn't care how, he just wanted you out. Gage asked what would happen if he didn't agree, and de Argos said he'd shut down the gate right then, trapping you all forever." She grimaced in his mind. "General Gage's blood pressure went way up and his system flooded with adrenaline, but he agreed.

They shook hands and de Argos suggested kidnapping as a possible reason for court martial. Gage's body temperature increased."

Faith faded a little as she zipped around the medical machines again. "Your I.V. drip has the anesthesia in it, and it's going to make you fall asleep again soon." She came back and Twitch had the strangest sensation of her hugging his brain. "I missed you. I'm glad you're back. Once you wake up again and we get the others and escape I want to hear what idiotic thing you did to get your arm cut off. Then you can be grateful to me forever for fixing it."

"What?" The medicine was making his brain fuzzy. He felt heavy, like his body was sinking into the bed. "Haider said it can't grow back."

"Stupid cat," she dismissed Haider's opinion. "He just means he can't. I can."

"Faith..." he trailed off, both his words and his mind fading.

He felt her holding his missing hand in both of hers. "I'm right here. I'm not going anywhere without you. You're not allowed to leave me behind ever again!"

He smiled at her, and then disappeared into the darkness of medicated sleep. His last conscious thought was hearing her mutter, "He doesn't understand what this means. We're in the dark, at the edge, and next comes the void."

ABOUT THE AUTHOR

Angela Day has loved fantasy ever since she was too young to read. Her father read the Chronicles of Narnia out loud to her when she was four years old, and she's had her nose in a book ever since. The only thing she wants to do more than reading is writing. Mrs. Day currently lives in Texas with the best husband in the world and two wonderful, brilliant sons of whom she is very proud. Visit her website at www.awriterbyday.com

www.ingramcontent.com/pod-product-compliance
Lightning Source LLC
Chambersburg PA
CBHW080814250626
47159CB00010B/3373